Prologue

Glen Loch, New York, summer 1812

ELEANOR CAMPBELL MACPHERSON sat in the gazebo that her late husband, Angus, had built for her and frowned at the sketch on her easel. This had always been her favorite place on the castle grounds to draw and to think. But today neither was going well. The story she was telling in the picture wasn't completed and neither was her mission.

Since his death a year ago, Angus had been visiting her in dreams and sending her visions that were helping her to right an old wrong. But for the last two months, the dreams hadn't been so clear. And she was anxious to finish. Wasn't she?

Or was she afraid that, once she buried the last of the Stuart sapphires, Angus would be lost to her forever?

When the pain around her heart tightened at the thought, she set down her pencils and walked over to sit on the stone steps that led into the garden. She missed him so much, and there wasn't anyplace on the castle grounds she could go that didn't bring back memories.

The gazebo had originally been her idea. She and Angus had chosen the spot for it together, because it offered views of the lake, as well as the castle and the stone arch, both of which he'd built to fulfill his promises to her. Of course, Angus, impulsive as always, had designed the gazebo and started construction immediately. He'd used stones for the foundation and chosen the sturdiest of woods for the benches, the railing and the roof. It had been his gift to her on their first anniversary.

Looking out on everything that Angus had built for her and everything that they'd created together, she recalled that long-ago day when the castle had still been under construction and the gardens had been in their infancy. It was their anniversary, and they'd placed the last stones in the arch together, stones that Angus had brought with him to the New World when he'd stolen her away from her home in Scotland.

He'd built the arch in a clearing at the far end of the gardens, just before the land sloped sharply upward into the mountains. It was almost an exact replica of the stone arch that had stood for hundreds of years in the gardens of the Campbell estate in Scotland. According to the legend that her mother and two older sisters had told her, the stone arch had the power from ancient times to unite true lovers. All you had to do was kiss your lover beneath the arch, and that was it. A *happy ever after* was guaranteed.

Well, she'd certainly kissed Angus many times beneath it. And she'd never forget the night she'd met him there for the last time. Having been promised to another man, she'd snuck out of the ball celebrating the engagement. She had been wearing her fiancé's gift to her—a sapphire necklace and earring set that had been be-

Bound by Passion

CARA SUMMERS
KATHERINE GARBERA
KATE CARLISLE

MILLS & BOON

First Published in Great Britain 2017
By Mills & Boon, an imprint of HarperCollins*Publishers*
1 London Bridge Street, London, SE1 9GF

BOUND BY PASSION © 2017 Harlequin Books S. A.

No Desire Denied, *One More Kiss* and *Second-Chance Seduction* were first published in Great Britain by Harlequin (UK) Limited.

No Desire Denied © 2013 Carolyn Hanlon
One More Kiss © 2013 Katherine Garbera
Second-Chance Seduction © 2013 Kathleen Beaver

ISBN: 978-0-263-92972-0

05-0717

Printed and bound in Spain
by CPI, Barcelona

NO DESIRE DENIED

BY
CARA SUMMERS

Was **Cara Summers** born with the dream of becoming a published romance novelist? No. But now that she is, she still feels her dream has come true. And she owes it all to her mother, who handed her a Mills & Boon Romance novel years ago and said, "Try it. You'll love it." Mum was right! Cara has written over forty stories for the Blaze line, and she has won numerous awards, including a Lifetime achievement award for Series Storyteller of the year from *RT Book Reviews*. When she isn't working on new books, she teaches in the writing program at Syracuse university.

To my three sons, Kevin, Brian and Brendan.
As you have grown into fine young men, I have
watched you cherish and protect the ones you love.
You have inspired my heroes for over forty books.
My wish is that you continue to care for each other and
for your families, and I know that it will come true.

To the best editor in the world, Brenda Chin. Thanks
for everything, especially your unwavering belief in me.

To Dr Tucker Harris. Thanks for everything.

queathed to his family for service to the Scottish court. Mary Stuart had worn the jewels at her coronation, and Eleanor's husband-to-be had insisted that she wear them at the ball as a display of his love for her.

With a smile, Eleanor recalled how fast her heart had been beating when she'd raced through the gardens to say a final goodbye to Angus. There could be no future for them, because she had to honor the arrangement her parents had made. Plus Angus's family and hers had been blood enemies for years. But before she could say a word, Angus had kissed her.

Even when she'd tried to say no, he hadn't listened. Impatient, impetuous and irresistible, Angus had simply swept her away.

Exactly what she'd wanted him to do.

Just the memory had her heart beating fast again.

That had only been the beginning of their story. Eleanor swept her gaze from the stone arch over the lush gardens to the castle and then back again. Angus had delivered on all of his promises. Her husband and lover of fifty years believed in building things that lasted—a marriage, a home, a family. Because of Angus's story-spinning talent, the legendary power of the replicated stone arch had taken root and spread. Their own three sons had married beneath the stones. Angus invited anyone to tap into the power of the legend, and many Glen Loch locals had taken advantage of his generosity.

Leaning back against a pillar, Eleanor closed her eyes, and let the scent of the flowers and hum of the insects help her find the inner peace the garden always brought her. She'd never once regretted her decision to leave everything behind in Scotland and come here to New York with Angus. In fact, it was the best decision she'd ever made. She had only one regret—on the night she'd run away with Angus, she'd taken the Stuart sapphires with her.

With her eyes still closed, she slipped a hand into her pocket and closed her fingers around the soft leather pouch that held the sapphire necklace that Mary Stuart wore at her coronation. Everything had happened so fast that long-ago night; once Angus had kissed her, she'd forgotten all about the sapphires. Only when it was too late had her conscience begun to trouble her. Any attempt to contact her family or return the jewels would have increased the chances that she and Angus would be found.

Her sons and her daughters-in-law believed the jewels had been her dowry, no doubt because she'd worn them in the formal portrait that hung in the main parlor of the castle. But they hadn't been her dowry. A man who'd loved her had given her the jewels, and she'd betrayed both his love and his trust. That made her worse than a thief.

Angus had always known about her troubled conscience, and he'd promised on his deathbed that he would help her right the old wrong. That was why he was visiting her now. The initial visions he'd sent to her had been so clear. In one, she'd seen a young woman with reddish-gold curls discovering a single earring in the stone arch. Eleanor had taken it as a sign to hide the first earring there. In the dreams that had followed, she'd seen a woman with long dark hair finding an earring in the old caves in the cliff face. So that's where Eleanor had hidden the second one.

But in her latest dreams, all she could see for sure were the blue stones of the necklace glowing so brightly that the features and surroundings of the young woman holding them were blurred. All Eleanor knew was that she had long blond hair, and she looked vaguely familiar.

A gull cried out over the lake, and squirrels chattered in nearby trees. Ignoring both, Eleanor kept her eyes closed and focused on bringing the girl's image into her mind again. This time it wasn't so blurry. She suddenly realized why the young woman had looked so familiar. She looked similar to how Eleanor herself had looked when she'd had that portrait painted.

As recognition slipped into her mind, she heard Angus's voice.

Her name is Nell, and like her sisters, she believes in the legendary power of the stones enough to put all her dreams and goals in them. She's a storyteller, like you. You'll know where to bury the necklace, Ellie. And you'll know how to make sure that she finds it. If you trust me, Ellie, the Stuart sapphires will at last find their way home.

He'd never left it up to her before. But he was trusting her, similar to how he'd asked her to trust him all those years ago, when they'd run away together.

Suddenly Eleanor knew exactly what to do so that the girl she was picturing would find the necklace and make everything right. Eleanor fetched her sketchbook from the easel and began to draw.

1

"I LOVED YOUR BOOK."

Those words were music to any writer's ears, and Nell MacPherson never tired of hearing them. She beamed a smile at the little girl standing in front of her table. "I'm so glad you did."

She took the copy of *It's All Good* the little girl held out to her and opened it to the title page. Her reading and signing at Pages, the bookstore—down the street from her sister Piper's Georgetown apartment—had run overtime. At one point, the line had spilled out into the street. The store's manager was thrilled, but Piper—who'd taken an extended morning break to attend—had glanced at her watch twice in the past fifteen minutes. She probably needed to head back to the office.

"What's your name?" Nell asked the little girl.

"Lissa. But I wish it was Ellie like the character in your book. Mommy says I look like her, but you do, too."

Lissa was right on both counts, Nell thought. They

both had Eleanor Campbell MacPherson's long blond hair and blue eyes.

"Mommy and I did some research. You're Ellie's great-great-great..." Lissa trailed off to glance up at her mother. "I forgot how many greats."

"Way too many," Nell said as she autographed the book. "I always say I'm Ellie and Angus's several-times-great-granddaughter."

"Did Ellie really draw all the pretty pictures for your story?"

"Yes. She was a talented artist. Every one of the illustrations came from her sketchbooks."

"And you live in her castle in New York," Lissa said.

"I grew up there, and I'm going back for a while to finish up another book." That hadn't been her original plan. The federal grant had given her a taste of what it was like to be totally independent, allowing her to travel across the country giving writing workshops to young children in inner city schools. For someone who'd been hovered over by a loving and overprotective family all her life, the past year had been a heady experience— one that she intended to build on.

But her sisters' recent adventures on the castle grounds—leading to the discovery of part of Eleanor Campbell's long-missing dowry—had caused Nell to question her plan of finding an apartment in New York City and finishing her second book there. Each of her siblings had discovered one of Eleanor's sapphire earrings. So wasn't it Nell's turn to find the necklace? Not that anyone in her family had suggested it. They had assumed she was returning home to settle in and take the teaching job that nearby Huntleigh College had offered her. But a week ago an anonymous letter had been delivered to her while she was teaching her last set of workshops in Louisville. The sender had used those exact words: *It's your turn.* Nell had known then that she had to return to the castle and find the rest of Eleanor's sapphires.

"Are you going to fall in love and kiss him beneath the stone arch that Angus built for Ellie?"

Nell reined in her thoughts.

"Lissa." The pretty woman standing behind the little girl put a hand on her shoulder and sent Nell an apologetic smile. "Thank Ms. MacPherson for signing your book."

"Thank you, Ms. MacPherson."

"Thank you for coming today, Lissa." Nell leaned a little closer. "Lots of people have kissed their true loves beneath that stone arch. My eldest sister, Adair, has recently become engaged to a man she kissed there. Cam Sutherland, a CIA agent. He's very handsome. And my aunt Vi is going to marry Cam's boss." Then she pointed to Piper who was standing near the door. "See that pretty woman over there?"

Lissa nodded.

"That's my other sister, Piper. She's a defense attorney here in D.C., and she just kissed her true love, FBI agent Duncan Sutherland, beneath the stone arch two weeks ago."

Lissa's eyes went wide. "And now they'll all live happily ever after, right?"

"That's the plan. In the meantime, my sister Adair and my aunt Vi are turning Castle MacPherson into a very popular place to fall in love and then have a wedding." She winked at the little girl. "When you're older and you find your true love, you might want to bring him up there."

"Can I, Mommy?" Lissa asked, a thrill in her voice. "Can I?"

"I don't see why not. But I can't see that happening for quite a while."

Lissa turned back to Nell. "What about you? Aren't you going to kiss your true love under the stones?"

"Someday," Nell said. But while her older sisters and her aunt might be ready for happy-ever-afters, Nell had much more she wanted to accomplish first. Finding Eleanor's sapphire necklace and finishing her second book were at the top of her list.

The instant Lissa's mother steered her daughter toward the checkout line, Piper crossed to Nell's table. "The Bronwell trial starts on Monday, and my boss is holding a press conference at five o'clock." Piper glanced at her watch. "I can treat you to a quick cup of coffee."

"No problem." Nell grabbed her purse and waved at the manager.

"You're great with the kids," Piper said. "They love talking to you about Eleanor and Angus."

She and Piper had nearly reached the door of the shop when a man rode his bike up over the curb and jumped off. A sense of déjà vu gripped Nell even before he had entered the store and she had read Instant Delivery on the insignia over his shirt pocket. The anonymous letter she'd received in Louisville had also been hand delivered.

"I have a letter for Nell MacPherson. Is she still here?" He spoke in a loud voice, his gaze sweeping the room.

"I'm Nell MacPherson."

The relief on his face was instantaneous. "Glad I didn't miss you. I was supposed to get here half an hour ago. The traffic today is worse than usual. If you'll just sign here."

As she signed, Nell's mind raced ahead. She hadn't told anyone in her family about the first letter. They would have wanted her to come home to the castle immediately so they could protect her. Worse still, now that her two sisters were involved with agents from the CIA and the FBI, they would have sent someone to hover over her. And the number one person they would have in mind would be Reid Sutherland.

Nell intended to avoid that at all cost. She also intended to avert their expectation that she and Reid live happily ever after. Just because her two sisters would soon wed Reid's two brothers didn't mean she had to marry the last triplet. No way was she ready for that fairy-tale ending.

This whole year had been about demonstrating to them that she could take care of herself. She took a quick look at the envelope held out to her. It was one of those standard-letter-sized ones used for overnight deliveries. The only return address was for the Instant Delivery office. She accepted it and tucked it under her arm.

"Aren't you going to open it?" Piper asked as they moved out onto the street.

"It's probably from my editor."

"Why would she send something to the bookstore? She'd simply call you, right? I think you should open it."

Curiosity and determination. Those were Piper's most outstanding qualities, and they served her well in her career. She wouldn't rest until she knew what was in the letter.

Nell pulled the tab. Inside was one page and the first four sentences matched the message in the first letter.

Your mission is to find the sapphire necklace that Eleanor Campbell stole from our family. Your sisters knew where to find the earrings. Now, it's your turn. I'll contact you and tell you how you can return the Stuart sapphires to their rightful owners.

Nell's gaze dropped to the last sentence. It was new, and an icy sliver of fear shot up her spine.

If you choose again to ignore your mission, someone in your family will die.

"ONE FOR THE ROAD," Lance Cabot said with a grin as he assumed the ancient fighting position, arms bent at the elbows and hands flexed.

Setting aside the file he was working on, Reid Sutherland stepped out from behind his desk and mirrored his adversary's stance. For seconds they moved in a small circle like dancers, retaking each other's measure.

"I can teach you the move," Reid offered as he had countless times before. Growing up as the oldest of triplet boys, he'd taken up martial arts as soon as his mother had allowed it. And he'd created the move by using his brothers for practice.

"Where's the fun in that? I think I've finally figured it out."

Reid blocked the kick aimed at his groin. "Maybe not."

They were evenly matched in height and weight, and Reid knew from experience that the baggy sweatshirt the man was wearing hid well-honed muscles. Reid was five years younger, so that gave him one advantage. And while four years at West Point and assignments in Bosnia and Iraq had kept his opponent fit, they hadn't provided the training in hand-to-hand combat that the Secret Service required of its agents. Another advantage for Reid. Plus Cabot's four-year stint in the United States Senate, not to mention a wife and two kids, could slow a man down.

A well-aimed foot grazed Reid's hip bone, making it sing. He feinted to the right, but the move didn't fool Cabot, and Reid had to dodge another kick. He blocked the next blow but felt it reverberate from his forearm to his shoulder. For two sweaty minutes, Cabot continued to attack, and Reid continued to defend himself.

Cabot had one major advantage. He was the vice president of the United States, and Reid's job was to protect him. Therefore, Reid kept his moves defensive. His office was not designed for hand-to-hand combat, but over the past year, that had meant squat to the VP. Thank God.

Reid feinted, ducked low and for the first time completely avoided Cabot's foot. The maneuver should have caused his opponent to stumble, but Lance Cabot merely shifted his weight and resumed his stance. "I like your moves."

"Ditto," Reid said as they continued their circular dance. He loved his job. Two things had drawn him to the Secret Service. First, the agency filled a need he'd had from an early age to protect those he cared about, and it allowed him to fulfill that need in a way that challenged him intellectually as well as physically.

Reid blocked a kick and danced to his right. Both of them liked a good fight, and neither wanted it to end yet. That was only one of the things that the two men shared. Like the VP, Reid knew what it was to balance family responsibility against that desire to push the envelope. He'd lived with it all of his life, and protecting the vice president had allowed him to push that envelope in ever new and exciting ways.

Keeping Cabot safe was first and foremost a mind game. It required the ability to foresee all possible scenarios in a given situation. Making sure that the VP could enjoy a Wednesday-night dinner with his wife in Georgetown posed almost as much of a challenge as his recent visit to the troops in Afghanistan. Plus the job offered the added bonus of protecting someone who was addicted to risk taking. Reid's boss had handpicked him to head up Cabot's Secret Service detail so that the VP's daredevil streak could be indulged—safely.

To date, those indulgences had included race-car driving, rock climbing and most recently skydiving. For Reid, it was the job of his dreams. And he'd learned that indulging the VP's danger addiction made him easier to manage when the threat might be all too real.

"We've been sparring like this for over a year. Are you ever going to show me your A game?" Cabot asked.

"Someday." Reid gave the man points: he wasn't even breathing heavily. "When it's no longer my job to protect you from serious injury, I'll be happy to oblige. Are you ever going to show me what you think my secret move is?"

"Soon," Cabot promised.

Unfortunately the clock was ticking down. Last night Reid had officially gone on vacation. Jenna Stanwick, an up-and-coming agent he'd been personally training for the past month, was heading up the protection unit in his place. She would keep watch over the VP and his family for the next two weeks while they vacationed in Martha's Vineyard. The Cabots were due to leave within the hour.

As if he too was aware that time was running out, Lance Cabot, quick as a cat, made his move, coming in low to grab Reid's arm. Reid countered it by pivoting, before he snaked his other arm around Cabot's neck and tossed him over his head. One of the chairs in front of his desk overturned and a paperweight clattered to the floor.

The door to the office shot open, and Jenna Stanwick strode into the room, gun drawn. With one sweeping glance she assessed the situation and reholstered her weapon. "Having fun, boys?"

"You didn't see this," Lance Cabot said as he got to his feet.

"See what?" Jenna asked.

Lance turned to Reid. "Maybe she will work out as your temporary replacement."

Shooting Jenna a look of approval, Reid said, "She will. She has four brothers. Plus I taught her my secret move. She'll teach it to you, if you want."

"Not on your life." But he studied Jenna with new interest. "How about if I practice on you, and you can tell me when I'm close?"

Jenna smiled at him. "I'd love to, but you'll have to check the schedule your wife has mapped out. It looks pretty full to me."

Once Jenna had stepped out and closed the door, Reid righted the overturned chair and offered it to Cabot. "You are going to have a good time with your wife and sons. Even if none of the planned activities offer much of an adrenaline rush."

Cabot grinned at him. "Oh, there'll be adrenaline rushes—they'll just be different. Isn't it time you explored the adventures you can have once you marry and have children?"

Reid raised both hands in mock surrender. "No thanks. I'm not cut out for family responsibilities." He'd decided that a long time ago, during the slew of repercussions that had followed his father's arrest for embezzlement.

With a grin, Cabot sank into the chair. "You just need the right woman to change your mind." He waved a hand at the photos displayed on the credenza beside Reid's desk. "Or maybe your brothers could do the job, seeing as they've both found that special woman in the past few months." He dropped his gaze to the duffel bag at the foot of Reid's desk. "For a man who's dead set on avoiding the whole marriage-and-family thing, aren't you running a huge risk spending your vacation up at that castle with those magic stones?"

Reid narrowed his eyes. "Who says I'm going to Castle MacPherson?"

Cabot's grin widened. "Elementary. Really elementary. I don't have to be Sherlock Holmes to figure out you're headed there. Not with the publicity your brothers have received lately. Each of them has been involved in the discovery of part of the long-missing Stuart sapphires. But the necklace is still lost. My bet is that sibling rivalry alone is pulling at you. I'm surprised that some enterprising reporter hasn't sought you out for an interview."

Reid's eyes narrowed. "My brothers have kept a very

low profile. You only know the extent of their involvement because I told you." So far, any publicity Cam and Duncan had garnered had centered on the romantic side of their adventures with Adair and Piper MacPherson, a slant that was encouraged because of the castle's wedding business.

Cabot raised both hands, palms outward. "Just saying. Last night one of the cable news channels did a Cliffs Notes summary of pretty much everything you've told me about unearthing the first two earrings."

Reid had caught the broadcast. The correspondent had laid out a coherent time line, starting with Adair finding the first earring after lightning had struck the stone arch, and ending with Piper and Duncan's discovery of the second earring in one of the caves on the castle grounds. The reporter's narrative had focused on the drama—the threats to the young women's lives. The villain who'd tried to kill Adair was in jail, and Deanna Lewis—the woman who'd subdued Duncan with a Taser shot and then had abducted Piper—was in a coma in a hospital in Albany. So far the press hadn't latched onto the fact that, for six months prior to finding the first earring, someone had been paying undetected nocturnal visits to the castle. Cam's theory was that the visits had been triggered by a feature article in the *New York Times* linking Eleanor's dowry to the sapphires that Mary Stuart had worn at her coronation. The piece had stirred up a whirlwind of interest in the missing jewels, and it had also enormously helped Adair and Viola MacPherson launch their wedding destination business at the castle.

"The anchor mentioned the fact that the youngest MacPherson sister had yet to pay a visit to the castle since the first earring was discovered," Cabot said. "The implication was that, when she did, the necklace might be found. If her sisters' experiences are any indication, she'll need some protection, so it's not a leap to think that the speculation might extend to you eventually."

Reid said nothing. He wasn't worried about the media getting around to him. But the cable newscast had certainly heightened the nagging worry he'd had about Nell. Cabot was thinking along the same lines that Reid was. Nell's two sisters had been lucky enough to find Eleanor Campbell's missing earrings. It definitely wasn't a stretch that anyone who wanted to gain possession of the necklace would be keeping an eye on Nell.

He intended to do just that himself.

Lance Cabot laughed. "That deadpan look works well in a poker game. And it may work with the media. But I know you. You're going to take a shot at finding that necklace. That's the real reason why you're sending me off with the very capable Jenna Stanwick."

Cabot was right about that, too. Reid *was* going to take a shot at finding the necklace. That was the second reason why his duffel was packed and waiting. He'd learned that Nell was heading to the castle on Sunday after her book signing today in Georgetown and a few days with her sister Piper. By joining her, he could kill two birds with one stone. Make sure she was safe and find the necklace.

The damn thing had always fascinated him.

The image flashed into his mind of the first time he'd seen the painting of Eleanor wearing her sapphires. He and his brothers had been ten, and their newly divorced mother, Professor Beth Sutherland, had made arrangements with A. D. MacPherson to research Beth's first historical novel in the castle's library. Part of the arrangement she'd negotiated had allowed her to bring her triplet sons along to the castle every day. Thus had begun a long summer of playdates that he and Cam and Duncan had shared with the MacPherson sisters.

Of course the oil painting had only hinted at the beauty of the jewels, but he'd felt something as he'd stood beneath the portrait that day and had listened to the story of Angus and Eleanor's flight from Scotland to the New World. The older girls had let little Nell do most of the talking, and all through the recital, Reid hadn't been able to take his eyes off the jewels.

Tradition held that this artwork in the main parlor was Eleanor's wedding portrait, and the priceless sapphires were her dowry. But after her death there was no proof of their existence. Reid imagined that her children and grandchildren had searched the castle thoroughly, but they'd never found the sapphires. The long-missing "treasure" had become the focus of many of the games he and his brothers had played with the MacPherson sisters that summer.

It was on that day, looking at the painting, that he'd made a promise to himself that one day he would find Eleanor's dowry. Of course life had interrupted. When the summer had ended, their mother had taken them back to Chicago and resumed her teaching responsibilities. But Reid had never forgotten the jewels or the story that Nell had woven about her ancestors.

Seven years ago, he and his brothers had returned to the castle for a brief visit on the day that their mother had married A. D. MacPherson beneath the castle's legendary stone arch. That had been the last time he had crossed the MacPherson girls' paths. He and Cam and Duncan had been seniors in college and totally focused on their careers. Cam had already interviewed at the CIA. Duncan had his sights set on working in the behavioral science division of the FBI, and Reid's own goal had been to land a job in the Secret Service. None of those careers left much time for family. So even though they were technically stepbrothers and stepsisters, it hadn't been until this summer that their lives had intersected again.

A tap sounded on the door, and Lance Cabot rose from his chair. "My vacation adventure calls." At the door, he turned back. "Good luck finding the sapphires. But in two weeks, I expect you back on the job. By then I will have figured out your secret move."

"Not worried."

"You should be."

Reid could hear Cabot's laughter even after he shut the door behind him. But he didn't smile. His conversation with the VP had only increased what his instincts had been telling him ever since Piper and Duncan had found the second earring. Nell could be in serious danger.

The cable news correspondent hadn't spent much time at all on Deanna Lewis. But Reid's family had been digging into her background for the past ten days. She'd been born and raised in London, the only daughter of Mary and Douglas Lewis. Deanna's mother had died when she was three, her father when she was a freshman in college. She'd been working as a freelance photographer when she'd sold the senior editor of *Architectural Digest* on the idea of doing a feature article on Castle MacPherson. In short, she was everything she'd represented herself to be when she'd appeared at the castle that day and abducted Piper.

And Deanna still had a partner out there. Someone who not only wanted the sapphires but who believed he had a right to them. Deanna Lewis had claimed that the sapphires had never been Eleanor's dowry, that she'd stolen them when she'd fled Scotland with Angus. It all boiled down to a priceless fortune in jewels and someone who was willing to do anything to lay hands on them.

That put the MacPherson sisters in serious danger. Fortunately his brothers had been on the scene when the worst of the trouble had erupted, and they were each sticking like glue to the older sisters. Cam had Adair with him in Scotland working with A.D. and their mother to see if they could find out who might claim the sapphires on that end. His brother Duncan was keeping a close watch on Piper now that she was working on a high-profile defense case in D.C.

That left Nell. Frowning, Reid picked up his pen and drew it through his fingers. So far the danger had been focused on the castle. But that could change. The sense of urgency that had been plaguing him for over a week now bumped up a notch when his cell blasted out his brother Cam's ringtone. His brother seldom called with good news. But he was in Scotland. It couldn't be about Nell. Taking the call, he spoke the standard phrase he and his brothers always used.

"Problem or favor?" And he willed it to be the latter.

2

"NEITHER," CAM SAID. "And this is a conference call. Duncan's on the line, too. Mom asked me to call."

Cam's tone had most of Reid's tension easing.

"Congratulations, Cam," Duncan said. "Usually Mom calls Reid to pass on the messages. Clearly the pecking order has changed."

Grinning now, Reid leaned back in his chair. The fact that their mom usually called him first was something that his brothers had razzed him about since they'd gone away to college. She'd been a very busy professor then, and since he'd been the firstborn of the triplets, she'd put him at the top of her phone tree. The habit had stuck. "Let me add my congratulations, too," Reid said. "I'm perfectly willing to hand that particular torch over to you, Cam."

"Of course, it could be a case of *out of sight, out of mind,*" Duncan said. "Cam's over there with her in Scotland. You're not."

That was true enough. Their mother had gained access to the library at the old Campbell estate that Eleanor had fled from with Angus so long ago. Beth was interested in uncovering the story that had led up to their flight to the New World to use in her latest historical novel. With the added information Deanna Lewis had brought to the table, they were all interested. "How can either of you be sure that Mom hasn't already called me?" Reid asked.

The beat of silence gave Reid great satisfaction. He leaned back in his chair.

"She hasn't," Cam said firmly.

Duncan laughed. "Keep thinking that, Cam."

"I know she hasn't called him yet because Adair and I were just with her when she discovered it in the library. Many of the books there were damaged or destroyed in a fire about six months ago, but leave it to Mom to dig up something."

Reid set down his pen. "What did she find?"

"Yeah." The teasing tone had disappeared from Duncan's voice. "Is it something that will help us identify the person Deanna Lewis was working with when she attacked Piper?"

"I'm hoping it will give us a start," Cam said. "Mom came across an old family Bible with part of the Campbell family tree sketched on the inside cover page. Eleanor's name is right there. She had two older sisters, Gwendolen and Ainslee." Cam spelled the names. "Both married and had children, and we can trace their descendants until around 1900. It's giving us some names to look at. Adair and I are going to start checking them out."

"Did one of them marry a Lewis?" Duncan asked.

"No," Cam said.

"Any more information on how the Stuart sapphires came into the Campbells' possession?" Reid asked. "If we knew that, we might have some idea why someone else believes to have a claim on them."

"Nothing yet," Cam said. "We're thinking that you might have a better chance of nailing down that part on your end."

"How do you figure?" Reid asked.

"I was here right after Adair found the first earring. Duncan and Piper found the second earring together. It's up to you to find the necklace. Along with Nell, of course. That should smoke out Deanna Lewis's partner, and you can get the story from him. Or her."

"Got to say, I'm siding with Cam on that one," Duncan said.

That was a new wrinkle, Reid thought. From the time they were very young, Duncan had made it a habit to stay silent and not side with either of them. The fact that his brothers' scenario matched up with the one presented on cable news only increased his worry that whoever was behind the attack on Piper and Duncan was thinking along the same lines. Nell might very well become their next target.

"Unless you are too afraid of those stones—and of falling for Nell," Cam said. "Oh, right. I forgot. You and Nell have been a done deal since you were ten."

Reid grimaced but said nothing. His brothers had teased him mercilessly that summer because he'd made it his priority to protect her.

"Afraid?" Duncan chuckled. "Not our brother. But our fearless leader is really going to hate following in our footsteps. Nell's visiting Piper right now in Georgetown. They're at Nell's book signing. But she's planning on going up to the castle Sunday afternoon. Daryl assigned himself to be there for the wedding Vi's handling this weekend and all next week. Cam has beefed up the security system on the castle, and Sheriff Skinner is using local volunteers to patrol the grounds. But Nell needs more protection once she gets to the castle."

That was the real reason behind the phone call from his brothers, Reid thought. They'd double-teamed him, and they'd known what buttons to push. Find the treasure and protect the youngest sister.

"I'll think about it." No need to tell them that he'd already decided to spend his time off at the castle.

"You have to do more than think about it. This person is dangerous," Cam said.

Duncan laughed. "He's pulling your leg, Cam. He's not just thinking about it. He's already got his bags packed. And I'm signing off. I'm getting another call."

There was a beat of silence before Cam said, "Duncan's right, isn't he? You do have your bags packed. Did A.D. already call you and tell you to get up there?"

"I'll never tell." Reid thoroughly enjoyed the annoyance he was hearing in Cam's voice. "That's why they call us Secret Service agents," he said and ended the call.

Reaching into the top drawer of his desk, he brought out the copy of Nell's book, *It's All Good*. Curious, he'd bought it a year ago when it had first been published, and when he read it, he'd thoroughly enjoyed it. She'd been six when he had stood beneath the portrait, and he had been as transfixed by the story she'd woven as by the sapphires. Even then she had had a gift for narrative, and in her book, she managed to bring Angus and Eleanor's story vividly to life. Despite the fact that it was a children's story, it had gripped his interest and his imagination right to the end.

Of course he'd known the ending ahead of time. The standard fairy-tale myth. True love would triumph over all and last forever.

Right.

In Reid's experience, nothing lasted forever, and true love was a rare commodity, if it existed at all. His mother's first marriage was testimony to that because it had nearly destroyed her. It might have destroyed them all.

Reid set down Nell's well-crafted fairy tale and let his mind drift back to the night when the police and the FBI had come to their home and arrested their father, David Fedderman. Reid and his brothers had been nine. Gradually they had learned the details behind the arrest. For several years, their father had been running a very successful Ponzi scheme in the investment firm that his grandfather had founded. Being born to wealth and privilege hadn't been enough for David Fedderman. He'd used his charm and intelligence to build a financial house of cards that had tripled the worth of Fedderman Investments.

At least on paper.

Duncan, the behavioral analyst in the family, believed their father was addicted to the thrill of running a con, and living on the edge had been worth more to him than wealth or family. Reid glanced down at Nell's book and wondered if David Fedderman had ever loved his mother at all. What he did know was that she had loved him, and he had broken her heart.

The image of his father being handcuffed and dragged from their home was indelibly imprinted on Reid's mind. He and his brothers had stood in a protective line in front of their mother, and that was symbolically where they'd remained during the turbulent years that had followed.

The Feddermans had sued for the triplets' custody, and what had begun with their father's arrest had changed all of their lives.

On the advice of her attorney, their mother had continued to pursue her doctoral studies. She landed a job teaching at a small college on the outskirts of Chicago, while Reid and his brothers had pitched in to help. Reid had been the idea man and organizer, and he'd been able to turn to Duncan for analysis and Cam to carry out any missions. Together they'd made sure that their mother had time for her academic pursuits.

In the preteen years that followed, Reid and his brothers had been as prone to mischief and getting into scrapes as most boys their age. More so. If two heads were better than one, three active and imaginative minds could hatch some adventures that, at the very least, might have distracted their mother. When they'd gotten into some of their worst scrapes, he'd run interference in an effort to protect them all. Perhaps because of that, she'd come to confide in him. The saddest thing she had ever told him was that she'd not only loved their father very much but believed that he'd loved her, too.

But their "true" love hadn't been enough.

One thing he knew for sure. What had happened had made his mother gun-shy with men. In fact, it was a key reason behind her love of research and choice to steep herself in scholarships and writing.

The triplets all believed that their mother and A. D. MacPherson initially fell in love during the summer that she'd first visited Castle MacPherson, but she'd waited over a decade to trust in the idea of true love again.

And though Reid had recently seen his two brothers take that risky fall and wished them well, Reid didn't have the time or the inclination to follow in their footsteps. He loved his career, and he was fully capable of allowing his work to consume him.

In that sense he believed that he was like both his father and his mother. He liked it that way, even though he'd seen up close what total focus on a career had done to his father, and the price his family had paid. He was determined not to risk boxing himself into the same position.

Still he had to hand it to Nell: in her book, she'd done an excellent job of making the myth seem real. As he flipped through the pages again, he noted the illustrations—the stone arch and other landmarks that surrounded the castle. He'd read in an article that the illustrations had been drawn by Eleanor herself. Nell's ancestor had the same talent Nell had for capturing significant details on the page. Studying them brought vividly to mind the little fairy-tale princess of a girl that he'd done his best to protect that long-ago summer.

He fervently wished that was the only image of Nell that lingered in his mind. But there was another one that he couldn't quite shake loose. At their parents' wedding, she'd still looked a bit like a fairy-tale princess with her long blond hair. But she hadn't been a little girl anymore. She'd been eighteen, just on the brink of womanhood, and she'd been beautiful.

Stunning actually. Her resemblance to Eleanor Campbell MacPherson had been striking. He'd caught himself looking at her more than once during the brief wedding ceremony, and when he'd met her gaze, for a moment he hadn't been able to see anyone or anything else. And he'd felt…well, the only way he could describe it was a kind of recognition—a knowledge that she was the one for him. It was as if they stood alone beneath the stone arch, and he'd wanted her with an intensity that he'd never felt before or since.

Later when he returned to college and the demands of finishing his senior year, he'd convinced himself that what he'd felt was a fluke, a onetime thing that had been triggered by the emotions of the day and his twenty-two-year-old hormones. Still he'd been careful to avoid Nell. A pretty easy task given the demands of his career.

But once the sapphires started popping up, he'd known that he would see Nell again—and he was enough of a Scot to believe that perhaps it was destined.

And if what he'd felt beneath the stones hadn't been a fluke?

Well, he wasn't twenty-two anymore, and he'd always been able to handle Nell. As he recalled, she'd been eager to please and meticulous about following orders, so he didn't expect any problems in that regard.

Rising from his desk, he tucked the book into his duffel bag. But the ringtone on his cell had him crossing back to his desk quickly. It was Duncan. Why was he calling again when his earlier mission had been accomplished?

Unless…

"Problem or favor?" Reid asked.

"A big problem," Duncan replied, his tone grim.

3

As a fiction writer, Nell knew that a good story always began on the day the trouble started. There was no mistaking that the letter with the threat to her family meant trouble.

If you choose to ignore your mission, someone in your family will die.

The numbing chill that had streaked through her when she'd first read the words hadn't surprised her. Neither had the fear she felt, fluttering like a trapped bird in her throat. Those were standard reactions any of her fictional characters might have felt. But the spurts of anger and excitement had been both unexpected and helpful. Because of those feelings, she'd been able to keep her smile in place, and get herself and her sister Piper halfway down the block and seated in the little sidewalk café before she handed over the letter.

Now, Piper, ever the lawyer, was reading it for at least the third time. Nell suppressed an urge to pinch herself to see if she was just imagining it all.

The setting couldn't have been more perfect if she'd been writing it. The morning sun was already high in the cloudless blue sky, the temperature was in the low eighties and the humidity tolerable. The sidewalks were bustling with happy shoppers and tourists. The whole lovely scene offered a stark contrast to the threat in the letter.

"I don't like this," Piper said. Then she read the message again, this time out loud.

Nell didn't like it, either. Hearing the threat helped her to focus on the fact that this wasn't some story she was making up. No need to pinch herself; this was real. And it was up to her to do something about it.

Excitement sparked again. She'd spent her entire life reading, imagining and writing stories, and now she was going to live one of her own. Wasn't that just what she wanted? Where would the adventure take her? Would she have the courage and the know-how to do what any one of her fictional heroines would?

One thing she knew for certain. No one was going to hurt anyone in her family—not if she could prevent it.

The waiter set down two chocolate and caramel Frappuccino drinks. Nell took a long sip of hers. She'd learned a long time ago that chocolate helped smooth over life's rough patches. Not that she'd had very many. As the youngest of three sisters, her life had always run pretty smoothly. She'd been a baby when her mother had died, and their father had turned into a recluse. So she hadn't known either of them long enough to really miss them. Then their aunt Vi had moved in with them, and Nell had always thought of Viola MacPherson as her mother.

People had always taken care of Nell. Adair had been the idea person, and based on her inspirations, Nell would invent stories that the three of them could act out during playtime. When Nell's plotlines had landed the MacPherson girls in trouble, Adair landed on her feet and thought of a way out. Or Piper, always the negotiator, would find a way to fix things with their aunt.

It wasn't until Nell went to college that she'd had to solve problems entirely on her own. Her goal from the time she was little had been to become a published writer and tell the stories she was always spinning in her mind. On the surface, the fact that she'd signed a publishing contract for her first book within a year of graduation might look like pretty smooth sailing. But she'd worked hard to achieve it.

The federal grant she had landed had allowed her to visit cities across the United States, offering writing classes to children and promoting her book at the same time. Several of the schools she'd visited had added *It's All Good* to their required reading lists, and they were passing the word on to other schools and libraries. Adair called what she was doing "networking."

The signing at Pages bookstore earlier today had been the last stop. It had only stalled her return to the castle by a few days. How could she have known that the delay could put those she loved in jeopardy?

"My best guess is that whoever sent this is the person Deanna Lewis was working with. Or at least someone who shares her belief that Eleanor did not have a right to the sapphires." Piper glanced up and met Nell's eyes. "Agreed?"

"Yes."

"One thing I don't get," Piper said. "Why did they send this letter to you? You've been traveling the country. And Adair and I have a proven track record. We each found one of the earrings."

They think it's my turn, Nell thought. What she said was, "The two of you stirred up quite a bit of publicity. Anyone paying attention knows that Adair is now engaged to a CIA agent, and you've hooked up with an FBI profiler. I don't come with that kind of baggage."

Piper studied her for a moment, before she nodded. "Okay. Makes sense. But another thing puzzles me." She tapped a finger on the last sentence. "Why do they say 'if you refuse your mission *again*'?"

Guilt stabbed at Nell, and she felt heat rise to her cheeks. She hadn't told Piper about the first letter. Whatever excuses she'd come up with in Louisville for keeping it a secret vaporized the instant she'd read that last sentence. She took a deep breath. "I received a letter very similar to that one a week ago."

Piper stared at her for two beats. "You what?"

Nell dug into her purse, pulled out the letter and laid it next to the other one so that Piper could read it. "I put it in a plastic bag, like the evidence bags they use on TV shows. Any fingerprints, including mine, are preserved. You can see it's the same message—except for the last line."

And the last line in the second letter was the kicker.

Piper frowned down at the first letter. "Why didn't you tell me or Aunt Vi immediately? We could have arranged for someone to protect you."

"That's exactly why I didn't tell anyone," Nell said, lifting her chin. "The last thing I wanted was for everyone to descend on Louisville. I'm not a child who needs to be rescued anymore. Besides, it could have been just a prank."

Piper took her hand and spoke in a tone that Nell remembered too well from her childhood. "Pranks have to be taken seriously when a fortune in sapphires is involved. Adair and I were both nearly killed."

Nell raised her free hand, palm out. "Point taken." The best way to handle Piper was to pretend to go along. But there was no way she was going to miss this chance to prove to them that she no longer needed to be sheltered and protected. They'd always taken care of her. Now she'd take care of them.

"It's going to be all right," Piper said.

Nell barely kept herself from rolling her eyes. How many times had she heard that sentence while she was growing up? She took a second sip of icy chocolate-flavored coffee and mimicked Piper's tone. "Yes, it is. I'll leave for the castle by noon."

Piper's gaze narrowed. "No, you won't. It's too dangerous. You'll stay here with me until we figure out what to do."

"I'll put all of us in even more danger if I don't go. I have to find the necklace, and we're not going to find it across the street in your apartment. Everyone agrees that Eleanor must have hidden the necklace somewhere on the grounds of Castle MacPherson."

"That's the problem. *Everyone* does agree it's there. Since the word leaked out that Duncan and I found a second sapphire earring in the caves, the treasure seekers are coming out of the woodwork, and the castle is getting more visitors and trespassers than usual. It's too dangerous up there."

Nell's eyes narrowed. "But it's not too dangerous for Aunt Vi or for Adair, who's coming back from Scotland soon. Or for you. I don't suppose it's too dangerous for Duncan or Cam Sutherland, either."

"Cam is CIA. Duncan is FBI. They're professionals. You're not."

Biting her tongue, Nell reminded herself of her strategy. *Pretend to go along.*

Piper released her hand and gave it a pat. "I'm calling Duncan. I wrote down the name of the delivery service that brought this to the bookstore. He'll know how to trace it, and he has a friend who works for the D.C. police, a Detective Nelson. He can check for fingerprints. Then Duncan can let both his brothers know about this, while I call Aunt Vi at the castle. She'll make sure the word gets passed on to Adair and Dad over in Scotland. We'll handle it. Don't you worry about a thing."

Don't you worry about a thing. Another familiar sentence from her childhood. In fact, the whole scenario, with her family sidelining her and solving her problems, had been the story of her life.

Until now.

Nell squared her shoulders and met her sister's eyes. "You *can't* handle this for me. I know that's what everyone has done all my life, but whoever wrote that letter wants *me* to find Eleanor's necklace. I was planning on looking for it anyway. Adair and Aunt Vi found the first earring in the stone arch. You and Duncan found the second one in those caves we used to play in. So it's my turn to find the rest of Eleanor's dowry. That's the way the story is supposed to go."

She paused to beam a smile at Piper. "Once I have the necklace, this person will contact me, and we'll find out just what he or she wants. I'm personally interested in discovering why they think they have a claim on the sapphires. Aren't you?"

Piper had retrieved her phone and now scowled at

her. "This isn't one of your stories where you can plan out the happy ending. The person who wrote this could be very dangerous, and he planned this meticulously. He knew you had that book signing today. He's probably watching us even now."

Nell ignored the chill that shot up her spine. "I know." That would be exactly the way she would write it. "There's this scene in an old Clint Eastwood movie, *Absolute Power,* where his daughter asks him to meet her at this sidewalk café right here in D.C. The FBI wants to arrest him, and two snipers are waiting to take him out. He escapes, of course."

"Of course he does. He's Clint Eastwood. And at the risk of repeating myself, you're not." Then Piper narrowed her eyes. "And what do you know about snipers? You write children's stories."

"Doesn't mean I don't read grown-up ones. My point is that it's not any more dangerous at the castle than it might be right here. There could be a sniper taking aim at us right now."

"All the more reason why you need protection. Ever since that article brought the missing sapphires to the public's attention, there are a lot of people, including some professional thieves, who want to get their hands on those jewels." Piper tapped a finger on the last line of the second letter. "This is a clear death threat."

"Yes." The chill Nell experienced was colder than it had been before. She firmly ignored it as she leaned closer and tapped her finger on the same line. "Piper, the writer is not threatening me. He's threatening all of you, if I don't find the necklace. So I'm going up to the castle, and I will find it. You're not going to talk me out of it."

"I'm calling Duncan." Piper punched in numbers.

While Piper relayed the situation to Duncan Sutherland, Nell studied her sister's face and delighted in the way it softened and then began to glow as she spoke to him. No one believed in the power of the stones more than Nell did. But as a writer, she also knew that the power of the legend didn't cover all scenarios. Her parents were a prime example of that. They had found true love, but her mother's death had cut their time short and had devastated her father. Life gave no guarantees.

That meant that she had to be very careful about the way she handled Reid Sutherland.

She reached for her drink and took a long swallow. She and Reid went back a very long time to the magical summer he was ten and she was six. She and her sisters had played games every single day with the Sutherland triplets, games that had opened up all kinds of story possibilities in her mind—posse and sheriff, pirates and treasure, good and evil.

That was the summer that she'd fallen in love with Reid. From a six-year-old's perspective, he'd been the personification of all the storybook princes and adventure heroes she'd ever read about. Whenever the games they had played had gotten too dangerous or too challenging, he'd been her protector or her champion. Guinevere couldn't have had a better Lancelot. Cinderella couldn't have met a more handsome prince at the ball. Princess Leia couldn't have fought side by side with a more daring Han Solo.

When that summer had ended and Reid had disappeared from her life, he'd remained the hero in all the stories she'd woven for years to come. Knowing full well that, at six, she'd seen Reid Sutherland through rose-colored Disney-movie glasses.

A dozen years later when his mother had married her father beneath Angus and Eleanor's stone arch, the way she'd seen Reid had been entirely different. He was no longer just a good-looking boy. He'd turned into an incredibly attractive man. While their parents recited vows, she found her gaze returning to him again and again. She hadn't been able to stop herself. Even now, years later, she could easily conjure up the image of that lean, raw-boned face, the tousled dark hair. The full, firm mouth.

And she could still remember what she'd felt—dryness in her throat, rapid beat to her heart and the strangest melting sensation in her body. When he had glanced over and met her gaze, she'd felt that flutter right beneath her heart, and she'd been certain that she was falling in love with him all over again.

A mistake that could be excused in a naive eighteen-year-old who'd never felt such strong attraction for a man before. Thank heavens she'd never let him or anyone else know that he'd twice been the object of her heart's desire. He always thought of her as a child; someone he felt indulgent toward. Someone he had to go out of his way to protect from harm. After their parents' wedding, he'd made his feelings for her quite clear when he'd kissed her on the nose and called her "my new little stepsister."

Those words had crushed her heart, and inspired by one of Adair's plans, she'd put pen to paper and created a very different narrative about Reid Sutherland.

Nell took another sip of her icy coffee as the memory poured into her mind in vivid detail. It had been midnight when Adair and Piper had come to her room and awakened her. The wedding guests had long-ago departed, and their aunt Vi was sound asleep. Piper had swiped a bottle of champagne, and they'd gone out to the stone arch, the way they'd done so many times growing up. But with cola or tea in their childhood years.

Beneath the stones, they'd shared their goals and dreams and secrets. More than that, at Adair's suggestion, they'd written down those goals and put them in their mother's old jewelry box. As children, they'd tucked the box behind some stones that were loose to tap into the power that resided there. Back then, Adair had come up with the idea of burying all their secret goals in the stones. The theory had been that, if the stone arch had the power to bring true lovers together, it might also have the power to make other dreams come true. Even the very practical-minded Piper had decided that it was worth a shot.

Nell had continued to tuck her goals into the box even after her sisters had gone away to college. Since it was divided into three compartments, it was perfect for their purpose. Adair had insisted from the beginning that they each use a different color paper to ensure privacy. Piper had chosen blue, Adair yellow and Nell had selected pink.

On the night of the wedding, it was Adair, of course, who had suggested that they cap the celebration by writing out their most secret and thrilling sexual fantasy. Perhaps Nell's fantasy had evolved as it did because she had been standing in the exact same spot when her gaze had locked with Reid's during the ceremony. Maybe because the memory of what she'd felt was still so fresh—that rush of desire, the glorious wave of heat and the flutter right beneath her heart. Or perhaps it had been the champagne. But, of course, her sexual fantasy had involved Reid Sutherland.

And that night she'd been creatively inspired. Her best story ideas came to her while she was actually writing. The physical acts of running her pen over the paper or her fingers atop the keyboard tapped into her creative imagination the way nothing else did. And she'd certainly tapped into it that night. Nell had been eighteen, a freshman in college, and what she'd written went far beyond her limited experience. The details of those original fantasies were a bit fuzzy now. But the setting she'd chosen and the broader picture were perfectly clear.

No longer was Reid the romantic hero of her childhood fairy tales. No, indeed. In her fantasy, seduction had been her goal. And she'd chosen the most romantic setting she could think of—Eleanor's garden. Over the years, she'd had plenty of time to embroider and expand on her original ideas. And those scenarios had been fueling her dreams, especially since the Sutherland men had reentered her sisters' lives.

Of course what she'd felt that day could have been a onetime thing. But working against that theory was the fact that every time she relived it in her mind, she felt the same things all over again. No one before or since had ever made her want with such intensity. With that feeling of inevitability.

The question was, when she finally met Reid again, what would happen next? Each time she asked it, a fresh thrill rippled through her system. As a writer, it was the question she always wanted foremost in her readers' minds. It was what made them turn the page. And she found that the more she thought about it, the more she wanted to turn the page in her own life and discover what would happen.

Just thinking about it had her reaching again for her drink to cool down her system. She hadn't seen Reid since their parents' wedding day. His job heading up the vice president's security team made him a very busy man. Still she had no doubt that they would meet again sometime soon, and she would have the opportunity to turn her fantasies into reality. And she'd made preparations.

A heady thrill moved through her at the thought.

"Earth to Nell."

Piper's words made Nell shift her gaze to the letters Piper was placing in her briefcase. Giving herself a mental shake, Nell refocused on the fact that she was currently involved in a much more pressing narrative.

"Duncan wants to see both letters. We'll take a taxi to Reid's office, and he'll meet us there." She left two bills on the table to pay for their coffees.

"Reid's office? Why do we have to go there?" Nell asked.

"It's halfway between Duncan's office and here. Plus Duncan says Reid's on vacation, and he's going to the castle with you."

In her mind, Nell pictured a guardian angel swooping down on her. "I don't need anyone to protect me. I can handle this."

"Don't be silly." Punching another number into her phone, Piper moved quickly toward the curb. "Abe, I'm going to be a little late for work. Family emergency."

Family emergency? Nell frowned. Nell grabbed one

last swallow of chocolate-laced caffeine and rose from her seat.

Piper turned back to her. "The best place to catch a taxi is at the opposite corner. Follow me."

Then she stepped in between two parked cars to wait for traffic to clear.

A horn blast drew Nell's attention. A few stores down, a dark sedan was blocking traffic. The driver behind him demonstrated his displeasure by leaning on the horn again. Piper glanced at the noise also and then turned her attention back to her phone call.

Nell had only taken one step when a woman came up to her. "Ms. MacPherson? You are Nell MacPherson, right?"

"Yes, I am."

The woman was a tall brunette in her early fifties who looked as if she could have stepped right off the cover of a high-end fashion magazine. "I missed your signing, and I was wondering if you could autograph a book for my granddaughter?"

"Of course."

While the woman fished in her bag for the book and a pen, Nell heard the horn again and the sound of a motor revving. She caught a blur of movement out of the corner of her eye. The image of the dark sedan shooting forward had barely registered, when she realized that Piper was directly in its path. Fear flashed so brightly in her mind that for a moment she was blinded. Pure instinct had her pushing past the woman and racing toward the street.

Piper seemed so far away, the sound of the car so close. Nell felt as if she was moving in slow motion, the car on fast-forward. She slammed into her sister, grabbing her around the waist and using Nell's momentum to hurl them both forward. They were airborne for a second. Holding tight to Piper, Nell twisted so that she took the impact on her side when they tumbled onto the pavement. Then with every ounce of energy she had, she rolled, dragging her sister with her. Hot wind seared her cheek, and she smelled burning rubber as the dark sedan whipped past and sped up the street.

"Nell? Are you all right?"

Pain was singing through every bone in her body, but Nell managed a smile as she opened her eyes and looked into Piper's. "I'm fine. You?"

"Yeah," Piper said. "Thanks to you."

"He was crazy," a man said as he helped both of them to their feet.

Piper ran her hands over her sister. "You're sure you're all right?"

"I'm better than I was a moment ago." Nell didn't want to ever replay those few seconds in her mind again.

For a moment Piper just held on to her sister's hands. There was a look in her eyes that Nell had never seen before. Surprise?

"You saved my life," Piper said. "I guess you were right about it being just as dangerous here as at the castle."

"It's all good," Nell said as she pulled her sister close and just held on to her for a minute.

"I wrote down his license plate number," a woman said. "It looked to me like he wanted to run you over, young lady. You should report him."

"I will." Pulling away from Nell, Piper took the slip of paper.

"I called 9-1-1," another woman said. "They're sending the police to take a report."

Glancing around, Nell noted that they'd attracted
quite a little crowd. On the edge of it, she saw a young
man pushing forward. As he reached her, she saw that
he had an envelope in his hand. "Sorry, lady," he said.
"The guy in that car gave me this to deliver to you after
you left the café. He paid me fifty bucks and told me to
wait until you crossed the street. I had no idea he was
going to try to run you down."

"Thanks," Nell said. But it wasn't her the driver had
been aiming for. It had been Piper.

"Let me open it for you," Piper said, then pulled out
her phone to call Duncan once more.

"No." This was her story, and if she'd had any lingering doubts about that, they vanished as she read the
message on the letter inside.

*You have forty-eight hours to find the sapphire neck-
lace, or you run the risk of losing another member of
your family.*

4

Horns blasted as Reid made an illegal left-hand turn that would cut five minutes off his trip to Piper MacPherson's apartment in Georgetown, near the latest Stuart sapphires crime scene. Now if he could just make it through the next few traffic lights. He cut off a car in the right lane, pressed his foot on the gas and shot through a yellow one. Duncan's ringtone had him grabbing his cell just as he headed into one of D.C.'s traffic circles.

"I'm still ten minutes out," Duncan said.

"I'll be there in less than five." Reid slammed on his brakes as the car in front of him slowed. "I'll let you know the second I arrive." He dropped his cell on the passenger seat and concentrated on snaking his way through the traffic.

He should have told Duncan to have the two women wait for him where they were, as soon as he'd first heard about the first two threatening letters. Why hadn't he? He seldom had to second-guess himself. His success in the Secret Service depended on him being right the first time.

But this particular scenario simply hadn't occurred to him. The writer of the letters had threatened Nell's family if she didn't locate the rest of Eleanor's sapphires and hand them over to their rightful owner. It was a good ploy. It would have probably scared her into taking a shot at finding the necklace ASAP. Who would have thought the writer would try to make good on his threat within the hour?

He should have, Reid thought. When his cell rang again, he grabbed it.

"Piper just called me again," Duncan said. "Nell asked the officer who responded to the attempted hit-and-run complaint to stay until one of us gets there."

"Smart," Reid said.

"Yeah, but we should have been smarter. I had Piper put the officer on the line. He filled me in on what the eyewitnesses saw. They say the driver of the car accelerated as soon as Piper stepped into the street—as if he'd been waiting for her. He would have run her down if Nell hadn't tackled her and gotten her out of the way."

Reid heard a thread of panic in his brother's voice he'd never heard before. "The important thing is that Piper's alive and unharmed." But he was thinking of Nell, the little fairy-tale princess of a girl he'd done his best to protect that long-ago summer. The image of her tackling her sister didn't quite gel with that. Nor did it fit with the fragile-looking teenage girl he recalled standing beneath the stone arch as their parents had taken their wedding vows.

"I knew there was another shoe that had to drop," Duncan said. "I should have known something like this might happen. The facts are all there. It's just that the attacks on Adair and Piper occurred at the castle, and only after they'd each found one of the earrings."

Reid had reviewed the same things in his own mind, until it had become a continuous loop. He'd first suggested they come to his office to get them out of the neighborhood. But he should have—

"I knew Deanna Lewis was working with someone," Duncan continued. "I knew they were obsessed with getting their hands on the Stuart sapphires. I should have—"

Reid cut his brother off by saying, "If it makes you feel any better, I've been blaming myself for not going there right after you called about the letters." Not that he would have gotten there in time. But he'd be there now.

There was a beat of silence on the other end of the line. Then Duncan said, "You've been blaming yourself?"

"That's what I said." With one hand, Reid eased the car out of the traffic circle.

"Wait. I'm going to punch the record button on my phone. Would you mind repeating that?"

"You can always dream, bro. And if you even breathe a word of that little confession to Cam, I'll deny it. Then I'll have to beat you up."

"*You* can always dream, bro."

With the panic in Duncan's voice replaced by humor, some of Reid's tension eased. But traffic had slowed to a crawl. Two blocks ahead, he saw the revolving lights of a patrol car. "I'm within sight of the apartment. I'll update you soon."

Reid jammed his car into a No Standing zone, jumped out and ran down the sidewalk.

NELL TURNED THE flame on beneath the teakettle on Piper's stove. She preferred coffee, but the ritual of making tea had always soothed her nerves. It brought back memories of the times she'd talked through her problems while she'd watched her aunt Vi brewing a pot in Castle MacPherson. Nell had spent a lot of time in the sunny kitchen after her sisters had left for college.

Adair had been the first to leave. Nell and Piper had shared one more year before Piper had deserted her, too. Then for her last two years of high school, she'd been alone. Of course, she'd still had her aunt Vi. And her father had been there, tucked away in his rooms painting or teaching some art classes at nearby Huntleigh College. But there'd been no one to sneak out to the stone arch with in the middle of the night, no one to laugh with as they'd written down their hopes and goals and dreams on different-colored papers and buried them.

Spotting the teapot in Piper's kitchen, Nell lifted it off the shelf, then nearly dropped it because her hands were trembling. So far she'd been able to hide that little fact from her sister. Since Piper's clothes looked as if they'd wiped the street, she was showering and changing before Duncan arrived.

Thank heavens Nell's own navy suit was made of some kind of miracle fabric she could roll up into a ball, stuff into a duffel bag and then shake out wrinkle-free. It had been perfect for her lifestyle during the past year. All she'd had to do to repair the damage from their close encounter with that wannabe hit-and-run driver was to sponge off a few spots of dust with cold water.

If only all her problems were that easy to solve. Tea, she reminded herself, as she searched through the cupboards and finally located the box. When it slipped through her fingers and landed on the floor, she retrieved it and set it gingerly on the counter. Pressing her palms flat on the ledge, she took a deep, calming breath.

She had to settle down. Once the nice young officer had taken their statements and escorted them up the alley stairs to her sister's apartment above a George-town boutique, her knees had begun to feel very weak.

A perfectly normal reaction, she'd told herself.

Someone was threatening her family. She hadn't heeded the warning in that first letter fast enough, and they'd taken action, nearly succeeding in killing Piper. Now that the initial adrenaline rush had worn off, shaking hands and wobbly knees were understandable.

But the butterflies in her stomach weren't just due to what had nearly happened in the street. They'd started frantically flapping their wings when Piper had told her that Reid Sutherland was on his way over. He would arrive momentarily.

Nell thought she'd have more time to prepare for meeting him again, time to think and to map out pos-sible scenarios. Find the necklace first. Then deal with Reid Sutherland. Closing her eyes, she drew in another breath. The way she saw it, her problem was twofold. If he came to the castle with her, he posed a threat to her plan to prove to her family that she could take care of herself. The other problem was more personal. She wanted very much to bring to life her fantasies about seducing Reid. They couldn't be denied. Wouldn't be denied. But the last thing she needed to deal with right now was her attraction to him. She needed to find that necklace.

On her own.

Reid might present a challenge there, too. The Reid

she remembered had made all her decisions for her. And she'd let him.

She couldn't allow that to happen again. No way was she going to slip into her old habit of letting others involve themselves in her life and control it.

The sudden shriek of the teakettle made her jump. But it also jarred a thought loose. In a well-plotted story, the heroine never has the luxury of time to plan everything out.

She had to face the unexpected—and improvise. That was the key to a good page-turner.

It was also the key to becoming the truly independent woman she wanted to be. A girl would want to separate the two problems and solve them one at a time. A woman would take on the challenge of juggling two or three agendas.

Anyway, why not? A thrill moved through her just thinking about it. There had to be a way to find the necklace and fulfill that fantasy she'd written seven years ago. She'd just have to find it.

Turning off the kettle, she refocused her attention on making tea and noted with some satisfaction that her hands were steadier as she poured water into the china pot. Though the specific details of the sexual narratives she'd buried seven years ago remained a bit fuzzy, her overall goal was still crystal clear. That one searing look Reid had given her ages ago had awakened a desire in her that couldn't be denied. Wouldn't be denied.

All she had to do was find a way to convince him. She measured out tea leaves into a tea ball. As she swirled some of the hot water in the teapot to warm it first, then tipped out the water into the sink, she noted that her hands were perfectly steady.

Good. But this was *not* the time to wonder how it might feel when she ran them over Reid Sutherland's skin. After carefully adding boiling water to the china pot then adding the tea ball, she turned back to face the table. She had a much more pressing problem.

Someone had tried to run Piper down with a car.

Before her sister had gone into the bedroom to change, Nell had spread out all three letters carefully on the table so that when Duncan and Reid arrived, they could examine the evidence. The third letter frightened her the most.

Losing another member of your family.

The man who'd gunned his car straight at Piper wasn't fooling around.

Neither was she. Nell welcomed the spurt of anger. She turned back to the counter, opened a drawer, and located a pad of paper and a pen. From the time she'd first learned to write words, she'd made it a habit to capture her ideas on paper. Moving to the table, she read the third letter again.

This time it was something else entirely that jumped out at her.

Forty-eight hours.

That was the important part of the message. Why hadn't she absorbed it sooner? A ticking clock was a literary device many writers and moviemakers used. She wrote the number on the pad. The writer of this story wanted to put pressure on her to find the necklace fast.

The sudden knock at the door had her nearly dropping her pen.

"Duncan made good time," Piper called from the bedroom. "I'll be right out."

Nell set down her pad and pen on the counter, before

she moved to the door and opened it. It wasn't Duncan standing there. It was Reid. For the first time in her life, she experienced what it was like to be struck dumb. She couldn't breathe, couldn't move. Lucky for her, his attention was focused on the young officer who'd agreed to stand guard outside on the landing.

Hers was focused on Reid. She might have been transported back in time. Except he wasn't the same. On that day, her eyes had been riveted on a twenty-two-year-old boy on the edge of manhood. Right now she was looking at a man. Perhaps the most intimidating man that she'd ever seen. His shoulders were broader, his face leaner, the angles more defined. Even the long rangy body was more muscled.

Harder. That's what it was, she decided. Reid Sutherland looked bigger and harder than she had remembered him being. He was definitely not storybook prince material anymore. Those characters were never scary. And Reid was—just a little. When he turned, and she met his gaze, she realized that one thing was exactly the same. He could still make her throat go dry, make her bones melt in that strange way, and she had to press a hand to her heart when it gave that little flutter.

"Nell?"

She realized that she wasn't going to get his name past the dryness in her throat.

"Reid, come in." Piper joined her at the door. "The letters are on the table. Duncan?"

"On his way."

As Nell stepped aside and let Piper lead Reid into the kitchen, she felt a rush of relief. Her legs were working. He was standing in the tiny kitchen shrugging out of his suit jacket. Just to make sure she could, she shifted her gaze to Piper. Then she thanked the young officer who'd allowed Reid up the stairs.

No worries. Her body was working again. Any moment now her brain would catch up. It was all going to be good. She turned back to the kitchen. Reid stood in profile, leaning over the table reading the letters. He looked every bit as attractive and dangerous from the side as he had face-to-face. Her gaze went to the gun that he wore in a shoulder holster.

Of course he wore a gun. And of course he looked dangerous and intimidating. That was his job. What surprised her was she found the whole package incredibly arousing. She was just going to have to get used to the dry throat, the heat pooling in her center and the fluttering sensation beneath her heart.

Focus.

Following the direction of Reid's gaze, she looked at the three threatening notes on the table. They were what she had to concentrate on now.

HALF AN HOUR later, Reid leaned a hip against the counter in the tiny kitchen. The table offered two seats and as soon as his brother had arrived, Reid had encouraged Piper and Duncan to sit. Both of them were shaken up. Not surprising since two attempts had now been made on Piper's life in the past ten days.

Duncan was currently on the phone with a friend of his, Detective Mike Nelson, who was officially handling the case. One of his officers had already placed the three letters in evidence bags and taken them away. Reid was sure there wouldn't be any prints, other than Piper's and Nell's. Whoever had orchestrated the one-two-punch attack on the MacPherson sisters today had planned it too carefully to make a careless mistake. According to the young officer on the landing, the second part of the punch had come within a hairbreadth of being successful. The bastard would have run Piper down on the street if not for Nell's quick thinking and amazing reflexes.

Reid shifted his gaze to where she stood arranging mugs on a tray and once more absorbed the overload to his senses. He was almost getting used to her effect on him.

Almost.

He certainly hadn't been prepared when she'd opened the door of the apartment. That first sight of her had hit him in the gut with the power a double-barreled shotgun. The sexual pull had been even more potent and primitive than he'd recalled. Seven years ago, he could blame it on hormones, but he found it harder to rationalize it now and impossible to deny.

Thinking back, he recalled that he'd sensed her the instant she'd opened the door—a tingling awareness along all of his nerve endings. And he'd caught her scent—something he couldn't quite describe. When he had turned away from the young officer and looked into her eyes, his mind had gone clear as glass, and all he'd seen was her.

All of her.

He was trained to take in numerous details in one glance, but they'd never registered so clearly on his senses before that he'd lost track of his surroundings. In that freeze-framed instant in time, he was completely absorbed in taking her in. The golden-blond hair that was clipped back from her face fell below her shoulders. The jacket and pants in some clingy fabric revealed a neat athletic body with more curves and longer legs than he remembered. Even as he registered all of that, his gaze hadn't wavered from her face. He couldn't look away from those eyes. They were still that dark, deep blue—the color of Eleanor's sapphires—and every bit as fascinating. Then there was the pale-as-milk skin, the soft unpainted mouth, the lips that were slightly parted. In surprise? Anticipation?

Nell? There was a question in the word he'd spoken, but he still wasn't sure what he'd been asking. What he knew was that for an instant he'd been tempted to step forward and take a taste of that mouth. It was fear that had kept him from moving. Fear that he might not be able to stop with a kiss.

No woman had ever made him afraid before.

Then Piper had come to the door, and he'd remembered who he was, where he was, and that this was Nell.

His stepsister.

He wished he could think of her only that way—the tiny and fragile girl who had to be cared for and protected. But the girl he'd carried around in his memory was turning out to be a sharp right turn from the woman who'd rescued her sister with a flying tackle. As a man who had fine-tuned his abilities to anticipate the future, Reid normally didn't like surprises. But in Nell's case, there was a part of him that was looking forward to them.

As long as they didn't distract him from the job he had to do. The MacPherson sisters were currently the priority he had to focus on.

He shifted his gaze back to the table where Piper was frowning down at her cell phone, examining the photos she'd taken of the three letters as if she had missed something. But she hadn't missed anything. The message was clear. Someone, and he was betting it was Deanna Lewis's partner, wanted Eleanor's sapphires badly enough to kill off the remaining members of the MacPherson family to get them. The would-be killer's focus seemed to be on the sisters for now, but the threats extended to their father, his mother, their aunt Vi. And because of their relationship with Adair and Piper, Cam and Duncan could also be on the list.

"Send me something as soon as you have it," Duncan said, then ended his call. "Nelson says that the car was just reported stolen from a hotel parking garage. But two of the eyewitnesses have arrived at the precinct. They're going to work with a sketch artist. If all goes well, they'll have something to put on the early-evening news."

"The sketch probably won't help us much," Nell said as she served tea to Piper and Duncan. "Both witnesses said the driver was wearing a hat low on his forehead, a beard and sunglasses. Those are pretty standard items for a disguise. In fact, he could even be a she."

Reid exchanged a glance with his brother. He was impressed with her analysis. And her focus. It was stronger than his was.

Piper frowned at her cell. "You should have told us the second you received the first letter."

Nell moved forward and rested a hand on Piper's shoulder. "I should have acted faster after I received the first letter. I won't make that mistake again. Whoever is behind the notes planned everything very carefully, and I must have been under surveillance. In Louisville, the letter was delivered to my work. To do that here in D.C., the job was trickier. The manager of Pages told me the sign's been in the window for almost a month, so the author of the letter knew exactly when I'd be there to sign for it. Arranging for the instant delivery was a piece of cake. But he had only a few hours to verify that Piper was with me and that we'd eventually have to cross the street to get to the apartment. It was a good bet that we'd stop for lunch or coffee at the café. We've done that every day since I arrived. All he had to do was wait."

"I agree," Duncan said. "He planned everything meticulously."

High praise from a profiler, Reid thought.

"But here's the thing," Nell said. "He couldn't have possibly known that Piper would step into the street alone. We could have been together just as easily."

As she described what had happened just before the attempted hit-and-run, Reid pictured it in his mind—something he should have been doing much earlier. "Why weren't you in the street with her?"

"She left fast," Nell said.

"And Nell always moves slow," Piper added.

"Wait. I remember now," Nell said. "There was a woman who came up to me and asked me for an autograph."

"I didn't see that," Piper said.

"You were talking to your boss on your cell. The woman said she'd missed the signing, and she wanted me to sign a copy of my book for her daughter. Then I was distracted by that horn again, and I heard the motor racing. I just pushed past her."

Reid reached for his jacket. "C'mon. Let's go down to the street and walk through it."

5

THE STREET IN front of Piper's apartment had returned to normal. Tourists and shoppers strolled along the sidewalks, some stopping to peer in windows. Nell noted that both Duncan and Reid were in full bodyguard mode, walking on the outside as they escorted the sisters across the street and along the sidewalk to the café.

They stopped just in front of the table where she and Piper had sat earlier. Reid made sure that she was just a bit behind him and to his left. That way he could shove her out of the way with his left hand and draw his gun with his right. Perfect, Nell thought. She had to stifle the urge to stop and make a note of it on her pad.

"Tell us what happened, Nell," Reid said, "just as if you were writing it. And we'll act it out."

Nell pointed to the street. "Piper, you were right there."

As Duncan and Piper moved into position between two parked cars, she said, "I heard the horn first and I glanced down the street to see this car holding up traffic. He was double-parked in front of the art store, and the driver behind him was getting impatient. I was about to join Piper when the woman came up to me with the book."

"And you signed it?" Reid asked.

Nell shook her head. "No. I was reaching for it when the horn distracted me again. Then everything happened at once. I heard the motor, saw the blur of motion, and I just ran toward Piper."

Reid took her arm and drew her with him toward the art store. When they reached it, he glanced up and back down the street. Then he signaled Piper and Duncan to join them.

"Nell says the car was stopped here blocking other cars when she first spotted it," he explained. "But he couldn't have been here long. Too much traffic."

"I bet he was illegally standing in that loading zone two stores down," Nell said. He could have idled there until Piper stood up. Then he pulled out into traffic and waited. That's the way I would have written it."

Reid glanced at her. "You could be right."

Nell heard something in his tone that she'd never heard before. Surprise? Admiration? Whatever it was, it sent a little stream of warmth through her.

"I'm sure she's right," Duncan said. "The guy's been watching her every movement since she arrived in town. He was watching her in Louisville, too."

"I'll bet the loading zone offers a good view of the café," Nell said.

When they reached the empty space two stores down and stepped into the street, Nell continued. "From here, he could see Piper drop the money on the table."

"Then I just walked away," Piper said. "I was totally focused on calling my boss to tell him I'd be late. Family emergency."

Reid could picture it very clearly in his mind—the driver pulling out and blocking the traffic. He should have seen it before. The problem was that his brain had been working in slow motion ever since he'd looked into Nell's eyes again. He had to change that—and fast.

"I'm about to join her when the woman comes up to me with the book," Nell said. "If it weren't for a driver who was heavy-handed with his horn, I wouldn't have turned to look. He would have had a clear shot to hit Piper."

"Gutsy bastard," Reid murmured. He pictured the acceleration, the collision. He frowned. "He wouldn't have been able to build up much speed. He couldn't have been certain he'd kill her."

"He didn't have to. All he had to do was make me think he *could* kill her."

They all turned to stare at her.

"He clearly intended to hit her. She could have been killed," Duncan pointed out.

"But hit-and-run is sloppy," Nell said. "Especially in Georgetown traffic. I think his real goal is to make me *believe* he's ready to pick off my family one member at a time so that I'll find the sapphire necklace for him and hand it over. Which is what I'm going to do."

"I don't think he's quite as nice a guy as you're imagining him to be," Reid said. "My guess is that he had murder on his mind, but he wasn't a professional."

"If he's anything like Deanna Lewis, he's not nice at all," Piper said. "Nell, it's too dangerous for you to go to the castle. You'll stay here with me, and we'll get protection. It's going to be all right."

Nell took her sister's hands. "You've been telling me that all my life. Now it's my turn to tell you this. I'm going to fix this. He's given me forty-eight hours. The clock is ticking. It's the oldest plot device in the world. But it works. So I'm going to the castle, and I'm going to find Eleanor's necklace. He'll follow me up there, because the Stuart sapphires are what he really wants."

Piper looked from Duncan to Reid and back to Duncan again. "One of you has to talk some sense into her."

Reid glanced at his brother, then said, "The thing is, she's making sense. At the very least, she has to go to the castle and go through the motions of looking for the necklace. That will buy us forty-eight hours to put an end to this. I'm going with her."

"In the meantime, we'll beef up protection for the whole family," Duncan added.

"IT'S GOING TO be all right," Nell said as she checked her suitcase for the last time. She was beginning to really enjoy saying those words to her sister. What she wasn't enjoying was the fact that Piper was so worried. Though there wasn't much space in the small bedroom, Piper was pacing just as she always had when something was really bothering her.

Nell glanced into the bathroom, checked the shelves one last time. The rest of her family would worry also. Duncan and Reid were filling them in on the plan right now. At least Aunt Vi wasn't alone at the castle. Daryl Garnett, her fiancé, who headed up the domestic division of the CIA, was with her. He'd taken some time off when Adair and Cam had left for Scotland to help Vi run the wedding business and make sure she was safe.

Piper stopped her pacing, sat on the foot of the bed and patted the space next to her. When Nell joined her, Piper said, "I just wish I could go with you."

"Your big trial starts on Monday. You need to be here. You'll be safer here."

"So will you. There are so many ways to sneak onto the castle grounds. And there's a wedding scheduled there on Saturday. A rehearsal tomorrow. Those will provide ample opportunity for someone to get close to you."

"I'll have two agents watching over me. And I'll know that Duncan will keep you safe."

Piper frowned at her. "Only because you're drawing this person away. You're making a target out of yourself."

"I'm also making a target out of Reid. I can't believe whoever this is will be happy that I'm taking a Secret Service agent with me. Deanna's partner will follow me to the castle, and I think he'll keep a close eye on me."

"You're not making me feel better," Piper said.

"I'm just thinking of their side of the story. Clearly they believe they have a right to those jewels, and if they turn out to be descendants of the Stuarts, they could be right."

"But we're Eleanor's descendants," Piper said.

"Exactly." Nell beamed a smile at her. "It will all boil down to a classic case of conflicting narratives. You deal with that in court every day. The thing is, they may have a more powerful claim on the jewels. Yet we've always believed that they were Eleanor's dowry."

"Well, the jury's out on that one."

"Agreed," Nell said. "But wouldn't the possibility make you just keep turning the pages to find out?"

Piper stared at her sister. "This isn't some story you're writing, Nell."

"No." But it was certainly a story she was thinking

of writing. The twist would fit well in the book she was working on—an adult thriller with a romantic subplot.

There was a knock on the bedroom door and Duncan said, "You two ready in there?"

"Yes." Piper rose and took Nell's suitcase. "The only reason I'm letting you go is because Reid's going with you. No one could be more devoted to protecting you than he is."

True, Nell thought. Yet having a guardian angel along was going to make it difficult to find the necklace on her own without being protected by Reid. But that wasn't her only problem. Difficulty number two was she wasn't sure she wanted to be protected *from* Reid.

But that was an entirely different story line, one she wasn't quite ready to share with her sister. She had to plot it out for herself first.

AN HOUR LATER, Reid found himself folded up like an accordion in the front seat of Nell's sporty little Fiat as she shot it up a ramp onto the beltway that would take them out of D.C. Using the side-view mirror, he checked the cars behind them.

"You think he'll try to follow us?" Nell asked.

"It's a good possibility," he said. "He'll want to make sure you're headed up to the castle."

"That's what your work is like, isn't it? Coming up with all the possibilities?"

"Yes."

"Writers have to do that, too. Except that we can choose one of the possibilities, and you have to deal with what you get. Like getting stuck with me and going up to the castle."

"I wouldn't call that getting stuck." But he was definitely stuck big-time in her little car.

The seat was pushed back as far as it would go, but he still felt as if he'd been stuffed into a shoe box. And he was listening to Bach or Beethoven or Brahms on the radio. He'd never been able to keep those classical composers straight.

He had no one to blame but himself for the cramped conditions. Nell had made several arguments while they'd taken the short walk to where he'd illegally parked his sedan. That was something she hadn't done when she was six. That summer she'd been willing and eager to do everything he told her.

First she'd demanded they take two cars. In separate vehicles, it would be less obvious that she'd acquired a bodyguard. He'd countered by pointing out that, once they got to the castle, his presence would be clear to anyone. Then she'd gone for the emotional appeal—she'd feel more comfortable if she had her own vehicle. After all, it had been the only steady companion she'd had for the past year when she'd toured the country teaching classes and promoting her book.

But if there was one thing he'd picked up on in the past two hours, it was that Nell was most interested in being a key player in recovering Eleanor's necklace. Bottom line—she wanted her own car, because it would give her a certain amount of independence. It was that desire to operate independently that was going to make his job more challenging. His knees were bumping against the dashboard right now because he intended to indulge her need for independence on the less important issues so that he could successfully block it on the more important ones.

That had always been his strategy with the VP. Nell was going into a dangerous situation at the castle. She'd put on a cheery act for her sister, and she might have an overly optimistic view on how everything was going to work out, but he didn't doubt for a moment that she had a clear outlook on the situation.

This couldn't be easy for her. One minute she'd been signing her books and looking forward to spending another few days with her sister. The next, someone had tried to run down Piper, immediately followed by another written threat against her family.

"We're going to find a way through this, Nell."

"I know."

The confidence in her tone had him looking at her. It occurred to him for the first time that her attitude might be fueled by more than her overly optimistic nature. "Do you have some idea about where the necklace is?"

"No." She shifted to the center lane as traffic began to clog the right lane. "But I've been thinking about it ever since Adair found the first earring. There's got to be a story behind the way Eleanor divided them up and hid them in different places."

"You think she had a method to her madness?" he asked.

"Exactly. With characters, motivation is always key. One of Eleanor's reasons for hiding the jewels had to be that she didn't want to pass them on to members of her own family. That has to be why she didn't hide them inside the castle. I think that once it was discovered that they were missing, the surviving children must have searched every inch of that place."

"Yet Cam believes that whoever is behind this believed that either she hid the sapphires or some kind of clue in the library."

"That's a very logical theory," Nell conceded. "If I were Eleanor, I'd want to leave behind something to point the way. Yet my sisters came upon the earrings without any clue at all."

Reid shifted to study her a moment. "Do you have a theory about that?"

"It's more of a story idea."

"Tell me."

She shot him a quick look. "Promise you won't laugh."

Intrigued now, he said, "I won't. Cross my heart."

"That's what you always used to say to me whenever I got scared that summer we played together. All those days when it was your job to get me up to the cave in the cliff face so that I could wait around to be rescued, you'd say, "You'll be safe, Nell. Cross my heart. Remember?""

Reid could hardly forget. Hands down, his brothers' favorite game that summer had been pirates hunting for treasure—the treasure being Eleanor's sapphires. Of course, any pirate had to kidnap and hold a fair damsel captive. After the first game, it had been Reid's idea that Nell should have the permanent role of kidnapped damsel. It had been the only way to keep her off the cliff face and safe. "I never lied. And you're stalling. Tell me your story idea."

She passed a truck, shifted back into the right lane and said, "Okay. First, Eleanor wanted to leave proof behind that the jewels existed and had been in her possession. That's why she wore them in the portrait. And she wanted the sapphires to eventually be discovered. She didn't just throw them away. The two earrings were very carefully wrapped in leather pouches and hidden in places built to survive time and weather. So far the jewels have been found in the places we played as children—in the stone arch and the cave."

"Correct."

"So—and this is the 'don't laugh part.' She hid each piece separately—so maybe she wanted them to be found now, and by my sisters and me."

"You're implying that she had some insight into the future."

"Something like that."

For a moment, Reid considered. "That idea might work very well for a children's story."

"But it's not a possibility that a Secret Service agent would entertain."

"No. We work in much more concrete scenarios."

"Hypothetical or concrete, we're both after the same thing," Nell said, easing the car into the center lane again.

"With one important difference. You want to discover the story about the sapphires, why Eleanor hid them, figure out who they belong to and why someone else believes they have a claim on them. My goal is much simpler. I want to catch a would-be killer and write 'the end' on the story."

She shot him a grin. "Works for me. And thanks for not laughing." Then she turned her full attention back to negotiating her way through traffic.

By the time they'd cleared the D.C. area and had entered Pennsylvania, Reid became aware that he had a bigger problem than the cramp in his leg. He'd been trained to use all of his senses, and sitting in the tiny space with Nell, he'd found that he was definitely using all of them.

First, there was no escaping her scent. He still hadn't come up with a description. But he'd smelled it before, perhaps in the gardens at the White House at night. He'd kept his eyes on the road, but he had excellent peripheral vision, and he'd been trained to use it. Therefore, in the space of thirty miles, he'd become very aware of the soft curve of her lips when she smiled, and that the sun lightened the color of her hair. He'd also had time to study her hands. They were small, the fingers slender. She wore her nails short with just a sheen of pink polish. A lady's hands. And twice so far, he'd caught himself imagining what they might feel like on his skin. He'd found out when they'd both reached to turn the radio station at the same time. Her fingers had just brushed lightly against the back of his hand, but the burning sensation had shot right to his loins.

"Sorry." They'd both spoken at once.

She'd laughed and held up one hand with her little finger extended. "Pinkie wish."

"Pinkie what?"

"We both said the same word at the same time. Now we're supposed to link our little fingers and make a wish. C'mon."

"Okay." He linked his pinkie finger with hers and felt the arrow of heat shoot through him again.

It gave him some satisfaction that her hand trembled just a little as she placed it back on the wheel. But he shouldn't be hoping she might be feeling even some part of the attraction he was feeling. Because he shouldn't be feeling this way; he shouldn't be wanting Nell MacPherson.

The problem was, like it or not, he did. And the desire to have her was growing with each passing mile.

"Well, are you going to do something about it or should I?" Nell asked him.

Everything in his body went hard as he turned to stare at her. "Do something about what?"

"The static on the radio. What did you think I was talking about?"

Not going there, Reid thought. "What do you like?" But even that question had his mind wandering beyond her taste in music. How did she like to be touched? Tasted?

"I have pretty eclectic tastes."

Good to know.

"But Piper's been listening to that classic station for three days now. I need a change. Do you like the Beatles?"

"Who doesn't?"

This time he kept his hands to himself as she punched some buttons and "I Want to Hold Your Hand" blasted into the small car. Listening to it didn't solve his problem. He wanted to do a lot more than hold Nell's hand.

She lowered the volume. He tried to do the same with the desire that was thrumming through him. He had only briefly touched the woman, not yet kissed her on the lips. His hormones hadn't run this hot since he was in college.

Not since the last time he'd seen Nell beneath the stone arch.

Grimly, Reid shifted his attention to the side view mirror again and watched that for a while. "Pass a few cars," he said.

While she did, he kept his gaze fixed. He saw what he was looking for when the highway began to climb.

"There's been a silvery-gray sedan three cars back for a while now," she said.

Surprised, he shot her a sideways glance. "You noticed it."

"You said it was possible he'd follow us, so I thought it might be a good idea to keep a lookout. That car was behind us when we drove onto the beltway. It got ahead of us about twenty miles back, but we passed it when traffic got congested again before the last exit."

The woman had good eyes. He, too, had noted the cars that had followed them onto the interstate, but he'd lost track of the gray sedan after it had passed them.

Because he'd been thinking of Nell.

A sign for the upcoming exit flashed by. "Cut back into the right-hand lane and take your speed down to just below the limit."

Nell did exactly as he asked. Within minutes, the car directly behind them cut into the passing lane and drove by. The gray sedan merely slowed and kept its distance. Before long, several more cars passed.

"What now?" Nell asked.

"A break," he announced. "We're going to take the next exit ramp and stop for some coffee, stretch our legs and see if the gray car follows us."

A break sounded like a very good idea. The fast-food chain they stopped at had a drive-through, so Nell was surprised when Reid told her to park. The gray car not only followed them onto the exit ramp, it turned into the restaurant behind them. By the time Nell eased her Fiat into the parking slot and turned off the engine, the gray car was moving past them toward the drive-through lane. Nell caught a glimpse of the driver in her rearview mirror and gasped.

"What?" Reid asked.

"The driver of the car that's been following us. It's the woman who came up to me in the café and asked me to autograph that book. I'm sure of it."

6

REID TURNED TO face Nell and blocked her view of the car. "Don't look at her again and stay right where you are. I'm going to get out and come around to your door."

Nell's mind raced almost as fast as her heart while Reid took his time extricating himself from the front seat and circling the front of the car. She summoned up the image of the woman who'd approached her on the sidewalk and compared it to the quick glimpse she'd gotten of the driver. The same hair, the glint of gold at her ear. It was her all right. Though Nell badly wanted to, she didn't look at the gray car again. Another vehicle drove past. In the rearview mirror she could see it was a big SUV with at least half a Little League baseball team packed into it. In her peripheral vision, she saw it follow the gray car into the drive-through lane.

Then Reid opened her door and extended his hand to help her out. When it closed over hers, the effect on her system was instantaneous. She stilled in her seat. All thought of the autograph lady faded from her mind as it filled with Reid. Just the sight of her hand lost in his had all of her senses heightening. She noticed the contrasts first. His hand was larger, broader, and his skin made hers look even paler. His palms were hard. She felt the pressure of each one of his fingers as they tensed on hers. There was power there. Danger. It pulled at her in a way nothing else ever had. Her body heated so quickly the hot afternoon sun felt cool on her skin. When she looked up to meet his eyes, she saw the same intensity that she felt in the grip of his hand. The gray of his irises had darkened. His hand tightened on hers and for a moment she thought he would help her up and then right into his arms.

She had to find out. Her mind was already racing forward, anticipating what would happen when her body was pressed fully to his, what she would feel when his mouth closed over hers.

Before she could move, he stepped back and shifted his gaze over the top of the car. Then he dropped her hand and closed the door. She made some kind of sound, but he was already moving around the front of the car. Biting down hard on her lip, Nell desperately tried to gather her wits. The time it took for him to insert himself into the front seat again helped. A little. But her heart pounded so hard and so fast she could hardly hear him when he finally spoke.

"She's gone around the corner, and she's trapped by the two cars that pulled in behind her. She's probably expecting us to go in."

His words and the brusque tone helped her to focus on reality. And on the woman who'd followed them from D.C. A woman who had played a role in nearly killing her sister.

Gripping the steering wheel, she forced herself to relive that horrifying moment when she was racing toward Piper, hoping and praying that she'd get to her before that car did. That did the trick. What she was feeling about Reid and what she wanted to do about it had to be shoved to the back burner for now. They had bigger and much more dangerous fish to fry.

"She can't afford to stay too close or to follow us into the restaurant. She has to be careful I don't recognize her," she said.

"Good point," Reid acknowledged.

"Still she's taking a risk. We could leave right now and be out of sight by the time she gets through the drive-through. But there may be another reason why she can afford to let us out of her sight for a few minutes."

"What are you thinking?"

Nell turned to face him. "She might not be our only tail. And you're thinking that, too. Aren't you? That's why we're still sitting here instead of going into the restaurant, isn't it?"

Surprise flickered in his eyes. "That's exactly what I'm thinking."

"I should have thought of it sooner," she said.

"Why would you?"

"Because one of my guilty pleasures is watching TV shows about crime fighters. I'm addicted to this one about this ex-CIA agent who's been burned from his job and is working for private clients in Miami. He and his pals use the double-tail strategy all the time. Police use it, too."

"So does the Secret Service," Reid said in a dry tone. "Let's put your theory to the test. If I'd set up the double tail, the second car would have pulled to the shoulder on the interstate and will be waiting to pick us up when we return. Back out and use the entrance to get us out of here."

Nell started the car, shot it into Reverse, then drove out the same way they'd come in. Turning left, she headed back toward the interstate. Three cars were waiting in a line to make a turn onto the highway. Other than that, there was no traffic, and no one had followed them out of the restaurant. "We're clear."

When she put on her signal to turn onto the interstate ramp, Reid said, "Keep going. You have a GPS system in the car, right?"

She glanced at him as she reached for the button to activate it. "What's the plan?"

"My guess is that the second tail is waiting for us near the entrance ramp, and your autograph hound won't panic until she picks up her drive-through order and notices that our car is gone. Her first call will be to the second tail. Keep your eye on the restaurant in your rearview mirror, while I find us a back-road route to Albany."

"Albany?" It was her turn to feel surprised.

Reid's fingers were busy on the console. "Just as soon as we're sure no one is following us, we're going to use an hour of the forty-four or so we have left to pay a visit to Deanna Lewis."

"She's still in a coma."

He pushed a button. "True. But I'd like to see her in person and talk to the staff. If we'd stayed on the interstate, we would have had to drive around Albany. This way our tail or tails won't know about our visit. Any sign of the gray car yet?"

She checked the rearview mirror. "No. And the three

cars exiting from the toll area all headed in the direction of the restaurant. We're still clear."

"Turn left at that intersection ahead."

Once she made the turn, Reid pulled out his cell. "Keep your eye out. I'm going to text gray car's license plate to Duncan." After a moment, he continued, "Can you describe the woman who asked you for the autograph?"

"Sure." After glancing in the rearview mirror again, Nell pictured in her mind the woman who'd come up to her in the café. "Long dark hair pulled back from her face with a gold clip. Not pretty, but very attractive. Early to mid-fifties, but she takes some care to look younger. Makeup, manicure and expensive clothes. She was wearing a silk shirt, gold necklace and earrings. And a ring on her left hand with some kind of insignia. Maybe a coat of arms."

She felt Reid glance up from his cell phone to look at her for a moment.

"Do you look at everyone you meet that closely?"

"I suppose," she said. "I never know when I might need those details for a character I'm writing."

"Did you notice anything else?"

"She spoke with a slight accent. British perhaps."

For the next fifteen minutes, there was silence in the car except for the low throbbing beat of the Beatles retrospective on the radio. With the road stretching out before her like an endless ribbon, Nell found her mind arrowing back to those few world-stopping moments in the parking lot when Reid had grasped her hand to pull her out of the car.

Earlier, when they'd made that pinkie wish, she'd nearly convinced herself that he hadn't shared that hot explosion of desire that she'd experienced. But during that space of time when she'd been anticipating the kiss she'd fantasized about for years, she hadn't been mistaken about his response. His intention. She couldn't have felt what she had if he had felt nothing. She'd taken enough chemistry in school to know the basics. Two substances had to interact for combustion to take place.

Just thinking about what might have happened if he'd kissed her triggered flames that licked along her nerve endings.

Breathe. She could barely feel her fingers on the steering wheel.

Focus. After checking the mirror again, Nell allowed herself a sideways glance at Reid. He was texting back and forth with Duncan. Doing what needed to be done. And what she needed to do was drive to Albany. But sooner or later, they were going to have to talk about what was going on between them and what they were going to do about it.

Just the thought of "doing something" was enough to release the floodgates again. She felt the torrid liquid heat flowing through her system, enough to make her shiver.

"You okay?" Reid asked.

It's all good, she told herself. "I'm fine," she said.

On second thought, perhaps it was best that they didn't talk about what was happening between them at all and just get to the *doing it* part. At any rate, now wasn't the time or the place. There were much better settings.

Once more, she checked the mirror. No sign of a gray car or any other vehicle. A glance at the GPS screen on her console told her that they were still ten miles from the outskirts of Albany. With nothing but a constantly unrolling ribbon of road in front of her, Nell increased the pressure on the gas pedal and thought of where at the castle she and Reid might have their "talk." Or not.

In the little fantasy she wrote about Reid all those years ago and buried in the metal box, the setting she'd chosen was in the gardens. She had to avoid the stone arch. Because the fantasies she'd spun about him had nothing to do with happy-ever-afters and everything to do with slow, teasing arousal and hot, unbridled chemistry.

Or at least, that's what she'd known about those things at eighteen. The gardens had always been her favorite on the castle grounds. There was one particular spot that had been her secret place—one she'd escaped to when she wanted to get away from her sisters and even Aunt Vi. She'd even plotted out the first draft of *It's All Good* there.

Little wonder her favorite place had come to mind when she'd written down her most secret and sexy narrative. There'd be moonlight, of course. A full moon over the lake and lots of stars. And the heady scent of flowers, some of which had been planted by Eleanor herself.

With the image fully delineated in her mind, she risked a quick glance at Reid. In her current reality, he was fully dressed in his Secret Service suit, all neat and tidy except for the loosened tie. He wouldn't need all those clothes in the garden. Not any of them, if her story line went according to plan.

She pictured taking his shirt off, exposing that tanned skin an inch at a time. The moonlight would play over it as she ran her hand over his shoulders, testing the smooth, firm flesh and the hard muscle beneath. Then she'd draw the shirt slowly down his arms until it hung from his wrists, trapping them. Yes, that would be good, she thought. He wouldn't be able to touch her as she began to explore his flesh with her mouth.

Nell? That would be the only word he'd say. The same way he'd said it when he had first seen her in Piper's apartment. It would have the same question in the tone. And this time she'd have the answer.

"Nell, are you all right?"

She tensed her fingers on the wheel and jerked herself back to her current reality. Then she slammed on the brakes to avoid running the red light ahead of her. "I'm fine."

"You seemed to be a thousand miles away."

Less than fifty, if she was judging the distance to the castle gardens correctly. "Just thinking."

"Here's more to think about. Duncan had some luck running the plates. The gray car is registered to a Gwendolen Campbell. And she spells it the same way one of Eleanor Campbell's older sisters did." Reid filled her in on the family lineage Cam had told him about that morning.

"What are the chances that two hundred years later we'd be tailed by someone who just happens to have the same name as Eleanor Campbell's sister? Right down to the spelling?"

"Duncan's going to do what he can to check her out. In the meantime, he's filling Cam in on the latest, and one of them will inform Daryl Garnett, so he's fully briefed when we arrive at the castle."

As the light turned, Reid noticed that the road had widened into four lanes. They were still on the outskirts of Albany, but he could see the capital buildings in the distance to his left, and the traffic had grown heavier. To his right he noted a sign that they were approaching a hospital.

"Well, with the CIA on our team both here and in Scotland, we ought to know more soon," Nell said. "In the meantime, we know that Gwendolen Campbell is definitely involved in this. The question is, how involved? Who is she working with besides Deanna Lewis and the man or woman who tried to run Piper down? And who's running the show?"

He shot Nell a sideways glance. He couldn't have put it better himself. Her questions were spot-on. "I should have seen she had to be a player when you first mentioned your autograph lady. Maybe the key player. More than that, we've been assuming that the *us* Deanna Lewis was talking about to Piper involved just two people, that Deanna had one partner. There could be three. But there could be more. That possibility should have occurred to me sooner."

"Well, if you want to play the blame game, I should have figured it out, too." Nell changed into the right lane. "I make up plotlines. And her request for that autograph had perfect timing. Plus, she looked so normal. All I saw was a woman who wanted me to sign a book for her granddaughter. And that makes her perfect for the role of villain."

She took a right turn toward the hospital. "I should have seen it. I was just too focused on Piper after the attempt. I wouldn't have even thought about the woman again if you hadn't probed."

The difference was Nell had good reason for her distraction. Someone had tried to run down her sister. But

Reid had only one reason for his lapse. Nell. He'd been thinking about her and wanting her ever since he'd seen her again. He couldn't seem to get any distance or perspective. It wasn't just the sexual attraction—although it was there, a steady burn in his blood. A strong part of his distraction was due to the fact that she'd changed in very surprising ways. He was constantly being delighted and fascinated by the way her mind worked.

"Something's bothering you," Nell said.

Then there was her talent for intuiting things about him: the way he was feeling and what he was thinking. Not even his brothers could do that.

And if he kept wondering how *she* could or what she might do next to surprise him, he wasn't going to be able to protect her.

"No one's following us." She turned into the hospital parking lot. "This was a great idea. Our quick exit from the fast-food restaurant bought us some time. At the castle, Daryl Garnett is with Aunt Vi, and from what Piper and Adair say, Vi is in very good hands. So even if autograph lady or one of her partners gets annoyed that we've taken this detour, I think everyone should be safe for the moment."

"You're the one I'm worried about. You're distracting me from this investigation, and that puts you in danger."

Nell's heart gave a little flutter, but she managed to keep her hands steady on the wheel as she drove down the line of cars and pulled into a parking space. Saying a little prayer that her voice would work, she faced him. "I can take care of myself. If it makes you feel any better, you're distracting me, too."

Reid frowned. "That only makes the problem worse. We have to sort this out and find a solution."

Nell knew exactly how she wanted to solve their problem. The image flashed into her mind of the scene she'd created earlier—the two of them in Eleanor's moonlit garden. She could almost feel the smooth taut skin of his bare shoulders beneath her hands. Reminding herself to breathe, she said, "The clock is ticking. We should discuss this after we get to the castle."

"We'll settle it now, in just a second. Stay right where you are." Reid opened the car door and climbed out to scan the lot.

While he did his bodyguard thing, Nell remained seated, gathered her thoughts. So much for the little garden in the moonlight scene. In that particular setting, she hadn't planned on doing a lot of talking. None at all, in fact. But any heroine worth her salt could adapt to the changing circumstances. All she had to do was tell him what she wanted.

Him.

When he climbed back into the car, he seemed to fill every inch of space until he was all she was aware of. His eyes were the color of smoke shooting up from a fire, dark and dangerous. And his lips were so close. The air in the cramped space had turned sultry. Stifling. She couldn't tear her gaze away from his mouth. It seemed to be the softest part of him; still, it looked firm and unyielding. What would it feel like pressed against hers? Gentle? Rough? Another inch and their lips would make contact. How long had she yearned for the moment? All she had to do was lean forward and...

Hard hands gripped her shoulders, making it impossible for her to move.

"I want you, Nell. I can't seem to change that. But

one thing I can control. Nothing is going to happen between us."

She felt as if he'd upended a bucket of ice water on her head.

Wanna bet? If she could have moved her lips, she would have said it out loud. She might even have stuck out her tongue. Neither was her best move if she wanted Reid to start thinking of her as a woman. A woman he was incapable of resisting. She needed another strategy. Fast.

"Nothing," he repeated as if he could read her mind.

She recognized the steely determination in his tone, and it only added fuel to her own resolve. During that long-ago summer, he'd used that same tone to convince her that she could reach any goal, conquer any obstacle. She'd obeyed him like a slave, taken any risk he'd challenged her with. Those days were gone.

"Why not? We're both adults. We want each other. What could be the harm?"

For an instant his hands tightened on her shoulders, and she was sure he was going to pull her closer. He gave her a hard shake.

Then he dropped his hands clenching them into fists. "You're family. Dammit, Nell, I don't want to hurt you."

Nell's temper flared. "You know what your problem is, Reid? Like the rest of my family, you're making some very false assumptions." She poked a finger into his chest. "One, you believe I'm still a little girl, someone you have to take care of. You're wrong. I can take care of myself."

"Maybe. But you deserve someone who'll offer you more than I can. You deserve what your sisters have found with my brothers. You'll expect that. Everyone in the family will. I decided a long time ago that I wouldn't be able to offer any woman that."

She poked him again. "You're wrong about my expectations, too. The last thing in the world I want is some kind of permanent involvement with a man. I'm three years out of college. I have to concentrate on my career. Besides, I tried the whole falling-in-love thing a few years back, and it drained too much time out of my writing schedule, not to mention the effect it had on my GPA. Even if I was ready for something long-term, you'd be the last man I'd choose."

"Why?"

"Because you're overprotective just like the rest of my family. It's bad enough that I'm stuck working with you to find the necklace. I intended to do that on my own."

After a beat of silence, his eyes narrowed on her. He was listening now. "The man you fell in love with— he hurt you."

"Yes, but I got over it. I'm a big girl. You're going to have to get used to that."

Another beat of silence.

"Is there anything else I got wrong?"

"Yes. You're absolutely wrong when you say 'Nothing can happen between us' because something already has. Back in the parking lot of that restaurant, I wanted to kiss you. And you wanted it, too. We're both thinking about what it would be like. I'm imagining one thing. You're probably envisioning another. In one of my books, this would be a plot point. The characters would have to make a decision. Either they find out and deal with the consequences, or they keep thinking about it. I would assume that, in your job, it pays to know exactly what you're up against. Right?"

"Close enough."

But *he* wasn't nearly close enough. The heat of his breath burned her lips, but she had to have more. And talking wasn't going to get it for her. If she wanted to seduce Reid, *she* had to make the move.

Finally, her arms were around him, her mouth parted beneath his. And she had her answers.

His mouth wasn't soft at all but open and urgent. His taste was as dark and dangerous as the man. That much she'd guessed. But there was none of the control that he always seemed to coat himself with. None of the reserve. There was only heat and luxurious demand. She was sinking fast to a place where there was nothing but Reid and the glorious sensations only he could give her. She wanted to lose herself in them. Her heart had never raced this fast. Her body had never pulsed so desperately. Even in her wildest fantasies, she'd never conceived of feeling this way. And it still wasn't enough. She needed more. Everything. Him. Digging her fingers into his shoulders, she pulled him closer.

Big mistake. In some far corner of Reid's mind, the words blinked like a huge neon sign. They'd started sending their message the instant he'd told her that they would settle what was happening between them now. He'd gotten out of the car to gain some distance, some perspective. Some resolve. But the brief respite had only seemed to increase the seductive pull Nell had on him.

He'd been a goner the moment he'd stuffed himself back into the front seat.

Long before that.

Oh, her argument had been flawless. Knowing ex-

actly what you were up against was key in his job. Reid
heartily wished it was her logic that had made his hands
streak into her hair and not the feelings that she'd been
arousing in him all day.

For seven years.

The hunger she'd triggered while she'd been talking so logically felt as if it had been buried inside him
forever. Then once her lips had pressed against his, he
forgot everything except that he was finally kissing
her. Finally touching her hair. He hadn't imagined how
silky the texture would be. One hand remained there,
trapped, while the other roamed freely, moving down
and over her, memorizing the curves and angles in one
possessive stroke.

She was everything a man could wish for; as small,
slim, and supple as he'd imagined. And he'd imagined
a lot.

Her lips were soft, too. Inviting, accepting, arousing—just as he'd fantasized. The first taste had been
sweet. Just as he had expected. But when he changed
the angle and used his tongue to probe farther, to tease
and to tempt, her flavors grew darker, stronger, hotter.
And beneath all those layers, he tasted not surrender
but demand. He had no choice but to answer it, taking
them both deeper until all he knew was her. His desire
only grew until it was huge and consuming. Not to be
denied. He wanted her—no, he needed her the way
a man needed sleep after a day of labor; the way he
needed water after a drought.

Unable to stop himself, he took more. Her hands
were on his shoulders, gripping hard. He wanted them
on his bare skin so that he could feel the softness of her

palms, the scrape of her fingers. Even through the layers of clothing, she made him burn.

Reid knew he had to get a grip or that burn would sear right through him and leave a scar. No other woman had ever seduced him this way: body, mind, soul. He'd never allowed it. He shouldn't allow it now. But he couldn't stop himself from releasing her seat belt. His hands gripped her waist, lifted.

A series of staccato blasts from a horn had him dropping her back into her seat. Reid glanced around, spotted a sedan two slots down in the row facing them with its lights blinking, the horn blasting. Behind it, a woman fumbled with her keys and managed to quiet the alarm.

Emotions shot through him. Relief that the noise had been caused by a woman who'd accidentally set off her car alarm. Fear that it could have been worse. Anger at himself that he'd let Nell so thoroughly distract him again.

He brought his gaze back to her. "Now we know what it's like." And the knowledge could change everything if he let it.

Perhaps it already had.

Nell felt like a diver resurfacing layer by layer from a very great depth. Her head was reeling. Good thing he hadn't asked a question. Since her lips were once more not taking commands from her brain, she wouldn't have been able to answer.

In contrast he seemed to be doing fine—except for the grunt he made as he extricated himself from his side of the car. She waited where she was, praying that her brain cells would click on and that she'd be able to move by the time he circled to open her door.

When he did, he didn't offer his hand as he had at

the fast-food restaurant. Instead, he stepped back while she made it out on her own. She tested her legs, while she pressed the remote to lock the door.

"One more thing," he said.

She met his eyes.

"Now that we know what it's like, we're going to put it in a file and forget it." Then he turned, scanned the area and gestured her forward.

Wanna bet? Once more she was grateful that she didn't trust herself to speak. What *she* knew was that she now had two conflicting narratives to deal with. In one her goal was to find a long-missing necklace, and in the other, her goal was to seduce Reid Sutherland. Plot and subplot. All she had to do was find a way to weave them together.

7

NELL STOOD IN front of a long glass window. Beyond it Deanna Lewis lay in a narrow hospital bed flanked by serious-looking machines that beeped and blinked continuously. A nurse was in the room replacing an IV.

Ever since they'd left the car, Reid had slipped back into the role of Secret Service agent. He'd introduced himself and shown his badge to the young officer who was standing guard at Deanna Lewis's door. Officer Jameson had been polite, but he'd asked them to wait while he contacted his superior officer.

Signaling them to join him, the young man said, "Sheriff Skinner over in Glen Loch has cleared you."

Reid nodded to him, then turned as the nurse opened the door. "How is Miss Lewis?"

"There's been no change in her condition since the surgery." The woman's name tag read Nancy Braxton. Nell estimated she was in her late twenties. Leading them back into the room, Braxton continued, "Dr. Knight stops in to see her every day. He's confident that she's healing, but there's no way to tell when she might come out of the coma."

"And there have been no visitors?" Reid asked.

"No. The police have been quite explicit about that. The only people who have been allowed in this room are doctors, nurses or members of our volunteer staff."

"There was a reporter from the *New York Times* who stopped by last week," Officer Jameson said from the doorway. "I told him about the no-visitor policy."

"A reporter?" Reid asked.

"Very polite young man. James Orbison," Jameson said.

"Can you describe him?" Reid asked.

"Medium height, short brown hair, slender build," Jameson said.

"Cute," Nurse Braxton added. "He wore preppy clothes, and the glasses added a geeky aura. Sexy."

Jameson glanced at the nurse with a raised eyebrow. "Sexy?"

Braxton shrugged. "Just saying."

Reid interrupted the byplay. "Anything else you can recall?"

"He said he'd written an article about Castle MacPherson a little over six months ago," Jameson said. "He'd convinced his editor to let him do a follow-up piece once some of the Stuart sapphires were discovered."

"You didn't let him visit Ms. Lewis?"

"No. He did see her through the glass. No way to prevent that. And he had questions about her condition. But I told him that he'd have to talk to Sheriff Skinner over in Glen Loch if he wanted any further information. He said that the sheriff was next on his list." Jameson's gaze shifted to Deanna. "She's such a pretty little thing. It's hard to believe that she threatened to kill someone."

Nell agreed with the young officer's assessment. Even with her head wrapped in bandages, Deanna Lewis was pretty. Hooked up to all the tubes and wires, she looked fragile and defenseless. Yet she'd taken out Duncan with a Taser shot and then kidnapped Piper at gunpoint.

"You mentioned that members of the volunteer staff are allowed in the room," Reid said. "Who are they exactly?"

"Oh, we have an amazing group of people who volunteer their services here at the hospital," Nurse Braxton said. "Many of them are senior citizens, but we also have college students who are required to do community service as part of their degree programs. Since Deanna didn't have any family visiting, Dr. Knight asked the woman who runs the service if she could find someone to spend time reading to her. He believes that the sound of a human voice often speeds the recovery of coma patients."

"And the volunteers do that?" Reid asked.

"One volunteer," Nurse Braxton said. "After her first visit, she said she'd try to come back every day. But the day before yesterday, she said she had to go out of town for a couple of days and not to expect her back for a few days."

Nell glanced at Reid, and she could tell what he was thinking. She asked the question. "What did this woman look like?"

"Brunette, tall and very attractive. In her early fifties, I'd say. Well dressed. Good jewelry."

"Did you notice a ring on her finger?" Nell asked.

Nurse Braxton nodded. "Yes. A gold one with a kind

of crest on it. I remarked on it. She said it was the family coat of arms."

"*Gwen* was on her name tag," Officer Jameson said. "She signed in as G. Harris."

Reid turned to him. "Was she ever alone with the patient?"

"No, sir. I always left the door open when she came, just as I'm doing now. All Ms. Harris did was read to her. The same book each time. A children's story with pictures. Sometimes she'd read it more than once."

"Do you remember what the story was about?" Nell asked. But she was pretty sure she already knew.

"It was a fairy tale about this Scot who stole his true love away from her family, brought her to the New World and built her a castle with a magical stone arch. Made me think of the one over at Castle MacPherson."

NELL WAS ASLEEP beside him when Reid turned down the dirt road that wound its way to the castle. He'd updated Duncan and Sheriff Skinner in Glen Loch before they'd left the hospital and then insisted on driving Nell's car.

If Gwen Harris showed up again at the hospital, Officer Jameson or whoever was on guard would contact Skinner discretely. Reid and Nell hadn't discussed what they'd learned; in fact, they'd barely spoken since they'd left the traffic of Albany behind. He could tell that, before she'd drifted off, she'd been doing exactly what he was doing—running through the possible explanations for the information they had gathered from their visit to the hospital. Nell's subconscious mind was probably still busily looking at the various story lines while she slept. The problem was there were too many possibilities, and so far they couldn't prove even one.

As the car crested a steep hill, he shifted his attention to the view. Below lay a postcard snapshot of Castle MacPherson tucked into the mountains on a rocky promontory overlooking a quiet blue lake. The image perfectly matched the one he'd carried around in his mind for seven years. The three stories of gray stone stood sturdy and strong, the sun glinting off its windows. Gardens stretched to the west, high cliffs to the east. He even caught a glimpse of Angus's legendary stone arch at the edge of the gardens before the road took the final steep dip that ended at the castle drive.

As he pressed down on the brake for a sharp curve, he glanced over at Nell. She slept like a child, her hand tucked beneath her cheek on the car door. Keeping her safe had to be his top priority, but he wasn't at all sure he could keep her safe from him.

File it away and forget it.

Excellent plan. Too bad he didn't have a chance in hell of sticking to it. When they'd tried that experimental kiss, *desire* seemed too tame a word for the gut-deep, soul-searing arousal he'd experienced. That wasn't the part that scared him the most. What did was that, at some point while he'd been kissing her, he'd wanted to give her more. He'd wanted to deny her nothing.

If that woman in the hospital parking lot hadn't accidentally set off the alarm in her car, he would have made love to Nell right in the front seat of her Fiat. He'd never done anything quite that reckless in his entire life. Not even when his teenage hormones had been at their peak.

Just the thought of it tempted him to pull off onto a side road, find a spot that was a bit more private and finish what he'd started in the parking lot. Reckless and impulsive were qualities he ruthlessly suppressed. Now Nell was making him want to set them free.

Even more troubling was what he had felt when she had mentioned the man she'd fallen in love with. Jealousy. The coppery taste in his mouth, the wrench in his gut—both had been unprecedented.

He might be able to get out of this unscathed. If he dropped her at the castle and never saw her again. That scenario wasn't open to him.

But if they started down the path where their desires were leading them, he didn't see a happy ending for either of them.

He didn't want to hurt her. She was young and idealistic, and she had this incredibly sunny outlook on life. There was no way she wouldn't expect a happy-ever-after. And she should have it. In many ways, she'd always reminded him a bit of his mother. He'd seen, perhaps more than his brothers ever had, the kind of pain she'd suffered when she'd learned that their father had never loved her. Reid never wanted to be responsible for hurting anyone the way his father had hurt all of them. Better not to go there. Nell deserved someone who would love her and have a family with her.

Ahead of him, the road leveled and the crunch of gravel beneath the tires told him that he was on the driveway. The moment he turned the car around the curve, he spotted Viola MacPherson just outside the front door. The dog sitting at her feet had to be Alba. Cam had filled him in on the dog that Vi had brought home from a shelter when she'd starting hearing noises in the middle of the night.

The fact that Alba was deaf made her a strange choice as a watchdog, but her instincts had turned out to be spot-on, because she had exposed the con man threatening Adair's life and wanting Eleanor's sapphire earring.

Reid shifted his gaze to the tall man with the silver-streaked hair standing next to Vi—Cam's boss at the CIA, Daryl Garnett. Reid knew Cam thought the world of him.

He pulled the car to a stop, then put his hand on Nell's. "Nell?"

Even before she turned her head, her fingers linked with his. Her eyes opened, and as he looked into them, Reid felt himself being pulled into that world where only the two of them existed. He'd felt desire before. And he'd experienced passion. But nothing this intense. Nothing this irresistible.

Then Vi was opening the passenger door and in seconds, the two women were in each other's arms, both talking over the other. The dog circled them once and then sat to watch.

When Reid climbed out of the car, Vi broke away from Nell long enough to envelope him in a hug. "Welcome back to Castle MacPherson." Then she turned to draw her niece into the house.

"They're going to need a few minutes," Daryl said. "Vi says she hasn't seen Nell for nearly a year because of that grant. In the meantime, I've got good news and bad news. Can I offer you a beer to wash both down?"

Reid smiled at him and extended his hand. "Cam said I was going to like you."

IT TOOK HALF a bottle of beer, but Reid was feeling more relaxed than he had all day. He and Daryl were seated at a table on the terrace outside the kitchen. Over

Daryl's shoulder, Reid could see the sun streaking the sky with pink as it sank closer to the lake. He'd been formally introduced to Alba, who'd sniffed his hand and then stretched out in a waning patch of sunlight and fallen asleep. Beyond her, through the glass of the terrace doors, he could see Vi and Nell chatting as they put together a meal.

"Vi roasted a chicken," Daryl said. "I think that's her version of killing the fatted calf."

Reid raised a brow. "If that's the good news, I'd rather it was related to the case."

Daryl grinned at him. "Vi's cooking is always good news. And she's celebrating the fact that the last of the Sutherland boys has finally returned to the castle. She's always thought of you three in a very special way, and since you're the final triplet to come back, that gives you prodigal son status. Don't knock it. As I recall, Cam got sandwiches, and Duncan had to grill his own steak."

Reid laughed. "Do me a favor and pass the word along to Cam about the chicken. It will just reinforce my status as the favored eldest son. But now, tell me you have something on Gwendolen Campbell."

"I do. Duncan forwarded me the text you sent him from the hospital, and once I had the name, it didn't take long to ID her. She had her name changed legally to Campbell six months ago. Before that, she was Gwendolen Harris."

"The name she used at the hospital when she was visiting Deanna Lewis."

"Turns out it isn't the only name she's gone by. Gerald Harris, the fifth Earl of Bainbridge, was her third husband," Daryl said. "He was twenty years her senior, and she inherited millions when he died."

"Explains the expensive clothes and jewelry."

"Husband number two, Martin Hatcher, wasn't short on money, either. Marrying him got her United States citizenship and she got his money when he passed on."

"Sounds like a pattern," Reid said.

"The pattern of a good grifter. But there's more. Husband number one was Douglas Lewis, and Deanna was just three years old when her widowed father married Gwen. Gwendolen's maiden name was MacDonald, and she was Douglas Lewis's second wife. That's why we didn't run across Gwendolen before this. Cam has discovered that she was born and raised in a village not twenty miles away from what remains of the Campbell estate in Scotland. He and Adair are looking into that end of it. But MacDonald isn't one of the names that pops up on the Campbell family tree that your mother discovered."

Reid took a swallow of his beer. "So this Gwendolen MacDonald Lewis Hatcher Harris is Deanna Lewis's stepmother. That would explain the visits to the hospital and offers a reason why they might be working together. But the question remains. Who is the man, or woman, who tried to run Piper down earlier today and how does he—or she—fit into the family picture?"

"We don't know yet. That's the bad news. Duncan says his friend at the police department will send us a rendering of the police artist's sketch of the hit-and-run driver as soon as it's completed. Then I'll give it to Sheriff Skinner, and he'll show it to Edie at the diner."

Reid grinned. "Edie is still running the diner?"

"She is, and besides serving up the best pancakes in upstate New York, she also provides better local information than the internet. If anyone who looks like this guy shows up, we'll get the news. It's her granddaughter Molly who's getting married here on Saturday, so Edie is especially interested in seeing that everything runs smoothly."

Reid sipped his beer. "Can we provide enough security for the wedding?"

"It's very small, and everyone is local. It will be impossible for someone to slip in unnoticed. The only outsider who might be attending is a young reporter from the *New York Times*, the one who did the original article that helped launch Castle MacPherson as a prime wedding destination."

"If you're talking about James Orbison, he dropped by the hospital to check on Deanna Lewis," Reid said.

"Sheriff Skinner told me. Last week Orbison dropped by to see him, and he also contacted Vi to arrange an interview tomorrow. He wants to shadow her for the day. I've done a background check, and he seems squeaky clean. He has a degree in journalism from Princeton. His uncle is a senior editor for the Sunday *Times* magazine section, and James started working for him right after graduation. We can meet him when he comes to interview Vi tomorrow."

"I want to ask him why he decided to write the original article on the castle."

Setting down his beer, Daryl said, "One more thing. Now that we know there's a connection between Deanna and Gwendolen and something about who they are, I've put some old friends of mine on it—a couple retired agents who are over in England. They're going to work with Cam and Adair."

Reid met Daryl's eyes. "They're going to have to

be fast. I'm not sure we have as much time as they've given us."

"What do you mean?"

Reid glanced to his right where he could see Nell and Vi moving about the kitchen. "Nell has this idea that she and her sisters are somehow destined to find the Stuart sapphires."

Daryl thought for a moment. "You think she's right?"

"I favor more practical scenarios, but I can't dismiss her idea," Reid said. "It sure didn't take Adair and Piper long to discover the two earrings once they returned to the castle. It was almost as if they'd been drawn to them like magnets. If Nell's right, she could discover the necklace very soon. Then she'll be disposable. If she doesn't find it fast, Vi could be in danger. That means that we can't let either of these women out of our sight, until we've got all the players behind bars."

He gestured to the two women in the kitchen. "As Nell has pointed out to me several times today—the clock is ticking."

"I hear you," Daryl said. "If there's one thing I've learned in the past few weeks, it's that things tend to move quickly here. I have one piece of advice to give you."

Reid turned to meet the older man's gaze.

Daryl smiled. "Beware of the legend. If you don't intend to marry a MacPherson woman, don't let her kiss you beneath the stones."

8

I'M HOME, NELL thought as she trimmed the ends off string beans and added them to a pot of water. A few feet away, Aunt Vi took a roasting pan out of the oven and placed it on top of the stove to cool. The scent of the chicken and freshly baked scones surrounded her with comfort and a feeling of safety. She'd spent her childhood, her girlhood, her adolescence, in this room. On rainy days, she'd played Scrabble with her sisters at the counter. Under her aunt's supervision, she had finished math assignments and had written her first short story at the kitchen table. After rinsing her hands in the sink, Nell sank into a chair to watch her aunt mash a steaming pot of potatoes. "You're making a feast."

Vi glanced up. "Tomorrow will be busy. There's a rehearsal for the wedding on Saturday. Very small. Edie's granddaughter Molly is getting married. So we're having a family celebration tonight. Reid hasn't visited since your father's wedding, and it's been nearly a year since you've been here—your longest absence yet. Your sisters were surprised that you completed your grant work. Very proud and pleased—but surprised."

Nell grinned at her. "Did they expect me to get home-sick and run back here?"

"Something like that. They were worried when you turned down that part-time teaching position at Hunt-leigh College. They saw it as the perfect job to comple-ment your writing career."

"And it would have kept me wrapped in a cocoon. I loved every minute of the year I spent on my own—no dorm supervisor, no one to report to except myself. No one to depend on except myself."

"No one hovering over you. The butterfly breaks free." Vi nodded in understanding. "You always had at least three of us looking out for you, telling you what to do."

Nell laughed. "*You* never hovered. You were much more subtle than Piper and Adair."

"I learned early on that it didn't do much good to argue with you once you had your mind made up. You were always your own boss, Nell. When you know what you want, you go after it, and you usually get it. So be-sides celebrating your independence, what did you enjoy the most on your cross-country tour?"

Nell smiled. "The settings, the people, and I kept a daily log. Now I have so much that will enrich my writ-ing. I'm trying my hand at writing a different kind of book this time. Romantic suspense for adults. It will be very different from my first."

Vi glanced over her shoulder. "I'm not surprised that you're taking on a new challenge. But it seems to me that *It's All Good* shares many qualities of the genre. Eleanor is a strong woman—just the kind of heroine a reader would connect with in a romantic suspense novel. As for Angus—he's a classic hero. He swept his true love off her feet and carried her off."

Nell thought of how different their situation was from her own. Fat chance that Reid was going to sweep her off her feet. In fact, she suspected that she was the one who was going to have to do the sweeping. "That makes Eleanor sound like a wimp. I want my heroine to be stronger."

"Don't sell Eleanor short. She left everything to go with Angus—her family, her home, the life she knew. To my way of thinking, that took a lot of courage."

Vi glanced through the glass terrace doors at the two men and then turned back to Nell. "They're about halfway through their beers. How about we have a glass of wine, and you can tell me what you're going to do about Reid Sutherland, and how you're going to find the necklace."

Nell tilted her head, studying her aunt as she opened a chilled bottle of white wine and filled two glasses. She hadn't missed the fact that Reid had come first on her aunt's list and not the necklace. "Reid's always been your favorite of the Sutherland boys, hasn't he?"

"He accepted the responsibility of taking care of my girls. You played a lot of risky games that summer."

Nell grinned. "You weren't supposed to know about them."

After taking a sip of her wine, Vi poured warm milk into the pot with the potatoes, then continued to mash. "It was my job to know. And I worried less because of Reid. He and his brothers were ten. And they were boys through and through. Mischief was in their genes. Reid could have made it his entire focus that summer to have fun. Instead, he made it his responsibility to keep all of you safe."

"He became my hero. My Prince Charming. I fell in love with him that summer."

"I fell in love with him a bit, too," Vi admitted. "He won my heart the day that Cam and Duncan decided you were all going to hike up Stone Mountain and find the source of the water that drops over Tinker's Falls."

Nell frowned for a bit as she searched her memory. "I remember we played at the falls a lot and in the cave where Piper and Duncan discovered the second earring, but I don't recall going to Stone Mountain."

"That's because you and Reid didn't go. He let his brothers go off with Adair and Piper. They were eight and nine. You were six. So he talked you into a day of playing tea party with your animals and dolls. I can't imagine that was the way he preferred to spend his time."

Nell grinned. "Now I remember that day. No one had been willing to play tea party with me before. Adair and Piper were always fascinated by the more danger-ous games the boys came up with."

"Reid knew exactly what bait to use to keep you from feeling you were missing out on the big adven-ture. I figured then he had to be pretty good at keeping watch over his brothers."

Nell shifted her gaze to the two men on the terrace. Vi's description of Reid rang true. He was a natural-born caretaker and it made him very good at his job. "He's still very much a protector."

"I'm depending on that." Vi set the pot of potatoes on a burner and sat down next to her niece.

A line appeared on Nell's brow as she continued to

study Reid speculatively. "That's posing a bit of a challenge for me."

"A challenge?"

"A big one. I was drawn to him when he was a boy because he was handsome and kind, a storybook hero. A fantasy in the flesh. Now what he makes me feel is entirely different. He stirs things up in me I didn't know were there. I didn't even know they were possible. I've never felt about anyone the way I feel about him."

Vi took Nell's hands in hers. "Does he know how you feel?"

"Oh, yes. And the stirring-up part is mutual. That's when our narratives start to conflict."

"How?"

"He's not happy about it. He doesn't want to hurt me. He thinks we should file away what we're feeling and what we could feel, and forget all about it. If Angus had been that kind of hero, this castle wouldn't be here. And neither would all of us."

Vi smiled at her. "You obviously take issue with Reid's solution."

Nell shifted her gaze to Reid again. "I do. I only have to look at him to want him. And I can't stop thinking about how much more we could stir up in each other. He kissed me today for the first time. I'm hoping that the forbidden-fruit thing kicks in, and he won't be able to resist taking another bite. I definitely want to kiss him again, and I want to know what comes next."

"Have you decided what you're going to do about it?" Vi asked.

"Yes." Nell thought of the scenarios she'd plotted out and hidden away on the night of their parents' wed-

ding, and of all the other similar ones that had fueled
her dreams for years.

Vi patted her hand. "Good. I'd act fast. That's what
I did with Daryl."

Nell's eyes widened. "You did?"

"I did." She grinned at her niece. "I knew I wanted
him the first time I looked at him, so I took him out
to the stone arch and kissed him there on the first day
we met."

Nell laughed as she hugged her aunt. "Well, that's not
my plan with Reid. He's made it clear that he doesn't
want the happy-ever-after part."

"What do you want?"

"More than anything I want to enjoy what he and I
can have together right now. And I have a plan."

"Of course you do. But don't kiss him beneath the
stones. Not until you're sure you want the happy-ever-
after part." Vi took another sip of her wine. "Do you
know what you're going to do about Eleanor's necklace?"

"Working on it." She slipped her hand into her pocket
and pulled out a folded piece of pink paper. "Remember Mom's old jewelry box that Adair and Piper and I
used to bury our goals and dreams in?"

"The one you buried in the stone arch? The one I
wasn't supposed to know anything about?"

Nell laughed. "You knew everything we did, and
you let us do it."

"So you've written down your goal to find Eleanor's
necklace, and you're going to tap into the power of the
stone arch to help you. That's a brilliant plan."

Nell glanced through the glass doors at Reid. Using
the stone arch to facilitate finding Eleanor's necklace

was only half of her plan. She had another piece of pink paper in her pocket. On that one she'd written her goal to seduce Reid and turn into reality the fantasies she'd written seven years ago. That way she could weave plot and subplot together. Since she could hardly seduce a man who wasn't around, any plan she might have entertained of slipping away from Reid and trying to find the necklace on her own would have to be modified. She'd have to work with him. She intended to place both papers in the jewelry box tonight because the clock was ticking.

THE CLOCK ON the parlor mantel struck the first of eleven bongs when Vi smothered a yawn and said, "Well, I'm ready to call it a night." Alba rose from her relaxed position in front of the fireplace and moved to Vi's side.

"When you hit a brick wall, sometimes the best cure is a good night's sleep," Daryl said.

They'd hit a brick wall all right, Nell thought as she hugged her aunt, and then Daryl surprised her by kissing her on the cheek. After dinner, they'd retired to the main parlor, reviewing everything they knew, didn't know, guessed or speculated.

Vi had even set up one of the whiteboards from Adair's office so that they could map out everything that had happened along a time line. However, at the end of more than two hours of studying the chronology of events, discussing, and theorizing, they weren't any further ahead than when they'd started. Reid followed Daryl out of the room. From the corner of her eye, Nell saw the two men pause to talk at the foot of the main staircase. Protection strategies, she thought.

There wasn't a doubt in her mind that Reid expected

her to join them so that he could escort her up to her room and "file her away" for the night.

Not happening. To distract herself from the flutter of nerves in her stomach, she moved closer to Eleanor's portrait. There was a part of her that envied the woman for having a lover who simply swept her away. The old Nell would have been thrilled by that. Recalling her aunt's comments on Eleanor's strength, she studied the painting more closely. At first glance, Eleanor appeared the same: beautiful, serene and very happy. But there was no denying the look of determination in her eyes, the lift to her chin.

All Nell needed was half the guts it had taken Eleanor to leave her family and home in Scotland to run away with her true love. Not that she intended to run away with Reid. All she wanted to do was give in to the yearning that had been growing inside her since the first time she'd seen him.

If Eleanor had felt this way about Angus, no wonder she'd risked everything to be with him. Again Nell checked the doorway to the main parlor. No sign of Reid. She glanced back up at the portrait and whispered, "At least you didn't have to deal with a reluctant lover."

REID WAITED UNTIL Daryl had disappeared around the curve of the landing before he turned and walked toward the open door of the main parlor. He'd successfully avoided being alone with Nell since they'd arrived at the castle. Not that the strategy had helped him control his preoccupation with her. While they'd been discussing the case for that last hour, he'd entirely lost the thread of the conversation. Twice.

That wasn't like him at all. In his job, he couldn't afford to lose his focus. Even when she wasn't looking at him, he still felt her in every pore of his being, and he felt that same sense of connection, which bordered on recognition, that he'd felt when they'd stood together beneath the stone arch seven years ago.

The Nell he'd known when he was ten was simple. The Nell he was coming to know was complex. He liked the way she looked—the delicate features, the fair skin, the hair that reminded him of spun gold. He also was coming to like and admire the way her mind worked. The problem was, the longer he was with her, the more he learned about her, the more fascinating she became.

He half hoped that she'd follow them out into the hallway, so that he could escort her safely up to her room and retire to his own. Separation and some distance were what he needed.

Right.

He wasn't a man who lied to himself. *Half hoped* were two telling words. There was a part of him that had wanted her to linger in the parlor so that he could be alone with her. Even though it meant playing with fire. Reid shoved his hands into his pockets. That wasn't like him, either. At least it hadn't been like him in a long time. Not since he and his brothers had been eight and they'd literally played with some matches they'd found in a kitchen drawer. Their father had been away, their mother working in her office. And she'd left him in charge. Her words had been, "Don't let your brothers burn down the house—or worse."

Cam had initiated the disaster by striking the first match. Then Duncan, usually the one to remain on the sidelines, had joined in. Finally Reid had succumbed to the hypnotic power of the bright flames. Their little adventure had progressed quickly from striking individual matches to starting a small blaze in a wastebasket which had severely damaged one wall of kitchen cabinets before the fire department arrived on the scene to put it out.

Even more than the scorched wood, he regretted the look of disappointment in his mother's eyes.

But he wasn't eight years old anymore. Dammit. Nell was changing him. There was something in her that tempted him to give in to that streak of recklessness that he suspected he and his brothers had inherited from his father. He wasn't sure he could resist her any more than he'd been able to resist striking that match on that long-ago afternoon. What he was absolutely certain of was that, if he started this particular fire, disaster lay ahead.

He didn't move into the room when he spoke. "You're not ready to call it a night yet."

"No." She flicked him a glance, then turned her attention back to the painting. "I want to start looking for the necklace."

"Tonight?"

"The clock is ticking. And this portrait is part of the story. For years it's been the only evidence that the sapphires exist. I think there's something in it that might provide a clue."

Intrigued, Reid joined her in front of the painting. "Why do you think that?"

"It's always been called her wedding portrait, but that can't be what it really is. True, she's wearing a white dress and there are flowers in her hair. But she and Angus ran away." Nell gestured to the upper right-hand corner of the painting. "You can see the stone arch that Angus built for her. So she sat for this portrait after they'd been here awhile. In my book, they married onboard the ship that brought them here. I had them renew their wedding vows beneath the arch once it was completed."

"In celebration of their first anniversary," Reid murmured.

She turned to stare at him. "You read *It's All Good?*"

He picked up a strand of her hair and rubbed it between his fingers. "Several times. I enjoyed it. Their story has always intrigued me, and you captured the heart of it in your book."

When she said nothing and continued to stare at him, he said, "You seem surprised that I enjoyed it."

"I'm trying to imagine you reading a children's story."

He smiled then. Because he wanted badly to do more than touch her hair, he dropped the strand and turned to the portrait. "Eleanor has always fascinated me. That summer when you and your sisters first showed us this painting and told us her story, my brothers immediately focused on finding the missing jewels. I was struck by the woman."

He had to wonder if that was because, even then, she made him think of the woman Nell would become. They had the same gold hair, pale skin, delicate features, stubborn chin. And the mouth. Eleanor's lips were slightly parted as if they were just waiting for a lover's kiss. His mind slipped back to that moment in the car when he'd been staring at Nell's mouth and nothing had mattered to him but kissing her. And more.

He could so easily have more. She was standing close enough that, if either of them moved, he would feel the brush of her body against his. If he turned ever so slightly, he could pull her into his arms. She wouldn't resist, and he could once more lose himself in the explosive heat of her response. Lose himself in her.

He shifted his gaze to the necklace. That was what he should be thinking about. "Perhaps the painting does hold the key. If we assume she was the one who hid them—"

"She did," Nell interrupted. "I'm certain of it."

"Why? Why not just pass them on to her heirs?"

Nell frowned at the portrait. "According to the story that was passed down, the jewels were Eleanor's dowry. But Deanna Lewis told Piper that they didn't belong to Eleanor, that she and whoever her partner was had a stronger claim. Maybe Eleanor felt the same way—that the jewels really did belong to someone else. After all, she eloped with Angus. That suggests that he may not have been someone her family approved of."

"Interesting."

"Deanna and Gwendolen may hold the answer."

He glanced at her. "What about your theory that you and your sisters are meant to find them? How does that fit?"

"I don't know exactly. But if I were going to hide something as beautiful as those jewels, I'd leave a clue. What better place to put it than in this portrait? Maybe that's why she had it painted in the first place and why she wore the sapphires. It's probably why this painting has survived all these years."

"Good point." Reid used her theory to study the portrait through a new lens. This time instead of focusing on Eleanor and her jewels, he concentrated on the other details. "She's sitting in the garden on a bench. There's a pile of books or notebooks next to her."

"Sketch pads, I'm betting. She drew," Nell said. "All of the illustrations in my book are based on her sketches."

"I read about that. The two of you share a talent for bringing images vividly to life. The location of that spot is somewhere in the gardens within sight of the stone arch, but I don't recall that latticework directly behind her."

"My father believed she was sitting in the gazebo," Nell said. "The wood structure rotted away years ago, but the stone foundation is still there." She sent him a smile. "You should remember it. You spent a day there playing tea party with me."

"What I remember is a pile of rocks."

"Beauty is in the eye of the beholder." Nell took a step back. "And so is the clue to the location of the necklace if we could just see it."

Still intrigued, he continued to study the painting. To hell with talking her into going to bed and getting a fresh start in the morning. His best strategy was to indulge her desire to be independent and encourage her to take the lead. And maybe it was time he surprised her. "If your theory is right and Eleanor is pointing the way to the jewels in this portrait, you'll want to start at the stone arch. Let's go out there right now."

She turned to stare at him. "I was going to suggest that, but I was sure you'd argue."

He grinned at her. "Waste of time. You were going to make the point that, as long as the autograph lady and company are depending on you to lead them to the necklace, you'll be safe. And if someone *is* out there watching, they'll see you're doing exactly what they want."

She shot him a frown as they moved out of the room. "I don't like that you can practically read my mind."

The feeling was mutual, but he wasn't about to admit that to her. Instead, he said, "Your mind works in a very logical way."

Her smile held a hint of mischief. "Not always. I think it's time that I filled you in on the fantasy box that my sisters and I buried in the stones a long time ago."

9

"I'VE ALWAYS LOVED the gardens," Nell said. "Especially at this time of night. All I have to do is take a breath and I can almost taste the roses and the freesias."

All Reid could smell was Nell, and his desire to taste her again was growing with each step they took. In spite of his belief that their trip to the stone arch put her in minimal danger, he still kept himself alert.

The full moon gleamed off the lake, and stars, undimmed by city lights, sparkled in the clear sky overhead. The illumination provided by Mother Nature made them fairly visible to anyone who might have stationed themselves in the hills that jutted up on three sides of the grounds. There could be someone up there right now, keeping an eye on the castle and specifically on Nell's movements.

When a sudden turn in the path caused her to brush against his arm, the desire that simmered constantly now in his blood shot to full boil. His awareness, previously attuned to their surroundings, narrowed to her as swiftly and dramatically as a spotlight on a stage. God, he wanted to touch her, really touch her. To slip that drab little suit off her and let his hands slowly, very slowly, mold every inch of her. Temptation grew as he imagined just how quickly he could edge her off the path and into the cover provided by the flowering trees that filled this particular part of the gardens. He wanted to give in to it—to throw caution to the wind, pull her into the shadows and just take her. It would be wonderfully crazy, and the certainty that she wouldn't resist him—that she'd deny him nothing—gave an unprecedented power to the images filling his mind. He might have made them a reality, if they hadn't stepped into the clearing in front of the stone arch.

Reid had to blink against brightness of the floodlights trained on the stones. They'd been installed after someone had planted a bomb inside the arch, once the first earring had been discovered. That person had nearly killed Alba. The sudden memory dragged him back to the real danger that still threatened Nell and her family.

When she started forward, he took her arm. "Let's keep to the edge of the light until we have to step into it."

"This is the first time I've seen them lit up like that. I think Angus would have liked it."

Reid recalled the first time he'd seen the stone arch. At ten he'd been impressed with the structure. It was a tunnel, really—ten feet long, ten high in the center and eight feet wide. He and his brothers had measured it off. It impressed him no less now that it was lit up like a monument. He was even more impressed with the man who'd built it. It had lasted two hundred years, and it would be here for years to come. So would the legend. "Not many men leave behind such a legacy."

"It's a real tribute to the power of love," Nell said.

"That kind of love is rare," Reid said. "A lot of people want it, but very few achieve it." He should tell her again that it wasn't in the cards for them. She had to want the rarified kind of love.

His mother certainly had. And now it seemed she'd found it with A.D., and Nell's aunt and sisters had found chances at their own happy-ever-afters. A.D. was a good man. So was Daryl. Cam and Duncan were good men. They'd never promise what they didn't think they could deliver on. But if the stats held true, two out of the four of those couples would be denied what they most desired. That's what he needed to tell her.

Before he could, she said, "I couldn't agree more. Even the few who are lucky enough to find true love can have it snatched away and be nearly destroyed by the loss. My father's a prime example of that. When my mother died, my sisters and I lost him, too. He was so devastated that he hid away in his rooms painting. I was too young to understand at the time, but when I finally did, I decided that true love isn't worth the risk. Not to mention the drama and the stress. And even with the legend, there are no guarantees."

Hadn't he always felt the same way? Why did it bother him that she'd simply voiced his own assessment? Or perhaps he was just annoyed by the impossibility of arguing with someone who shared his opinion.

Nell took a deep breath and told herself to shut up. She'd made her point, and she was starting to babble. The walk through the garden had taken its toll on her concentration. She'd lied about loving the scent of the roses and the freesias. She'd barely noticed them compared to Reid. He smelled of soap: simple, basic. Wonderful. When he'd accidentally brushed up against her arm, she'd lost her train of thought completely.

Not good.

She needed to keep her head as clear as one of her heroines if she was going to achieve all her goals tonight. Slipping her hand into her pocket, she fingered the two slips of pink paper that had been burning a hole there all evening. The action helped her refocus.

They reached the far end of the clearing where the distance to the opening of the stone arch was only about twenty-five yards away. She needed to get to the fantasy box. "My sisters and I used to sneak out here late at night when we thought Aunt Vi was asleep. The instant we stepped out of the gardens, we always used to race for the stones." She flicked him a look. "Bet I can beat you." She took off.

The element of surprise should have guaranteed her a victory. But Reid was fast, his reflexes honed to perfection. He clamped a hand on her arm within the first ten yards, and they ended the race in a tie. When they finally stood beneath the arch, she was breathing hard. He wasn't.

"You've got to remember to let me do my bodyguarding thing." His hand was still wrapped around her arm, but his grip was no longer as firm. So there was no reason at all for her to feel the pressure of each one of his fingers. Even less reason for her knees to turn to water.

Then she made the mistake of looking at him. He'd turned to scan the clearing, and the memory of him on their parent's wedding day superimposed itself over what she was seeing now. He'd been standing in profile that day, too. His hair had been longer then and more tousled. She'd wanted so much to touch it. To touch him. The urge had been so acute that if the bridal couple hadn't separated her from him, she was sure she would have.

Nothing separated them right now. They were alone. She could do exactly what she'd wanted to do that afternoon seven years ago, what she'd started to do in the hospital parking lot. All she had to do was lift her hand. But when she pulled it out of her pocket, she was holding the two slips of pink paper, and her grip on reality and her goals came back into focus. First things first.

"Nell…"

She met his eyes, and for a moment she wavered. It would be so easy to step into his arms and kiss him again. So easy to just lose herself in that whirlwind of excitement that was waiting for her. She certainly wanted to. But if she did, they'd do more than kiss. Then he'd have second thoughts again, just as he had in the car. Worse still, he'd regret it. That was the kind of man she was dealing with. A man who lived by a very strict code. A man who didn't want to hurt her. A protector.

She was pretty sure that the fantasy she'd begun all those years ago was the perfect solution. But first she had to set up the story line.

"I have to tell you about these pink slips and the fantasy box," she said. "From the time we were little, my sisters and I used to sneak out here, write down our goals and dreams and put them into this metal box." Turning, she dropped to her knees and ran her hand along the base of the arch. "I'll show you."

Reid stayed right where he was, hoping to get a grip on his resolve. And his sanity. A moment ago, he'd nearly lost both. Dragging his eyes away from Nell, he glanced around the stone arch.

It would be dangerous and reckless to drag her into the shadows in the garden and make love to her. But to do the same thing beneath the arch that Angus MacPherson had built for his true love? That was just crazy.

Saved by two pieces of folded pink paper. And a box of fantasies?

Curious, he squatted down and tried to get a better look at what she was doing. "Can I help?"

Her first response was a grunt, followed by, "I think I've got it."

Stone scraped against stone. Then Nell turned, sat on her heels and set a small metal box on the stone floor. When she opened it, Reid saw that it was divided in three sections with folded sheets of colored paper in each one.

"It was Adair who thought of it." Nell explained her sister's plan. "To make it even more adventurous, we would all meet in Piper's room and then climb down from her balcony. Hers was closest to the ground."

As he listened, Reid was just as fascinated by the story as he was by the play of shadows and muted light on her face. She had a gift with words that drew vivid pictures of the three sisters climbing down the balcony, then racing through the gardens to bury their deepest and most heartfelt desires in the stones. He'd been touched when she'd told him that the box had originally been their mother's jewelry box. Amused when he'd learned that they'd each used a different color of paper to guard their privacy and that her color had turned out to be pink.

"Some of my goals were pretty frivolous," she admitted with a wry smile. "One of my early ones was to just be taller than my sisters."

"When did you achieve it?" Reid asked.

"Six years later. Of course, I was hoping for an overnight change. At twelve, I was wishing I'd set my sights higher. My sisters didn't offer much of a challenge in the height department."

Reid laughed. "With siblings it's always about competition and pecking order."

"Even with triplets?"

"Especially with triplets."

After glancing at the slips in her palm, she handed one of them to Reid. "I'm going to use the box again and tap into the power of the stones."

And it was going to work. Whatever doubts she'd had, whatever nerves plagued her had begun to fade the moment her fingers first brushed against her mother's jewelry box. There was a power here that had never failed her.

While he leaned toward the mouth of the arch to maximize the light, she glanced down at the folded pieces of pink paper she'd written her sexual fantasy on. They were easy to identify because all the other goals were written on small single sheets. She'd filled two large pieces of paper with her plans for Reid, and over the years she'd expanded them a lot.

"'My goal is to find Eleanor's sapphire necklace before sundown tomorrow,'" Reid read aloud. Then he refolded the slip of paper and passed it to her. "You're being more specific with your time frame, I see."

"A lesson learned the hard way." She placed the goal on the top of the pile.

"You really believe that putting that into the box

and tucking it into the stones is going to help you find the necklace?"

"I know it is. There's a power here." Positive of that, she placed the second slip of paper she'd brought on the top of her pile and closed the lid.

"Don't I get to read that one?"

"I'll tell you all about it." *Just as soon as I get it buried.* She slid the box into its niche and replaced the stones. Then, still on her knees, she faced him. "That final piece of paper was a sexual fantasy I wrote about you on the night our parents married."

"Nell—"

She stopped him by placing a hand over his lips. "Let me finish. I knew even then that you would be a reluctant lover, so I wrote about seducing you. I'd never before imagined myself in that kind of role, but with you it was easy. Let me turn that fantasy into reality. Just one night—no harm, no foul."

When he said nothing, she moved her hand to his shoulder, then down his arm and closed them around his fingers. Triumph thrilled her when his fingers gripped hers hard. "I've waited so long to touch you, and it's the perfect time. Once we find the necklace and everyone's safe, we'll go our separate ways. End of story."

"Life doesn't work like a story line, Nell. Shit happens."

"I'm a big girl. I can handle shit." She raised his hand to her mouth, kissed their linked fingers. Then she placed her free hand on his chest. His heart was beating as hard as hers. "My story line in my fantasy is all about enjoying each other for as long as we can."

With his free hand, he simply took a strand of her hair. "People leave."

"Of course they do." There was no mistaking the flash of pain she'd seen in his eyes. Odd that she'd never thought of Reid as being vulnerable. But it occurred to her that he might be just as afraid of being hurt as he was of hurting her.

Her instinct was to soothe. "People walk in and out of our lives all the time. I lost my mother before I could even remember her. Adair and Piper missed her terribly. But they at least had the memory of her. I don't. You and I can have each other now. I'd rather live with the memory of that than with regret, wouldn't you?"

Regrets. Reid was sure he'd have them. He already knew he wanted to give her more than she was asking for. More than he was capable of giving her. "You win."

When he leaned toward her, she placed a firm hand on his chest. "We have to find a better place for me to seduce you. We don't want the legend kicking in." Rising, she tugged him with her and stepped out of the stone arch. "In my fantasy, I started my seduction very slowly. Just a stolen kiss in the gardens. Come on. I'll show you."

"I can't wait." He'd been wanting to kiss her ever since they'd left the castle. Ever since the last time he'd kissed her. For seven long years.

Forever.

In one quick move, he pushed her into the shadows at the side of the arch and caged her against the stones. Her eyes darkened; her breath caught. He could have sworn he felt her body melting into his until every soft, round curve fit perfectly.

"Wait. In my fantasy, I'm supposed to be the seductress."

"You've done your job." He streaked his hands up her

sides and thrust his fingers into her hair and crushed her lips with his. The low purr in her throat shot fire straight to his loins. The desire he'd felt for her, already consuming, became even more raw, more impatient, more primitive. Undeniable. It beat in his blood, in his mind, until he couldn't think. He could only want. Take.

He inched them farther into the shadows, but she slowed his progress by fisting her hands in his hair to keep his mouth on hers. Gone was the slow, gentle seduction she'd begun beneath the arch. Her tongue met his, tangling, tasting, testing. Her hands were just as demanding, tugging his shirt free from his pants so she could run her hands up his back.

And those nails. Each scrape, each little stab fanned the flames she'd ignited with her story. He couldn't stop touching her. She was stronger than he'd imagined and more agile. She moved against him, not in submission but in aggression. Give me more, she seemed to demand. As if there were something he was holding back.

He wasn't. He couldn't. He thought he'd known all the variations of desire before, but it had never sliced at his control this way. As he dragged her closer, he thought that maybe she was all he'd ever wanted—the softness, the fire. When she was pressed against him like this, it was easy to block out the past, the future, and think only of now. Of having her right now.

Nell told herself she had to think. She had to breathe. But the searing heat he created was burning her seduction plans with the ferocity of a wildfire. When he tore away his mouth to run kisses over her face, her throat, she dragged in a breath and willed the oxygen to her brain. She needed a new plan.

"Wait."

"Nell...." His grip on her tightened. "You want me to stop?"

"No. I just want you to let me show you another fantasy I've dreamed of." The night air filled her lungs, and the sound of her ragged breathing mingled with his was erotic, tempting. "I've dreamed so often of doing this." She pulled his belt free. "And this." She unsnapped his jeans and tugged down the zipper. "And finally this." She freed him and wrapped her hand around him. The instant she did, she revised the rest of her plan because she simply couldn't wait another moment. "Now you can kiss me again."

The instant his mouth crushed hers, she did her best to melt into him. Her body had never felt this alive. She could even feel her blood racing through her veins. There was so much to absorb—every hard angle and plane of his body. The roughness of his hands as he gripped her hips to pull her closer. The sharp, unyielding press of the rocks at her back. Each separate sensation brought its own unique thrill.

He tore his mouth from hers to run his lips over her face as if he was determined to absorb every texture through the sense of taste alone. Then he kissed her again with a thorough, feverish fury as if he were looking for some flavor that she might deny him.

She denied him nothing. He was showing her more than anyone ever had, opening doors she hadn't known existed. And he could give her more. More than she'd ever imagined. The very thought that he might take her here and now, with such urgent need and desperation, sent her own desires spiraling. She raced her mouth down his neck, sank her teeth into the curve of his shoulder. The flavors were amazing. Addicting.

Now. The word hammered in her blood, pounded in her mind, as she dragged her mouth free of his. The cool night air eased her burning lungs as he dealt with her clothes. She thought she'd never felt anything more erotic than the slide of her dress over her arms and head. Once free of it, she wrapped her arms and legs around him.

They'd waited too long. A lifetime. He lifted her hips; she wrapped her legs around him.

"Now."

When she said the word, fresh needs exploded inside of him. Reid could see her eyes in the muted light, needed to see them as the last of his control shredded. He plunged into her. She surrounded him. For a moment, neither of them moved.

If he could have, he would have held on to the moment forever. But she'd weakened him when she'd begun to strip him. Unable to resist, he began to move, quickly, fiercely. The sultry sound of her moans fanned the flames as she matched him thrust for thrust until he knew nothing else, wanted nothing else. He swore once without knowing what he cursed. Then savagely he increased the pace. Faster and faster, harder and harder, they raced into the vortex of a storm—a place where neither of them had ever been. Then they shattered.

SANITY SLIPPED IN SLOWLY. Reid had no idea how long he'd stood there, pressing her into the stone arch as bits and pieces of reality trickled in. She was still wrapped tightly around him, her head on his shoulder. His breath was still coming in gasps. His heart was still hammering against his chest. He still couldn't think clearly.

And he was trembling.

No woman had ever made him tremble before. Somehow he found the strength to angle his head so that he could look at her. Her eyes were open, dazed. A fresh wave of desire shot through him. He felt himself grow hard again inside her.

Good Lord, he needed a moment. Just a moment, he told himself. Or he was going to take her again like a madman.

Murmuring his name, Nell ran her hand down his back. There'd been something in his eyes when he'd looked at her—vulnerability. It had her nestling closer. The gesture flooded him with warmth.

"It wasn't exactly what I'd planned."

"I'll take it. Gladly." Reid tipped her chin up. "Are you all right? I wasn't careful."

She smiled at him. "Neither was I."

"I wasn't careful about something else. Protection."

She cupped his face in her hands. "I have it covered."

His body jerked, pressing her hard into the side of the arch. The pinging sound registered in her brain at the same instant that she felt the sting on her cheek. Reid pivoted, holding her tightly against him as he sprinted into the stone arch. Then she was on the ground, his body on top of hers and her breath whooshed out.

"Don't move," he said.

Not a possibility. She could barely drag in a breath. Her mind was racing to process what had just happened—the jerk of Reid's body, the sound like stone hitting stone.

"What happened?" she asked.

"Someone took a shot at us." He'd lifted his head and was staring beyond them through the other end of the tunnel at the wooded hillside behind the stone arch. Her lover was gone and the Secret Service agent was back.

"The floodlights don't spill in this far," he was saying, "so I think we're safe for the moment. Stay put."

When he moved, she gripped his shoulders and held tight. "You shouldn't leave again. You said we were safe here."

"Cell phone," he said. "I'm calling Daryl. He can douse the floodlights."

That was when she realized that her hand was wet. Sticky. When she saw the dark color, fear fluttered in her throat like a trapped bird. "He...hit you."

"A scratch." Without bothering to check the wound, he spoke into his cell. "Daryl, we've got a problem. We're in the stone arch. Someone took a shot at us a couple of seconds ago. He nicked my upper arm, but Nell's fine. I figure the shooter was in the hills behind the arch. About twenty-five feet up and maybe fifty feet to the right."

The floodlights went out.

"Thanks. We were beneath the stones for five to ten minutes, and when we stepped out, we lingered at the side of the arch for a minute or so."

Lingered.

She could only seem to process one word at a time. From the moment she'd felt Reid's blood, it was as if her brain had been frozen. As he outlined to Daryl what had happened, reality sank in. While they'd made love, someone—a sniper—had taken aim at Reid and shot him.

A wave of dizziness struck her.

They'd lingered.

To fulfill her fantasy. Her fault. They'd made love

right out in the open when someone was threatening to kill off her family. And Reid. Her fault again. She tightened her grip on him and held on for dear life.

"Relax," he murmured, pulling off her hands. Then he shifted so that he could keep an eye on both entrances. "Daryl will be here in a moment, and we'll get you safely back to the castle."

But it wasn't *her* safety that had been threatened. She'd put her subplot in front of her plot, and it had nearly cost Reid his life.

10

"WHOEVER IT WAS, they're a damn good shot." Daryl studied the extra whiteboard he'd dragged into the main parlor from Adair's office. On it he'd sketched the clearing, the stone arch and the hillside beyond. He pointed to the place where he thought the sniper had taken his shot. "I bet he was standing right here."

Reid's mind flashed back to the instant he'd felt the fiery sensation sear the side of his shoulder. He remembered that, and the icy stab of fear that had pierced right to his core—and then nothing until he was standing by Nell midway beneath the stone arch. Even now, he had no recollection of how he'd gotten her there.

That was a first for him. He took a sip of the brandy Daryl had poured him after Vi had tended to the scratch the bullet had left.

A bullet meant for Nell.

In the bright lights of the kitchen with Vi and Nell, he'd seen how tired Nell had looked. There'd been dark circles beneath her eyes, and for the first time he'd glimpsed fear in them. His fault. He'd never treated a woman with less care. And he'd never been this careless on a job.

Vi had agreed with his assessment of Nell's exhaustion, because she'd hurried her niece upstairs, so that she could shower and change and get some rest. The dog had gone with the women.

In the parlor, Daryl drew his finger down to where he'd sketched the stone arch. "If you were here, you would have been out of range of the floodlights. I'll bet he was wearing night vision goggles."

"Which means he's either a pro or he's had military training," Reid said.

"Agreed."

Reid wanted badly to pace off his nerves. Another first for him. He never paced.

"While Vi was patching you up, I updated Sheriff Skinner. He's got a man stationed there right now to guard the area."

"At first light, I want to search for the bullet."

Daryl met his eyes. "My thoughts exactly. It might shed some light on who we're dealing with." Then he tapped on the sketch again. "By then, Skinner will have volunteers patrolling the hillside and searching for any casing. He said he'd have no trouble getting the manpower. Edie's a popular woman in Glen Loch, and no one wants trouble at her granddaughter's wedding rehearsal. Everyone in town's grateful for the economic boost that this wedding business has given the local community."

"Nell is not going to want to stay inside the castle," Reid said. "She's determined to find the necklace, and I'm worried about the number of strangers who will be here tomorrow."

"With the extra manpower Skinner is mustering up, we ought to be able to handle it. I'll print up copies of the police artist's sketch that Duncan sent us so Skinner can distribute them to his volunteers. Not that it will help much since he was wearing sunglasses and a beard. That reporter from the *Times* will be here at ten to interview Vi and shadow her for the rest of the day. I'll stick with them. Vi has two appointments with prospective clients, and the wedding rehearsal starts at four. That will involve less than a dozen people, and none of them will be strangers. I'll also have a man at my office check more deeply into Gwendolen Campbell's known acquaintances. He can take another look at Deanna Lewis's circle. Someone with a military background might pop up."

Reid could hear the clock ticking in his head. "I never should have agreed to take her out there tonight. I let her convince me that they wouldn't want to eliminate her until she'd found the necklace. I've never been this off my game."

Daryl turned to him. "You're not off your game. The shooter didn't want to hit Nell. He wanted to hit you."

Reid stared at him. The man was right. And he should have realized it sooner. He was definitely off his game. That had to stop.

"What did we miss?" Nell asked as she and Vi joined them.

"You should be in bed," Reid said.

"Save your breath," Vi said. "I lost that argument ten minutes ago."

"I was just telling Reid that he was the shooter's target and not you," Daryl said.

"I know," Nell said. "It's my fault for convincing Reid to go out there."

"No." Reid waited until she met his gaze. "I'm responsible for what happened, and I'm going to make sure it doesn't happen again."

Nell felt a band tighten around her heart. He was talking about more than the shooter, and he was right. Hadn't she already realized that she had to modify her subplot? She couldn't, she wouldn't put him in danger again. If that meant she had to put her garden fantasy on hold until she'd figured out where Eleanor had hidden her necklace, she could live with that. She'd waited seven years. She could certainly wait to seduce him in the garden until after sundown tomorrow. If all went well, she'd find the necklace by then.

At least that was the argument she'd made to herself when she had been in the shower.

So why did it hurt so much that he'd come to the same conclusion?

"The person responsible for all this is the person who thinks they have a right to Eleanor's sapphires," Vi said as she urged Nell toward sofa. "The best way to put an end to it is to catch them."

Daryl poured two brandies and handed them to the women. "Reid and I agree that the shooter is either a professional or perhaps ex-military."

"What if it's someone who shoots for sport?" Nell asked. "Gwendolen and Deanna are both from Great Britain. Perhaps they hunt or skeet shoot. Obviously Deanna couldn't have been out there on the hillside tonight, but Gwendolen could."

The two men exchanged a look. "Nell could be

right," Daryl said. "I'll have my man check it out." Then he turned to Nell. "How did you think of that?"

"The characters I create for my stories all have backgrounds, and we've pretty much established that the villains in this case have a connection to Eleanor and Angus that reaches back to Scotland." She smiled at Daryl. "Plus hunting and skeet shooting are big on British television."

"Reid tells me that you think the clue to the location of Eleanor's necklace is in the painting," Daryl said.

Nell moved so she could stand directly beneath the portrait. As she passed the second whiteboard that Daryl had used to sketch out the time line of events, she gave it a glance and once more experienced that little tug on her memory that she'd experienced earlier in the evening, but whatever was lingering at the edge of her mind stayed there. Shifting her gaze to Eleanor, she tried to focus.

Finding the necklace had to be at the top of her priority list. "She was so careful hiding the two earrings. She wanted them to be eventually found. So she had to have left clues."

"Cam is sure that's why someone was paying those nocturnal visits to our library six months ago," Vi said. "Trying to find those clues before Adair found the first earring."

"The stone arch is definitely in the portrait," Daryl said. "But what about the cave in the cliff face where Duncan and Piper found the second earring?"

He was right, Nell thought with a sinking heart. In the beats of silence that followed Daryl's comment, she waited for Reid to say something. Anything. When he didn't, the little band of pain tightened around her heart.

The necklace, she lectured herself. Plot before subplot. But no matter how hard she stared at the portrait, she couldn't make the cliffs appear. If Eleanor was seated in the gazebo as her father had always insisted she was, there was no way to fit the cliffs in the background.

"If she left the jewels behind in different places, maybe she didn't feel the need to put the clues all in the portrait," Vi said. "Maybe that's why our nighttime visitor spent so much time in the library."

No one said a word, but Nell was sure they were all thinking the same thing. If there was a clue in the library, discovering it would be like finding a needle in a haystack. Someone had spent six months working there and had come up empty.

A wave of exhaustion suddenly hit Nell. An arm went around her shoulders. Not Reid's but her aunt Vi's.

"We need to sleep on it," Vi said as she drew Nell toward the door. "Let our subconscious minds sort through it. Things will be better in the morning."

They'd better be, Nell thought. Then she remembered the notes she'd tucked into her fantasy box, and her tiredness began to fade. She was going to find Eleanor's necklace by sundown tomorrow.

And she was going to seduce Reid Sutherland tonight, just not in the garden. Yet.

REID STOOD ON the balcony of his room, his hands gripping the stone railing like a lifeline. He'd stepped out because it was as far away as he could get from the connecting door to Nell's bedroom. The cold shower he'd already taken hadn't done a thing to lessen his desire. While the water had poured down on him, he had reviewed the reasons why it would be a mistake to go to her. She needed sleep badly. He needed some distance to regain his perspective. Making love to her again would only increase her expectation that he could give her something that he was incapable of. He didn't want to hurt her more than he already had. Etcetera, etcetera and so forth.

Cut the crap, Sutherland. The real reason you're holding on to the railing like a lifeline is because you want more than to make love to her again. You simply want to be with her. To lie beside her and hold her. To talk to her. Not just about the case or the sapphires. He wanted to know more about her. What she'd shared with him beneath the stone arch had only made him more curious.

Pillow talk. It was an old-fashioned and clichéd term that his mother had used to describe one of the joys of her marriage to A.D. The fact that he could envision himself doing it with Nell scared the hell out of him. Spending the night with a woman had been near the top of his never-do list. He'd never brought one to his home because he valued the freedom, the flexibility to leave before morning. Staying the night built the kind of intimacy he'd never desired.

With Nell, he wanted to spend the night, to wake in the morning holding her close, to see her face in the light of a new day. He wanted intimacy.

Damn her. No other woman had made him want more than he could have.

Lifting his hands from the stone railing, he found that his fingers had gone numb from the tightness of his grip. He had to think of something else. Vi had been right. He needed to sleep. While he slept, perhaps his unconscious mind would let him know what to do about Nell.

But the thought of going to an empty bed kept him lingering on the balcony. The night was so quiet that he could hear individual waves licking the rocks along the shore. Flexing his fingers, he shifted his focus to the gardens that stretched from beneath his balcony to the stone arch and the hillside in one direction and the lake in the other.

The stone arch was clearly visible in the floodlights, and the moon spilled enough light to make out the tops of the trees and the shadowy paths that wound through the gardens. Nell was so sure that Eleanor had left clues in the painting, but Daryl had been dead-on. The cliff face was on the opposite side of the castle from the gardens. If Eleanor had intended to leave clues to the location of the sapphires in the painting, she'd left a big one out.

And if he stayed on his balcony all night, he definitely wouldn't be at the top of his game tomorrow. He was about to turn and head for bed when his cell phone rang. A quick glance at the caller ID told him that it was Cam. He must have news.

"Problem or favor?" Reid asked.

"Neither. Adair and I discovered something…curious."

Reid knew his brother well enough—Cam wouldn't call in the middle of the night unless he thought it was important. Aware of how sound could carry over water, he stepped back into his bedroom and slid the balcony doors shut. "Tell me."

"It was Adair's idea," Cam said. "Mom's been in the library ever since she got permission to visit the Campbell estate, and A.D.'s been in the gardens. Neither one of them has gotten a tour of the castle, so this afternoon Adair convinced the housekeeper to give us one."

"You found something on our Gwendolen," Reid said.

"Not exactly. We learned the estate has fallen on hard times. The story in the village is that it started to decline about two hundred years ago—just about the time of Angus and Eleanor's flight to the New World. Due to the lack of a male heir in Eleanor's generation, the castle and the estate went to a cousin, but the money just wasn't there. The present housekeeper says that her mother worked here after the Second World War when most of the furniture was sold or taken by debt collectors. She's still alive, and we're going to visit her first thing in the morning. But it's what we didn't find on our tour that's curious."

"What did you not find on your tour?"

"About the only things that didn't get sold are a series of portraits in the upstairs ballroom. It's a regular rogues' gallery of Campbell heirs and family members. Each generation has a family portrait with the male heir and his wife and children. The last one has Eleanor in it—the same long blond hair. The housekeeper says the family wouldn't sell them, but it's more likely that the pictures wouldn't be of much value to anyone but the Campbells."

It was unlike Cam to take so long in getting to the point, and that fact alone had Reid's curiosity growing.

"The thing is, none of the wives are wearing the sapphires—not even Eleanor's mother," he said. "Adair's been nagging me ever since we left the ballroom to call you about it. She says that the sapphires should be in the paintings, and she claims their conspicuous absence means that Deanna Lewis might be right. The sapphires were not Eleanor's dowry because they never belonged to the Campbells."

"There's certainly an argument to be made for that theory," Reid said. In his mind he could hear Nell making it. If the Campbells had been in legitimate possession of the Stuart sapphires, surely a record would have been displayed in the family portraits.

"Yeah," Cam said in a resigned tone. "It opens up a whole new can of worms. If the Stuart sapphires didn't belong to the Campbells, who the hell did they belong to and how did Eleanor get hold of them?"

"That's what you need to find out. And fast," Reid said. "Anything else?"

"Now that you mention it, I am curious about whether or not you've read the fantasies in the MacPherson sisters' fantasy box."

Reid let a beat of silence go by. Of course, Cam would know about the box. Duncan would probably know about it, also. "No, I haven't."

"Well, you have a treat in store. Long story short, the sisters got together on the night our parents married and wrote some very explicit sexual fantasies. Then they buried them in the stone arch so that they would eventually come true. Nell wrote hers on pink paper, and it's very interesting."

Reid frowned. "Are you telling me that you've read them?"

"Hey, I'm CIA. I'm trained to leave no stone unturned."

Reid couldn't identify all the emotions that shot through him. Fury that someone had invaded Nell's privacy was the first one. "You had no business reading Nell's."

"Whoa, big bro. Calm down."

Reid was shocked to find that he needed to. He was pacing, and his free hand had clenched into a fist. If Cam had been in the room, that fist would already have collided with his jaw. He stopped short and drew in a deep breath.

"You're in love with her, aren't you?" Cam asked.

Reid found he couldn't answer. He was very much afraid that the answer was yes. And if he said it out loud...

"I'm going to take your silence as an affirmation," Cam said. "I bet Duncan that you'd be a goner within the first twelve hours of your arrival at the castle. The profiler believes that you're a cautious man, and it would take at least twenty-four hours for you to take the fall. I win." Cam was chuckling as he ended the call.

Reid stood there for a moment staring down at his cell phone. Then he reached deep for his control. He couldn't, he wouldn't think about his feelings for Nell right now. He had a forty-eight-hour countdown clock to deal with, which left them only thirty-six hours at most. When he glanced up, he discovered he was standing right in front of the connecting door to Nell's room, his hand on the knob. But before he could turn it, it opened, and he barely recognized this version of Nell, who took one of his hands and drew him into her room.

11

NELL'S HEART THREATENED to pound right out of her chest.
She was not going to let Reid spoil her plan this time.
Not after all her careful preparations.

He'd taken forever to get to his room. She'd used
the time to light candles, chill champagne and dress in
the black lace designer lingerie she'd purchased in the
boutique below Piper's apartment. When she'd put it
on and looked at herself in the mirror, she hadn't even
recognized the old Nell.

Perfect. The lacy tank top stopped just short of the
string-bikini-style panties, leaving the skin at her waist
exposed. She placed a hand there now to help her focus.

It wasn't just black lace that she'd armed herself with.
She also had plenty of other ideas. But there was a world
of difference between imagining something and actually doing it. In her daydreams she'd never had to deal
with the effect of his gaze as it swept down her body.
Flames licked first along the nerve endings at her throat,
then flickered lower to the sensitive skin at the tops of
her breasts. She sucked in a breath when she felt the
fire reach her belly, then sear her legs right down to

her toes. He was still fully clothed, and that made her remember her plan.

Strip him. You can definitely do that. Just talk your way through it.

Careful not to look directly into his eyes or at his mouth, she said, "I intend to seduce you, Reid. I wanted to do it in the gardens, but it may be a while before either of us is safe there."

Good. Words had always come easily to her.

"You have too many clothes on." She reached for the first button on his shirt and slipped it free. "Better."

She could do this.

"Nell—"

"Shh." Tamping down on the impulse to meet his eyes, she concentrated on the second button and felt a spurt of triumph when she freed it. "You don't have to say a word. You want to tell me that we both need our sleep if we're going to find the necklace tomorrow. And you're expecting that I'll obey like the good little girl I was at six. But I'm not that girl anymore."

As if to emphasize her point to both of them, she ignored the last button, and in a move she'd dreamed of forever, she shoved the shirt down his arms so that it trapped his wrists at his sides. When he sucked in his breath, the thrill shot straight through her.

Turning him, she placed a hand on his chest and urged him toward her bed. "Do you know how long I've dreamed of getting you out of your clothes?" The fast thud of his heart against her palm was rewarding, arousing. When she backed him into the side of the mattress, she slid her hand down his now-bare chest to his belt. Thrilled at his quick expulsion of breath, she lingered there, tracing her finger along the top of his waistband.

"I wanted to do this on the day our parents were married." Taking her time, she unfastened the buckle, then pulled the belt through the loops. Slowly. "I described the way I would strip you in one of the fantasies I wrote about you that night."

Moonlight streamed through the glass doors, highlighting all the planes and angles of the skin she'd exposed. She simply had to touch him again. Tossing the belt aside, she ran her hands from his waist to his throat. It wasn't just the sight of him that fascinated her. She loved the contrast in their skin tones. His was tan; hers was pale. Pleasure sharpened at each response. The sound of his breath expelling when her nails scraped down over his nipples, the rapid hammer of his heart against her lips, the way her name caught in his throat when she unsnapped his jeans and slid the zipper down—each separate sensation thrilled her, enchanted her.

"Nell…"

The desperation in his tone was contagious. And it was all so incredibly good. Glorious. How had she managed to wait for so long? His hands rested on her shoulders, but without the strength that she'd felt before. Her confidence surged. "There's more." Impatient now, she shoved his jeans down over his hips.

And there *was* more.

Her gaze froze on silky black jockeys. The material was sheer and revealing. "I never imagined the full impact of being with you."

How could she? At eighteen, her experience had been limited. Now, she realized, it still was. There'd been no time to see him during that firestorm of desire at the side of the stone arch. No time to touch him. Craving tore at her. She'd take the time now.

"Nice," she murmured as she danced her fingers down the length of him.

"Nell…"

The word came out on a moan, delighting her and encouraging her to press her hand more firmly against him. "Very sexy. And we're so compatible. Who would have thought?"

Because her mind had begun to spin, she was having trouble thinking at all. She couldn't stop touching him. Was it her imagination or had he grown even harder as she stroked her fingers up and down the length of him? "This… You…go beyond anything I dreamed of."

Her hands moved of their own accord, her fingers slipping beneath the waistband of his briefs. "I wrote about doing this.

"And this."

When she dropped to her knees and began to use her mouth on him, Reid slid his fingers from her shoulders into her hair and held on. Helpless. That's what she'd made him. The sensation skittered in his stomach, melted his muscles, burned through his brain. He should tell her to stop. But if he could have spoken, he would have begged her to continue on. And he'd never begged a woman before. He'd never wanted one so desperately.

The sensations she brought with a flick of her tongue, the soft wet caress of her mouth, the scrape of her teeth steeped him in pleasures he'd never known. Agonizing. Outrageous. Magnificent. He'd never allowed another woman to seduce him. He'd never been willing to hand over the reins of control.

With Nell he hadn't had a choice. She'd cast a spell

on him from the moment that he'd opened the door to her room and seen her standing there in those scraps of black lace. He'd literally ached for her, and that had stunned him as nothing else ever had.

People were only turned to stone in legends and myths—or in the Bible. That kind of thing didn't happen in real life. And certainly not to him.

Until that moment she'd opened the connecting door. Since then, he hadn't been able to move or think or say anything but her name since. He couldn't seem to talk at all now. Nor could he stop her when she rose and pushed him back on the bed.

Everything about her bewitched him. As she climbed onto the mattress and straddled him, he wanted to reach for her, but the weakness in his limbs persisted. She'd trapped him in a world of pleasure, a world where her goal seemed to be to fulfill every desire he'd ever had. All he could see was her face above him. The play of moonlight in her hair shifted the color from pale gold to silver. When her mouth hovered over his, when their breaths mingled, he said, "I want you, Nell."

"Soon." Her lips brushed his, then she linked their fingers and pressed his hands into the mattress. "You should relax. I'm just getting started."

"Kiss me."

"My pleasure." She was careful to avoid his mouth, nipping his chin instead. As she took her lips on a slow journey along his jaw, down his throat and across his shoulder, she absorbed the sound of his ragged breathing. She lingered at the bandage, kissing it softly.

"I've fantasized so often about tasting you." Inch by inch, she moved her mouth down his chest, licking here, nipping there. "So many flavors." She took his nipple into her mouth and suckled. Then, shifting her body downward, she delighted in the rich dark taste beneath his pecs and in the rapid beating of his heart against her lips.

Even in her wildest fantasies she hadn't anticipated the thrill she experienced when the hairs on his chest brushed against her own nipples or the excitement when his fingers went lax in hers. Lost in him now, she moved lower, exploring his body with her mouth alone.

When she slid her tongue into his navel, his fingers gripped hers hard. "Nell…"

She raised her head, met his eyes and what she saw ignited a flame that threatened to melt her. She tried to refocus on her plan. "I'm still just getting started. I poured some champagne, and I have so many ideas."

As she wiggled up his body and lifted the glass from a bedside table, a shock wave of heat melted his bones, his will. Through a haze of desire, he watched her dip her fingers into the flute. When the cold drops hit his face, his lips, his neck, they sent a blast of fire right to his core. Even though his hands were free now, he couldn't seem to lift them, didn't want to.

She leaned down and began to lick at his lips. "Mmm. You taste even better mixed with champagne." She traced her tongue over his mouth. "Delicious."

Then she sprinkled his chest with champagne and took her mouth on the same journey as before. Reid found himself totally trapped in a world of ice and fire. Tremors danced along his skin. A searing heat shot through his body. The sounds of pleasure she made as she used her mouth on him vibrated through his system and smoked through his brain.

She was devouring him as if he were some rare treat

that she'd waited all her life to sample. Just as he'd waited all his life for her.

He had to have more. Gripping her shoulders, he drew her up so that she met his eyes.

"I have more ideas," she said with a smile.

"So do I," he said as he hooked an arm around her and shifted her beneath him on the mattress. "Let me show you."

His intention had been to go slowly, to mimic the method she'd used on him. But the instant he pressed his mouth to hers, he felt his control stretch to the breaking point. At the first possessive sweep of his hands, her response tore through him. She arched against him, demanding more, as if there were something he was holding back. He wasn't. He couldn't.

They rolled across the bed as if they were combatants instead of lovers. As soon as he could, Reid tore at the silk that still covered her breast, then used his mouth on the skin he exposed inch by inch by inch. Any thought he might have had of savoring the rich, ripe taste of her skin vanished in a savage attack of hunger.

More.

He wasn't sure who said the word or if he'd only thought it. But everywhere he touched, everywhere he tasted, she showed him more, enchanting him all over again. Her scent was lightest at her wrist, heavier at her throat and addicting beneath her breast. She was generous beyond any man's fantasy. But each sigh, each shiver, each scrape of her nails or nip of her teeth left him wanting more. And more.

So he took. And took. Though he had no idea how, they were now in his bedroom, on the floor in a pool of moonlight when she finally rose above him. She filled his vision. Her skin was sheened with moisture, her eyes filled with his reflection. He tried to say her name, but the air burned so fiercely in his lungs that it came out on a gasp. Guiding her hips, he plunged into her, felt her close around him, and once more he felt as if she'd turned him to stone.

He wanted more than anything to hold on to the moment—to make time spin out. To hold them both there on that delicious, dangerous edge where she belonged only to him.

She moved first, arching on top of him, and he watched her eyes as her pleasure built and peaked. Even as her climax abated, he held himself still, determined to extend the moment when she thought only of him. Then her eyes cleared, and she began to move again. "More."

His control snapped as did any grasp he had on civilized matters. *Mine.* It was the only word he could think of as he thrust into her again and again. But as pleasure exploded and sent them both shooting over the edge, he poured more and more of himself into her. The last word he thought of was *hers.*

NELL MOVED IN a dream world where mists swirled, thickening in some places, thinning in others. She tried to wake up, but couldn't seem to break free. Her limbs felt heavy as if she were walking through water. The strange sensation should have frightened her, but all she felt was a burning curiosity. She searched for some sign of where she was.

Nothing.

With her vision totally impaired, she concentrated on her other senses. She smelled wood burning, heard it snap and crackle, and there was music—a tune she didn't recognize from an instrument she thought she did.

Bagpipes?

As the sound grew stronger, the mist thinned enough for her to make out the silhouette of a couple dancing. Over their heads, candles flickered in crystal chandeliers. At the far end of the room, a fire roared in a huge hearth. There were other people in the room, but they stood in the shadows watching and whispering as the man and woman turned this way and that, moving gracefully to the music.

It was like a fairy tale, Nell thought. She might have been witnessing Prince Charming and Cinderella dancing at the ball—a Disney movie come to life. Except the woman was familiar.

Though she could only see her back, Nell was certain she'd seen her before. Her frame was slender. Blond hair tumbled in loose curls below her shoulders. When her partner turned her, candles struck brilliance into the sapphires that dangled from her ears and nestled at her throat, and recognition had Nell's heart taking a leap.

Eleanor.

She was younger than the woman in the portrait and even more beautiful. When the music had the couple turning again, Nell caught a quick glimpse of the man's face. He was much taller than Eleanor, his hair dark, his features handsome. He turned again, giving Nell a second look.

Not Angus. He bore no resemblance to the likenesses that remained of her several-times-great-grandfather. Still, he too was familiar. Nell was certain she knew him.

She had to get a better look, but before she could move, the mists descended, blanketing the scene in front of her with the finality of a curtain falling on the final act. The air chilled. Gone was the scent of burning wood and the music. She smelled jasmine and roses now, and the only sound piercing the silence came from a breeze rushing through the trees.

Nell felt a surge of urgency as she pushed her way forward. There was something more she had to see. She was sure of it. When the mist finally abated, she recognized the stone arch immediately. Beneath it stood a couple. The man's back was to her, but Eleanor was bathed in moonlight. She wore the same white dress she'd danced in, and the sapphires gleamed bright at her throat and ears. But her expression was troubled. Then the man lifted her off her feet, pressed her close and kissed her.

Eleanor kissed him back, wrapping her arms around him and holding on for dear life. Though she hadn't been aware of moving, Nell realized that she was closer now. The couple stood in profile, and Nell saw that the man kissing Eleanor was Angus and not the man she'd been dancing with. But even as the certainty of that flashed through her, the mists swirled in, thick and gray.

This time when they cleared, her vision remained blurred. The image in front of her took form slowly, one detail at a time. She was still standing in front of the stone arch. And there was still a couple beneath it. But it wasn't Angus and Eleanor who stood so close they might have been one.

The man was Reid. And she was the woman he was kissing. She knew because she felt the searing brand of his mouth pressed to hers, and she felt her own response break free and wild. She tightened her grip on him and let the mists sweep them away.

12

THE EASTERN SKY was barely pink with the promise of the sun when Skinner had pulled into the driveway just as he and Daryl had stepped into the clearing in front of the stone arch. Reid had filled them in on what Cam and Adair had discovered in Scotland. Reid split up from Sheriff Skinner and Daryl to begin searching for the bullet that had grazed his shoulder the night before.

When they'd left the castle, Vi had been in the kitchen making scones, and even though he knew the two women were perfectly safe, he'd asked Vi to take Alba up to Nell's room to guard her.

Better to be doubly safe than sorry. Better still to find something that might identify the shooter who'd aimed a bullet at him. The hills on this side of the castle kept the area around the stone arch blanketed in shadows, adding an extra challenge to the job. Moments earlier Daryl had suggested they divide the area into three concentric half circles.

Chances were good that the bullet had ricocheted off the stones, so Skinner was looking in the outermost half circle, ten yards out; Daryl was examining every inch of the middle one, five yards out; and then Reid was searching the area closest to the arch itself. If they didn't find it, they'd widen the search area.

He ran his hand over the stones at eye level where he estimated he and Nell had been standing the night before, and he felt his fingers brush against the coolness of steel. Stepping back, he took out his penknife and used the flashlight at the end of it. The glint of metal was unmistakable. Seconds later, he'd managed to free it from the rocks. Keeping his voice stage-whisper low, he said, "I've got it."

Daryl reached him with Skinner two steps behind. Reid passed the bullet to Daryl first. For a few moments, there were only the sounds of the gentle lapping of the water in the distance and the chirping of morning birds.

"Nothing I recognize on sight," Daryl said. "That pretty much eliminates most of what the military is using as well as what the pros are favoring. My office can get a lab in Albany to take a look at it, but that will take time. Overnighting it to my office in D.C. might get us quicker results."

But not quick enough. Reid heard the clock ticking in his head. The sound had been there since he'd awakened, beating in rhythm to the pumping of his blood.

"Benjy Grimshaw might be able to help us out," Sheriff Skinner said. "He's the father of the bride, and he manages the sporting goods department at our general store. Guns have always been his hobby. His grandson helps him with his blog, and a lot of collectors visit his site."

Reid met Daryl's gaze. "We might as well have him take a look before we send it anywhere."

When Daryl handed him the bullet, Skinner said,

"If my men find a casing up there in the hills, I'll send that along to Benjy, too."

"If you've got a minute, I'd like to run over the schedule for the wedding rehearsal with you," Daryl said. "When Reid and I left the kitchen, Vi was putting a tray of scones into the oven."

Skinner's smile spread slowly. "You've just successfully bribed an officer of the law."

"Save one for me," Reid said. "I'm going to take a short detour over to the old gazebo. Nell's going to want to pay it a visit, and I need to check out what I'm up against in terms of security."

Daryl stopped and looked at Reid. "You should be safe enough right now with the sheriff's volunteers up in the hills. But no promises on the scones."

"I'll have to rely on my prodigal son status." Reid shot Daryl a smile before he veered off on a path that led deeper into the gardens. He wanted to visit the gazebo alone, and Daryl had been astute enough to realize that. Cam was a lucky man to have Daryl for a boss. Reid hoped he'd be half as lucky finding the ruins of the old gazebo. He'd been ten the last time he was there.

The hedges lining the path rose high enough in places to mimic a maze, preventing him from having a clear view of where he was going. And providing too damn many places to hide. Relying on instinct, Reid angled his way to the left of the stone arch and closer to the lake.

He'd told Daryl the truth. He did need to check out any security problems. But that wasn't the only reason he wanted some time by himself. If he went back to the castle right now, he wasn't sure Vi's scones could prevent him from going back to Nell.

When he'd awakened, her head had been tucked in the crook of his shoulder, and he hadn't been able to take his eyes off her. In the thin rays of morning light slipping through the drapes of his bedroom, she'd looked outrageously beautiful. The pale gold hair and porcelain skin made her appear fragile and delicate. But he'd learned her strength, experienced the passion of those frantic hands, those wild lips. During the night, she'd seduced him the way any man dreamed of being seduced, and layer by layer she'd stripped him of any claim he had on sanity. More, she'd unlocked a place inside him that he hadn't even known was there, and for a moment he'd glimpsed what his life might be like if he could wake every morning with his arms wrapped around her.

It was fear that had galvanized him enough to get out of bed. But he wasn't sure what he was more afraid of—the new desire he'd discovered in himself or the possibility of it being denied?

And what did Nell want?

What she'd told him or something else?

And where were the ruins of the old gazebo? He was certain he'd gone too far and was about to retrace his steps, when he spotted the rubble through a narrow break in the hedge. At first glance, the area looked as though it had been abandoned for a long time. Flowers grew everywhere, poking through rocks and at times totally obscuring what appeared to be a low circular wall of stones. The circle was uneven, and there were breaks where it totally disappeared. But Reid knew that, with a little digging, he would find stones beneath the earth that had covered them over time.

When he'd completed a walk around the perimeter,

he was sure of three things. Though there were many more flowers than he recalled, this was the place that Nell had brought him on that long-ago summer day. He could even identify the exact spot where she'd invited him to sit and drink tea.

There was no sign left of the wooden latticework or even what had been the floor of the structure. But Reid would have staked money on A.D.'s theory that this was where the gazebo in the portrait had once stood.

Allowing Nell to linger here for any length of time would be dangerous. He swept his gaze along the top of the hedge. Anyone approaching would be totally blocked from view, and there were areas where someone could see in, just as he had. A hedge would provide no protection from a bullet.

Reid ignored the icy fear that slithered up his spine. He needed a cool head. His best option would be to refuse to let her come here. Since that had no chance in hell of flying, he'd have to go with option two. Minimize the risk, and that always had to do with timing. Three years of heading up security for a vice president who disliked playing it safe was going to come in handy again. The trick would be to bring her here when the visitors to the castle were at a minimum, and to get her in and out as quickly as possible.

Quickly reviewing the schedule in his head, Reid calculated that perfect window of opportunity for Nell's visit to the old gazebo would be while the reporter from the *Times* was interviewing and shadowing Vi. James Orbison was scheduled to arrive in less than two hours. That meant Nell could sleep for a while longer. Then Daryl could keep his eyes on the writer and Vi, while

Reid and Nell tried to uncover what Eleanor wanted them to see in the place she'd chosen for her portrait.

He swept his gaze around the area again.

Carefully making his way into the center of the circle, he wished for a step stool. The hedges surrounding the area were high enough to block any view he might have of the stone arch. He figured the floor of the gazebo would have been level with the top of his thigh, the bench Eleanor was sitting on even higher. From that vantage point, the stone arch would have been clearly visible to anyone in the gazebo. And so would the south facade of the castle and the cliffs beyond.

It should take about fifteen seconds for Nell to figure that out. But he knew her well enough now that she'd want to linger a bit longer. In fact…chances were good that this had been the destination she'd had in mind last night. *The gardens*. She'd wanted to seduce him right here.

Was that all she wanted? Just a few days of indulgence—and then they'd go on their separate ways? That's what she'd said, and the words had perfectly matched his own desires. Or so he'd thought.

Frowning, he looked in the direction of the stone arch. There was one way to find out exactly what she wanted. Cam had claimed she'd written her desires down in explicit detail. As Reid pushed his way through the hedge and headed toward the arch, he wondered if reading her fantasies had been his goal from the moment he'd stepped out of the castle this morning.

NELL WOKE UP as she always did with her sensory perceptions just a few seconds ahead of her mind and her feelings. Her view of the ceiling told her that she was at the castle. But not in her own bed.

Because she'd finally seduced Reid.

The memory rushed in along with delight and triumph. And joy. She wanted to savor what had happened, celebrate it and relive each detail, but a jingling bell had her sitting straight up in bed. Alba rose from her prone position in front of the door and padded to her side.

That's when it sank in. "Reid's gone." The tightening around Nell's heart had her pressing the heel of her hand against her chest. She noted the indentation in the pillow, but when she explored it with her hand, it was cold.

"He left you here to do the bodyguard work," she said to Alba.

Why did that hurt so much? Disappointment she could understand. If Reid had been here, she would have seduced him again. Happily.

But what she was feeling cut deeper. She wanted him here. Needed him here.

"Loss," she murmured as she patted the bed so that the dog would join her. Alba jumped up, circled once and settled next to Nell's thigh.

"I suppose that, since you came from a shelter, you've experienced your share of rejection," Nell said. "But I've been lucky." She scratched Alba behind the ears. "There was that cad I thought I was in love with in college. He told me that he loved me, and I believed him. Everyone has always loved me, so I was sucker enough to believe him. Once I went to bed with him, I found out that I was just one more notch on his belt. Classic story."

Alba plopped her head on Nell's lap.

She frowned. "It's absolutely unreasonable that this

hurts more." It wasn't as though he'd left her. He took his job as bodyguard too seriously. The dog was proof of that.

To confirm her suspicion, she grabbed the sheet, wrapping it around herself as she hurried to the sliding glass doors. Even as she slid them open, she spotted Reid sitting with Daryl at the far end of the kitchen terrace. "See," she murmured to the dog who'd joined her. "From where he's sitting, he can keep an eye on all the balconies on this side of the castle. The perfect Secret Service vantage point."

Was that all she was to him? A job? When she caught herself rubbing her chest again, she jerked her hand away and frowned down at it. "There's no reason to feel bad because he left me with you." She hadn't lost Reid.

Yet.

The band around her heart tightened even more— because she would lose him. Hadn't she explained it very clearly to him? Once they found Eleanor's necklace and everyone was safe, she and Reid would go their separate ways. Seduction had been the plan, not a lifelong commitment. If she wanted that, all she would have had to do was follow her aunt's advice and kiss him beneath the stones.

Panic replaced the tight feeling around her heart as she remembered doing just that.

In a dream, she reminded herself. It had all been a strange dream that had started out with Eleanor dancing with another man and ended when Eleanor had kissed Angus beneath the stones.

And then you kissed Reid.

She couldn't deny that. Nor could she deny what had happened right after that, when the dream had drifted, and she had lost herself in the reality of Reid. Their lovemaking had erased everything else from her mind. Even now, she was thinking of Reid instead of finding the necklace. That had to stop.

As if he could sense her presence, Reid chose that moment to shift his gaze to the balcony of his room. When his gaze locked on hers, she felt her heart take a long tumble.

"Oh, my God," she whispered.

Alba rubbed her head against Nell's leg while she concentrated on drawing in a deep breath. When Reid turned his attention back to Daryl, she glanced at the dog. "It was only a dream. I didn't actually kiss him beneath the stones."

But in your heart you did. And in your heart...

Nell sank to her knees beside the dog. "I've fallen in love with him."

For a second, as the whispered words hung in the air, she felt her heart tumble again.

Maybe she'd never fallen out of love with him.

Following fast on that realization came a second. *Another day or two at the most—that's all you'll have.*

Pain sliced deeper this time. Alba licked her cheek. A few days. Beyond that, it was all blank pages.

Pages that you could write a different story on.

This time when she pressed a hand to her heart, it wasn't because of pain. It was because she was sure it had skipped a beat.

First things first.

She had to find that necklace. Rising, she shifted her gaze to the spot in the garden where the old gazebo had stood. Last night Daryl had made a salient point. If Eleanor had intended the portrait to be a treasure map to the location of the sapphires, she'd left the cave out. But there had to be some reason why Eleanor had chosen that spot to sit for her portrait. So it was still going to be the starting point of her search this morning.

Alba rubbed against her leg and whined. Glancing down, Nell saw that the dog had risen to her feet and had her eyes riveted on the terrace. Shifting her own gaze she watched Reid and Daryl rise from their chairs. A second later they were joined by her aunt Vi and a young man. A stranger.

"Good girl," she murmured as she patted the dog's head. "But you don't have to worry. He has to be the writer from the *Times*." As the young man sat down and crossed his legs, Nell felt a little flicker at the back of her mind. She'd experienced the same thing last night when she was looking at the time line Daryl had drawn. Narrowing her eyes, she studied the man more closely. He was several inches shorter than either Daryl or Reid and built along more slender lines. Nell agreed with Nurse Braxton—his face was indeed pretty, and the glasses added a geeky sexiness.

He was here to interview and shadow Vi, so then he could write a follow-up story on the discovery of Eleanor's earrings. And Nell was here to find the necklace and write The End on that story, she reminded herself. Her glance strayed back to Reid. The fastest route to filling in the blank pages on her subplot was to finish writing her main plot.

"The clock is ticking," she murmured to Alba. As she turned, her gaze ran over the writer from the *Times* again, and she remembered what it was that had been tugging at her mind. "The beginning," she said to the dog. "Every story has a trigger. I have to get dressed so I can talk to Reid." Then she dashed for the connecting door to her room.

REID KNEW THE instant that Nell disappeared from the window of his balcony. Not only had she vanished from his peripheral vision but he'd felt an immediate chill in the temperature of his skin when her gaze had left it.

Though Reid hadn't thought it possible, reading the fantasies she'd written on those pink sheets of paper had increased his desire for her. When he'd first caught sight of her on the balcony, he'd had to hold tight to the arms of his chair to keep himself from going to her.

Earlier when he had told Daryl his plans to take Nell to the gazebo, the older man had asked him to hang around long enough to get a personal impression of James Orbison. While Daryl had filled him in on the data the CIA had gathered on the young man, Vi had packed a canvas tote bag with a thermos of coffee and some of her scones so that he and Nell could head out to the gardens as soon as she woke up.

Ten minutes. That's what he'd give her to shower and dress. Ruthlessly he refocused his attention on the young journalist, and he found himself in agreement with Nurse Braxton's description—"pretty and preppy." The eyeglasses emphasized the intelligence in his eyes. Adding that to his unassuming air and enthusiasm about the castle, Reid understood why both Adair and Vi had been amenable to showing him the castle and the grounds, so he could write the initial story on their business and Eleanor's jewels.

What would Nell think of him?

Realizing that his thoughts had once more gone to

Nell, Reid prevented the frown from showing on his face. He hadn't been able to completely rid his mind of her, since he'd dug her mother's jewelry box out of the stones and unfolded those pink sheets of paper.

Entranced. Enchanted. Electrified. Those were just three of the words that described what he'd felt while he'd read them. She had an exceptional talent for creating images, and he'd recognized all of the settings—they were the places he and his brothers had played with the MacPherson sisters that long-ago summer. He'd never look at them the same way again. Especially not the gazebo. The memory of that tea party he'd attended when he was ten would be forever replaced by the scene she'd painted of undressing him slowly, inch by inch. Just thinking about it made his skin heat.

Instead of providing an answer to his questions, invading Nell's privacy had only complicated his problem. Now he burned with a desire to fulfill every one of her fantasies.

And more.

How in the hell had it come to this? Where had it all begun?

When Reid found himself tapping his fingers on the arm of his chair, he stilled them.

"You stopped by the hospital in Albany to see Deanna Lewis," Daryl was saying. "Why was that?"

Five more minutes, Reid decided. If Nell didn't appear, he'd make some excuse and go get her.

"Background information," Orbison said. "I like to be thorough in my research."

Reid thought of his mother's current project, and for the first time, his entire attention was captured by

James Orbison. "Have you had a chance to visit what's left of the Campbell estate in Scotland?"

"No. Much as I would like to go there, my editor couldn't approve that kind of expense. At least not yet. If I can parlay my articles into a book deal, that might change." He turned to Vi. "In the meantime, I'm perfectly happy to be doing research on *this* castle. I understand that your niece Nell is here visiting. I brought a copy of her book so she could sign it for me. I'd love to talk to her."

"I'm afraid that Nell won't be available. She's on a deadline." Reid leaned forward. "I can tell you what she'd ask if she were here. A writing question. What triggered your interest to write a story about the castle?"

"The Stuart sapphires, of course," Orbison replied with a smile.

"Where did you first hear about them?" Reid asked.

"I was a history major at Princeton, and I wrote my senior thesis on Mary Stuart. That's when I came across a photo of that painting that appeared in my article—the one of Mary Queen of Scots on her coronation day. When I saw Eleanor's portrait, I recognized the jewels immediately."

"Did you ever come across the means by which the sapphires came into the Campbells' possession?" Daryl asked.

Orbison shook his head. "No."

"What led you to Castle MacPherson?" Reid asked. "Before your article, the story of Eleanor's jewels has always been a local one."

Orbison's face brightened. "It was by pure chance. I was driving through the Adirondacks on an impromptu vacation, and I stopped at the diner in Glen Loch. They were talking about the new wedding destination business that was being launched at the castle. By the time we finished our pancakes, I'd heard all about the legend and the story of how Angus built the castle for Eleanor. The owner of the diner, Edie, even had a copy of Nell's book. When someone mentioned the sapphires' connection to Mary Stuart, I called my editor and pitched him the idea of writing a feature article on the castle. He went for it."

The explanation was plausible enough. Reid knew Daryl by now, and he would check every detail.

And where was Nell? More than ten minutes had passed. Had she gone out to the gazebo on her own? Panic had him rising from the table abruptly. "Excuse me," he murmured as he strode toward the sliding glass doors to the kitchen. "There's a call I have to make."

On his way through the kitchen, Reid grabbed the thermos of coffee Vi had made and then increased his pace as he entered the hallway to the central foyer. He was three strides past the open door to the main parlor before he fully registered that Nell was standing in front of Eleanor's portrait.

Stopping, he made himself draw in a deep breath. A cool head was essential if he was going to be able to do his job. When he stepped into the room, she didn't move. Neither did Alba, who was lying at her feet. "I thought you'd gone ahead without me," he finally said.

"No." Nell didn't turn to face him. She was too busy analyzing why it hadn't even occurred to her to go out there to the gazebo by herself. A few days ago, the story would have been different. She would have snatched the opportunity to prove that she could find the necklace on her own. Now Reid's opinion and his ideas were important to her. She'd even grown impatient while she'd been waiting for him to join her.

"I stopped here to gather my thoughts before joining you on the terrace." Clasping her hands together, she finally met his eyes. "But if I *had* left you behind, it would have been tit for tat. You left me to meet with that journalist."

"I was doing my job." He opened the thermos and poured coffee for her while he filled her in on their successful search for the bullet. "What thoughts are you gathering? Have you changed your mind about the gazebo?"

"No. I still have a feeling that it plays an important part in the message that Eleanor left. It has to be a part of the puzzle. Otherwise, why choose that place to sit for her portrait? But seeing that journalist made me think about Daryl's time line and where everything to do with Eleanor's sapphires started." She pointed at the whiteboard. "We've been concentrating on Adair's discovery of the first earring and the *Times* article that made everything public. Those two events triggered all that's happened here at the castle. But my thought is the real beginning has to go back to when Eleanor first wore those jewels. We know that she had them with her on the night she and Angus eloped. But we still don't know how the Campbell family came to possess them."

Reid turned to study the portrait. "Right. Cam called last night and told me there's a portrait gallery of all the Campbell heirs and their families, including one of Eleanor's parents and her sisters. The sapphires don't appear in any of the paintings."

"What if they had never belonged to the Campbells? If they had, surely the family would have wanted it known. Mary Stuart wore them in a painting celebrating her coronation. Eleanor wore them in this portrait. And she was wearing them in the dream I had last night."

"What kind of dream?"

"She was dancing in a massive ballroom with a man. Not the ballroom here. There was a huge fire burning in a fireplace and candles everywhere. I'd swear that the dress she was wearing is the one she's wearing in the painting. He looked familiar, but it definitely wasn't Angus. Then the ballroom faded. Eleanor was kissing Angus beneath the stone arch, and she was wearing the same dress and the sapphires."

When Reid said nothing, Nell shot him a sideways look. "I know dreams aren't evidence. I know their meaning is at best symbolic. But look at the evidence we do have.

"No one is wearing them in the portrait gallery. Your mother hasn't found any mention of them in the records that remain in the library. And she hasn't come across any stories about them that have been handed down orally. Jewels like those sapphires generate talk. The legend of the stone arch is still being told—there and here. But the only place where there are stories about the Stuart sapphires is here."

"Mom isn't having any luck discovering the story behind Angus and Eleanor's flight, either." He poured her a refill out of the thermos. "Deanna Lewis claimed they were never Eleanor's dowry. What do you think happened?"

After taking a sip of coffee, she said, "Maybe they were a gift from this strange man she was dancing with in my dream. I might write it that way. It would certainly complicate everything."

"It would explain why the jewels didn't appear in any of the Campbell portraits," Reid said.

"But it doesn't explain the lack of stories. Whoever they belonged to must have been furious when they disappeared. Murders have occurred for less. Wars have started for less. Someone must have gone to a great deal of trouble to keep that story hushed up."

"Someone may still be trying to keep it a secret. That may be why there was a fire in the library on the Campbell estate six months ago," Reid mused. "It might also be a reason why someone spent so much time searching through the library here at the castle. Eleanor and Angus had to have known the story behind the sapphires. If she kept a journal…"

Nell grabbed his hand. "That's what they might have been looking for. If this Gwendolen 'Campbell' really is a true descendent of the Campbell line, she wouldn't want anyone to know who might have a better claim on those sapphires."

"It still doesn't explain why she thinks she has a better claim than you and your sisters," Reid pointed out.

"Once we find the necklace, and she makes a play for it, we can ask her. Let's go."

The moment Nell opened the front door, Alba nosed her way through it, then turned and waited for them to follow.

Nell sighed. "Like it or not, it looks like I've picked up another guardian angel."

Reid laughed as they headed toward the gardens.

13

THE MOMENT HE pushed aside the branches of the hedge so that Nell could slip through them, Reid's senses went on full alert. Even as he tightened his grip on her hand, he noticed the disturbed dirt in the spot where he'd unearthed the flat stone step. "Someone has been here since I left."

Nell sent Reid an amused glance. "I would imagine so. I can't recall the last time I visited this place."

"I was here about an hour ago to check out security." Keeping her close to his side, he circled to the spot and pointed at it. "I pushed enough debris away to uncover what must have been one of the steps that led up to the wooden floor. Someone has shoved it all back in place."

"You were here alone?" She poked a finger into his chest. "Who checked out the security for you?"

When she poked him again, he captured her hand. "I had to look at the place, make a plan to keep you safe." He swept his gaze along the top of the hedge to the hills beyond. "The sun was barely up. Skinner's men would have still been looking for the casings in the area above the stone arch. Whoever it was used the shadows and the trees for cover." He cursed himself silently that none of that had entered his mind while he'd been checking out the security. He'd been too distracted by the idea of reading Nell's fantasies.

Nell slipped her hand into his and held it tight. "He was probably watching you from the time you left the castle this morning. When you came here alone, he could have killed you."

"Or vice versa. I wouldn't have made such an easy target this morning. And while Skinner's men might not have spotted him, they were up there in the hills. Any kind of noise would have brought them down."

Nell swept her gaze along the tops of the hedges. "I'm betting he never left the area. After he shot at you last night, he could have slipped down into the garden and just waited."

She was right. There were plenty of places to take cover in the garden. In his mind, Reid planned the conversation he'd have with Skinner and Daryl. Some of the volunteers would have to patrol the paths, especially during the wedding rehearsal.

"I want to get you back to the castle, but we have to look for the necklace," Nell said.

Reid looked at her. "You want to get *me* back to the castle? Who's the bodyguard here?"

"We both are. But you're the one who got shot at. Whoever he is, he's smart. But he's not here now. We can relax for the moment."

"Why do you say that?"

"If he were still here in the garden, Alba would be raising the alarm." She patted the dog's head. "Vi claims her instincts are spot-on."

Reid glanced around. The sun was higher in the sky.

Even in camouflage, an intruder was likely to be spotted by the volunteers patrolling the hills. Alba was walking around the perimeter of the stones that had formed the base of the old gazebo, sniffing as she went. Every so often, she paused to dig in the dirt, but she showed no signs of alarm.

"Let's just make it fast," he said. "I was thinking about Daryl's point that the cliff face isn't in the painting, and I want to show you something." He led her to the far side of the circle formed by the stones. "Turn around." Once she had, he gripped her waist and lifted her up so she sat on his shoulder.

"I'm thinking this is about the height of the bench Eleanor sat on for her portrait. The stone arch is beyond her right shoulder. Tell me what you see."

"The castle, the woods and the cliffs beyond. To the right, I can see the arch, more hills above it, to the left, the lake. She could see pretty much everything from here."

"Think of the position of her head in the painting. What is she directly facing?" Reid prompted.

Nell shaded her eyes. "The top of the cliff where the cave is. It's directly beyond the third floor of castle. She must have been looking straight at it." The thrill in her tone gave Reid a great deal of satisfaction. He lowered her then. Her feet had barely touched the ground when Alba began to bark excitedly.

Reid shoved her behind him, pulled out his gun and fanned it in a quick circle. Then he pushed Nell down behind the biggest pile of stones and checked the garden paths on each side of the tall hedges. No sign of anyone. Only the continued barking of the dog marred the silence.

Turning back, he saw Alba pawing the dirt near the stone step he'd uncovered on his earlier visit.

"She's found something." Dropping to her knees, Nell pushed more dirt aside. Sunlight glinted off metal as she lifted Alba's unearthed treasure in the palm of her hand.

"Another earring. And it's not Eleanor's." She met Reid's eyes. "My autograph lady was wearing this when she asked me to sign that book."

Alba barked as she pawed at the dirt again. Sunlight glinted off metal again as Reid squatted down beside Nell. But it wasn't jewelry he saw in the little depression. It was a very sophisticated electronic listening device.

"What—?"

Reid silenced Nell by putting a hand over her mouth. Keeping her eyes on his, she wrapped her fingers around his wrist and tightened them. *Good girl,* he thought. He mouthed the words, "Follow my lead."

Something flashed into her eyes. Not fear, but excitement.

He wanted to kiss her. *Later,* he promised himself.

Someone had listened to everything they'd said. In his mind, he quickly reviewed the essentials of their conversation and wished he had more time to strategize. "Well, now our villain has a face. That will make it easier for Sheriff Skinner's men if she tries to get on the grounds again."

That would give her something to worry about. She would know now that they'd put it together that she had to have been involved in the attempted hit-and-run on Piper.

"We just need to find out who she is." He wanted

their listener worried but not in panic mode. "How sure are you that the necklace has to be here in the foundation of the gazebo?" he asked Nell.

Reid saw the surprise flash into Nell's eyes, then something else. Understanding? Amusement? She didn't miss a beat before saying, "I'm absolutely positive. I think Eleanor planned where she would hide the jewels right from this very spot. It's just a matter of finding the necklace before someone else in my family is hurt."

"C'mon," he said. "Let's go fill your aunt in on our discoveries."

AN HOUR LATER, Nell sat on the couch in the main parlor trying to make her mind go blank. It was a technique she sometimes used when she had to write a scene and too many possibilities were flooding her mind. Daryl and Reid had been discussing them nonstop since Reid had hurried her back to the castle. As a precautionary measure, the two men had searched the room thoroughly for any listening devices, and now they were on their cell phones. Daryl had his pressed to his ear while he stood sentry at the French doors that connected the parlor with Adair's office. Through the sheer curtains on the panes of glass, he could keep an unobtrusive eye on Vi and James Orbison as her aunt dealt with a young couple interested in scheduling their wedding at the castle.

At least that meeting seemed to be going well. She only wished her meeting with Daryl and Reid had gone as well. But from the moment Reid had rushed her away from the gazebo and back to the castle, he and Daryl had done all the talking and decision-making. The only time they'd paid her any heed was when she'd advanced the possibility that autograph lady had been the shooter.

Two full beats of silence followed her suggestion. She'd almost heard the wheels turning in their heads as she'd made her case. "The dropped earring makes us assume she lost it when she was planting the listening device. Why didn't she assign that task to her 'accomplice' with the military training? Unless there was no accomplice?"

At that point both men had gone to their cell phones. Neither had spoken to her since. She was beginning to feel like Jane Eyre standing out in the cold and peering through the windows at the life she would never be a part of.

Her gaze settled on the gold earring on the coffee table, and once again she experienced the same icy sliver of fear she'd felt when she had first recognized it. It was her desire to keep her family safe that had kept her from getting angry that the two men were excluding her.

But she had spent the past year establishing an independent life for herself and wasn't going to let anyone make all the decisions for her again. She would have to show them that her ideas were just as good as theirs. Maybe better.

"The landscaper will begin excavating the foundation within the hour," Reid said as he pocketed his cell phone and joined Daryl at the French doors. "That should buy us some time."

Nothing to argue with there, Nell thought.

Daryl removed his cell phone from his ear. "Skinner's men will have pictures of Gwendolen within the hour. My man is still researching, but her most recent husband had a brother who served in the British army. U.K. special forces. But the brother-in-law died six months ago."

Enough, Nell thought. Once again, they were talking as if she weren't in the room. Rising, she said, "He could have taught her to shoot, supplied her with a weapon and night vision goggles at the very least. And six months seems to be a magic number in all of this."

When both men turned to look at her, it gave Nell a great deal of satisfaction. While she had their attention, she moved quickly to the original time line that Daryl had drawn on the whiteboard. "The article in the *Times* that triggered all the interest in the Stuart sapphires appeared about six months ago. The fire in the library on the Campbell estate in Scotland occurred six months ago. And now we find out our lead suspect's brother-in-law with a military background died at roughly the same time. Coincidence? I sure couldn't sell it that way in a book."

"You think our Gwendolen was behind that fire?" Daryl asked.

Reid turned to Daryl. "I share Nell's aversion to coincidence. Her theory is that someone discovered something about the location and the story behind how the sapphires came into Eleanor's possession in the library at the Campbell estate, and then set a fire to suppress the details. Before that they may have discovered a clue that pointed toward where the jewels are."

"And they believed that the library here might also contain some of the details," Daryl said. "Or hold the key to the location of the jewels—until they started popping up elsewhere."

"So far I'm just thinking about possible story scenarios," Nell said. "But if Gwendolen is the master-mind behind everything, as a successful grifter, she's become very adept at using what comes to hand—circumstances, people. I'll bet Duncan would agree."

"I'll update him on what we're thinking." Reid punched a number into his phone. Then he turned to Nell. "In the meantime, fill us in on what you're thinking."

The type of warmth that flooded her at Reid's words was new. "As a con woman, she's played a lot of different roles, probably picked up many skills along the way. The image she presents to the public—the fashionably dressed matron—is only one of her personas." Nell leaned over and picked up the gold earring, holding it so that it caught the light. "My first impression was that she would make a great villain because she looks so *normal*. A matron who dresses well, who wants a book signed for her granddaughter, who does volunteer work at hospitals. But she also has a string of dead ex-husbands. Not to mention a deceased brother-in-law."

There was a beat of silence as the two men exchanged a glance.

"Nell is very good at spinning stories," Reid said. "I don't like this one, but it fits the facts."

"There's another thing," Nell said. "The person who visited the castle library over a period of six months was patient. She's not patient anymore. She sent her stepdaughter in to kidnap Piper. She had another accomplice try to run Piper down. Now she's doing things herself."

Reid looked at Daryl. "I don't know why we need Duncan when we've got a behavioral analyst right in the room."

She was back in the game, Nell thought. Now, if she could just convince them to let her go to the gazebo…

"I'll put another man on it. I want to know how those husbands died, and what kind of skill sets she might have picked up from them." Daryl was punching a number into his cell when Alba rose to her feet and whined. He glanced through the French doors, then at his watch. "Vi is through with her clients, and the wedding party should be arriving at any minute for the rehearsal. She'll want to greet them. I'll go with her and Orbison. I want the two of you to stay here." He shifted his gaze from Reid to Nell and then back again. "Consider yourselves under house arrest."

"But the sapphires aren't in the house," Nell said. "And I'm supposed to find them. Reid?"

"I agree with Daryl. More than twenty-four hours have passed. Once we start excavating the old gazebo, Gwendolen may decide we know where the necklace is, and we're finding it. Or she may believe we've already found it and we're stalling. Either way, she's going to have to make a move soon. Planting that listening device was very risky. And you're dead-on about her waning patience. If she still believes you're the key to the necklace, she'll make a move on you."

The words chilled Nell to the bone. Reid was right. She couldn't have written it any better. But how was she supposed to find Eleanor's necklace if they kept her locked up in the castle?

"The castle's security is state-of-the-art," Daryl said. "She's not getting in here. Skinner will have men posted at every entrance during the wedding rehearsal. And that will take place at the stone arch. All you have to do is stay put."

When Daryl exited through the French doors, Alba gave a whine, but she stayed right where she was.

"Looks like the dog agrees that we're the ones in danger," Nell said.

"Her instincts are good. And you can save whatever arguments you're summoning up. I'm not going to take you to the gazebo." He began to pace. "If your theory is right, she's not just a class A con woman with some idea that those sapphires belong to her. She's a stone-cold killer. When she tried to have Piper killed yesterday, it wasn't just because you didn't get up here to the castle fast enough. I'm betting it was because Piper was responsible for putting her stepdaughter in a coma. It was a pretty good plan. Motivate you and get revenge at the same time."

Nell thought she couldn't feel any colder, but his words about her sister made her tremble. "I didn't even think of that. You're scaring me."

"Good." Reid moved to her, then pulled her into his arms and held on tight. It was something he'd wanted to do ever since he'd gotten her back safely into the castle. "I'm scaring myself."

"Piper—"

"She'll be safe. Gwendolen is here focused on the necklace." Which meant that Nell was the one in danger.

When she wrapped her arms around him and held him as tightly as he was holding her, he couldn't have named all the feelings rushing through him. Not the passion that he'd felt, not the explosion of desire that she could so easily trigger. This was what he'd felt when he'd awakened with her in his arms—that warmth moving through his veins with the slow but powerful strength of a river that couldn't be held back or denied.

He wanted this; perhaps he'd wanted it from the first moment he saw her.

He would want this always.

Drawing back, he met her gaze. What he hoped he saw was that she was experiencing the same thing he was.

He wanted to ask her. But the timing was wrong. Her life was in danger. He knew that. But he also knew that it wasn't just fear for her safety that was holding him back. It was his fear of her answer. It was that and that alone that made him release her for the moment and step back.

"We need to find the necklace." He put his hands on her shoulders to turn her to face the portrait. "You believe she put the clues in the portrait. So let's go back to square one. What story is Eleanor telling in the painting?"

Nell had to shove down the urge to object. He was correct. But if he hadn't drawn back, if he hadn't turned her to face the painting, the desire to stay in his arms would have kept her there. She might have given anything to stay right there. She might have given *everything*.

That realization helped her focus. Everything wasn't what he wanted. It wasn't what she believed she wanted, either.

"Tell me Eleanor's story," Reid prompted.

Pushing everything else from her mind, she tried to imagine she was seeing Eleanor's portrait for the first time.

"Talk me through it as if you were writing about it."

"I see a beautiful woman. My eye is drawn immediately to her. And then to the sapphires."

"What do you notice next?"

"Her hair, the dress. It's white like a wedding dress. She wants to remind us of her story. The stone arch in the background—that's her history, and it's the symbol of the love that triggered everything."

"Go on."

"The expression on her face. She's glowing. So are the sapphires. She wants us to know how happy she is, and she wants to tell us about the sapphires. A picture limits the scope of the story she can tell. That makes the details even more significant."

"What else?"

"Her— How slender she is, how small her hands are, the way her fingers curl over that pile of books." Nell felt her hands tense. "I'm starting to babble."

Reid squeezed her shoulders. "Relax. Don't think or edit. Just list the details."

"The flowers. She's sitting in the gazebo in a garden that she designed and planted. She's looking right at the cliff where the cave is. The third floor of the castle is also in her line of vision. But…"

"What?"

"The stone arch is in her past. I'm not surprised that she hid one of the earrings there because it's the connection between where she and Angus fell in love and the life they built here. But her present and her future—that's what she's looking at. It's almost like another painting. The castle is in the foreground and the cliff beyond. The cave must have meant something to them. Perhaps it was a place where she and Angus could sneak off to."

"Keep going."

Nell closed her eyes and reimagined the view she'd

had in those moments when she'd sat on Reid's shoulders at the gazebo. "She can see the glint of water at the top of Tinker's Falls. The lake. The hills surrounding the castle—they're all there either in her line of vision or in the painting." Her stomach sank. She opened her eyes to focus on Reid. "Thinking of it that way, she's got everything in there but the kitchen sink. How in the world are we supposed to figure out where she hid the necklace?"

"Look again."

She stared at the portrait once more. Her gaze focused automatically on Eleanor first. "Odd. She's so relaxed but her hands are tense on those books." Nell felt her own fingers curl and grow tense again. "She's the focus of the portrait, and other than the sapphires, they're the closest thing to her. Why are they even there?"

"The illustrations in your book—could those be the books you found them in?" Reid asked.

"They could be. They're in my mother's room." The image flashed into her mind of exactly what she'd seen when she'd been sitting on Reid's shoulders in the gazebo. And she could have sworn that the glow on Eleanor's face grew even brighter. Excitement bloomed inside Nell as she grabbed Reid's hand and pulled him into the foyer. "She wasn't just looking at the cliff face. She was looking right at that room."

14

REID HAD TO hurry his pace to keep up with her. To his surprise she didn't stop on the second floor where her own room was and instead climbed a third flight of stairs. At the top was a double set of doors carved in oak. Opening them, she brushed aside cobwebs, then led the way down a dim hallway.

"When my mother was alive, the nursery was on this floor and so was the master suite my parents used. When she died, my father declared the whole third floor of the castle off-limits. He locked up the library, too, because it had been her favorite room."

The room she ushered Reid into was dim. Sunlight struggled with grime on the windows and barely illuminated the dust motes in its path. He took in the perfectly made bed, the robe that still lay across its foot. His heart twisted when he made out the tiny white crib tucked into a book-lined alcove in one wall.

"As far as I know, I'm the only one who's visited this place since my mother died."

"Your sisters never came up here?" A rumble of thunder had him striding to the windows that ran along two walls. Alba followed, her collar jingling. "It's just a storm, girl," he murmured as he patted her head. He knew that she couldn't hear the thunder or his words but could feel the rumble effects. Still she jumped up and settled herself on the window seats that lined one wall of windows. On the other, sliding glass doors opened onto a balcony with a stunning view of the lake. From this height, he could clearly make out the hedge circling the old gazebo. Beyond that, a small group of people had gathered around Vi and Daryl in front of the stone arch. The wedding rehearsal was about to begin. Thunder rumbled again. He patted the dog's head. There wasn't a cloud in the sky.

"Adair and Piper said coming up here would make them too sad."

Turning, he watched her run her hand along the railing of the tiny white crib. "How old were you when she died?" he asked.

"Six months. I don't remember her at all. I must have been four or five when I realized Piper and Adair did, and I couldn't. It made me feel left out, so that's when I started sneaking up here. I suppose I was hoping something might trigger a memory. I even tried playing dress up in her clothes. Nothing worked."

"But you kept coming back anyway."

She smiled as she joined him at the windows. "It was forbidden. That held a great deal of appeal. And I found other things I liked to do. Like reading. My mother's favorite room was the library, and I pretended the books on those shelves in the alcove were her favorites. I read them all. On rainy days, I used to sit on this window seat and write. Eleanor did some of her sketches right from this vantage point."

"The sketchbooks. You found them in the alcove?"

"No. I found them in what I've always imagined was her secret cupboard. You've seen Angus's secret cupboard in the main parlor."

Nell moved to the stone fireplace that took up a great deal of the wall opposite the alcove. "It's different than Angus's. It's built right into the side of the fireplace."

Angus's secret cupboard had fascinated Reid's brothers and him when they were ten. Only it wasn't a secret. According to Cam, Piper had made a show-and-tell video when she was in fifth grade that was available in the local library.

By the time he joined Nell, she had swung open one of the square flat stones on a central hinge just large enough to allow her to slide the sketchbooks out. Dropping to his knees, he ran his hand along the inside of the space. His best guess was that it was about two feet square. Smaller than Angus's. Smooth stones lined the walls, and not one of them budged.

"If Eleanor's necklace were in there, I would have found it when I discovered the sketchbooks." Nell carried them to the window seat.

"Just checking. Why don't we split these up?" As he sat beside her, there was an ominous roll of thunder. Alba inched close enough to make contact with his thigh. Sunlight still poured down on the gardens, but he could see a line of black clouds on the far side of the lake rolling forward like invading tanks. A car pulled into the drive and a young woman stepped out, followed by two older women. Reid recognized one of them as Edie. He noted that Daryl was talking with Sheriff Skinner. Thunder growled again and wind gusts disturbed the leaves in the garden.

"I hope that storm doesn't interfere with the rehearsal," Nell said as she passed him a book.

Reid began to turn the pages. Some of the drawings he recognized from Nell's book. Other places captured in the sketches he remembered seeing the summer he was ten. "I'm noticing a pattern. Many of them are drawn from the vantage point of the gazebo. But Eleanor must have done others right on the scene. It's almost as if she was using the drawings the way a photographer might use a camera—taking the wide angle shot and then zooming in.

"You're right." Nell pointed to the page she was studying. "Here's the one of the castle and the cliffs. Then on the next page there's one of the beach that had to have been drawn from that ledge in front of the cave. Then there are several of the interior sections of the cave. I'll bet one of them was where Piper and Duncan discovered the earring. It's almost as though she's drawing a treasure map right to that earring with her sketches."

Reid turned to look at her, once again all admiration at the quick way her mind worked. "Did you ever tell anyone about these drawings or show them to anyone?"

"No. When I was trying to convince my editor and publishers to use the drawings, I showed them enlarged photos. I never told anyone about the secret cupboard, either."

"Not even your sisters?"

"Especially not my sisters. I told my publisher and the marketing people that I'd found them in the library. Sometimes I felt guilty about not telling Piper and Adair. But by the time I had found them, I'd begun to think of this place as mine—a secret I shared only with my mother and Eleanor. Don't you have secrets you've kept from your brothers?"

He smiled. "I treasure each and every one of them." Setting aside the book, he rose and walked over to the fireplace. Kneeling down, he pushed the stone back into place. The mechanism worked smoothly. Even when he ran his hands over it, he felt nothing that indicated that there was a secret cupboard behind it.

"It's constructed very well. Assuming that Eleanor hid the sketchbooks here, I still wonder why no one ever found them or why this secret cupboard didn't become part of the family history the way Angus's did. How did you discover the way to work that stone?"

"Totally by accident. There was a huge rainstorm that day just like the one that seems to be blowing in now. We lost electricity for a few minutes. During one flash of lightning, I noticed a glint along this side of the fireplace. When the lights came back on, I investigated. The stone swung open quite easily, and there they were."

Thunder clapped overhead, and wind howled its way past the windows. Alba pressed closer to her. For a while Nell watched Reid try to find the way to open the stone and was surprised that he couldn't.

"I'll show you." Nell joined him and slipped just the tips of her fingers between two of the stones. The stone swung open again.

"Let me try." Once he closed the stone, he did try, but the size of his fingers prevented him from getting any traction. "It seems to require a woman's touch," he murmured.

The ringing of his cell was nearly drowned out by another clap of thunder overhead.

Reid held the phone so Nell could hear. "Change of

plans," Daryl said. "Vi's bringing the wedding rehearsal inside to the ballroom. Skinner will make sure the rest of the castle is blocked off, but his job will be easier if you and Nell join us. That way we can all multitask."

"Agreed." He ended the call and the instant he studied Nell's eyes, he saw mirrored in them exactly what he was feeling—disappointment and frustration.

"I need to keep looking through the sketches. The answer is in them somewhere."

"I think so, too." There wasn't a doubt in his mind that Eleanor was somehow going to guide Nell to the necklace. "We'll come back just as soon as we can. And we'll come back together, Nell. Promise?"

"Promise. Let me put the sketchbooks back."

Once she did, he signaled the dog, and they left the room.

"YOUR AUNT VI'S a genius," Sheriff Skinner said.

"Yes." Nell had always known that, but the quick way Vi had improvised to go forward with the wedding rehearsal in the ballroom confirmed it in spades. Nell could only hope that the rest of the rehearsal would go as swiftly. She needed to get back to those sketchbooks.

There were twenty or so people in the ballroom. They'd all pitched in to line up folding chairs into a makeshift aisle. Now they were standing in small groups laughing and chatting—totally ignoring the storm that raged outside. Daryl had shut Alba away in the kitchen because she'd started growling and barking when the wedding party had descended on the castle.

At the far end of the room, Vi stood in a huddle with the bride and groom and the minister. Nearby, Nell spotted Edie with a concerned look on her face as she gave

James Orbison a pat on his arm. The young journalist was maximizing on the chaos produced by the sudden change of venue to speak to as many guests as he could.

Reid and Daryl stood nearby the line of French doors that opened onto a long terrace with a view of the lake. Rain pounded against the windowpanes, and lightning crisscrossed the sky. A pretty young flute player began to play softly—Beethoven's "Ode to Joy" as Edie and the groom's father, Benjy Grimshaw, joined Reid and Daryl. From this distance, Nell could see that Edie was making the introductions. The conversation was brief, but when the couple walked away, both Daryl and Reid reached immediately for their cell phones.

Turning to Sheriff Skinner, Nell asked, "Do you know what Benjy Grimshaw discovered about the gun the shooter used?"

"One of his blog followers in England is all but positive that the bullets were manufactured there," Skinner said. "He claims he has a rifle in his pawn shop that uses that particular caliber. The weapon is a favorite with upper-class Brits who love to hunt."

"Gwendolen could have access to that kind of bullet. She might even own that kind of gun. But it's not proof."

"No," Skinner agreed. "But the evidence is piling up."

Not fast enough, Nell thought. Thunder continued to rumble as Reid and Daryl talked into their cells, gathering that needed evidence. Frustration that she had thought she'd quelled rose up again. Not because Daryl and Reid were leaving her out. Their splitting off made perfect sense. As long as there was an unplanned event going on in the castle, they had to focus on security. For everyone.

The source of her frustration was more personal. Oh, she wanted to tell herself that it was because she was so close to finding the necklace, and she wanted Reid's perspective on the sketches. He would see things that she couldn't. The last thing she'd expected was that they made a good team. They were so different. But somehow they fit. Perfectly.

He stood not fifty feet away from her, and yet she missed him.

How in the world had it come to that? What had become of her goal to operate independently? How had she gotten to the point where she wanted to be with him all the time? She hated to think of herself as that… immersed.

She studied his frame in the window, the darkness of the storm at his back. The toughness and the strength in his face and his body offered such an appealing contrast to the kindness she'd always known was there. A kaleidoscope of images flashed through her mind. His face as it had looked on the day their parents had married and again when she'd first seen him talking to the policeman at the door of Piper's apartment. The expression in his eyes when he'd walked through the door to her room last night, and finally what she'd seen in his eyes after he'd held her in the main parlor only hours ago.

Her heart took a long bounce. There was a story in the way he looked at her, but she'd avoided thinking about it. Afraid that she might be seeing in his eyes what she wanted to see—the narrative of her own developing feelings and not his. Images always told stories, but love was blind. Her heart bounced again, and fear bubbled up.

The slow crescendo in the sound of a flute had the

guests quieting, and Nell's attention switched to Vi as she led the bride, her father and two other young women to the end of the makeshift aisle. The groom-to-be and another man stood to the left of the minister. While the music played softly, Vi orchestrated the seating of the groom's parents and then the bride's. Two young men were quietly capturing each moment on their cell phones.

Something flickered at the edge of her mind, then faded before she could grasp it.

Focus, she told herself. Find the necklace, and then you'll figure out what to do about Reid Sutherland.

REID PUNCHED HIS contact button for Cam. Calculating the time difference, he figured that his brother and Adair were meeting with the housekeeper's mother right now, and depending on where the woman lived, cell reception could be tricky.

A few minutes ago, he and Daryl had discovered they'd been told a lie. Not a major one, but it was enough to put his senses on full alert. Daryl was checking it out. But Reid had an urgent question for his brother. His gaze swept the room. As the flute player segued into the wedding march, Vi gently urged the first bridesmaid up the aisle.

"Problem or favor?" Cam asked in his ear.

"Both. What have you found out about the sapphires?"

"A word to the wise—housekeepers and servants know everything. Delia Dunsmore is ninety-four years old, but her mind still works like a steel trap. Mom's in love with her, and A.D. wants to paint her."

Reid suppressed the urge to tell his brother to hurry

up. He knew from experience doing that would only have the opposite effect. Instead, he checked the room once again. Everyone was accounted for. Security was tight. Skinner was still at Nell's side. Reminding himself of those things only increased the urgency he felt in his gut. Time was running out.

"Is that the wedding march I hear in the background? You're not getting hitched to Nell, are you?" Cam asked.

Ignoring the question, Reid took a risk. "Could you give me the *Reader's Digest* version? Was this Delia able to recall anything about how the Campbells gained possession of the sapphires?"

"They were a betrothal gift from Eleanor's groom-to-be, one Alistair MacGregor. He'd been invited to the castle and had fallen in love with Eleanor on sight. On the night of the ball celebrating their engagement, he gave them to her and insisted she wear them. Evidently, his family had been staunch supporters of the queen, and the sapphires had been a gift to his great-great-grandfather from Mary Stuart herself. According to Delia, the marriage would have brought money and land to help the Campbells over a rough patch."

Reid recalled Nell's dream. "So she was wearing them on the night of the big betrothal ball, and that was the same night she ran off with Angus."

"Correct. Technically, it could be argued that she had a right to take the jewels with her."

"I wonder if Eleanor would make that argument. Or her betrothed. If those sapphires were mine, and the woman I loved ran off with them and another man, I wouldn't take that generous a view. Why wasn't more of a stink raised?"

"Alistair MacGregor hanged himself. One of the servants discovered him on the morning after the party. According to Delia it was all hushed up. Guests at the betrothal bash were told that the bride and groom had decided to elope and move immediately to his isolated estate in northern Scotland. Since Alistair was an only child and the last of his line, no one from that side offered a different version. Scandal avoided. Delia says that for months the Campbell family waited for Eleanor to return. If she had, they probably would have hidden her away in a nunnery and kept the jewels."

"Who inherited on the MacGregor side?" Reid asked. "Seems to me that part of the family might think they have a claim, especially if there's no written record to support the story that the sapphires were a gift to Eleanor."

"We're all going to work on that. But if there was a written record, that might have been what Castle MacPherson's nocturnal visitor was looking for in the library."

"And it may be the reason why a fire came close to destroying the library at the Campbell estate," Reid pointed out. "That's why I called. I need to know if anyone visited the Campbell estate six to eight months ago. Nell and I both think that the fire in the library is related to what's going on now."

"Hold on," Cam said. "I can ask the housekeeper right now."

While he waited, Reid glanced around the ballroom again. The second bridesmaid was halfway up the aisle. Sheriff Skinner still stood at Nell's side. Everyone else was focused on the progress of the rehearsal. Nothing he saw triggered an alarm. Still, a sense of urgency rolled through him, and he willed Cam to hurry.

His gaze settled on Nell. More than anything he wanted to go to her and just carry her away. But he couldn't. Gut instinct told him that she was very close to figuring out where that necklace was. He was as sure of that as he was that something unforeseen was about to happen.

"How are you holding up?" Skinner asked.

Nell dragged her gaze away from the two young people at the altar to look at Sheriff Skinner. "I just wish this was over. I need to find that necklace."

"If anyone can figure out where it is, you can," Skinner commented.

Surprised, she met his eyes. "You sound so sure of that."

"You're a lot like your mother."

"You knew her?" Even as she asked it, she realized it was a foolish question. She judged Sheriff Skinner to be close to her father's age, and everyone knew everyone in Glen Loch.

"I dated her a few times in high school before your father snapped her up."

Something in his tone made her ask, "Were you in love with her?"

"Enough to start thinking I should seal the deal by kissing her up here under the stones. She was sixteen, I was seventeen, and I thought I had time."

"What happened?"

There was a twinkle in Skinner's eyes. "Your father had some fast moves, and he had the home-court advantage."

She'd never thought of her father in that way, as a young man in love. And she'd certainly never thought of him as having fast moves. "Maybe it was my mother who had the fast moves."

Skinner chuckled. "You could be right. Once she set a goal for herself, she never let anyone stop her."

When the flute player segued into the bridal march, Nell shifted her gaze back to the wedding rehearsal just in time to see the bride-to-be and her father start up the aisle.

"Molly's two younger brothers are getting everything on their cell phones," Sheriff Skinner commented. "With that newfangled technology and zoom feature, those little phones can do videos and stills, and they don't have to run around the way wedding photographers had to do in my day."

A zoom feature. Now Nell knew exactly what she'd been trying to remember just before the sheriff had joined her. She and Reid had already theorized that was exactly what Eleanor had done. The location of the necklace had to be in that final sketchbook. If she couldn't get to the sketches, she'd just summon them up in her mind. Closing her eyes, she focused on the drawings in the last book.

The location of the necklace would be in one of the close-ups. Not in the gazebo. She couldn't recall even one sketch that Eleanor had made of it. But from that perspective she'd sketched the castle several times. Then Nell remembered one series of drawings and a close-up, one that she hadn't used in her book because she had never wanted to share it.

The necklace would be there. She was sure of it.

A spattering of applause broke out as the bride-to-be's father handed her over to the groom-to-be. Then glass shattered and screams mingled with the sound of glass shattering again.

"Get down," Skinner shouted. "Everybody, get down."

Nell had no choice when the sheriff shoved her to the floor. "Stay here," he said as he crouched low and moved away. Keeping her head on the floor, Nell searched for a glimpse of Reid. Too many chairs stood in the way. Lightning flashed as another pane of glass splintered into shards. Fear froze Nell's stomach as she saw the silhouetted figure and the rifle poised on the far end of the terrace just where the land dropped away to the lake below. Another pane of glass on the French doors shattered very close to where Reid had been standing.

A hand clamped on her wrist and a voice rasped in her ear. "My partner's next bullet will hit Reid if you don't come with me now."

AT THE SOUND of the first shot, Reid pitched to the floor, and rolled twice until he could use a potted plant for some cover. Then he pulled his gun. He couldn't see anyone outside the French doors, but the sniper could be crouching behind the stone wall that ran the length of the terrace. The lights inside the ballroom made them all sitting targets. A quick glance over his shoulder assured him that Nell was out of sight.

There were woods to the right of the terrace. In his mind, he could see just how the shooter had taken advantage of the storm and gotten in position. Wait for everyone to be on the move, take out the volunteer Skinner had stationed at the back of the castle and then wait for the moment to shoot.

Nell. A mix of panic and fear sprinted up his spine as he twisted to pinpoint her location. He spotted Skinner crouched low near one of doors leading out of the ballroom, but Nell wasn't with him. A second later the sheriff reached up to douse the lights.

"I'll cover the terrace doors." Daryl called to him from behind another plant. "Go find Nell."

Crawling on his belly, he moved quickly to the spot where he'd last seen her. The wood beneath his palms was still warm from her body. Fear pumped through his veins like a flooding river. His cell phone rang.

Not a number he recognized.

"Yes," he said.

"Keep everyone in the ballroom and tell Skinner to call off his volunteers. My partner will shoot to kill the next time. Nell has ten minutes to give me the necklace."

James Orbison. Reid barely recognized the voice because of the tone. Gone was the eager young scholar and journalist he'd questioned on the kitchen terrace earlier.

If he'd only acted sooner—he'd had all the evidence he needed seconds ago, when Cam had given him the description of two people who'd visited the Campbell estate seven months ago. And Edie had told him minutes before that Orbison had lied about coming to Edie's diner alone. According to Edie, he'd been with an older woman who'd acted besotted with him. She'd matched Gwen's description.

Ruthlessly, he shoved aside the recriminations. "Let me talk to Nell."

A beat went by, then Nell said, "I'm fine. I'm going to take James to where Eleanor hid the necklace."

An icy blade of fear sliced through Reid right to the

bone. The excitement in her voice told him that she'd figured out Eleanor's hiding place. But once she handed the necklace over, Orbison would kill her. Reid's only hope was to get to her first. Praying that the lack of light in the ballroom would cover his movements, Reid belly crawled his way back to Daryl and filled him in on his plan.

NELL STOPPED SHORT just as she and James passed the staircase in the foyer.

"Keep going." He jabbed the gun he was carrying into her back. "Giving me the necklace is the only way you're going to save the people you love. My partner will shoot someone the second I tell her to. Do you want a demonstration?"

His tone had Nell whirling to meet his eyes. There was a hardness and a steely determination that contrasted sharply with the one that her sister Adair and her aunt had described to her. Stiffening her knees to hide the shaking, she said, "The necklace isn't in the gazebo."

He grabbed her arm. "Don't toy with me. I know it's there."

Nell swallowed to ease the dryness in her throat. She was taking a huge gamble. Reid would come after her. Would he figure she was stalling and go to the gazebo? She had to bank on the fact that his instincts would guide him. "I discovered the listening device, and I said that to throw you off."

His eyes narrowed as his fingers bit into her arm. "If you're lying, all I have to do is press a button on my cell and someone inside the ballroom will die— starting with Reid Sutherland."

Nell pushed past the panic. "I'm not lying. Let me show you."

After a beat, he gestured with the gun. "Eight minutes—that's all you have left."

Past James's shoulder, she could see Eleanor's painting. She was acting on instinct and a guess, and everything depended on her being right. Taking a deep breath, she said, "Eleanor hid the necklace in her bedroom. There's a secret cupboard that Angus built for her."

"A secret cupboard."

Nell could almost see the wheels turning in his head.

"That would make sense," he said, a thread of excitement in his tone. "During those months when I was doing nightly research in your library, I looked for a second cupboard in that fireplace. Angus was the kind of man who would want the woman he loved to have one of her own. Then to make sure it remains a secret, he makes his own public knowledge and keeps all the attention on that. Distraction. Magicians use that same technique. Clever."

Nell climbed the stairs as slowly as she could. All she had was a theory. She had to keep him talking. "How do you know so much about Angus?"

"Research." He pushed her toward the stairs. "Eleanor Campbell kept diaries. I discovered them when I visited the Campbell estate in Scotland. She wrote about everything, including the story of the sapphires and how they came into the possession of Alistair MacGregor."

Nell stopped and looked over her shoulder at him. "Who is Alistair MacGregor?"

James jabbed the gun into her back. "Six minutes."

His cell phone rang.

"Have you got it?" The voice was faint but Nell could hear it.

"Not yet. She has six minutes left to give it to me. Let's give her an added incentive. Fire another bullet into the ballroom."

Nell stumbled at the sound of the shot. She had to buy more time. James Orbison wasn't a big man, but she doubted she could get the gun away from him. She'd already given him a hint of where to look for the necklace. The moment she led him into the bedroom, he might risk killing her and going after the sapphire necklace on his own.

"Five and a half minutes."

Get his mind off the clock. Keep him talking. "Who is Alistair MacGregor?"

"He was my great-great-great-great-grandfather's cousin, several times removed. I grew up hearing stories of how Mary Stuart gave her sapphires to his father in payment for saving her life, and how they mysteriously disappeared after Alistair's death. I've spent my life studying Mary Stuart and trying to find some trace of them. They belong to me."

"How did Eleanor get them?" Even as she asked the question, Nell thought of her dream and believed she already knew.

"Alistair fell so hard for Eleanor that he gave them to her as a betrothal gift. And she betrayed him." Hate and anger were clear in his voice. "Your beloved ancestor had no right to take them and run off with another man. They were never heard from again. There was no contact with the family as far as I could discover. Alistair hanged himself when he discovered what she'd done. That part wasn't in her diaries. She never knew she had caused that man's death. I found out from descendants of the servants." As they reached the door of the bedroom, he jabbed her with the gun. "I want what's mine."

Closing her hand around the doorknob, Nell swallowed hard. "You burned the library at the Campbell estate. Why?"

"To destroy any record legitimate heirs might use to claim the sapphires. They belong to me. Only me. She's appeared to me in dreams and told me that she wants me to have them."

Nell ignored the chill that flooded her. He was crazy. Obsession could do that to a person. Reminding herself to breathe, Nell opened the door to Eleanor's bedroom and crossed to the fireplace. He was right behind her, the gun in her back. *Stall.* "How in the world did you ever get mixed up with Gwendolen?"

"I came across her in my research. She's a true descendant of the Campbells. My plan was to use her and her stepdaughter and then let them take the fall when I disappeared with the sapphires. She also fancies herself in love with me, and she'll do anything I ask."

Or at least that's what she's made you believe. "Who's idea was it to run down my sister?"

"My suggestion. But Gwen was very agreeable. She blames your sister for putting her stepdaughter into a coma. I blame your sister for distracting Gwen. She's been less efficient since her stepdaughter went into the hospital. She was supposed to kill your boyfriend last night. But she intends to rectify her failure today. I wouldn't be surprised if she took him out with her first shot."

No. Nell had to exert all her self-control to prevent herself from shouting the word out loud. Not Reid.

Please not Reid. She would know if Gwen had succeeded in killing him because part of her would die, too.

"Three minutes."

15

In his mind, Reid could hear a clock ticking as seconds sped away. He'd left taking out the shooter in Daryl's and Skinner's capable hands, but it had still taken precious minutes to get out of the ballroom. No time for second-guessing now. Not that he needed to. The Nell who he was coming to know would take Orbison straight to Eleanor and Angus's bedroom. Hitting the foyer at a dead run, he took the stairs three at a time.

Stall, Nell. Stall.

The words became a chant in his head as he reached the third floor and pushed through the double doors. Then he slowed his pace. He couldn't afford to alert Orbison. At the inner door, he paused. It was open a crack, which was large enough to reveal Nell kneeling at the left side of the fireplace. Orbison stood less than an arm's length away, his gun pointed at her back. Ruthlessly, he pushed feelings aside. A cool head was what he needed now. Slowly, he drew his weapon, aimed it and weighed the risks. If he took the shot, there was a chance Orbison's gun would go off. If he walked in, Orbison could grab Nell and use her as a shield.

If she found the necklace, Orbison would be distracted. That would be his moment to act. But that was a big *if.*

A trickle of sweat ran down his back as the ticking clock in his head grew louder. Nell traced her fingers along the stones of the fireplace. Not the side that opened Eleanor's cupboard. It was the side like the one used when Angus had built his secret cupboard in the main parlor. Of course. He'd built another one in this room so that Eleanor could hide her necklace in it. And Nell was going to find the priceless sapphires. When she did, he had to be ready.

"TWO MINUTES," ORBISON SAID.

Nell felt the jab of a gun in her back and fought against panic. She'd run her fingers over the rows of stones twice now, trying to find something that would open the cupboard. Had she been wrong?

Orbison jabbed her with the gun again. "Stop stalling."

"I'm not." Pushing against panic, she summoned up the image of the sketch that she was certain held the key to finding the necklace. Eleanor had drawn the fireplace at an angle that highlighted the left side. She ran her fingers over the first row of stones again. "It has to be here."

"Has to? You haven't seen the necklace?"

His voice had risen in pitch, and Nell swallowed hard against fear. "You said yourself that it makes sense that Angus would build a secret cupboard for Eleanor, then publicize his own to protect its existence. A classic case of distraction. I just need another minute."

"Thirty seconds."

As she began to search the third row, she caught a flicker of movement out of the corner of her eye. Reid. He was outside the door.

Fear stabbed sharper than ever. She had to buy time. "You said you researched the story of the sapphires and Alistair MacGregor. What did you find?"

"I found out who has the strongest claim on the sapphires, and it isn't you and your sisters or even Gwen. Although I convinced Gwen that her claim was stronger."

"Why is that?" Saying a little prayer, Nell continued along the third row.

"She is a descendent of Eleanor's oldest sister. I found proof of that. And Eleanor ran off with the jewels. Had she stayed in Scotland after Alistair MacGregor's death, the sapphires would have belonged to the family. So in a sense she stole them. It would have made a strong legal argument, but once we found out that someone had a stronger claim, I convinced Gwen that a much better plan would be to simply take them."

Nell feathered her fingers down to the final row of stones. "Who has a stronger claim?"

"Are you just playing dumb? Or are you simply stalling because you think someone is coming to rescue you?"

"No." Her heart jumped when she felt the tiny depression in the stones. But she needed a minute. "What are you talking about? Who has a stronger legal claim than Eleanor's descendants?"

"Alistair MacGregor's true heirs. After his death, his estate went to a cousin twice removed, Ennis Sutherland. Your friends, Reid, Duncan and Cam, are the only remaining Sutherlands left in that line. But the jewels belong to me. And your thirty seconds are up."

The gun stabbed sharply into her back. Even as panic threatened, she felt the tiny gap between the stones. Easing her fingertips into it, she pulled. A foot square section of the fireplace swung silently open. When she saw the suede pouch lying inside, her heart skipped a beat. Fingers shaking, she opened the flap and slipped out the necklace. The jewels caught every bit of the light in the room, gleaming as blue as the surface of the lake at its deepest point. They grew warm in her hands, and for a second she was sure she felt the presence of the woman who'd so carefully hidden them away. And she felt the love.

"Mine."

The rasp in Orbison's voice brought reality back with a snap. Reid. He hadn't made a move yet because of her. And when he did, Nell didn't doubt that James Orbison would shoot him. She had to distract Orbison. Clasping the necklace tightly in her left hand, she held it to her side out of his sight as she rose and turned.

"Let me see it."

Slowly, she raised her hand, the jewels dripping from her fingers. Orbison's gaze dropped to the sapphires— just as she'd hoped.

"Lovely," he murmured. "They're more beautiful than I imagined. You can carry the memory of them into the next world."

Out of the corner of her eye, she saw the door swing open and a figure step into the room. But Orbison caught the movement, also. The hand that was reaching for the jewels was suddenly around her neck and the muzzle of Orbison's gun pressed hard into her temple.

"How nice of you to join us, Mr. Sutherland. It will be better for Nell if you put the gun down right now."

Don't. Nell tried to get the word out, but the arm around her neck cut off her breath.

Reid let one full beat go by before he let the gun drop. Then he raised his hands, palms outward. "Let her go."

Orbison laughed. "After all the trouble she's caused?"

"She found the necklace."

"Good point. I'll make her death as quick and painless as possible."

"You won't get away with it," Reid said, his voice calm. "You'll never make it off the castle grounds. And you haven't killed anyone yet."

"High time I did then." Orbison took the gun from her temple and swung it toward Reid.

The instant his grip on her loosened, Nell used all her weight and the adrenaline of terror to stomp hard on James Orbison's foot. Twisting, she grabbed the arm that held the weapon with both hands. The sound of the shot deafened her as she used all her weight to shove him to the floor.

She was barely aware of pain and the coppery flavor of fear in her mouth as she scrambled to straddle him, never losing her grip on the wrist that held the gun. "You are not going to shoot Reid. He's mine."

They rolled once, twice. Nell used all her strength to hold on. But her hands had become slippery, and Orbison was strong. She couldn't keep him from raising the gun again. In seconds, he would have it pointed at her.

Reid stood frozen. He'd retrieved his gun, but he couldn't get a clear shot. Then everything happened so quickly that immediately afterward he wasn't sure of the sequence. Nell still had the sapphire necklace wrapped around one of her wrists, and suddenly it caught all the light in the room and nearly blinded him.

It did blind Orbison. Fully.

"Mine." The greedy voice was almost drowned out by the clatter of his gun hitting the floor when Nell knocked it out of his hand. He reached for the necklace. As Reid moved for him, he saw Nell smash her fist into Orbison's face. Reid kicked the gun aside and pulled Nell off. He made quick work of using Orbison's belt to secure his hands.

Pushing her hair out of her face, Nell watched Reid work quickly, efficiently. She felt as if she were watching a movie. It was over. And Reid was alive. Relief. That's why she felt dizzy. And her arm was stinging. Glancing down, she saw the red stain on her shirt. "Reid…"

He turned to face her. "I had it under control. You could have been shot."

"I think I was shot." She might have laughed if it hadn't been for the second wave of dizziness. Then all she felt was Reid's arms around her as the world went black.

With fear snaking through his gut, Reid pulled Nell into his arms and cradled her on his lap. Feeling the warmth of her blood on his hands, he had to swallow hard. He should have protected her from this, and he hadn't. Not that she'd needed him. She'd fought Orbison like a demon.

Ignoring the thoughts of blame, he ripped off the sleeve of her shirt and made himself examine the wound. The bullet had gone cleanly through the flesh. Nell's flesh. His stomach rolled.

It was only slightly deeper than a scratch, he told himself as he used her shirt to bandage it tightly. By the time he finished, his throat was dry from the rawness of his breathing. He heard footsteps pounding in the corridor outside. While he waited for the cavalry, he held her close, rocking her. "You're going to be fine. You're going to be fine."

"Yes," she murmured without opening her eyes. "He wanted to kill you. I couldn't…let him do that. Because I love you, and I never kissed you beneath the stones."

Reid felt his heart take a long tumble. He opened his mouth to say something, but before he could even form a word, Daryl burst into the room.

"She took him out, but not before he shot her," Reid said. "A flesh wound. She's going to be fine." If he said it often enough, he'd start to believe it. "We need a doctor."

"Glad you left something for me to do," Daryl said as he punched a number into his cell phone. "Our Gwen is neutralized thanks to Skinner. That man has good moves. If he were twenty years younger, I'd recruit him."

REID PACED BACK and forth outside the door to Nell's bedroom. A headache pulsed at his temple as thoughts and fears danced through his mind. When he'd lain her on the bed, she'd looked so small, so pale, she might have been dead. The moment the doctor from the clinic at nearby Huntleigh College had arrived, she'd cleared the room of everyone but Vi. That had been nearly half an hour ago.

"Nell is going to be fine." Daryl pocketed his cell phone and leaned against the wall. "Our local doctor is very good. The college hired her when she retired from the E.R. at Boston General. Her record there was stellar. I checked her out."

Reid ran his hands through his hair. "We didn't check deeply enough into Orbison."

"I agree that we didn't do it quickly enough. But the reports that I've had in the past half hour from Cam and my man in D.C. substantiated everything he told you. Your maternal grandfather is a direct descendant of Ennis Sutherland, so you and your brothers have a legitimate claim on those sapphires."

Reid waved a dismissive hand as he continued to pace. "Do you think I care about that?"

Daryl chuckled. "Not yet. But it was the main motivation behind everything Orbison did. Obsessed as he was with getting his hands on the sapphires, he did everything he could to destroy any evidence of that claim."

As Daryl answered a call on his cell, Reid's mind veered once more to what Nell had told him just before she'd lost consciousness. She loved him. The emotions those words had triggered were still spinning through his system. He also recalled what she'd told Orbison in those seconds when Reid had stood helpless and watched her struggle with Orbison. "He's mine." But she'd spoken in the heat of the moment. She might not even remember.

"That was Skinner," Daryl said as he pocketed his phone. "Gwen is furious with Orbison, and she's singing like a bird. The only thing more dangerous than a woman scorned is a con woman who's been outconned."

The doctor stepped out of Nell's bedroom. When Reid made a move to go in, she placed a firm hand on his chest. "She's a lucky girl. She's going to be fine, but she needs her rest. I cleaned and bandaged the wound and left her a sedative."

"I have to see her," Reid said.

The doctor stood her ground. "She won't take that sedative if you go in there. Whatever it is, it can wait until morning."

No. It can't. Reid barely kept himself from shouting the words.

"I'll make some tea," Vi said, drawing the doctor down the hall. Reluctantly, Reid followed to the head of the stairs. Then he paused, waiting until the two women rounded the landing and began their descent to the foyer. "I have to call Cam," he said to Daryl.

"I'll tell the doc that you'll join us shortly." Smiling, he patted Reid's shoulder before Cam ambled after the two women. At the landing, he paused. "If you're smart, you'll take her out to the stone arch. That's where I would have taken Vi if she hadn't beat me to it."

The stones. Daryl was right. Whirling, he strode back to Nell's room. The only way to settle things between them was to talk beneath Angus's arch. He was reaching for the knob when the door swung open.

"We have to talk." They spoke the words together. When Nell grabbed his shirt to pull him into the room, he swept her up and into his arms.

"Where—"

"We're going to finish this once and for all under Angus and Eleanor's stones."

Finish? A band of pain tightened around Nell's heart, and it sharpened with each step Reid took. He was down the stairs in seconds. Tapping in the security code delayed him only a few more, and then he was running with her through the gardens.

He wanted to finish things between them.

Nell drew in a breath and felt the burn in her lungs. Night sounds filled the air—the hoot of an owl, the soft rush of wind through the trees, and farther away, the lapping of the water against the shore. She had to think. If he wanted to end things between them and walk away, doing it beneath the stone arch made some sense. To her knowledge, no one had ever used the stones that way before. But if kissing beneath the stones bound you to a person for life, breaking up beneath the arch might also tap into the power of the legend.

She could imagine Reid developing a strategy like that. She could even see herself writing it that way. In fact, for her book, it would make a great opening scene. Her hero and heroine who'd kissed beneath the stones would break up there, trying to undo the spell. It would definitely add a layer of conflict to the plot, and it would serve as a trigger to the romance. And Alistair MacGregor's tragic love story would serve as a background to everything. It would add a layer of tragedy to her book.

A mix of panic and fear bubbled up when he stepped into the wide arc of light that surrounded the stone arch. This was *her* story. And it was not going to end the way Alistair's had. Nor was she going to allow Reid to break up with her. She was going to use the power of the legend before he could.

The instant Reid stepped beneath the stones, she grabbed his face, drew his lips to hers and planted a kiss. She'd meant it as a statement, but the moment his mouth covered hers, her intention changed. Everything else faded but Reid, and she let herself simply sink into him—his scent, his taste, the strength of his arms wrapped so tightly around her. This was what she wanted. This was everything she wanted. She was never going to let him go.

When he finally drew back, she had to tell herself to breathe, to swallow, to think. She was stunned, when he dropped his hands to his side, to discover she remained upright.

"Nell…"

Shadows prevented her from reading his eyes. But his action had been clear. How could he have kissed her like that and still want to finish things between them?

"Nell," he repeated. "I brought you out here to talk."

A flare of anger stiffened her spine, and she jabbed a finger into his chest. "Save your breath. No amount of talking is going to change what's between us. I kissed you, and you kissed me back. It's settled."

"Nell…"

She poked him again, hard enough to send him back a step. "You're going to say you didn't want this. Too bad." Whirling, she paced to the side of the arch and then turned back, her chin lifted. "Neither did I. But a girl has a right to change her mind. And now it's too late. We're stuck with each other. End of story."

Reid walked toward her then. It wasn't what he had planned, but then nothing had been from the day he'd encountered her again. "Okay." When he took her hand and linked their fingers, the surprise in her eyes gave him some satisfaction.

"You're not going to argue?"

Raising their joined hands, he kissed her fingers. "You kissed me under the stones. I love you, Nell MacPherson. We are definitely stuck with each other."

She gripped his fingers hard as if she were determined to never let him go. "Then why did you stop kissing me?"

"Because in another moment, I was going to do more than that." He lifted her in his arms. "You've been shot. I have to get you back to the castle."

"Wait." Her grip on him tightened.

"Nell…"

Her smile had his determination wavering. "I'll go quietly on two conditions. First, I get a rain check on the kiss and 'more than that,' and second, we just sit here on the ledge for a minute."

Reid sat and settled her on his lap. When she snuggled her head into the crook of his shoulder, nothing had ever felt so right.

"I love you, too," she said.

His laugh blended with the whisper of the wind in the trees and the far-off sound of the water. "I got the message when you kissed me." He tipped her chin up. "I brought you out here to talk you into marrying me and beginning a new life together. Thank God you are a woman of action."

"That's just what Angus must have done with Eleanor."

Reid glanced out over the gardens to the castle and the lake. "I can almost feel them here."

"Can you? I thought the practical Secret Service agent didn't believe in that kind of woo-woo."

"It gets better. Remember that theory you had that Angus helped her hide the jewels so that you and your sisters would find them? I'm willing to buy into that, too. It's the only scenario I can come up with to explain how they ended up back where Eleanor would have wanted them—with Alistair MacGregor's heirs.

I don't know how he did it, but Angus found a way to help her deal with the guilt she felt."

"It makes sense. When you consider that Angus spent his entire life granting Eleanor's every wish, it's a logical conclusion. I am sure I can use it in the book I am writing. I'm going to weave in all the aspects of Angus and Eleanor's story—even the tragedy of Alistair's death." She reached up to place her palms on his cheeks and looked into his eyes. "And, of course, the hero and heroine, after fighting against it for the length of the story, will find their happy ending, as we finally have."

"No." Reid brushed his lips softly over hers. "Not an ending. This is just the beginning of our story."

Then he kissed her again beneath the stones.

* * * * *

ONE MORE KISS

BY
KATHERINE GARBERA

Katherine Garbera is a *USA TODAY* bestselling author of more than forty books who has always believed in happy endings. She lives in England with her husband, children and their pampered pet, Godiva. Visit Katherine on the web at www.katherinegarbera.com, or catch up with her on Facebook and Twitter.

I have to thank Julie Leto who was very helpful when I asked for her advice on writing for Blaze. She gave me her insights, which as always were spot-on. Also thanks to Brenda Chin and Kathryn Lye for liking my idea when I sent it to them!

This book is dedicated to my sister Linda and her family, James, Katie and Ryan, who made us so happy to call Southern California home and who shared their friends with us and they became our friends, as well. So a shout-out to Brit, Amy and Jason, who made us feel welcome.

1

"MARRY ME," Gunnery Sergeant Mac said as he took the small box filled with four of her signature chocolate "sin" cupcakes. They were her number-one seller in the bakeshop, Sweet Dreams.

"I can't, Mac, you only love me for my cupcakes," Alysse Dresden replied. The uniformed Marine came in here once a week and every time asked her the same mock question.

"We can work around that, I can come to love you for your other assets," he said as he headed toward the door.

Alysse laughed as the soldier left and she turned to her next customer. Sweet Dreams was the culmination of four years of hard work. She got at least two marriage proposals a day at her bakery and usually a few professions of undying love. Her mother hadn't been wrong when she said the way to a man's heart was through his stomach.

If only her mother had told her how to keep a man once she got his attention with food. Alas, she hadn't, and Alysse had one failed marriage behind her. But that disaster wasn't one that should be dwelt on.

"You should take him up on his offer," Staci Rowland said as she came in from the back with a tray of red velvet cupcakes.

"Mac?" Alysse asked. She wasn't about to marry a man she barely knew. She'd been there, done that and had burned the T-shirt.

"Yes, or any of the other guys who come through here," Staci said as she placed the tray in the display counter.

Staci was her business partner and the cocreator of Sweet Dreams. They'd met almost four years ago in a local baking competition. They'd competed with each other for a few years trying to outsell and out-create each other around town before they'd decided to work together and open the bakery. The rest, as they say, was history.

"They aren't serious. They just like my cakes," Alysse said, knowing what she said was true. Though she wished sometimes that some of the men were at least interested in a few casual dates, they never were.

"Of course they do, but unless you go out with one of them you're never going to find the one guy who wants more than baked goods from you," Staci said.

Staci was five foot four and had short black hair that she wore in a pixie cut. She was petite but had more curves than Alysse, who was tall with a more athletic build. Where Alysse overanalyzed every action before she took it, Staci tended to jump and then hope a net would appear. They were opposites in everything except their desire to make Sweet Dreams a success.

"That guy was pretty hot, you should have—"

"Ugh!" Alysse said to Staci. "Besides, hot doesn't mean he's the right guy for me."

She was living proof of that. Damn. Why was she dwelling on her ex today? She wanted to pretend she didn't really know, but this week…it was the four-year anniversary of her waking up alone in the honeymoon suite of the Golden Dream Hotel in Vegas.

"It doesn't mean he's the *wrong* guy for you, either," Staci chastised. "You have a thing against men in uniform. Why?"

"They're cocky and they really can't commit to a woman. And for the record, it's not like I don't go on dates," Alysse said. She'd never talked about her brief marriage.

"You've given the usual dating websites a try and I'll admit they aren't exactly gleaming with amazing guys, but I think you don't want to find a man."

"Do you?" Alysse asked. To be honest, there were times when she was lonely, but the risk of falling for the wrong guy was too high for her to take the chance. She didn't ever again want to feel the way she had when Jay had walked away. *Ever.*

"No, but I at least enjoy being single," Staci said. "Going out to clubs. And you don't."

"I'm sorry I couldn't go with you last night. I had already promised my brother that I'd hang out with him."

"Well, I'm surprised you went since it was just your brother and about fifteen hot guys."

Alysse shook her head. "Toby's friends are my friends. We grew up surfing together and playing beach volleyball. Going out with them…it's fun."

"It's safe," Staci said. "There's no risk for you. Why do you do that?"

Alysse shrugged. It was safe going out with them because Toby's friends treated her like their little sister. And when she was out on the waves, surfing with them they treated her like an anonymous person—just another surfer.

"Most people don't want to risk their hearts," Alysse answered.

Staci came over and gave her a hug. From the beginning, Staci's caring heart had surprised Alysse, because her friend looked tough. Her hair was cut in a trendy fashion but she presented herself to the world as if she were a badass.

"Honey, safe isn't doing it for you. Something is missing in your life. I just want you to be happy," Staci said.

"Me, too." Alysse really craved happiness but had no idea how to get it. She'd thought that the bakery was the solution but the longer they worked at it and the more success and accolades she achieved at Sweet Dreams, the bigger that longing inside of her grew.

The phone rang before Staci could respond and Alysse reached around her to answer it. The phone was an old-fashioned wall-mounted unit that had come with the bakery when they'd bought the property.

"Sweet Dreams Bakery, home of the incredible red velvet dream cupcakes."

"Hello," the caller said. His voice was deep and raspy, vaguely familiar, but then she talked to men on the phone all the time.

Staci just mouthed over to her that the discussion

wasn't over and went to help a customer who had entered the shop. Alysse leaned back against the wall and twirled the phone cord around her finger.

"What can I do for you today?" she asked.

"I have a dessert emergency," he said.

"An emergency? Well, we will be happy to help you out," she said. She liked creating desserts that were unique to the person who would eat them. It wasn't always easy to do, but she'd done it more than once with a lot of success. In fact, she'd been featured in a regional magazine after she'd made an anniversary cake for the deputy mayor of San Diego.

"I was hoping you'd say that," he said.

His voice was perfect, she thought. She closed her eyes and just let the sound of it wash over her. This was what was wrong with her, she thought, snapping her eyes open and staring at the photo of cupcakes mounted on the wall behind the phone. She was afraid of a man who walked into her bakery but one she could flirt with on the phone, one who was safely isolated, she could handle.

"What can I get for you?" she asked. She pulled a prestamped notepad closer and got ready to jot down the details. She and Staci had made these forms up after they'd botched an order writing it down on napkins. That had been a long time ago, but they still wrote everything down on the notepad.

"I need something…different. I made some mistakes where my lady is concerned and I want to make it up to her," he said, his voice low yet sincere.

Alysse knew she was a softy when it came to men making big romantic gestures. One time she'd stayed up all night making an anniversary cake for a man who'd forgotten to order it in advance and needed it first thing in the morning. She'd charged him double to justify staying overnight to bake it, but in her heart she liked that he'd realized he'd screwed up and tried to make up for it.

"Then this is going to have to be a really special cupcake or maybe a cookie. Tell me about her," Alysse invited.

Sweet Dreams had cultivated a reputation in San Diego of being the place for one-of-a-kind desserts, mainly because she and Staci both believed that making something special was more than worth their time. People would pay for good food and that was what they delivered.

"Hmm…that's not easy. She's kind of elusive and hard to figure out."

It was always interesting to her the way men described the women they loved. She and Staci had an annual Valentine's Day contest where couples competed to come up with the perfect treat for each other by describing what the other person was like. The winners were chosen from those who described their mate and picked the perfect dessert.

"That's probably why you like her," Alysse said. "Men like a mystery."

He sighed and she thought she heard a honking horn behind him. "That we do. But I'm used to solving them."

She jotted down *mysterious* on the order form. Every guy thought women were hard to figure out, but if they just paid attention, she thought, it would be mystery solved. She'd never known a woman yet who didn't in her own way tell a man exactly what she wanted.

"What else can you tell me about her?" Alysse asked.

"She's feisty and spicy in bed," he said. "She knows how to both satisfy a man and leave him wanting more."

She made a few more notes and then put her pen down. Well, it sounded as though he had found him a woman who met all of Alysse's own perceptions of what the male fantasy was.

"Is she sweet?" Alysse asked.

"Semisweet," he said. "She's got a kind of gentleness to her that is at odds with that fiery temper of hers."

She turned to look at the stainless-steel counters of the kitchen area of the bakery.

"Okay, I think I've got it. Do you want a small cake or a cupcake?" she asked. She already had an idea in mind for the batter—a kind of a riff on her Redemption Cake. She made it often enough out of a basic chocolate cake recipe and added special ingredients to make it personal to the couple.

"Surprise me," he said.

"I will. When do you need it?" she asked. She figured she'd work on the recipe overnight and try a couple of variations so that she got the perfect recipe for this guy. She was going to be charging him a high price for this unique cake and she wanted to ensure he got his money's worth.

"This evening."

"Uh…I'm not sure I can do that. We close at six,"

she said. She could also spend the afternoon in the kitchen working on this special order instead of helping customers and listening to Staci tell her she didn't date the right guys, which—she wasn't going to lie—sounded ideal. But this guy was asking for the moon.

"Perfect. I'll pay you to deliver it to the Hotel Del Coronado—the Beach Villas."

"Um…we don't usually do that."

"Please," he said, his sexy voice dropping a bit to become even deeper. "I won't ask again."

A shiver spread down her arms and across her chest. There was something familiar about that low tone but then she always associated sexy with Jay Michener, her ex-husband. And Jay was the last man who'd be pulling out all the stops to win back a woman. That wasn't his style. No. Walking away without looking back was his style, and she needed to remember that.

"I think you might be my only chance," he said.

Alysse shook her head at her own weakness for romance. What was her deal?

"Okay. I'll do it," she said. "Should I leave it at the desk?"

"No, I'm having a dinner catered for us on the beach. Can you bring it down there?"

She should say no, but this man who was going to such lengths to win back his lady intrigued her. "I'll do it. What's your name?"

"Just ask for the Marine," he said.

"Okay. I'll need your credit-card information," she said. She wasn't about to do all that work without being paid.

"I'll pay when you get here."

He hung up before she could get any more details. She turned around to see that the shop was empty again and Staci was watching her.

"Order?" she asked.

"A mystery order from a sexy-voiced guy," Alysse said, trying to sound light. But this Marine and his order was affecting her and making her think of things that she usually kept tucked away. She decided to trust that he could pay her; he was staying at the Coronado and it wasn't exactly cheap.

"Tell me more."

She shrugged. How could she describe what he wanted her to do without letting Staci know that her hard heart was melting? "He wants something special to try to win back his girl."

"What are you going to make?" Staci asked, focusing on the food like a good baker.

"I don't know. I was going to go and pull ingredients that fit his description of her." She liked this part of the process. Baking was as easy to her as breathing. She knew the recipes and then just changed up the ingredients until she had something unique.

"And that would be?" Staci asked. "Let me guess, sexy?"

Alysse laughed because so many guys said that when they were asked about their women. But once the probing went a little deeper the answers started to vary.

"More specifically, spicy, unpredictable and semi-sweet," she said.

"Sounds like a challenge. When do you need it?" Staci asked, wiping down the counter.

"Tonight. I told him I'd deliver it to the Hotel Del Coronado."

"Why are you delivering it?" Staci asked. "Girl, be serious here. We don't do this kind of thing."

"He had a really sexy voice and he said please," Alysse said. It sounded lame as a reason even to her.

"He's taken," Staci said, shaking her head as she walked across the room. "He wants a dessert for his lady."

"I know. I just… It's romantic, isn't it? That he'd go to that much trouble to get her back," Alysse said.

"He must have really made a mess of their relationship," Staci, ever the realist, said.

Big-time, Alysse agreed. But that didn't change the fact that he was trying to make up for it. That earned him major points in her book.

"Probably. Would you take a guy back if he planned a dinner for you at the Coronado on the beach?" Alysse asked her friend.

"Not sure. I guess it would depend on the guy," she said with a shrug. "I'm not much on forgiving."

"Me, neither," Alysse said.

Maybe that was why she had said yes to delivering the dessert. She wanted this couple to have a second chance at love. A second chance at making their relationship work—because her own lover had never even tried for a second chance.

Even if he had she would have said no, she thought. She left the store area and went back into the kitchen. It was time for her to do the one thing that she was genuinely good at—taking ingredients and mixing them into something edible, something mouthwatering and delicious. It wasn't lost on her that she used her baking to escape from the real world. In here she was in charge and if anything went wrong she could toss it out and start over.

She weighed and measured the cocoa and the flour and sifted them together, taking a kind of comfort from the mixing. She tried to keep the image of Jay from her mind but she couldn't. The memory of the tough-as-Pittsburgh-steel Marine Corps sniper was hard to ignore. She knew that was why she'd failed at blind dates and speed-dating. She measured every man she met by the yardstick that was Jay, or by what she'd thought Jay was when she'd married him, and no one, not even Jay, would ever measure up.

JAY MICHENER TOOK a swallow of his beer and leaned back against the wall behind him. The bar was more open than he felt comfortable in; since he'd gotten back from Afghanistan he couldn't relax. There were three other guys at the table with him.

Lucien he knew well as they'd been in the same unit for two tours. They'd been to the Middle East and back several times. Lucien had gotten out of the Corps two years ago and had started his own security business with the other two men at the table.

Jay didn't know either man well, but they felt like guys he'd known before. But then, Jay had spent all of his adult life in the military so there weren't many enlisted men he couldn't relate to. The two men got up to play pool and Lucien took a sip of his beer before turning to Jay.

"Why don't you come by my office tomorrow and

I'll give you the tour? Show you what life is like on the outside," Lucien said with a wry grin.

"The outside? It's not like I've been in prison," Jay said. The Corps was his life not because he had no other choices but because it was where he wanted to be.

"It sort of is. You've been in since you were eighteen and you're pushing thirty now. Isn't it time you tried something else?" Lucien asked.

"Maybe," Jay said. "I'll try to swing by tomorrow."

"Don't 'try to,' be there around ten, Lance Corporal," Lucien said.

"Okay," Jay told him, giving in. It couldn't hurt to check out Lucien's place.

"You free for dinner?" Lucien asked.

"Why?"

"I want you to meet my girlfriend," Lucien said. "She's always bugging me to bring home the guys I talk about."

"I can't tonight," Jay said. *Or ever,* he thought. He couldn't think of anything more torturous than spending the night with Lucien and his girlfriend talking about the old times.

"I've gotta go," Jay said, glancing at his watch. He wasn't a guy who normally took gambles, so this one with Alysse was odd. But she had always made him feel differently than other women did, which was probably why he'd married her four years ago. That was probably also the chief reason he'd left her after only one week.

He was dressed casually in a pair of faded jeans and a T-shirt but he felt naked without his rifle in his hand. How was a man supposed to live when he was always on edge? With Alysse, he had hoped to find something more normal, but the week they'd spent together had made him realize that he felt even more vulnerable with her.

Now he was stationed at Pendleton in Oceanside, California, about a twenty-minute drive north of San Diego. Pendleton had an idyllic setting right across the 5 from the Pacific Ocean and it was easy sometimes to forget that there was anything else but the beach and an endless horizon.

But his mind hadn't let Alysse go as easily as Jay had hoped. Every night she sneaked into his dreams—and the sexy ones weren't the problem. It was the normal-life ones that really disturbed Jay. The ones where he pictured Alysse in an apron with a few kids at her feet were the worst because he didn't believe he was ever going to be the man who gave her those things.

"You're on leave, Lance Corporal, I didn't think you had anywhere to be," Lucien said.

"I do tonight."

There was a lot of laughing at the table as the men all made some comment about women and hot dates. He smiled and let them think it was just a casual hookup. He waved goodbye and walked out of the bar in San Diego's Gaslamp district.

He got on his Ducati 1100s motorcycle and drove to the Hotel Del Coronado. He didn't make a lot of money as a sniper in the U.S. Marine Corps but Jay didn't spend a lot of money either. He didn't have an apartment or house of his own, preferring to stay in hotels when he was on leave. Since he had always planned to be a career military man, he used base housing and stored his Ducati when he was deployed.

But something had changed in him on this last deployment. He had no idea if it was the fact that he'd turned thirty or the fact that he was at a crossroads. He could get out of the Corps now, find a civilian job and maybe have a shot at normality. Though he wasn't convinced he was cut out for normal.

Tricking Alysse wasn't the answer, but the last time he'd had a shot at a real life had been with her. His commanding officer would say he was being a, well… a coward, for lack of a better word, and Jay knew the CO would be right. But he wanted Alysse back.

His plan—and he always had a plan—was to spend his leave here with Alysse Dresden and figure out if he was meant for this life or if he should stay being a warrior.

Still, he needed to make up for how he'd left her. He hoped the romantic setting and the surprise of the grand gesture would be enough of an olive branch to persuade her to give him a second chance.

He pulled his bike to a stop in front of the villa he was renting and went inside and showered and changed. He'd spent a lot of time thinking up this strategy. He knew better than just to call and ask Alysse out. He'd hurt her and he knew it. The fact that he'd thought of nothing but her for the last four years had sent a strong message to him that he needed some kind of closure with her.

He took his time setting up the area, just as he would to get ready for a target. Planning and execution were the keys to success and he never forgot that. The staff had laid out a bamboo rug and then set the table up on that. Twinkle lights hung from the ceiling of the cabana. There were curtains which had been drawn back to let the breeze flow through the structure.

Jay was a little wary of having so much open space around him, but he was on leave and he tried not to let it bother him. He hated how on edge he always was when he came in from the field. And tonight he was doubly edgy because of Alysse.

He scanned the beach and the area where he was standing looking for the best strategic advantage. He sat at the table but felt stupid just sitting there, so he got up. He checked the wine chilling in the freestanding ice bucket and then walked to the edge of the cabana to lean against a palm tree.

Just as he decided he looked like someone in an all-inclusive resort commercial, Alysse appeared. He realized all at once he wasn't as prepared as he'd hoped to be, because he'd forgotten how beautiful she was.

She arrived just as the sun was starting to set. She wore a casual skirt, and a blousy shirt. But it wasn't the clothes—more the body underneath it. She was tall—almost five-foot-seven—and had an athletic build. She moved with grace and confidence and he couldn't tear his eyes from her.

He had his sunglasses on. Her long ginger hair blew in the wind, a tendril brushing over her cheek and her lips. She moved with fluid grace and ease. She stopped on the path and glanced at the cabana. Was she wary of coming out here on her own?

"Hello? Marine?" Alysse called out.

Jay stayed where he was, watching her, feeling a little like a voyeur, but this was probably the only chance he'd have to observe her before she recognized him. He could turn around and walk away from this beach and this woman, just walk back to his Ducati and get the hell out of here.

"Hello?"

There was a catch in her voice and he knew he couldn't just leave. He didn't want to. There was a reason he was here and the reason had everything to do with this woman.

"Hello, Alysse," he said, stepping from the shadows.

She shook her head and then pushed her sunglasses up, revealing her narrowed eyes. She took two angry steps toward him.

"Jay?" she asked. "Is that really you?"

He took a step closer to her. He was so close he could smell the homey scent of vanilla and see the freckles that dotted her cheekbones.

"Yes."

She threw the cake box on the table and clenched her hands. "You ass."

"I guess I deserve that," he said.

She shook her head. "You deserve a lot more than that."

"Yes, ma'am."

"I never thought I'd see you again," she said, more to herself. She took a step back from him and then pivoted and he realized she was leaving.

"Wait."

"Why should I?" she asked.

He took two steps toward her and reached out to touch her but she flinched away.

"I...I'm sorry for the way I left," he said.

She nodded, but he couldn't tell what she was thinking. "I had to get back to base. The way we met and married I never had a chance to tell you I only had a week of leave."

"You couldn't wake me up to tell me or maybe leave me a note?" she asked.

Of course he could have, but Alysse had made him think about something other than getting laid, and no woman had done that before. "I didn't mean to marry you."

"I know that. It was Vegas that made us both act the way we did," she said. "Here's your dessert. I guess your technique with women hasn't improved if you needed something special to win her back."

"It's for you," he said.

"It's going to take a hell of a lot more than a cupcake to win me back."

"I know. Stay for dinner tonight."

She shook her head. "Give me one good reason. Why should I stay with the man who abandoned me?"

"We have unfinished business, Aly, you know it and I know it. That's why I left the way I did."

"I've moved on."

He knew she meant it to hurt him and it did. But he'd already recognized that this was going to be one of the toughest missions he'd ever been on and he didn't mind working to get Alysse back.

2

ALYSSE DIDN'T THINK as highly of Jay's idea now that she realized she was the woman in question. There wasn't any dessert in the world that would make a woman forgive being left on the last day of her honeymoon by her husband. Especially not if the woman in question was her. A cake couldn't fix the way he'd abandoned her.

Last night she'd had a good time hanging out with her brother and his friends, who were all extreme athletes. Two of them were pro surfers, another two pro skateboarders and Toby was a semi-pro beach volleyball player. She understood that men could let something other than a woman dominate their lives—for Jay it was service to his country. But all of the men she knew had learned how to balance their careers with a relationship. Something that Jay seemed not to have done.

A part of her still wanted him, though. He was dressed in a skintight black T-shirt that showed off his muscles, he was cleanly shaven and she noticed a new scar along the left side of his jaw. How had he gotten that?

He was a Marine who had been in a combat zone; she knew that from trying to track him down to get their divorce finalized. He held himself tensely. His eyes were narrowed and, though he kept his attention on her, she knew he was aware of their surroundings.

"Why are you looking at me?" he asked as he held the chair out for her to sit down. "Do you want to curse at me again?"

She felt a little embarrassed at what she'd done but mostly she felt justified. It was better than her other impulse which had been to start screaming at him. Or worse, to start crying. She doubted that he'd believe how deeply he'd hurt her. After all, as her mom had pointed out, they'd only known each other for a week. But that week had changed her life.

"Maybe," she said. But she knew she wouldn't do it. She wanted answers from him. And if she got nothing else out of this dinner, she promised herself at least she'd leave with a better understanding of why she'd been attracted to him and why even a divorce didn't seem final enough for her to forget him.

He set the bakery box on the table between them. She looked at the bottle of wine chilling in the ice bucket and realized he'd remembered what she drank— Santa Margherita pinot grigio. *Good for him,* she thought, trying not to let it matter.

"I really am sorry about the way I left," he said. "It was a cowardly thing to do."

"I'd have thought your Marine code would have a rule about that."

"Not a rule exactly," he said wryly.

She didn't want to flirt with him and talk about the

Corps. That easy charm was part of what had attracted her to him in the first place, but she knew now that there was nothing easy about Jay Michener.

"Why did you do it?" she asked. She couldn't figure out why he'd asked her to marry him. She'd accepted because it had fitted into her plans. She'd just finished cooking school and the next thing on her to-do list was to start a family. She'd always wanted one and when she'd met Jay in Vegas it had seemed as if fate had stepped in.

"I don't know," he said.

"Honestly? You must have some clue," she said. She wasn't going to let him get away with lying to her. *Not now.* He'd broken her heart. That wasn't right.

"No. That's not true. I left because you tempted me to stay," he said. "And I had a job to do. And in the end the job won."

Brutal.

But what else had she expected? That was another little nugget for her to tuck away and make sure she never let this man's charm win her over again.

"Why am I here now? Are you on leave again and thought we could hook up?" she asked.

"Yes, I'm on leave, and as you pointed out I owe you some explanations."

She leaned back in her chair and took in the scene. The table had been set up with a pretty white damask tablecloth. With the setting sun and private beach, he'd gotten the romance of this moment perfect. But she no longer believed that Jay was the right man for this kind of special moment.

"I'm not sure I'm following you—you came back to explain?"

"No. I came back to see if you would listen to me. Maybe give me a second chance."

"At what?"

He arched one eyebrow at her. "At us."

She shook her head. "You want to get married again?"

He shrugged. And her heart fell. He wasn't here for her. He was here to bring closure to his past. And if she was honest with herself, she'd already let Jay use her enough for this lifetime.

"No thanks."

She honestly believed that Jay was a warrior. A man more at home with his unit on a mission. Having been a soldier his entire adult life he had no idea how to share himself with others.

"I asked around, you're still single."

"I own my own business, which takes up a lot of my time," she said, not sure how she felt about him asking about her.

"Granted."

"What do you want me to say, Jay?"

"That you'll give us a second chance."

"But you're making no promises? I'm not an idiot," she said.

"I know that. Neither am I. And I'll tell you this, I've never been able to forget you, Aly. There's not a day that goes by that I don't think about you. I know I hurt you and don't really deserve a second chance, but I'm asking you to give me one."

He was sincere; she could read that easily enough

in his eyes. But she didn't want to trust him again. For some reason she'd fallen for him—the quiet loner with the easy charm instead of the outgoing athletic guys she usually hung out with.

"I'm sorry. But I don't think I should be here. You enjoy the dessert and have a great life, Jay."

She grabbed her purse and started to walk away and he followed her again, this time when he grabbed her arm he wouldn't let her shake him off.

"No, don't leave. I'm sorry. I'm not handling this right, but I don't know what else to do. I need to figure out things that have nothing to do with the Corps."

"I don't see how that affects me," she said. She tried not to let it bother her that he thought about her.

"I guess I want you to give me a second chance, not to leave you again but to love you."

"I don't think I can do that, Jay," she said. "You broke my heart and didn't have the guts to stay and tell me you were leaving."

"I can't tell you how sorry I am for that," he said. "But I can show you that I've changed."

"Have you?" she asked. Because so far she wasn't seeing any big differences.

He started to nod, but then stopped. "I hope so. But I really don't know. I've been on back-to-back deployments so I haven't had a chance even to breathe since the last time I saw you."

She tugged her arm from his grip and stood staring at him in the fading light. She could use some closure herself. Maybe then she'd be able to really move on from Jay.

For too long he'd been the reason she'd stayed single, afraid to risk herself again. He'd changed her from the girl who'd always said yes to life to someone who'd started living in the shadows. That was it, she thought as she stood staring at him in the fading twilight.

She'd given him her heart after a whirlwind courtship and gotten burned and now…now she wanted a chance to reclaim her heart and her faith in men. Because her short marriage was the reason why she was too afraid to let anyone in.

Maybe this would heal her.

"If I give you this chance, it might not work out for you," she said. "I'm not sure I can ever trust you again."

"I understand. It's my mission to make you trust me," he said.

She had to think this through. On the surface it seemed the perfect way for her to get on with her life. She had poured her heart and soul into Sweet Dreams and now the bakery was doing better than she or Staci had ever hoped it would. But what was next? They had been talking about opening a second location, but that was more work. She used work as the excuse to her family and friends as the reason why she didn't date. Now Jay was back and until she resolved her past with him she'd never be able to move on. He was offering her a lot more than he probably realized.

"There was something powerful between us or we wouldn't have been attracted to each other the first time."

"We can try to get to know each other again, Jay, but I'm going to use this time to get over you."

Jay crossed his big-muscled arms over his chest. It would help her to get over him if he'd let himself go physically in the four years since she'd last seen him. But no, he was still in top form. His thick brown hair was still military short and his eyes had a few more sun lines around them than he had before.

And he looked older, but not in a bad way. He had more experience and he wore it with an ease that she hoped she did, as well. She still wanted him. She had wished she wouldn't.

The thought of those big arms wrapping around her and holding her made her close her eyes. She remembered the way his legs had tangled with hers and how they'd fitted together perfectly.

"Fair enough," he said, holding up his hands. "If I can't convince myself we deserve a second chance then how the hell am I going to convince you?"

He was asking her to trust him, though he didn't recognize it. She had to believe she was strong enough to protect her heart this time. She had to believe that she was strong enough to resist the lust and emotions he drew effortlessly from her.

And yet, she wanted him. It had been four long years since she'd been in the same space as this man. She'd never admit it out loud, but she had sort of feared he'd die on deployment and she'd never know. That she'd spend the rest of her life wondering what had happened to him.

And though she still wasn't sure this was the wisest course of action, she found that that one thing hadn't changed in four years.

It was her intent that this time she'd walk away the winner. She was intrigued enough by Jay to want to stay, and having a plan made her feel that much better about it. But the truth was he was her fatal weakness and something she was determined to change.

JAY KNEW HOW FRAGILE his control over Alysse was. He had thought an apology would be enough at least to get them back to a nice place to start over. But now he was admitting that wouldn't do it. How out of touch he was struck him.

How could he convince her to trust him when he wasn't too sure that leaving the Corps and starting over was what he truly wanted? He should have dinner with her and then send her on her way. She deserved a new start without him possibly dragging her down.

And that was the rub. In the field he was confident of his abilities. All the training and missions he'd had ensured that when he took aim he hit his target. But alone on the beach with Alysse, now that was something he wasn't as confident of.

"Will you come back and have a glass of wine with me?" he asked.

"Yes," she said. "But I don't think I should stay for dinner."

He escorted Alysse back to the table and for the first time understood how hard this mission was going to be. He wanted a second chance to make things right with her. He'd never meant for her to get hurt the way she had.

He poured them each a glass of wine. Their two-day affair had led to marriage and one week of red-hot sex in the honeymoon suite. He still couldn't believe that he'd married her. When he'd been with her, he'd felt young—though he was only a year older than her.

He'd always felt older, but not during that week. He'd felt young and a little bit carefree. That had all changed on the last night.

But he didn't want to think about that now. Instead he looked at the way her pretty red hair blew around her shoulders. That attraction hadn't dulled at all. She was dressed casually and had clearly been working all day but she was still the most beautiful woman in the world to him.

"Tell me about your job. Are you a baker or what at Sweet Dreams?" he asked. He'd found her the old-fashioned way. Followed his lawyer's address that she'd used to send him the divorce papers. He'd been surprised she'd used a business address but really shouldn't have been. She'd been very clear in her letter to him that every conversation between them go through their lawyers.

"I own the bakery with a partner. We've been open almost three years," she said as she took a sip of her wine. There was a faint smile on her face and she traced the raised lettering on the dessert box she'd brought.

"From what I hear on base and around town, you're very successful."

He'd asked about the bakery and had heard tales of the sexy redhead who worked behind the counter. He'd been jealous of the admiration that the other men had for her. She was his, but he knew he'd given up any claims to her when he'd walked away. And that hadn't sat well with him.

"We are," she said. "But then we put everything we have into it. Staci and I have to be at the shop every morning by four to start baking. Usually we try to have a seasonal cupcake so we brainstorm ideas for our next one and then once a week do a sample in the store to judge its success."

"That makes for a very long day." She would have to be pretty tired come evening.

"But I love what I do," she said, then flushed.

There was passion in her voice and something that sounded like joy. She'd found her calling and clearly loved her life. But it seemed as one-sided as his was. "It really gave me something to focus on."

"I'm sorry for the way I left you. Why did you marry me?" he asked. "I've always wondered. You didn't seem like the kind of woman to fall so quickly."

She shrugged and looked away. "You know. I was excited about finishing cooking school and celebrating in Vegas."

"Vegas was a riot, wasn't it?" he asked.

"Definitely. I guess I forgot that it wasn't real, you know. The lights and the people, and you were so good with the grand gestures. I don't even remember you asking me to marry you but I do remember standing in that chapel."

"Me, too."

"Why did you marry me?"

"You made me feel like I was a part of the world and not just an observer," he said.

He'd known from a very early age that he was bound for the military. He'd always had an affinity for weapons and had gone hunting with his dad and uncles from the time he was eight. A certain sense had enabled him to sight his target and make his shot.

"I know you're in the Marines, Jay, but I know so little else about you."

She pushed a strand of hair behind her ear and tipped her head to the side to study him. He wondered what she saw when she looked at him. He knew he was in top physical form thanks to the rigorous requirements of the Corps, but beyond that what did she see?

"I'm a sniper. And have been just about my entire career."

He didn't talk about his work and wouldn't do it now except to give an overview of what he did. This was one part of his life that he never wanted Alysse to be too familiar with.

"Oh. And you like it?" she asked.

"I guess," he said. He wasn't about to reveal his near miss in Afghanistan or how it had hit him hard that he might die and no one would even care. That changed a man, but not in a way he wanted anyone else to know. Especially a woman he was hoping to woo back into his arms. It had made him return to the past and acknowledge he needed to make amends for how he'd left her.

"I don't know, Jay. If you want me to trust you, you have to open up a little more than that," she said.

"You're not going to make this easy, are you?" he asked.

She shook her head. "Nope. I know that it's not very nice but we did easy the first time and look how that turned out."

He doubted that she didn't really care. He'd hurt her and he wouldn't blame her if she wanted to wound him the same way. He deserved that for running out on his marriage to her.

He was relieved when he heard the sound of footsteps behind them and glanced over to see the waiter from the hotel delivering their salads. Food was the distraction they needed so he didn't have to continue to answer uncomfortable questions about himself.

He wasn't sure that this plan of his was being executed to its best advantage. He needed to regroup. But he didn't want just to approach Alysse as though she was a mission. He kept getting distracted by the scent of her perfume and the way her hair blew in the wind.

After the waiter left, he lifted his glass toward her. "To second chances."

"To *earned* second chances," she said, taking a sip of her wine. "I'm sorry if I sounded mean before…"

He had to laugh. It was not Alysse's nature to speak harshly to anyone. He'd learned that during their week together. "You didn't. Don't apologize for your anger at me. I feel incredibly lucky that you agreed to stay for dinner."

"I'm not sure I agreed, but I do have a lot of questions about the way our marriage ended and about you," she said.

"You deserve to have them answered and much more. But not tonight," he said.

She gave him a hard-level stare and he knew she was searching for answers in his eyes. He didn't know what the future held so he tried to convey the only thing he was certain of, which was his sincerity.

They ate dinner and talked about things that didn't really matter to him. Books and movies that he hadn't seen or read; he was behind on his popular culture. And there was a little awkwardness to the evening. But that was to be expected. What he hadn't anticipated was how much he wanted her still. And that that was the only thing he could think about.

"How long are you on leave?" Alysse asked after the waiters had left.

"Two weeks. I'm actually due to sign my reenlistment papers soon," he said.

"And what?" she asked. "You want to spend them with me?"

"I'd like to."

"I'm not changing my life for you, Jay."

"I don't expect you to," he said. "I know that I'm very lucky that you agreed to have dinner with me."

She gave him a half smile. "You *are* lucky. Are you thinking about getting out of the Corps?" she asked.

"I really don't know. When we're done eating I'll take you on a ride on my Ducati, so you can let the wind clear your mind."

"Um…a ride on a motorcycle will likely make me feel like I'm going to die," she said.

"Ah, I won't drive like a maniac, you'll be safe with me. I promise."

She didn't want to believe him, but she did. She wanted to hold on to her anger and just stew in it for as long as she could, because being angry was insulation against starting to feel again.

"I'll think about it. If you don't go back in the Corps what will you do?" she asked.

"A lot of that depends on you."

"It can't. You have to want to get out for yourself."

"I don't really know," he said, then pushed his hands

through his hair. "I hate being indecisive but my future isn't as set in stone as it once was."

"Why?" she asked. "Did something happen? Our marriage wasn't enough to change your mind?"

"Nothing happened," he said. Nothing he wanted to talk about at least, she thought. He'd been raised to be strong and he wasn't going to admit to her that he was a little scared of the future. "I'm just getting older," he told her.

She knew there was more to it than that but he was still not ready to really talk to her. She put her napkin on her plate and stood up.

"It's been nice but I think I'll be going," she said.

"Why? What did I say?"

"It's what you're not saying. You ask me to give you a second chance. Telling me nice-sounding platitudes and then when I ask you for something real, it's back to the smoke and mirrors."

She stared down at him. And then, when he kept silent, she shook her head. "Good luck, Jay."

"Wait. Let's go for a walk… I'll tell you what's going on," he said.

"Okay, but you asked me to trust you, and I'm not sure I can but I'm at least trying. I need to know that you're doing the same," she said.

"I'll try, I'm not any good at this sort of thing, which is why I probably should have just stayed out of your life."

"If you believe that, why are you back here?" she asked. "Why did you call Sweet Dreams and order dessert for a woman—me—to try to win her back?"

"I want something more," he said. "I had a close call

on my last deployment and I realized that I really don't want to live the rest of my life alone—without you."

She didn't either, which was why she'd always been…waiting for the right guy.

For honesty, that was pretty much on the mark. And his words made her admit that she didn't want him to be alone, but that didn't mean that she wanted to be the woman at his side. Jay was difficult to get to know and it was only tonight that she was coming to understand how difficult. That week together had been almost a fairy tale and she'd seen in Jay only what she'd wanted to. A man who was enamored with her and as caught up in the whirlwind romance as she had been.

"What do you want?" she asked.

"I have two weeks to figure it out," he said. "I'm having lunch with some buddies who got out last year," Jay said. "Something might come of that. If I can't find work do you think you could use another cake-froster?"

"Cake-frosting is a delicate art. It requires a skill set you might not have." He'd given her a little nugget of truth and then turned the topic to something safer and she let him do it. She wasn't sure how much "truth" she could take tonight. Seeing him was enough of a shock, learning that he'd almost died before he could come back to her… Well, that was something she didn't want to dwell on.

"What skills exactly?" he asked. "I have steady hands."

He held his big hands out to her. They were tanned and had blunt-trimmed nails. They were the hands of a man who took care of himself. No metrosexual manicure, but looked after all the same.

"That's only part of it. I'd have to see how good you are using them," she said, flirting just a little because she wanted him. And to be honest, flirting was safe. She flirted with uniformed Marines every day and nothing came of it.

"I thought that would be the one thing you'd know I could do," he said.

She shivered as she remembered his hands on her body. He was very good at using them. He was a thorough lover who had taken his time with her, every time. The attention he'd lavished on her had made her feel like the most fascinating woman in the world.

"That's a different type of hand work," she said.

"Really?" he asked in a teasing smile.

"I didn't mean it that way!"

"Of course you didn't," he said with a laugh. It sounded rusty.

"You'd be bored," she said. "It's quiet and repetitive. Most of the stuff we do for decoration is simple flowers or candies. Staci and I do all the work ourselves because it's our favorite part of the job."

"I get your passion. You both have a stake in making sure the business is successful, I'm sure it shows in your work," he said.

"Yes, it does. You'll be able to tell when we have dessert," she said.

"What did you make for my mystery woman?" he asked.

"Wait and see."

"About working at the bakery, I don't think I'd get bored. Plus, you'd be there…we'd have some frosting."

"Okay, enough with that. This is a first date not—"

"Not what? Our last first date ended pretty well."

"The date did, but what happened afterward is something I'm not looking to repeating."

"Me, neither," he said.

He took her hand, cradling it in his own. He ran his finger over her knuckles. She felt an electric charge go up her arm and then shivers across her shoulders and chest. Her nipples tightened and her breasts felt fuller.

She remembered how one simple touch could lead to much more. She pushed her fingers through his and held his hand in hers. He tightened his grasp on her fingers and lifted her hand to his mouth.

The warmth of his breath brushed over the back of her hand. He looked up at her as he kissed her hand and then her wrist.

She pulled her hand from his grasp and put it in her lap. She wasn't ready to rekindle the sexual flame that had always been between them. Not at this instant. But to reclaim herself she knew that she was going to have to. And she was afraid that when she did she'd lose a little bit more of herself.

3

JAY LEANED BACK in his chair, lacing his fingers over his chest. Granted, she couldn't see his eyes in the growing darkness, but still she felt the weight of his gaze on her. He looked aloof and dangerous and though she knew he wouldn't hurt her she felt that he wanted to keep the world at bay.

"So…how did you start a bakery?" he asked.

"With a lot of loans from the bank," she replied with a wry grin. Her parents had offered to help by cosigning but she'd refused. After the debacle of her "marriage" to Jay she'd needed to do something on her own.

"Was it hard?" he asked.

"You have no idea," she said.

"That's why I'm asking," he said. "The woman I married was looking for a family and wanted to settle down."

"Well, that didn't work out, did it?" she asked.

She was starting to feel annoyed. She had enjoyed Jay's company, but a part of her hadn't wanted to. She wanted Jay to have turned into some kind of jerk so she could stand up and walk away. Instead he'd been nice and kept the conversation going when all she wanted was…well, some awkward silences.

"No, it didn't. So tell me, what happened? I want to know what I missed," he said.

She tried studying him. The new him. But memories of the old him were bonded deep within her. She felt vulnerable and unsure. She pulled her sunglasses off the top of her head and put them on.

"I started doing bakery competitions in the area and winning some of them. Then I was invited to be a part of *Good Morning Los Angeles*'s cooking segment and gained some notoriety that way. But there was another cupcake girl, Staci, and we kept bumping into each other. And one thing led to another until one night, after a few too many margaritas, I found myself agreeing to be her partner and open a bakery with her."

He just continued watching her and she fiddled with her fork. She didn't like his attention on her because she didn't want to feel even a bit of attraction for him. But it was crazy to try to deny it. She did want him.

There was something exciting about him—there always had been. He exuded male confidence, and he had from the moment he'd walked up to her at the roulette table and teasingly asked her for a kiss. She'd given it to him and he'd placed all his money on the table and won. He'd called her his lucky charm and spent the rest of that night and the next four days wining and dining her. He'd made her feel as if she was the most beautiful and exciting woman in the world.

And she'd heard the saying "older and wiser" but somehow, where he was concerned, she wasn't any wiser. She wanted to walk over to him, turn him away from the table and straddle his lap while she kissed him long and deep.

"Margaritas, eh?" he asked.

"I've got to lay off the margaritas," she said, trying to sound wry but knowing she just sounded a little pathetic. It was after a night of drinking one too many strawberry margaritas that she'd agreed to marry Jay.

"I don't know about that. Sweet Dreams seems to have paid off," he said. "And everyone's heard of your bakery. Although it wasn't what I'd expected."

"What did you expect?" she asked.

He shrugged and looked away from her. "I don't know. I was kind of hoping you'd be waiting for me to come back."

"You left me," she said, not able to keep the incredulity out of her voice. "And I divorced you, remember?"

"I know. It was a fantasy," he admitted. "I knew you wouldn't be. You have a very strong sense of self. I think that is part of what made me leave. You had your own dreams. Your own desires."

She nodded at him. She didn't want to travel or be a military man's wife. Her life had been rooted here in Southern California long before she'd opened Sweet Dreams.

"You surprised me, Alysse. You still do. I'm very proud of your success even though I know I have no right to be."

She picked up her glass and took a dainty mouthful of wine. Trying for an attitude of sophistication she didn't really feel at this moment. "If you hadn't left me…I wouldn't have the bakery. So I guess I owe you some thanks for that."

She hadn't gone to a therapist after what had happened but she had started reading a lot of self-help books. At first she kept waiting for him to walk back into her life and then after three months of that kind of hopelessness, she'd decided she needed to move on. All her life she'd had a plan for herself and it had always involved a white knight riding in and scooping her up on his horse. It was odd, but she'd always wanted to be lifted onto a horse by a big, strong warrior man and carried out of her dull ordinary life.

After Jay…it was clear that no white knight was coming and that her warrior man was just a man with issues and flaws. She'd also come to the realization that her man hadn't had the same dream of a life together that she'd had. So she'd had to readjust. And baking, not to mention graduating from cooking school, had helped her do that.

Now, she was self-supporting and happy with her career. She could easily see herself owning Sweet Dreams and baking for the rest of her life. That thought often made her smile when she was feeling alone.

But Jay was back and he was offering her a chance to mend her broken heart and finally reclaim a little of her feminine pride. Though she'd never admit it out loud, having him leave her the way he had had made her doubt her own attractiveness to the opposite sex. Had made her wonder if she had some kind of flaw that she'd never noticed before.

"Alysse?" he asked in that deep voice, reminiscent of the way he'd sounded on the phone this afternoon when he'd pleaded with her to deliver the dessert.

"Hmm?"

"I asked if you were done with your salad. The waiter wants to clear our plates and bring out dinner," he said.

"Yes, I am. Sorry about that," she said. She really needed to stop daydreaming and pay attention. This was Jay Michener and he wouldn't hesitate to use any weakness he spotted against her. She knew him well enough to know he was back here to win. "I was lost in the past."

"I understand that," he said. "I've spent a lot of time in the past."

The waiter cleared the table and laid down the dinner plates. He removed the covers and she saw that there was a pan-seared tuna with a creamy risotto and asparagus. It smelled heavenly and she stared at her plate, trying to make the evening about food instead of about the past. But she knew that was a lie.

The waiter offered cracked black pepper and refilled their wineglasses before leaving. She stared at the empty beach. The sun still shone but it wasn't very bright.

"Alysse?"

"Yes?" she asked. It was silly to still be wearing sunglasses, she thought as she focused on Jay's face.

"Are you okay?"

"No," she said. "I'm not. This is the most surreal night of my entire life and that's counting the night I married a stranger."

His mouth tightened but then he relaxed his shoulders. "I guess I'm glad it's not boring for you."

Just that one sentence shocked her and made her smile. Then she started laughing though it wasn't that funny and she felt the sting of tears and the very real urge to start crying. Damn. She turned her head away from him, pushed her sunglasses up on top of her head and wiped her eyes.

"You do know how to show a girl an interesting time," she said. "What have you been up to?"

"Fighting," he said. "That's what I do."

She arched one eyebrow at him. That was almost too straightforward, especially for Jay.

"Sorry. It's on a T-shirt that a guy in my unit gave me last Christmas."

"Oh," she said, realizing there was a possibility of him having a life outside the Corps. "I have one that says 'I dream in dark chocolate.'"

He smiled and they started eating. She gave Jay props for keeping the conversation light and she found him charming. Too charming as he recounted some humorous pranks he'd played on his buddies. That was how he referred to them. No names or any other identifiers.

"Why don't you call them by their name?" she asked as they were finishing up dinner.

"I don't know why, I just think of them as they are, like *sniper-scout*. He's the fourth one I've been paired with since I've been in the Corps."

"What does he do exactly?" she asked.

"He's my partner in the field. He helps me sight the target by gauging wind and other factors. He's got my back, you know?"

She shook her head. "In the movies, snipers are always loners, but it doesn't seem like you are."

He shrugged again and she noticed the way his massive shoulders moved. He was still in top form, with muscles bulging under that black T-shirt of his. "Sort of. We work in pairs but because of burnout and other issues we don't always develop deep bonds. I'd work alone if I could."

"Why?" she asked, putting her silverware down to concentrate on what he was saying. To be honest, his answer didn't surprise her. There had always been something solitary about him, even in Vegas when he'd been on leave.

"That way I don't have to depend on anyone but myself."

She tipped her head to the side to consider him. "Was that why you left me?"

"I have no idea. I've never been a coward, but walking away from you was the only thing I could do."

"Why? Because you didn't want to have to depend on me?" she asked.

"No," he said, putting his sunglasses back down over his eyes. "I didn't want you to depend on me and then let you down."

JAY DIDN'T LIKE admitting his weaknesses out loud but he knew that lying to Alysse wasn't going to win him any favors. He'd planned what he'd say and how he'd say it, but he hadn't been able to plan for her reactions.

She was hard to get a bead on tonight as she was both angry and sad and at times almost relaxed. And seeing her behavior tonight made him wonder if he should have just stayed gone. Selfishly, for his own peace of mind, he'd had to see her again.

He'd had to try to make things right. He wasn't a

complex man and Lord knew he didn't have any real idea of how a relationship should work, but having seen his buddies and their wives, Jay knew that it was possible for a guy to be a soldier and have a life outside the Corps.

"So you decided just to let me down and get it over with."

In this respect she was right, although there had been so much more to the decision. Now he was paying for it. He wondered sometimes if he'd be just better off staying to himself. His dad had always said he was a lone wolf who wasn't fit for socializing and at times like this Jay believed that. "I think we've both gone around this long enough. Tell me more about the woman you are today."

She took a swallow of her wine and then gave him a half smile. He couldn't stop staring at her mouth. She'd had some kind of lipstick on earlier, but during the meal it had worn off. And left just the natural color of her lips, which brought an image to his mind of her tight nipples.

Damn. He wanted her.

"I work, I meet friends at the beach, I go to my parents' house for dinner. I have a normal life."

"Are you happy?" he asked.

"Most of the time. What are you trying to ask me?"

"Am I screwing your life up again by coming back?" he asked, being as blunt as he could. "I didn't think that you would be so—"

She laughed quietly, and this time not with the strained quality she'd had before. "So...what?"

"So real," he said at last.

"How did you expect me to be?" she asked. Then she leaned her elbows on the table and looked him straight in the eye. "Vegas wasn't real for either of us."

"I know that now, but I didn't at the time," he admitted. He'd been seduced by the lights of Vegas and that attitude the city had of everything seeming possible. He'd felt the pull of Alysse so strongly he hadn't thought beyond his time there and having her in his arms. And that had been a mistake because he'd ignored the fact that he wasn't the kind of guy that women liked having around. His own mother had proven that point a long time ago.

Alysse put both hands on the table and continued looking at him. He knew she couldn't see his eyes but he wondered what she was searching for in his face. He knew he was very good at not giving up anything, but he still wished that maybe she'd find whatever it was she needed to see.

"Why? Even I knew it was just a fantasy," she said.

"I didn't. If I don't have a weapon in my hand and a target in my sights I don't know what's real," he explained.

She sat back in her chair and he knew he hadn't given her the answer she'd been wanting. Still, he didn't have any explanation other than the truth. "Why did you take a chance on me if you knew that Vegas was all lights and make-believe?"

She tucked a strand of her long pretty hair behind her ear and nibbled on her lower lip. "I thought…I thought that after the glitter of Vegas faded away we'd still have the connection. I thought we'd formed a bond so quickly because it *was* real."

Fair enough, he thought. Both of them were living their own fantasy and their perceptions had led to…him leaving. Not her actions, she couldn't have been more perfectly suited to him during that weekend.

"Where do we go from here?" she asked.

"We're going to date. *Real* dating. To see if our bond was real," he said.

Alysse shook her head and pushed back from the table. She paced to the edge of the cabana where she looked out at the shore. Waves gently lapped on the beach.

He stood up and walked over to her, putting his hand on her shoulder. She shrugged his hand away and he realized for the hundredth time what a monumental task he'd set for himself.

"What are you thinking?" he asked.

"That I'm not sure I can do this," she said. "I know that I have said that before but the more time I spend with you, the harder it is to remember that I have moved on."

Her words cut him, but he knew that they shouldn't. He was lucky she'd stayed for dinner. He knew each date would be a test to pass, he thought. That was motivation enough. It gave him something to focus on, something concrete that didn't make him feel so unsure.

"We *are* going to figure this out. If for no other reason than that we both need to resolve what happened."

"How do you mean?"

"I don't want to be the man who hurt you and you don't want to be the woman with the broken heart."

She pursed her lips as she turned and looked at him.

"It's the truth."

"Yes, it is. I just don't want it to be. But you're right, I need something that only you can give me, and I'm going to be ruthless about taking it, Jay. I won't make this easy for you."

He smiled and felt something tight in his chest relax. "I wouldn't want you any other way."

"Do you want me?" she asked. "Or do you just want a version of me? This isn't Vegas. I'm not going to have time to just lie in bed with you and have sex all day."

He hardened at the thought of that. That was one of his fantasies, but he also wanted more from her than the physical. Their bond had started with light flirting and kisses that he still didn't quite believe were real. No one had ever tasted as good as Alysse or had fitted into his arms just the way she did.

"Who said anything about sex?" he asked.

She closed the gap between the two of them. He held himself still as she ran her finger down the center of his chest, poking him. "This entire setup is about seduction and we both know it. So give me the truth, Marine."

He took a deep breath. "I don't know how to handle you without the sex," he said. "In bed I know what I'm doing and…well, it makes our relationship a lot easier."

"That's not a relationship," she said.

"I know. Believe me, if it was we'd still be together and the last few years would have been much different."

She smiled at him. "I don't understand you, Jay."

He didn't understand himself. This crossroads had started in the desert sand but it was turning into a crisis inside him. Something that he had to resolve, or he knew he'd end up just as bitter and lonely as his old man had been. Having a chance at happiness with Alysse—he knew he couldn't, wouldn't, give that up.

"I don't either, but we can do something about it," he said.

"You are very confident about this."

"It's the only plan I've got. I'm kind of invested in making it work."

She nodded. "Things are going to be different this time."

"I get that," he said.

"Good. I'm not the passive person I used to be."

He laughed that she said that with a straight face. "You are so far from passive. From the beginning you had me wrapped around your little finger."

"Did I?" she asked. "It felt the other way around to me."

In that instant he knew that the bond they'd formed had its grounding in something beyond just sex. He had always known it deep inside because she'd never left his thoughts even when they had half the world between them. But she'd made him very aware that the feelings weren't one-sided. And that gave him more hope than he probably deserved.

THE WAITER LIT the tiki torches near them and delivered a coffee service. She glanced at her watch, knowing she should be leaving, but she didn't want to go just yet. Jay made her feel as if this was the first day of the rest of her life.

She wanted it to be worth something. She thought about how one-sided her life had been since she'd started working at the bakery. How when she went to the beach to play volleyball with her friends and family she always felt like the odd person out because everyone else had a partner and she was afraid to risk herself again.

Jay had stolen a little of that happiness from her and she wanted it back. She wanted everything life had to offer and the only way she would get that would be to take it back.

Jay had been right when he'd said she wasn't passive. She liked to pretend she was easygoing and just went with the flow, but truly, she was determined to have everything her own way.

And maybe Jay had sensed that and he'd left her because he knew she wasn't going to be content just to let him be her lover and rule her life the way he had that week in Vegas. She had changed in the last five years and she hadn't even realized how much until she'd been sitting across from him at dinner. She wanted things now that she hadn't understood were important back then.

It was humbling to discover that though she'd felt so adult and grown up in Vegas she was only now catching on to how much she still had to learn. It had been easy to fall for Jay because she'd never really lost before. Were her expectations too high? Not high enough?

"Come back and sit down," he said.

She nodded and returned to the table. No matter how much she wanted to run away and leave him she knew she wasn't going to do it until she'd gotten some more information from him.

"What are you thinking about?"

"Just wondering how difficult the last few years have been for you," she said.

"Not too bad," he answered. "A lot of routine and discipline."

"Do you like the routine?"

"Love it. In the Corps there are rules and if you follow them you get the expected results."

"Just like baking," she said.

He chuckled and she caught her breath as she recognized just how handsome he was when he smiled. She stared at him and noticed again the new cut above his lip. Just a small scar, not recent, but it hadn't been there the last time she'd seen him.

Suddenly she had a vision of a warrior, battered and bruised, but continuing to fight because he didn't know anything else. She wondered if Jay had a code of honor and then realized what a silly thing that was to consider: she knew he had a code of honor. He'd left her to keep from hurting her.

That was what he'd said. And in a way she could see the logic in it, but in another way she didn't get it. She truly didn't understand this man.

"I guess it is like baking," he said at last. "I like the order of it."

"Me, too. But I also like coming up with my own variations. I use the recipes for the basics, then I build on them."

He shook his head. "There's little room for variation when you are fighting a war."

"I wouldn't know about that. But I think I want to. Tell me about yourself, Jay."

"There's not much to tell," he said.

She frowned. "I'm not going to let you push it aside. I need to know what you're really like."

"Fine. I wake up at five-thirty even when I'm on leave and run five miles. Then I shower and eat breakfast."

"What do you have for breakfast?" she asked, suspecting he ate the same thing every day. After all, he'd admitted he liked routine. It was just the Jay in Vegas that had been spontaneous.

"Cereal. I like it and it tastes the same wherever I am in the world."

She wanted to ask him more questions, but he seemed lost in thought. She could almost see the gears in his mind turning as he mentally went through his routine.

"I report for duty when I'm not on leave and check my weapons and get my assignment. Depending on what my mission is I follow the parameters of that. Then, at the end of the day or mission, depending on how long it lasts, I return home."

"What kind of assignments do you have?"

"You don't want to know," he said.

"Yes, I do."

"Tell me about your day," he said.

She narrowed her gaze on him. "You're stubborn. More so than I am."

"Damned straight."

She just sat there knowing that she'd play this out to the end by not budging an inch. But then if she did and kept up the stone wall around her emotions, was he going to leave her exactly the same person she was when she arrived here? Alone and not trusting any man.

"Fine. I wake up at four and hit the snooze button twice before I finally have to jump out of bed and hurry through my shower. Once I get to the bakery I am almost awake. I have a cup of coffee and start making the pastries we need for the morning. Staci gets there about the same time as I do and the first fifteen minutes are eerily quiet until we both wake up and then we start talking."

"What do you talk about?"

"Anything, everything and nothing. You know? We just talk and then the day speeds by and when it's six we close up and head home."

"That's a long day," he said.

"Yes, but I like it. We're closed on Sunday and Monday and I always wake up at four and can't go back to sleep. It's so frustrating."

He chuckled, and for a moment she forgot the past and the baggage they both had. She felt as though she was on a date, and she relaxed for the first time in more than five years.

"I hate that."

"Does it happen to you?" she asked.

He shook his head and she had to laugh. It figured. He was the kind of man who was too regimented ever to have that kind of sleeping issue. He probably ordered his body to exercise and it did it.

But he wasn't a machine, no matter how much he might seem so on the surface. She knew that he was a man and he wanted—no, needed—something from her. Some sign that there was more to life than what he'd known, and she was so afraid to go down this path with him.

But she wasn't about to let herself chicken out.

4

JAY DIDN'T BELIEVE in luck. He'd seen too many guys with four-leaf-clover tattoos leaving in body bags to think that there was anything in this world that could influence his fate. He'd kind of always known he made his own luck and sitting across from Alysse on the beach with the waves crashing on the shore…well, it was about as lucky as he'd ever felt.

Tonight he'd realized how little he knew Alysse and that had maybe been why he'd left. Perhaps that panicked sweat he'd woken up in the last morning he'd been in Vegas had had nothing to do with her large family and the expectations she had for him, and everything to do with the fact that he didn't really know her outside of that king-size bed they'd shared.

He wanted to believe that. Truly, he did. But at the end of the day he'd taken one look at the sweetly sleeping woman and known deep in his soul he was going to hurt her. So he'd done it the quickest way possible. Got it over with and got out.

But then that damned IED had changed his life. And now he was back trying to carve something from the past that he should never have given up. It wasn't as simple as reliving what they'd had because they couldn't go back. He wanted to know if he could have the life he'd never experienced with her.

"So tell me about your near miss," she said in a careful tone.

Alysse was the prettiest girl he'd ever known. He'd seen beautiful women before but there was something about her that had drawn him from the moment their eyes had met. And sitting across from her now, he was still enamored with her. She had mellowed toward him during dinner, though he knew he was still on the hot seat and she'd walk away from him without looking back.

"There's not much to tell. The logistics of it won't matter to you. Just know that I was lying in the sand, sun in my eyes and for a minute I thought I was dying. In that instant it came to me that I had no one. It sharpened all of my desires and all of my ideas of what life was about."

She reached over and rubbed her hand down his arm, taking his fingers in her grasp and squeezing them gently. "I'm sorry you were alone."

He nodded and looked away. Even though the sun had started to set, he'd kept his sunglasses on so she couldn't read his emotions or see the fear he knew was in his eyes. She was too good for him, he thought, the way she was upset about him being alone even though he'd tossed her aside.

"It's my own fault."

"Yes, it is," she said. "So you almost died and thought you needed someone to mourn you?"

"Nah. I almost died and I thought, Really, man, this is all you want out of life?" Faced with his own mortality, he'd acknowledged he wanted more than what he had. Yet he wasn't too sure what he'd do with more if he got it.

The one thing he was sure of was that Alysse was the key to understanding that. She truly was the only woman he'd spent more than one night with. But he wasn't about to tell her that. She was looking skeptical enough about his entire proposition.

"What answer did you find?" she asked.

"I haven't. But the last time I was happy outside of the Corps was with you, so…"

"I can't believe you," she said, shaking her head. "You're back here hoping for something."

"That *is* what I said," he reminded her gently.

She withdrew her hand from his.

He looked away and then pushed his hands through his hair. He'd rather face an entire unit of well-trained guerillas than this woman. The fact that he was still scared of her after all this time made him realize that there was more to Alysse than sex. He wanted more from her than physical pleasure, though that was still a big part of why he was here.

"I get that you are afraid to trust me, Alysse. I know that I don't deserve the slightest kindness from you—"

"Don't. Don't say things like that because you make me want to feel sorry for you," she said. "And that's not right."

He stepped toward her. "Let's go. I need to get away from here. I feel exposed."

She nodded. He saw her long hair blowing in the

wind and he had the feeling that he'd said the wrong thing. But at this point there was nothing else he could say.

"I can't…I'm not sure I can do much more tonight. I guess you can call me tomorrow," she said backing away.

He knew he had to let her go. At least until he figured out what he wanted from her and for her, as well as how to have peace in the future.

But that wasn't about to happen tonight. He knew better than that. "Can I give you a ride home?"

"No. I have my car," she said. "Thanks for dinner."

"Hey, I'm not about to let you treat this like some casual date. I want to know what you are feeling."

"Feeling? I have no idea what I feel at this moment. I'm scared and nervous and excited. I don't have any idea what will happen next and I'm not entirely sure that I'm not making a stupid decision because…well, because I never actually got over you, Jay."

"That's good," he said, feeling more confident than he had since she'd arrived on the beach.

"I'm glad you think so. But you are here to sort out your life and I already have one. One that you didn't want to be a part of."

"We don't know that. This second chance—"

"Is for you," she said. "It's not for me and I have to remember that. I'm not going to let you hurt me again."

The very last thing he wanted was to hurt Alysse, but he wasn't about to let his chance—his chance at… what?—go. He had no idea what she going to be to him, though his gut said she was his golden ticket and a man didn't get too many of those.

"I get that," he said. "Thanks for staying for dinner."

"You're welcome," she replied, making ready to leave. Then he noticed the Sweet Dreams bakery box.

"Dessert!" he said. That was the excuse he'd used to get her down here and maybe now it would be reason enough for her to stay. He could only hope so.

"Dessert?" she asked.

"We haven't had whatever you brought for us yet," he said. "You can't leave until we have dessert."

With an almost sad look on her face, she pushed her sunglasses to the top of her head and he saw her pretty blue eyes. Saw the pain and fear she'd alluded to earlier and he knew he was a goner. He was never going to be able to make an unbiased decision where she was concerned.

He was alive but not well and he wanted to take care of himself and find out if he had any chance at life, a real life, but he wasn't going to be able to put himself before her.

"Please," he said at last, because any other words were beyond him.

She blinked and then nodded. "We have to get past this."

"I know," he said. "You're afraid I'm going to hurt you and I'd rather die than do that."

"You can't be vulnerable to me," she said slowly. "If you are…we will both lose."

"This isn't about winning," he said, closing the gap between them and pulling her into his arms. "This is about…"

She tipped her head back and put her hands on his shoulders. Going up on tiptoe she leaned up and brushed her lips over his. Then she slowly opened her mouth and her tongue sneaked out to touch his and he melted.

He forgot that he didn't want to screw this up and went with his gut. And his gut said this woman belonged in his arms. She belonged with him.

ALYSSE KNEW SHE'D MADE a huge mistake by coming here. She'd already been in a "romantic" mood, thinking that this Marine was going to make a gesture that would win back his woman. Being the woman in question…well, a cupcake wasn't enough, but sadly Jay was. He was the guy she'd been waiting for and now she found she was ready.

Her control of the kiss lasted briefly and then Jay's hands were on her hips and he pulled her off balance and into him. She wrapped her arms around his shoulders and was overcome with an emotion that was embarrassing. She felt the sting of tears so abruptly she stopped the kiss and rested her head on his shoulder.

It had been too long. She took a deep shuddering breath. She refused to cry. But she couldn't help it when he slid one hand up her back to her neck and rubbed her shoulders.

"Ah, Aly. I'm so sorry."

"Me, too," she admitted, the truth finally revealing itself. Jay wasn't someone she could be casual about, as he'd said. If she couldn't walk away now and not look back, she was never going to be able to do it.

She might want to pretend that she had some say over her emotions, but truthfully she didn't, not where he was concerned.

He tipped her chin up, looking down at her with those big dark chocolate-brown eyes of his and he kissed her. His hands framed her face as his mouth moved over hers with the confidence and surety she remembered.

But then his tongue slid against hers and she stopped thinking. She just let her feelings take over. Shivers spread down her spine. Her breasts felt full and needy. She shifted her shoulders to rub against him and he moaned deep in his throat as he widened his stance so that his hips cradled hers.

She felt the nudge of his cock as he hardened and she moaned a little as he rubbed himself against her.

She was alive and nothing else mattered to her in that moment. Jay's hands were under her shirt and sliding over her back. His big calloused hands caressed up and down her spine until she was arching against him, trying to get even closer.

He lifted her off her feet and took a few steps before sitting down on the closest chair. She straddled him and looked down at him, smiling.

"I want you," he said. He took the tip of his finger and drew it down the center of her throat and then caressed the skin where her neck and throat met. It was a particularly sensitive spot for her and she shuddered with awareness.

"I can tell," she said, rocking her hips over his erection.

"I never could hide the way you make me feel," he said.

"I'm glad," she said. She didn't want to talk. If they did, she'd start thinking and worrying and she'd have to leave. And right now she was remembering that it had been a very long time since any man had touched her this way.

She leaned down, dropped nibbling kisses against his jaw, and slowly worked her way to his lips. When she met his mouth, he tunneled his fingers through her hair and tangled his tongue with hers. She shifted on his lap and knew she was close to climaxing.

She reached between them, running her hands over his chest encased in that black T-shirt. He was a fine-looking man, she thought. She reached for the hem of the shirt and lifted it up and over his head.

She sat on his thighs and looked down at the light smattering of hair on his chest. The muscles pulsed as she moved her touch over him.

She traced the line of hair that narrowed over his hard stomach before it disappeared into the waistband of his jeans where flesh met fabric. His stomach tightened and he let out a long, low breath.

"Damn, woman…"

"Like that?" she asked, feeling a heady sense of power over him. This was what she'd wanted. She needed to be in control.

"Love it."

"Good," she said, shifting on his lap to lean forward and kiss his chest. She kissed each pec and then used her tongue on his brown nipples. Gooseflesh spread down his body wherever she touched him.

His hands tightened on her waist and then he swept his hands up her back, taking off her shirt. He tossed it to the side and brought his hands around to her breasts. He cupped them and leaned into her.

She felt the arousing warmth of his breath on her skin before the brush of his lips. He kissed the scalloped edge of her lacy bra over one breast and then the other. She shuddered on his lap, fighting to control the sensations that threatened to overtake her.

He put his hands around her midriff and then brushed his thumbs up until he found the center of her nipple under the lacy fabric of her bra. Using his thumbs, he stroked back and forth and she found his mouth.

His tongue sucked hers strongly, and again she shuddered. Frustrated by her jeans and his, she wished they were both naked. She needed more from him and she needed it now.

She reached for his zipper, but he stopped her. "Not yet."

"Why not?"

"I want this to last."

"I don't think I can wait," she confessed. She was on the edge of coming just from this little bit of temptation and she didn't want to draw it out. She wanted to take her orgasm now.

"It will be worth your while," he said.

She smiled. The sound of his words affected her as much as his touch did. He unhooked her bra with a quick flick of his wrist. The cups stayed in place on her breasts and she saw him glance down at her.

She felt his cock twitch against her, and knew the sight of her breasts had turned him on. She reached behind her to brace her hands on the table so she could lean back and give him a better view.

"Aly, you are gorgeous," he said, his words low, husky.

"Am I?"

"Hell, yeah. I'm almost afraid to touch you. Afraid to let you touch me because I'll wake up and find out this is just another fantasy."

His words were penetrating. She didn't want to find out this wasn't real either. And she needed this night. The fantasy of Jay and this moment.

She brought her hand up and covered his lips with her fingers. "Don't talk. Just make love to me, Jay. Make me forget everything but this."

He put both hands over her breasts and slowly peeled back the lacy cups. He stopped when the areole of her left breast was revealed and leaned in to tongue the fabric out of the way. He teased it with his mouth and then slowly closed his lips around her nipple.

Alysse felt her arms tremble and then a minute later, Jay's arm was around her to support her while he pleasured her. She slowly slipped a hand to touch him while he continued to caress her breasts.

She undid the button at the top of his jeans and gradually lowered the zipper, caressing him through the barrier of his boxers. He shifted his hips and she gripped his cock. It was hot and hard and she slid her hand up and down its length until his hips bucked forward and a drop of moisture was at her fingertip. She rubbed it over the head of his cock and then stroked him again.

He found the fastening of her jeans and undid them. She moved, trying to get her pants off but it wasn't going to happen while she was sitting on his lap. She pushed herself to her feet and shimmied out of her jeans and then turned back to him.

"I can't believe we're here. Like this. After everything that's happened," he said. He reached out and trailed his fingers down her stomach and around her belly button. Then his touch moved lower and he cupped her intimately.

His fingers gently stroked against her most sensitive flesh. She wanted—no needed—more and she wouldn't be denied any longer. She pushed against his shoulders, urging him back to his chair but he shook his head.

"No way. I've dreamed of this moment for too long," he said.

She was taken aback at his words. Soon she felt his mouth against her shoulder, kissing and suckling as he continued along her arm. He kept that one hand between her legs, fingers teasing her, as his other hand slipped her bra away.

His eyes narrowed intensely as his gaze fixed on her exposed torso. She splayed her hands on his chest and, in a reverent way, opened his jeans. She pushed them down his legs along with his boxers. He stepped carefully out of them while continuing to explore her body with his mouth.

She touched his cock. He stopped then, and lifted her up to carry her. She put her arm around his shoulders to steady herself as he strode to the table. He set her on her feet next to it. Then he walked around the gazebo and lowered the curtains so that no one could see in. She watched every movement, admiring his fluid grace.

"Like what you see?" he asked when they were closed off from the world.

"Very much," she admitted.

"Good," he said. He returned to her side and kissed her. His hands were on her waist and he raised her up onto the table. She felt a little uncertain, but when he stepped between her legs and she felt the hot nudge of the tip of his cock she stopped worrying. She knew this was right.

He cupped her bottom and drew her closer. She responded, wrapping her legs around his hips, but he pushed them down and away. Instead, he took her hands in his and placed them on the table on either side of her. "Lean back."

She did and her breasts jutted out, as if on display, her nipples painfully tight. He leaned down and kissed each nipple, scraping briefly, carefully with his teeth before he nibbled his way down to her stomach. His tongued dipped into her belly button, readying her instantly. Then he nibbled her hip bone before gently tonguing his way to her center.

She felt his fingers first, then the brush of his tongue against her clit. She screamed his name and immediately put her hands to his head. She needed to touch him as he found that sweet bud of passion and sucked on it. She knew she was close to climaxing as soon as the tip of his finger penetrated her and the rolling wave of her orgasm began to wash over her.

Eagerly, her body responded, desperate for more. He lifted his head.

She stared down at him. "Take me, Jay."

He nodded and reached for his jeans. She saw him draw out a condom from his pocket. He opened the package and put the protection on quickly before returning to her.

He spread her legs and then she felt him tap her clit with his cock. She shivered as he rubbed himself against her and then she caught her breath as the tip of his cock entered her. But he paused there and she shifted under him, trying to get all of him.

"Beg me," he said.

"Please...take me, Jay."

He slid another tiny inch inside of her. "That's not begging," he said, leaning forward so that his chest teased her tingling breasts.

He whispered naughty, dirty sexual ideas in her ear and her muscles clenched around him. She felt his hips jerk, and she bit the lobe of his ear.

She could sense the shiver that went through him and then a moment later he filled her completely. She tightened her legs around his waist as he took her, relentlessly moving in and out of her body.

"Come for me," he said.

She was already from the moment he'd first thrust inside her. What control she had left was quickly slipping away. Her clit was pulsing as one sensation after another claimed her. He leaned down and kissed and sucked the side of her neck as his hips pistoned forward. On a breathy cry, her name passed his lips, and she felt his hard, smooth cock spilling into her.

Alysse ran her hand up and down his strong back and buried her face against his chest. His breath sawed in and out of his body and she relished the afterglow.

He held her loosely in his arms and then brought her to the chair with him where he'd cradled her earlier. He held her to him and she let him. She rested her head against his chest and pretended she was never going to have to leave this spot.

She wanted to stay with him, like this, and remember that one perfect week they'd spent in each other's arms.

But that wasn't going to happen. She sat up and faced him.

His expression went from relaxed and sated to guarded. "I guess that was a mistake?"

She shook her head. "Not at all. But I think that's all we are ever going to have."

"Sex? It's more than sex, Aly."

She frowned and got to her feet. She felt vulnerable and raw as she moved around gathering up her clothes, dressing as quickly as she could. She heard Jay behind her, dressing as well, and by the time she turned around he was fully clothed and looking every inch the Marine that he was.

This wasn't the sexy, demanding lover of only minutes ago. This was the man who'd called her down here with a mission in mind. She had the feeling that lovemaking hadn't been his objective.

"I want more than sex. It wasn't some hot lover I

was missing when I was lying in the desert sand feeling like I was going to die."

"Who were you missing?"

"You."

"You had me," she said, trying to objectify what had just happened so it wouldn't mean as much to either of them.

"I did. I made a mistake. I'm trying to make up for that."

She laughed because he sounded so wounded and so…well, not like himself. "You said sex was the only place we communicated honestly."

"I was a guy looking to get laid when I said that."

She raised her shoulder and tipped her head to the side. "Isn't that who you were tonight?"

"No."

She arched her eyebrow at him.

"Well, yes, but I want more. Dammit, Aly, nothing is going the way I planned."

"Welcome to the real world, Marine. It's not like the Corps where there are rules and everyone follows them."

He stalked over to her and put his hands on her waist and lifted her off her feet to kiss her. She could have ignored it if it was hard and demanding, but instead it was soft, seductive. It was every tender feeling she had burning inside her, waiting to get out.

She almost put her arms around him, yet she knew she had to get away. She needed to get some distance between them or he was going to have his willing little Vegas-minded sex-crazy wife back. And she wasn't that woman.

Really, she assured herself. Tonight was her chance to have Jay one last time before she set about curing herself of caring about him. Curing herself from wanting that hot body of his pressed against her again. Curing herself of the broken heart that she'd never been able to heal.

5

"THE REAL WORLD?" he said, grasping her hand and stopping her before she got too far away. "I know more about reality than you do. You are about to go happily back to your safe, happy life never knowing what I've done to keep you secure."

"That's not what I meant. You think you can plan out every detail and I'll just fall in line like a good little girl."

"God knows that you are a good girl, aren't you?" he asked sarcastically.

She stopped abruptly. He knew he was pushing her into a corner. He didn't care. He felt so out of control right now he wanted to see her lose it a little, too.

"I always have been, but then following the rules didn't exactly help me out with my marriage," she said.

"I never intended to hurt you," he said.

"Well, you can't be blamed then for your actions, is that it?" she asked.

He pushed his hands through his short-cropped hair and realized this conversation was on a downward spiral. "No, that's not what I meant."

"What did you mean? You have no defense, you walked away and left me and now you're back… I'm entitled to be angry."

"Yes, you are," he said, letting his own anger abate. He knew Alysse hadn't meant that the way he'd taken it.

"Come on, let's go back to my room and we can talk about it. This isn't the place for us to do that and we have too much to hash out."

"No," she said as she deliberately pulled her hand free. "I don't think we have anything more to say to each other."

"Why not?" he asked, but he already suspected he knew the answer.

From the second they'd met in Vegas he'd promised her the world to get her into his room and kept her there as long as he could. Not just because of the physical pleasure but because in his room, when it was just the two of them, he could keep the real world at bay. The reality that spoke of the group of friends she had who wanted them to go clubbing or gaming with them. The reality that spoke of the community of people that she surrounded herself with. The reality that spoke the truth—that he didn't really fit in her life.

"Jay, I don't want to hurt your feelings but you have to know that I had sex with you tonight to regain my ego, the ego you bruised so badly when you left me. I needed to prove to myself that you still wanted me."

"Ah, hell…"

He could see the slight red abrasion that his beard had left on her neck. "That about sums it up."

He had wanted tonight to be the romance he needed

to get back into her life and he feared that once again he'd underestimated the parameters of this mission.

"I'd say I'm sorry but I don't think it would help," he said at last.

"You're right. I know you're searching for answers for your future and I get that, believe me, I do. But for me, right now, I need to… I just need to figure out some things about myself."

Jay looked at this woman and knew that if any other girl were standing there he'd write tonight off as a one-night stand and let her go. But this was Alysse. The one woman in the world who had haunted his dreams for the last five years, and somehow, if she needed to use him, well, then he was okay with it.

"So you want to use me for sex?" he asked, a teasing note in his voice that he hoped would mask his own desperation for her not to dismiss him. Sex was the one place in his relationship with her where he felt secure.

Finally, he understood a little of what she must be feeling and he was humbled by her courage. The fact that she must feel at least a hint of what he felt and she'd stayed and had dinner with him anyway…well, that spoke to him.

"Leave it to you to boil it down to sex," she said. "But yes, I am going to use you to figure out why I don't want another man to touch me, why I haven't been able to go on more than one date with any guy. I'm stuck and I'm ready to move on."

He nodded. It was a gamble he was taking and he knew that. What he didn't know was if Alysse would ever be able to really forgive him. And what about a future for them? Was that even possible? After everything he'd been through, could he stay here and live some kind of normal suburban life? For now though, he could help her out and maybe figure himself out at the same time.

"Okay."

"Okay?" she asked.

"I'll let you use me for sex."

"Oh, Jay. I wish it were that easy," she said. "I'm going to use you to get over you."

Jay pulled her into his arms because she looked so small, so fragile, standing there and he needed to touch her. Really touch her, not just hold her hand. He hugged her and ran his hands up and down her back and then leaned away to see her eyes.

"You are going to get over Vegas Jay who wasn't ready for you," he said. "But I am a different man today, Aly, and I'm not letting you go."

She pulled away from him and adjusted the strap of her purse on her shoulder as the cool evening breeze stirred her long ginger hair. She studied him for what felt like an eternity.

"I'm not sure that I'm going to give you the chance to keep me," she said. "You're going to have to prove you're worthy of me this time."

She walked away then and all he could do was watch her leave. He understood the path he'd started down was going to be hard and fraught with obstacles but he did know one thing with utter certainty. He wasn't about to back down from this.

For the first time since he'd lain in that hospital in Afghanistan he felt truly alive, and he had Alysse to thank for that. He knew that had to mean something important and he was determined to understand what.

She wasn't about to make it easy for him and he knew he didn't want easy. He wanted a path to lead him to answer what she meant to him.

FOR ONCE SHE HAD no problems getting out of bed at 4:00 a.m. Considering she'd tossed and turned all night it was a relief when the alarm went off and she jumped out of bed. Alysse took a quick shower and stared at herself in the mirror as she put on her makeup. She looked tired and tense. Last night had been…

Don't think about it, she ordered herself as she went out to her VW convertible and drove to work. There wasn't a lot of traffic on the road at this time of the morning, which was a good thing because her mind was definitely not on the road. Instead she thought about last night and hoped against hope that she hadn't made a huge mistake.

But she suspected she had. She'd let lust rule and now she was regretting it. She shouldn't have slept with Jay because objectivity had left him. *Ha,* she thought. Objectivity had left her a long time before they'd had sex together.

She unlocked the back door of the bakery and let herself in. She grabbed a cup of French roast from the Keurig machine and got started on the Danish dough. But that didn't distract her because she could do the morning baking on autopilot and all she could think of was last night and Jay.

It didn't matter that she thought she'd made a huge

mistake. A part of her wanted to see him again and only regretted that she hadn't stayed and slept in his arms.

She groaned out loud. What was wrong with her? Was she destined to be a fool forever where Jay was concerned?

"You okay?"

Alysse jumped and turned to face the doorway where Staci stood. The other woman looked just as sleepy as Alysse felt. But she went straight to work on her morning baking.

"Yes. Why?" Alysse asked. She was having lunch with her mom later today and if she couldn't fool Staci into thinking nothing was up, then she didn't stand a chance with her mom.

"You have been staring at the flour for about five minutes, and unless you are trying to use your mind power to make the Danishes this morning…"

Alysse dumped the flour into the mixer and then added the other dry ingredients. She cursed under her breath as she realized she hadn't sifted the dry stuff together. She had to get her head into baking and off a certain good-looking Marine.

"Sorry. I'm not myself today."

"Are you getting sick?" Staci said. "If you are, I can handle this and you can head back home."

"No, I'm fine. I'm just a little off my game."

"Good. Because I want to hear about the guy last night," Staci said. She started pulling things from the pantry area and bringing them to her own station. "Was he the big romantic you thought he'd be?"

"Ha, no," Alysse replied.

"Sorry he was a dud. Did he pay you?" Staci asked.

Given everything that had happened last night she'd forgotten about charging Jay for the cupcake. She included that on his list of offenses.

"It was a setup, Staci. I never told you but I'm divorced. And the guy was my ex-husband. I never thought I'd see him again."

Staci was staring at her as if she'd grown a second head or maybe really had created Danishes with just her mind power. She should have kept that special nugget to herself, Alysse thought. But Jay had rattled her. She had no idea if using him was going to help her out or if she was out for revenge, even though that wasn't her style.

"Sorry. Forget I said that. Let's get the baking done," she said, eyeing the butter she'd need next.

"Oh, hell, no," Staci said, coming over to Alysse's station. "You can't drop a bombshell like that and then say never mind. I want details."

Alysse paused and leaned back against the counter. Maybe talking to Staci would help. Although logically, she already knew what she should do—never see Jay again. "Like what?"

"Let's start with your marriage," Staci said. "But we have to work while we talk or we won't be able to open on time."

Her friend returned to her station and picked up where she'd left off. That she was being so matter-of-fact enabled Alysse to regain her equilibrium. She knew she had to work, the bakery's fate rested on the two of them getting their products made each morning.

"We met and married in Vegas and spent a fabulous week in the honeymoon suite of the Golden Dream

Hotel. When I woke up on the day we were supposed to go home, he was gone. No note, nothing. Just disappeared."

"Oh, my God. That's… How did you cope with it?" Staci asked. "I would have hunted his ass down and reamed him a new one."

"He's a Marine…a warrior. He'd be hard to take in a fight." To be honest, that had been part of what had drawn her to Jay. Being athletic she was hard-pressed to find a guy much better than her at most sports and one who didn't treat her like one of the guys. From the beginning Jay had treated her as though she was special—a lady.

"I don't care. What did you do?" Staci asked again. She had all of her ingredients assembled.

"I channeled that anger into baking and beating you at regional competitions," Alysse said. She flipped on her mixer to combine the wet and dry ingredients. Staci did the same, but came over to her.

"Because you are in pain I'm going to let you get away with saying you always beat me," she said, giving Alysse a quick hug before going back to her station.

Alysse realized then that she hadn't shut out everyone when Jay had hurt her. Just men. She'd formed this bond with Staci and she was close to her brother's girlfriend, too.

She and Staci removed their dough from the mixers and started rolling it out. One of the things that Alysse loved most about baking was how she could take a bunch of separate things and make them into something whole. Something good. She liked seeing the dough form.

"So what happened then?" Staci asked.

"I divorced him while he was on tour in Iraq. He signed the papers and my attorney said he reenlisted but went to Afghanistan this time. I have tried to put him out of my mind but I don't know that I was too successful."

"Given the string of lackluster dates you've been on, I'd say you haven't been. So why's he back?" Staci asked.

Alysse paid close attention to the individual Danishes she was starting to create on her baking sheets. She went to the refrigerator to get the different fruits that she had prepared last night while she'd been waiting for Jay's cake to bake.

"I don't know," she said.

She didn't want to tell Staci he wanted her back and was determined to win her over. She didn't want Staci to know how weak she was where Jay was concerned and that she was contemplating letting him into her life, considering how badly he'd hurt her.

"Yeah, right."

Staci was preparing croissants and had set the dough aside to rise, now she moved on to the doughnuts.

"Did you sleep with him?" Staci asked in a low voice.

"Staci!"

"Well?"

Alysse bit her lower lip. "I'm not going to answer that."

"That means you did. You still want him. Do you still love him?" Staci persisted.

"I don't know. I think he's the reason all my dates

have sucked so much and I want to be able to move on. I'm still not sure I can trust him or myself. He's come back to figure out if he can have a life outside the Corps and apparently he wants me to be a part of it."

Alysse wasn't too sure that was really what Jay was after, but that was what he'd said. She trusted him to a certain extent but it was hard to see him as the settled-down type. He hadn't been four years ago; had what happened in the Middle East really changed him?

"That's great for him, but what do you want?" Staci asked. "I don't know that guy, but you do. I'm not going to judge you."

"I thought I was over him," Alysse said.

It had been really disheartening last night to admit she wasn't. She'd thought she had better self-preservation skills than that. "He broke my heart and I should have moved on, but he's still there in the back of my mind and I judge every guy I meet by the man he was in Vegas."

"Not the man he is today?"

She shrugged. "I'm not really sure who he is. I don't know that he knows either. I'm telling myself that I'm going to see him and sort out how to…"

"Hurt him?" Staci supplied.

She shook her head. "I thought so, but I couldn't do it. I just want to be able to move on with my life. I want to enjoy being single and I can't until I know what it is about Jay that makes me like him."

"I hope it's that easy," Staci said.

She did, too, but if the sleepless night she'd spent was any indication, nothing was going to be easy about this thing with Jay.

JAY RAN ALONG the beach and tried to clear his mind. Frankly though, there wasn't a safe place for it to go. He'd already scanned the area in front and behind him. It didn't matter that he was in San Diego on Coronado Island, a part of him just couldn't relax. The other part of his mind kept replaying last night—every damned second of it. Physical exhaustion had seemed like the only means out of the endless cycle of images of Alysse, but it wasn't. His room felt like a prison when he got back there and he wondered what normal people did on vacations. He couldn't imagine spending too much time in this place. He felt boxed-in and edgy.

He showered and changed and got on his bike and drove without a destination in mind, but he wasn't too shocked when he found himself parked down the street from Sweet Dreams. It was the one place he wanted to be. But he knew that he couldn't just show up at her bakery. She was working and he had commitments of his own.

He was meeting Lucien at ten this morning and he decided that had to be his priority right now. But Alysse was winning the battle in his mind. He had let things go too far last night and, as hard as it was for him to admit, making love to her might have actually hurt his chances of getting back together with her.

He cast aside the disturbing thought, put his sunglasses on and roared away from the curb. He drove to the offices of Company B. The name gave Jay a chuckle since Lucien and the other men who'd formed it were all from Bravo or B Company. He parked the bike and entered the impressive office building, feeling the cool air conditioning brush over his skin. The receptionist was a pretty California blonde.

She smiled up at him and Jay wondered why everything couldn't be as uncomplicated as this girl. Why hadn't he just taken those divorce papers from Alysse and moved on?

"Can I help you, sir?"

"I'm Jay Michener, I have an appointment this morning with Lucien DuPoin."

"I'll let Lucien know. Please have a seat over there. Can I get you anything to drink?"

"I'm good," Jay said. He moved toward the guest chairs but they were lined up against the glass windows and there was no way he was sitting with his back to the street. Didn't matter where he was, he couldn't switch off his instincts.

Instead he walked to an interior wall that had the Company B logo on it and their mission statement— Securing What's Important to You.

Vague, Jay thought. No clue as to what the company actually did, which was exactly as it should be.

"Jay, buddy," Lucien DuPoin greeted him.

Lucien was six feet tall, with more muscles than seemed humanly possible. His head was shaved and he wore a mustache that Jay knew hid a scar on his upper lip.

Lucien held out his hand to Jay. Jay took the hand and leaned in to bump chests with Lucien. They'd served together on Jay's third tour. "What's up?"

"Not much. Glad to see your ugly mug," Lucien replied. "How'd your plans go last night?"

"Not as I'd expected."

"What do you think of the place?" Lucien asked.

"Cushy setup you have here. Not bad for a guy from the First," Jay said. They'd served together in the First Recon Battalion in 2006.

"You have no idea," Lucien said. "Come on back and I'll show you what we're all about."

Jay followed his friend down the corridor to a high-tech, windowless conference room. Jay heard the solid thump of a bulletproof door closing behind him. There was a video wall along the right side of the room, and on the left, a huge Company B logo was displayed.

"Have a seat," Lucien said, gesturing to the leather armchairs around the table.

Jay sat down. He took his sunglasses off and set them on the table in front of him.

"Let me tell you a little about what we do and what we can offer you," Lucien said.

"Who are 'we'?"

"Myself and four other guys—two of them were Army Rangers—you met them yesterday at the bar, one was a SEAL and the other is ex-CIA. We are a unique private security force and we operate as a team or unit the way we would in the Corps. That much would be the same. We want you to be a sniper but you won't be working with a scout—we don't have the staff for that."

"What kind of missions are you taking?"

"High-risk, high-pay missions from the private sector."

"Really?"

"Yes, usually we protect or rescue ordinary citizens when our government can't go in and do so. The families or companies have the money to afford us," Lucien said.

"Like who?"

"Usually executives kidnapped in South America or kids who go missing or land in trouble. We've had a few jobs that involved the DEA and Border Patrol, but to be honest I think we've all agreed those aren't our favorites."

Jay chuckled. "I can understand that."

"Your role, if you choose to join us, would be to use the skills you have now, mainly as a marksman," Lucien explained.

Jay was one of the top-rated marksmen in the world.

"Okay. I'd be the sniper. How often do you need one?" Jay asked. Rescue missions didn't always require a man with his skills.

"More often than you'd guess," Lucien said. "T-bone, the SEAL, is good with long-range shots, but he's not you. And we need him in other roles. You'd provide expert cover. If you decide to come on board you'd be paid a monthly salary plus a bonus based on the danger factor of the mission."

The amount that Lucien mentioned was eye-opening; Jay had had no idea his skills with a weapon were worth that much. But he was looking for a change in lifestyle, not just his income bracket. "How often would I be gone? And what would I do when we aren't on a mission?"

Lucien leaned back in his chair. "We monitor security and provide bodyguards for the affluent in Southern California. Also, when dignitaries are visiting we're usually the detail assigned to guard them. So that keeps us busy. You'd have two days off a week, unless we are on a mission, and you would work regular hours."

"Sounds tempting," Jay said. Really tempting. It would mean closing one chapter of his life and starting another. Here. This job would give him a way to romance Alysse and do it right this time. But he hadn't stayed in one place since he'd left North Texas. And he had a really hard time picturing himself in a home.

"Good, I want you on my team, Jay," Lucien said.

"When do you need to know if I'm in?" Jay asked.

"When are you due to re-up?" Lucien asked.

"Two weeks. I'm on leave until then."

"Why don't you think it over tonight and let me know tomorrow?" Lucien said. "Then you can come and work with us for a few days, see if it's really what you want. I'd hate to have you regret leaving the Corps."

"Do you regret it? I thought you were going to be a lifer," Jay said.

"At first I hated it. I just wasn't cut out for civilian life, but then, once I got involved with these guys at Company B, I found my place. It's helped me a lot to be able to still use my skills but to sleep in my own bed each night," Lucien said. "Plus I have a steady woman in my life. She's more important than the Corps. For a while I didn't think she would be. Oh, I'm making a mess of saying this."

"Nah, I get it. Women are complicated," Jay said.

"You spoke a mouthful," Lucien said with his smooth Cajun accent, and Jay smiled. They'd had a lot of fun in the old days even when they were on missions, and there was something about working with his friend again that appealed to him.

"I'll call you tomorrow and let you know what I think," Jay said.

He left the offices a few minutes later and drove toward the Hotel Del Coronado but that wasn't really where he wanted to go. He wanted to see Alysse again, and if nothing else, at least talk to her.

Lucien's offer sat squarely in the front of Jay's mind. He wasn't convinced he'd be happy on a security detail, but if he knew he'd be coming home to Alysse each night, maybe he could be.

6

THE END OF THE LUNCH HOUR signaled the end of their busy time at the bakery. During the school year they'd sometimes have a rush of after-school moms and kids, but it was summertime and the afternoons were slow-paced. Staci was in the kitchen trying to perfect a recipe she'd been juggling with for days. It was a main course, not a dessert.

Alysse was afraid sometimes that Staci was getting restless in the bakery. One of her greatest fears was that Staci would move on and leave Alysse alone with Sweet Dreams. She knew she could handle the shop, but she had come to really depend on having her friend around.

But that worry wasn't foremost today, she thought, as she cleaned the counter in the empty shop front.

Okay, so she'd gotten the usual professions of love from men who liked her baked goods. However, today it hadn't seemed as much fun as it always did. She'd had a hard time flirting, knowing that Jay was back. Since their divorce had been final he'd been in the far recesses of her mind. But last night had changed all of that.

Meanwhile, her brother had called and invited her to join him and a group of their friends for a bonfire on the beach later tonight. She'd started to make her usual excuses but then decided to go. What was she going to do? Stay home and stew over Jay?

The doorbell tinkled as someone entered the shop. "Welcome to Sweet Dreams…"

Jay.

He stood backlit by the summer sun, looking totally out of place in her shop. He had on a pair of faded skin-tight jeans, a form-fitting khaki T-shirt and, despite the heat outside, a leather jacket. His aviator sunglasses were on so she couldn't see those dark chocolate eyes of his.

Why was he here? This was her Jay-free zone. She didn't want to talk to him or see him right now and certainly not in her shop.

"Why are you here?" she asked, knowing she didn't sound hospitable but not really caring. She was tired from last night, edgy about Staci's future plans and he was the source of a lot of her unease about her own future.

"I wanted to talk to you," he said as he stepped into the shop and removed his sunglasses. He opened up the side of his jacket and put them in an inner pocket. "I don't have any other number for you."

"Oh. Right." She wasn't ready to deal with Jay. Not now. Possibly not ever.

She wished she could be cool and calm, instead she figured she was coming off as more than a little flaky.

Get it together, she admonished herself.

"So, what's up?"

"I think we still need to talk. And I didn't feel comfortable about the way you left last night," he said.

"I can't really do that here because if I have a customer they have to be my priority." Thank God. The last thing she wanted to do was rehash last night and her bold proclamation that she was using him for sex.

"Can you take a break?" he asked.

"Can't this wait until later?" She needed a good twenty-four hours of sleep and some distance between them so she could forget about how those big muscled arms of his felt around her. But right now all she could see was him last night as he'd moved between her legs and made her his once again.

"It could," he said, moving slowly closer to the counter.

"Great," she said.

"I can come back when the shop is closed and take you to dinner," he offered.

She wanted to do that. Have a private dinner with him, but she knew she'd end up making love to him again. She needed to get out and do things with him that brought other people into their company. Otherwise, she'd fall back into bed with him and in two weeks he'd be gone and she'd be wondering why the hell she'd let him dominate her life again.

"I can't tonight," she said.

"Do you have plans?" he asked.

"Yes. I have a very busy life. You got lucky last night when you asked me to bring you that cupcake, which you never paid for," she said.

"Let me rectify that now," he said, taking out his credit card and handing it to her.

She went to the cash register and rang up his order from the night before and then slid the card through the credit-card machine. She focused on every detail of the mundane task, ignoring the spicy scent of his aftershave and the fact that he was so close she could reach out and touch him.

"I'll need your signature," she said as she tore the receipt from the machine.

She pushed the paper across the counter to him and handed him the pen with the flower on top of it that they kept in a jar by the register. His fingers brushed hers and a little electric tingle went up her arm.

How could one man's touch affect her so much?

"What are you doing tonight?" he asked.

"I'm going to meet friends at the beach after work. We're going to surf and do some paddleboarding."

"Sounds interesting," he said.

He was so close she could see the scar on the left side of his face more clearly. Last night when she'd been kissing him she'd concentrated on other places, but today in the bright sunlight that scar seemed more prominent.

"How did you get this?" she asked, reaching up to touch it.

"Our convoy was attacked. I went out looking for high ground to get a good shot, ran into an enemy combatant with a knife. We fought. He cut me."

The words were sparse but the image in her head was horrifying. She reached over and touched the scar again. She didn't know what to say. He stood there and

let her touch his face. There was so much more to her
ex-husband than she'd ever guessed.

"We're planning to have a bonfire on the beach tonight. Do you want to join us?"

He shook his head. "That's not what I had in mind.
I wanted a private night with just you, me and not on
the beach this time."

As empathetic as she felt toward him right now, she
wasn't about to have another night alone with him.
They needed to be with other people or they'd spend
the entire time naked. And she'd learned more about
Jay in the last five minutes than she had all of last night.

"My offer is the only one that's on the table at this
time," she said.

"Fine, but I want to have a chance to talk to you
properly," he said, handing her back the pen. "I need
to get your opinion on a job offer I got today."

"Really? I thought you were just thinking about
leaving the Marines," she said.

"I was. But near misses like this one," he said gesturing to his scar. "Make me think I might need to
change professions."

"That's very true. But you've only been here one
day… I didn't think you'd started job-hunting."

"Well, one of my buddies owns the company so it
wasn't exactly hunting that had me find it. He knows
I'm due to re-up and wanted to see if I'd be interested
in joining him instead," Jay said.

She wasn't sure what any of this had to do with her
but she did know it would be helpful for a long-term
relationship if he got out of the Corps and took a job
here. That was an interesting tidbit.

"What is the job?"

"Can you take a break? I don't want to talk about it in the store," he asked.

"Let me check with Staci," Alysse said. She left the shop to go into the kitchens and found Staci standing right inside the doorway, clearly eavesdropping.

"What are you doing?" Alysse asked her friend.

"Listening in on your conversation, obviously. So that's the guy?"

"Yes," Alysse said. "I guess you aren't working now."

"No. I hit a snag and need to think about what I want to do. I really want this dish to be more than a main. But it just tastes so bland... Not enough wow," Staci said.

"I'll give you a hand if you want," Alysse offered. Even though she knew Staci would decline the help. Staci was always trying to prove something to herself with her cooking, and, Alysse suspected, to the world.

"Nah, I'll figure it out. So are you going to do it, go talk to him?" Staci encouraged, peeking around the corner at him.

Alysse wanted to, but a part of her thought getting to know him better was stupid. He was the one man who'd hurt her worse than any other. Was she really going to open herself up to that kind of pain again?

"He is one hot-looking guy," Staci said.

"Yes, he is."

"I can see why you fell for him, but you aren't the same person you used to be. I think you are in the right place to deal with him," Staci said.

"Me, too," Alysse said with a confidence she was far from feeling. "I'll be back in twenty minutes or so."

"Take your time," Staci said. "It's not like we're busy right now."

Alysse took off her apron and went out front where Jay was still waiting. He was studying the glass cases but she sensed his attention was really on her.

"I'm ready to go," she told him.

"Good. Do you want to go someplace on my bike? Or we can walk," he suggested.

"Let's go to Old Town. It will be busy but there are a couple of quiet streets where we can walk and talk," Alysse said. Her plan to use Jay made sense when she was in the throes of wanting him sexually and trying to justify that to herself. Now, in the bright light of day, she wanted more. She wanted to find out what kind of man Jay was.

Finding out more about Jay would be hard and she'd have to stay focused because Jay didn't give up much information about himself and she didn't blame him because she also played her cards close to her chest.

She'd learned the hard way that being as open as she used to be didn't pay off. And she hated that she'd become so guarded and afraid to risk herself. Jay had stolen that confidence from her. She wanted it back, but she also wanted to fix him.

Oh, my God, she thought. That was what this was about. Jay was her latest project. Someone who needed her help. But she wouldn't fix Jay for herself. She'd help him so he could move on and so she could finally be over him.

JAY WATCHED ALYSSE out of the corner of his eye as they strolled down the hilly street. The weather was a temperate eighty degrees today and as he watched other people nearby he felt almost normal. For the first time in a long time he was exactly where he belonged, but he knew that was false. He didn't really belong with Alysse and even though to the world they probably looked like every other couple walking through town on this nice afternoon, he knew they were different.

She led him to a quiet park where an empty bench stood under the shade of a tall tree that he didn't know the name of. She sat down and stretched her legs out in front of her, then tipped her head slightly toward him.

"So, talk," she said.

She seemed relaxed, but in spite of her posture he could sense the tension in her. She wasn't sure of him and didn't trust him, and he knew that he would have to earn back her trust. He just wasn't sure he deserved it. Didn't even know how he'd go about winning her over because for years he'd been alone. And though he wasn't happy about it, there was a part of him that could get along just fine with Fantasy Alysse running through his mind.

It was safer that way. For him, certainly, and also for her. He didn't want to disappoint her again or hurt her anymore than he already had.

"Are you going to say anything?" she asked. "Or just keep staring at me?"

"I don't know how to begin. I've been thinking of the way you left last night. How you said you were going to use me."

"Maybe that wasn't the nicest thing to say," she admitted. She tucked a strand of her hair back toward the high ponytail it had escaped from and then rubbed her hands along her thighs.

"But that is who you are now. I made you into a woman who wants to use someone else. I did that," he said. He hadn't thought of anyone but himself when he'd left her in Vegas and he regretted that now.

He'd told himself he was doing it for her. That he wasn't the right guy to make her dreams come true. But he knew he'd left because he'd been unsure of what to do next.

She straightened up, twisting to face him. "I did that. Not you. I'm the one who put myself in a place where I can't find my way back to who I used to be. I'm not ever going to be that girl again."

She carefully put her hand on his wrist. "I need to do this and you're looking for answers, too. Don't worry too much. We'll do this together."

"I do worry. And I'm not someone who's ever anxious, but with you—I am. I am afraid I'm too hard for you. I already hurt the woman you used to be."

She bit her lower lip and he saw her hesitate and then she smiled over at him. "I've never complained about your hardness."

He chuckled. "I guess not. In fact, it probably works for your plan to use me for my body."

"It does," she said. "It definitely does."

"So where does that leave us?" he asked. Because, as he'd discovered last night, sex wasn't necessarily the answer to what he was searching for from her.

"It leaves us where we are. Two people who are

both trying to get who we are and where we're going, who enjoy sex."

"I need more than sex from you," Jay said. "You're different for me."

"You were for me, too, but then you became someone I didn't know. Let's try to start over."

"I don't know if we can," he said.

"We can. It won't be easy, but it will work. You told me you have a job offer…."

He pushed his sunglasses up on top of his head and turned to face her full-on. "I do. I'm not sure if it's the right thing for me or not."

"What is it exactly? I know we talked about you being a cake froster but I don't imagine you went out and found that kind of job opening."

He gave her a wry smile. "Your cookies are the only ones I'm interested in frosting."

She just shook her head and waited.

"It's a private security firm. They take on missions, some similar to what I've done in the Corps. They want me to be a sniper, which is what I've trained for and what I know."

"Sounds like what you're doing now, just that you'd be based here."

"Sort of. They aren't always deployed, so when they are here they do security for celebs… That sounds lame. Could you imagine me guarding some pretty face on the red carpet?" he asked.

She shook her head. "Definitely not. I'm sure they have stuff that's not that high-profile. Doesn't seem like sending you to a red-carpet event would suit your personality."

"Yeah, I'd have to ask about that. Lucien offered to let me try it out for the next few days until I have to re-up. That way I can see what they do."

She crossed those long legs of hers and swung her foot as she listened to him. Distracted, all he could think about was pulling her onto his lap, putting his hands around her waist and holding her close to him.

"I think you should give it a try. You said you were back here to see if there was something else for you— that you were at a crossroads. I can't imagine a job that would make your transition easier. I mean, you could try a government job, but I don't see you as a desk man."

"I'm definitely not a desk man."

"So, I guess that's settled," she said.

"Is it?" he asked.

"Isn't it?"

"Yes, it is. I want to give it a chance. But the crazy part is I don't even have a house. I always live in hotels when I'm on leave. If I do this it will mean a complete lifestyle change."

"You don't own a house?"

"I've never needed one," he said.

"What about an apartment?" she asked.

"No. I'm seldom in the States and when I am I use temporary quarters on base."

"Jay—no wonder the idea of being married to me sent you running. You've never had anything in your adult life like it," she said.

"I take it you own a home?"

"Yes. And a rental property with my brother," she

said. "Do you still want to come to the beach with me tonight?"

Hell, no. He had just established that he liked being apart from others and keeping himself removed, but he did want to spend more time with Alysse. So, he'd go to the beach tonight. Five years ago, it had been the thought of her big network of friends and family that had partially driven him to leave and this time…well, he guessed it was time to face them.

"Yes, I guess I do. But I don't have a surfboard or a wet suit. And I haven't surfed in over a year."

"No problem. I'll take care of that for you."

He walked her back to the bakery and then rode away on his motorcycle, pondering the fact that in the course of a few hours he had a job offer and a date with Alysse and her friends. He certainly wasn't in the Corps anymore.

ALYSSE HAD GIVEN Jay directions to the beach. It wasn't the one that the Marines stationed at Pendleton used. This one was farther up the coast near San Clemente, which was where she'd grown up. They were meeting Toby, her older brother, his girlfriend, Molly, Tommy and Jean, who'd gone to college with Toby, and Paulo and Frida, who they'd met at the beach about eight years ago and had started playing volleyball with.

Toby was a marine biologist as were Molly, Tommy and Jean. His true passion was the ocean and he spent as many hours on the water as he could. Tonight he'd spotted a new grouping of sea lions and they were all going to paddleboard out to look at them.

Paddleboarding consisted of standing on a board—

similar to a surfboard, and using a long pole to steer and move the board along. Alysse usually avoided going to these events even though Toby, who was two years older than she was, called her at least twice a week and invited her to do something with him and Molly.

And she usually went but lately she'd been busy at Sweet Dreams. Though it pained her to admit it, she was also a little jealous at Toby and Molly.

"'Bout time you showed up," Toby said, giving her a hug as she unloaded cookies from the back of her car.

"I'm early," she pointed out.

"I meant after putting me off for days. What made you change your mind tonight?" he asked as he grabbed her board from the roof of her car. She slung her beach bag over her shoulder and locked the car.

"I invited a guy to come along and join us," she said carefully. She hadn't realized that she was sort of setting Jay up by bringing him to meet her brother until she'd arrived here.

"Great. It's about time. So who is he?"

Toby knew about her marriage so she had a feeling that he'd be less than welcoming, which was why she'd come early.

"It's Jay."

"Your ex?"

"Yes. He's back in town."

"I don't like the sound of that," Toby said as they reached the beach area where he already had a small bonfire burning. He put her board down and turned to her with his hands on his hips. "Are you sure about this?"

"No, I'm not. But the bakery is a success now and I really don't know what to do next. I want to date, have a relationship, I thought, now I just don't know. I'm going to spend some time with Jay and see what happens."

Toby grimaced and stared out at the ocean. "God knows I don't have any advice for you on marriage, but I don't want to see you get hurt again."

"Me, neither," Jay said, joining them on the beach. "Sorry to interrupt."

She glanced past her brother at her lover. He wore a pair of khaki shorts and a Marine Corps T-shirt. He had those aviator sunglasses of his on and he looked every inch the tough badass that he could be. Toby glanced over at him.

"I've got my eye on you, Michener, and if you hurt Alysse again I promise you there is nowhere you will be able to hide from me."

"Good. That's how it should be," Jay said.

"Well, then…are you much of a surfer? I've brought a spare board you can use," Toby said.

"I've surfed a time or two." Jay stood taller than her brother and he had a more muscular build. For the first time in a long time she was seeing a man next to Toby who could hold his own. The few guys she'd brought surfing didn't really have what it took to cut it on the waves or with her brother. But Jay looked like he could.

"Great. You want to hit the waves with Alysse and I until everyone else gets here?"

Jay glanced over at her and she nodded. She and Toby had spent a lot of time surfing in their youth, waiting for waves and just talking quietly about whatever was happening with them. Their parents had divorced when they were four and two years old respectively, and their teenaged years had been interesting, to say the least.

"Love to. But I'm not really prepared, I don't have a wet suit," Jay said.

"I'll hook you up. Come with me," Toby offered.

Jay looked at her, and she said, "Go ahead. I'll change in my car and be right back."

"Sounds good," Toby said and led the way.

She admired Jay's backside and his muscled body as he followed Toby. She was definitely going to enjoy every moment she had with him because the last four years of her dating life had left her parched. And Jay was exactly the man to quench her thirst.

She grabbed her wet suit and then decided she'd just get changed right there on the beach. She should have put her bikini on before she drove up to meet Toby but she had wanted to get here before anyone else.

She donned her bikini under her sundress and then pulled on the bottom part of her wet suit. Most of the other people on the beach were doing the same thing. The families with young children had left for the day and the older crowd was coming out...well, young adults anyway.

"You ready?" Toby asked when he came back.

Jay was wearing the wet suit her dad used when he came to visit, and he had Toby's spare board tucked under his arm. He tossed his sunglasses in her bag and gave her a rakish smile.

"I like the way you look in that wet suit," Jay said, giving her a hot once-over with his dark chocolate gaze.

She blew him a kiss. "You look good, too, hot stuff."

Toby made a gagging sound, which was typical of her brother. Alysse laughed, thinking how perfect this moment was with her brother and Jay and the waves at their toes. She was so afraid to believe that things were good. And that worried her because with Jay she was always going to be waiting for him to leave.

7

JAY HAD SURFED off and on since he'd been stationed at Pendleton. Growing up on a ranch in North Texas he hadn't ever thought of surfing or the ocean much at all. Put him on a horse and point him toward some cattle and he felt at home.

But as he watched Alysse on her board catching the waves he was in awe. He caught a glimpse of how natural she was in this setting. This was a side to her he'd never seen before and he just sat back and lapped it up.

Toby had put on a friendly face in front of Alysse but in private had told Jay he was watching him. And Jay had to respect that.

He didn't have any friends or close confidantes that he'd mentioned his brief marriage to, but she had family—close family and friends. People she socialized with today who knew he'd married and left her.

Thinking on that made him wonder if he should just leave now. Alysse was way too good for the likes of him and the burden of being accepted by her friends was a high one. But then she paddled her board over toward him and sat up and smiled. Really smiled all the way to her soul, he imagined.

"Are you having fun?" she asked. The sun was behind her, casting her face in shadow, but he knew that she was enjoying herself. Her body language and easy laughter were all indications.

No, he wasn't having fun. But he did enjoy watching her enjoy herself and that made it worth it. He'd wiped out twice and even though it was just water swirling around him he felt as if he'd gone ten rounds with Lucien in a mixed-martial-arts match and gotten his ass handed to him.

"I'm a bit rusty," he said at last.

"Ah, that's not a big deal. Last summer we were slammed at the bakery, lots of weddings and special events, and I didn't get to surf once all summer. Come September Toby 'kidnapped' me from work and made me come out. I wiped out three times before I got out of my head. Maybe that's your problem...you seem to be weighing something very heavy."

He shrugged. There were a lot of positives about the Corps to him and one of them was that he didn't have to think about what to do next. If he reenlisted he'd have everything just the way it had always been.

If he didn't...he might have Alysse, a new job, a house... "There's a lot to think about."

"Of course there is. But this is a moment when you can let go and just for these few hours forget everything else and have fun with these people."

"There is only one person on this beach I'm interested in having fun with," he said.

"Me?" she asked, giving him a sultry look.

"Hell, yes," he admitted. "But you know that already, don't you?"

"I do," she said. "I am very interested in you, too, Jay but I don't want to make the same mistake I did before."

"It did sort of work for a while," he said.

"It didn't work at all. It was nice until reality started closing in. This time I want to know the real Jay. Who is the man with his clothes on?"

"And here I'd rather let you see me with my clothes off," he said.

"I like that, too, but today I learned that you don't own a home… That's huge."

"Is it?"

"Yes," she said, riding the swell of a wave that bobbed their boards. "It tells me you don't like roots."

He couldn't believe she was talking about this now. He wasn't prepared for it, but as natural as Alysse was on the water it probably felt like sitting around a kitchen table to her.

"That's true."

"What else don't I know about you?" she asked.

"You two going to take any waves or just keep talking like old women?" Toby called as he paddled over toward them.

Alysse called back, "We'll take a wave when we see one we like."

"Whatever," Toby said, paddling to catch the first in the next set that rolled under them.

"You should try to get to know some of the people in the group tonight. It's hard, believe me I know, but you'll enjoy it."

"Will I? Is that a guarantee?" he asked.

She leaned over and kissed him quickly on the lips. "Nope, but if you try it and it works, that's way better than the alternative. You taking this wave?"

He glanced back, thinking of what she'd said. He didn't have any answers and only knew what he wanted to happen but Alysse was right; he couldn't control any of that tonight. "I am."

He paddled toward the wave and his instincts and athletic ability kicked in.

The wave swelled behind him and he felt the board moving the way it was supposed to; he stood up and rode it. The sun was setting behind him and the beach seemed far away and there was no real noise around him except the sound of the water. This all felt so unreal. Not even a week ago he'd been up to his ass in desert sand without a drop of water in sight and now he was immersed in it. Alysse had been a memory; now he was with her, next to her, and who knows…

He tumbled off his board and was pulled into the water. The wave crashed over him and dragged his board; he felt the tug on his ankle strap. He held his breath and then swam to the surface watching out for his board so he didn't get conked on the head with it. He made his way to the beach and took off his ankle strap before picking up the board.

"You okay?" Toby asked from a distance.

Jay nodded and put the loaned board off to the side. There were other people there at the bonfire and they looked up at him with tentative smiles, but the conversation had ground to an abrupt halt as he'd approached.

Immediately, he turned away from the group and

began walking down the beach. He didn't belong in Alysse's life, did he need more evidence than what he'd just seen? This was a big part of her world and he was never going to fit in here.

He didn't understand its currents and patterns the way he did the corps. It didn't matter that he'd spent all his adult life in the Corps, he should be able to adapt to almost anything. What was the matter with him? Did he really not want to be with Alysse?

That was the answer he'd been searching for, and it'd been right here in front of him the entire time. He didn't fit in Alysse's life because he couldn't adapt the way she did. He'd seen her go from the bakery, where she was very at home, to the beach, and she probably had a dozen other roles she filled with ease.

He only had one. Marine. Did he want to leave the Corps behind and take a chance with Lucien and Company B? Or was he simply going to continue his same path? Honestly, he just wanted to stay where he was, but he knew that wasn't the way to a successful life, not anymore. Not for him, anyway.

"Jay?"

He turned and saw Alysse jogging toward him. She still wore her wet suit, which lovingly hugged every inch of her body. Her ginger hair appeared darker, almost brown, as it hung in long, wet tendrils around her face and his heart soared. He didn't want to leave her and yet he had no idea if he could stay.

There was no way he could ask her to be a part of his life while it was a mess. And tonight had proven beyond a shadow of a doubt that his life was really still FUBAR.

ALYSSE HAD THOUGHT TWICE about catching Jay, but in the end he'd looked so forlorn that she had no choice. He carried himself with pride. The man was an island and she felt acutely that he didn't want or need her or anyone else. But she couldn't just leave him to it.

Admittedly, she hated that she cared about Jay, because she shouldn't. He'd hurt her and she knew better than to trust him. But there was a part of her that understood the struggle he was going through.

"You okay?"

He clenched his jaw and she saw a glimpse of a man she'd never seen before in his eyes. He was a hard man and she had no doubt that he could survive in any dangerous situation he was dropped in, but seeing him now, like this, made her pause. He didn't know how to get along here.

She reached for his arm. He flinched away. She pulled her hand back and wrapped her arms around her waist, comforting herself. No matter what she projected on Jay, he was still a man whom she barely knew outside the bedroom. And though he'd never hurt her physically, he seemed to have an uncanny ability to find the right gesture to cut right through her.

"Of course I'm okay," he said, his tone terse.

"Whatever. So you're fine. If you don't want to talk to me I'm happy enough to just walk back. Is that what you want?" she asked. She was setting herself up here. It was a big gamble, giving him an ultimatum. But she had to try something. She hadn't even had a chance to introduce him to the others.

He didn't react and she started to return to her friends.

"No, wait. I don't want that."

She stopped and faced him. "What *do* you want?"

She wasn't sure what she'd expected tonight. Only knew that she needed to keep from being alone with Jay. But seeing him like this—uncomfortable and not himself—wasn't what she'd had in mind.

Even suggesting that he let himself forget about his troubles and just enjoy the waves hadn't helped for long. He wasn't like everyone else and she suspected that was part of the reason why she was so attracted to him. Yet that difference was something she didn't know how to bridge.

"I don't know," he admitted at long last.

"You're the only one who can actually fix that," she said. "Listen, I've got a short fuse where you're concerned so maybe I'm not the best one to be here with you right now."

He turned his head to the sea and she stepped closer to him, putting her arm around his waist because he seemed so alone. She wanted to comfort him. To take care of him, and she had a revelation that that was one of the very things that she'd always wanted to do for him.

"What do you want from me?" she asked.

"I don't know that either," he said. "Hell, I've gone from a man who had a career path he was sure of and a life that worked for him to this. I have no idea."

"That's okay," she said. "You're figuring it out. One thing I do know is that you can't keep hiding all the time. You need friends and you need to meet people who aren't in your line of work. Come back and eat with my friends. You *will* like them."

She tried to lead him back but he refused to budge. She sensed there was more to it than just being around strangers.

"What were you thinking on the waves?" she asked. "You were doing really well and then all of a sudden…"

"I wasn't thinking, like you said, and then I realized how ironic it was that I had been surrounded by sand not even a week ago and here I was on the water. It was just a surreal moment and I couldn't shake it. It got me thinking about going back and then I fell and you saw the rest."

"Wipeout," she said. "The water is a good place to think."

"Unless thinking makes you drown," he said.

She laughed because she thought that was what he intended her to do. But it was forced and she had some doubts that she was the right woman for Jay. For the first time she understood why he'd left her; her life was so different from his.

"I guess so. You're used to always being on edge. Maybe one of the other guys has a better surfing tip for you."

"I don't give a crap about surfing, Alysse. I'm not going to be out here all the time. I came here for you. I want—no, need—to be with you. That's all that really matters to me."

She wasn't sure how to respond to that. His words touched a place deep inside her that she was afraid to admit she still had. And she wanted him to really be here for her but she wasn't too sure he could be.

"I can't promise you anything. I'm seeing now how different we really both are," she said. She understood that her dreams of the future were bound to be very un-like his because he had never even had a home of his own. How could he possibly look at her and see plans for a distant future together?

"Why just now? What did you see that you didn't before?" he asked her.

"I thought we had some kind of common back-ground, but I'm beginning to suspect we don't. I never asked you about your past. We never did the fifty-questions thing that most couples do when they first meet."

"Well, we sort of did, but the questions were more, do you like the way my mouth feels on your neck?" he said.

She shivered as a pulse of desire went through her. It would be easy to let this be about sex, but she refused to let it go that way right now.

"We both know I like it," she said.

"No, we never did the getting-to-know-you part, did we?"

"So…" she said, not about to let him divert her again. There was so much more happening with Jay right now than a bonfire on the beach. This was her chance to really get to know him and she wasn't about to pass it up.

"My family's from Texas, the northern part near the Oklahoma border. My dad had a ranch," he said, his voice taking on a reminiscent quality. "Our family had been ranching there for over a hundred and fifty years."

"Why aren't you a rancher?" she asked.

"We lost the ranch in my senior year of high school.

Had to move into town and live over the diner where I worked as a dishwasher."

"What kind of work was there for your dad?" she asked, trying to imagine how horrible it must have been to move during your senior year of high school.

"He took to the rodeo circuit taking care of the livestock on the road," Jay said.

"At least you had your mom with you," she said. "That kind of change must have been hard."

"It was."

Silence grew between them and she realized that Jay wasn't going to offer anything else. Good thing she had a million questions.

"What did your mom do for a career?" she asked.

"She was a bank manager," Jay said.

"They make pretty good money, why did you have to live over the diner?" Alysse asked.

"Because she left us when I was eight. Had enough of the dusty, isolated ranch," Jay said. "Dad had to mortgage the ranch when she left and by the time I was in high school he'd fallen behind on the payments."

"That's horrible. Why didn't your mom take you with her?" Alysse asked. Jay's childhood had been so different from hers. Her dad had owned a car dealership and made good money. He and her mom had doted on both her and Toby and they'd had a fairly good life.

"Who knows? She always said I was a handful and more like my dad than like her," Jay responded.

"In what way?" she asked, trying to understand how a mom could leave behind her eight-year-old son. She tried to see the boy Jay must have been, but he was too much a man for that to happen. Any softness in him had been burned out long ago. He was a tough Marine through and through, and she saw the evidence with her own two eyes.

"Just rough, I guess. We hunted and took care of the ranch together. I was his little shadow. Everyone said so. I guess she thought I needed to be with him."

Alysse hugged Jay close to her, trying to comfort the little boy who had been abandoned. But she knew that she couldn't. That event had changed Jay. Could he ever trust, be with anyone?

She was beginning to wonder if she was fighting a losing battle where he was concerned. She knew she'd wanted to mend her broken heart but a part of her had hoped to find the keys to real happiness with Jay and she was beginning to believe that would never happen.

JAY LIKED THE FEEL of Alysse in his arms and knew that he was winning her over not by doing anything but simply by showing her parts of himself that he usually kept closed off. He hadn't wanted her to see the lost little boy he'd been, but he knew that this time he had to do things differently.

It occurred to him that they were finally alone. Exactly what he'd wanted all day. He pulled her closer, skimming his hands down her back until he could cup her buttocks. He wanted her.

He felt his cock stir and wished they were really alone. He scanned the area, hoping for an isolated place that would allow them to be all but invisible. He wanted to carry her away from here and make love to her and reinforce the bonds that were already there between them. His caring was the first step to winning her back.

"You okay?" she asked. "I didn't think I'd ever feel… sympathetic toward you, but all of that has changed. I want to know more about your past and more about the person you really are. Want to walk for a while and talk?"

No, he wanted to slowly strip the wet suit from her body and kiss her until they both forgot their names and where they were.

"I don't see why the past should have anything to do with you and me," he said.

"Well, maybe you left me before I left you…maybe the little boy you—"

"Stop. I don't think that has anything to do with it. I don't want to talk. I want to take you away from here and go someplace where we can make love and leave all the obvious differences behind us."

"You're running away again, Jay."

He knew he was. He'd probably always run away from her. She made him uncomfortable in his own skin, but at the same time he couldn't imagine not having her in his arms.

"I need more," she stated.

"I know that," he said. "Tell me about your upbringing. Where did you grow up?"

"Right here. Well, Oceanside, not San Clemente. My dad owned the local Chevy dealership and my mom did the books for him, even after they'd divorced. My brother and I got into the usual mischief but nothing too crazy. He went to UC Santa Barbara. I did one year at Berkeley before I flaked out and came home."

"Berkeley? You must be pretty smart," he said.

"Sort of. But I hated it. I came home and my dad

said I'm not supporting you if you aren't going to school and so I enrolled in cooking school. Found I really loved it."

"Looks like you ended up where you needed to be," he said. "What does your dad think of you now?"

"I imagine he'd be pretty proud of me," she said. "He died of a heart attack before I graduated cooking school. It was a huge shock for us. He went out jogging one morning and that was it."

"I'm sorry," Jay said. "My dad died on the road."

"How?"

"Drunk driver." He didn't like to think about that too much. It had happened during his first six months in the Corps and after that, Jay had nothing to come back home to.

"I'm sorry," she said.

For the first time ever, Jay didn't mind talking to someone about the past. There was something about Alysse that made some of the rougher parts of his life seem okay.

"Let's go back and join your friends," he said, taking her hand and leading her down the beach.

"Do they all know that we were married?" he asked, stopping before they got to the group. "I don't want to have to do the whole thing I did with your brother with each of them."

"Only Toby and his girlfriend, Molly, know," she said. "Don't worry, if this doesn't work out, we can go back to my using you for sex—but not tonight." She laughed.

"Why not tonight?"

"Because you'll leave and I'll stay here and paddle-board and pretend that I'm happy."

His gaze narrowed on her. "Why pretend?"

"Because I think you need something from me that has absolutely nothing to do with making up for the past. And no matter how hard I try to be objective, I just can't and that makes me just a little sad."

He swallowed hard, listening to the honesty that came so easily to Alysse and that made him feel small and ashamed. He wanted her, and he wanted his life to be so much easier than it could be right now. He was at a crossroads, she wasn't. So he could either be the man she needed him to be or he could move on.

"Fine, let's go back to your friends."

"Not like that," she said. "I didn't say that to force you."

"But you did. You're taking control of this relationship and I don't blame you. Just give me some time to adjust as we go along, okay?"

He saw her weighing it over and thought she might say no, and tonight, as aggravated as he felt at the world in general, he almost thought that it was okay if she said no. Major decisions could be influenced by things smaller than this moment. And if she said no now he would have no reason to stay.

"Sure, it's okay. This isn't easy for me either. I am still trying to find my way forward," she said.

He knew that and he understood that his coming back into her life had seemed to spur her on some sort of quest.

"Did you invite me tonight to see how much I didn't fit in or to get back at me?"

"No. I invited you because I thought it'd be nice for you to see what my life is like. To get a chance to know the people in my life and, as much as I want just to get over you, I also have a hard time not liking you."

"You are a paradox," he said.

"I'm not. I'm simple and straightforward. You just have to look beneath the surface," she said, leading him over to her friends—and he let her.

He wanted to go wherever she led him. Which was a sobering discovery because he'd thought he was back in San Diego to make a tough decision but more and more he was coming to realize he was back here because this was where Alysse was.

8

JAY HADN'T EXPECTED to be able to relax with the group at the bonfire, but one man stood up as soon as they arrived and greeted Alysse with a warm hug.

"How are you, *amiga?*"

"I'm good, Paulo," she replied. "I want you to meet Jay. Jay, this Paulo Ramones. Paulo, this is Jay Michener."

Jay shook the other man's hand. "It's good to meet you."

"You, as well," Paulo said. "This is my wife, Frida."

A lovely woman with dark hair and olive-colored skin walked over to them and shook his hand. "So nice to meet you."

Both Paulo and Frida had heavy Spanish accents and were fit and lean.

"The pleasure is mine," Jay said.

"This is Tommy and Jean. They both work with Toby. And this is Toby's girlfriend, Molly. She works with them, as well," Alysse said.

He waved at the group. "What do y'all do?"

"Marine biology. Currently, we're studying changes in migration habits of whales."

"Interesting," Jay said. "You, too, Paulo?"

"Nah. I play volleyball with Toby. We're on a competitive team in the Cal King tournament."

"Everyone ready for a veggie burger?" Toby asked.

The food was served and Jay found himself sitting on a large blanket with Alysse on one side and Paulo on the other. The group was all sitting fairly close together around the fire.

"Are you a baker like Alysse?" Paulo asked, after taking a huge bite out of his veggie burger.

Jay shook his head. "No, sir. I'm a Marine."

"Really?"

"Yes. Does that seem hard to believe?" Jay asked.

"No, it's just that I never thought a military man would be Alysse's type," he said.

"I guess I am," Jay said. Focusing on his plate.

"I meant nothing by that comment. I was in the special forces before we moved here. Have you been to Iraq?" Paulo asked.

"Yes," Jay answered, and saw the other man in a different light. They started talking about their respective deployments and places they'd been to. Paulo had gotten out and no longer did anything vaguely resembling what he had in the past.

"How do you like being out of the military?" Jay asked. He wanted to know how other people made the adjustment. It would give him some ideas on how he'd be able to do it if he decided to leave the Corps.

"I love it. But I went in because I'm the second son in my family and I was expected to have some military training. Though I play volleyball with Toby on the weekends, my real career is in wine. My family owns vineyards in Spain and here in California," Paulo said. "Is it like that for you?"

"I am just a military man," Jay answered. "Don't have anything waiting for me outside the Corps."

"I don't know about that," Paulo said, glancing around him toward Alysse who was having an animated conversation with Molly.

"It's complicated," Jay said. He didn't want to discuss his brief marriage to Alysse with a man he'd only just met. In fact, Jay knew he never wanted to discuss that one week in Vegas with anyone, ever. But he did like the thought that other people looked at him and Alysse and saw a couple.

The thought pleased him more than he'd expected it to. This night, while wildly different than any other he'd spent with her, was turning out to be really enjoyable.

"I'm not surprised. I liked the order of military life," Paulo said. "The discipline I learned there has helped me in my business. And I found that I liked stepping out of the traditional role my family had planned for me."

"Where is your vineyard?" Jay asked.

"Temecula. Have you been down there?"

"No. I pretty much stay near the base or go into San Diego," Jay said.

"You should take Alysse to Temecula and go up in a hot air balloon. You will get a nice view of the entire valley. If you do this, you call me and we will treat you to lunch at the vineyard."

"I will do that," Jay said, wondering if he could convince Alysse to take a balloon ride with him. He wasn't good at making romantic gestures and he wasn't even sure that she'd welcome them.

"Do what?" Alysse said.

"Bring you to my vineyard for lunch," Paulo said.

"That's a wonderful idea," Frida agreed, joining in the conversation.

"I guess that's decided then," Alysse said. "When?"

"We'll have to discuss the details later," Jay said feeling a wave of panic washing over him. He was still struggling to figure out him and Alysse. Adding more people to the mix right now might be too soon.

"Alysse has my number. You will call me, yes?" Paulo said.

"I will," Jay agreed.

Toby stood up and everyone finished up the last of the dinner and joined him. "Jay hasn't been paddleboarding before so I'm going to give him a quick lesson. Anyone else need one?"

Frida raised her hand. "I'm afraid I've never done it before either."

"Follow me," Toby said.

Jay glanced back at Alysse and she just smiled at him. He knew he was making her happy by doing this and even though it was outside his own comfort zone, he followed her brother down to the water. He wasn't sure when it had happened but he'd come to realize that he'd do anything to see Alysse smile.

That was a dangerous thought.

She'd been important enough for him to come back

here and try again, but he hadn't understood how important until this very moment.

ALYSSE WASN'T SURPRISED when Jay followed her home from the beach. The evening had turned out differently than she'd anticipated. She'd thought that Jay wouldn't be so comfortable so quickly even once she'd introduced him. But after the initial hesitancy on his part, Jay had really made an effort. It hadn't been easy and luckily Paulo's military experience had made Jay feel right at home. But that had only underscored to Alysse the difference in the two men. Despite his time in the military Paulo was open and gregarious. He was affectionate and doted on Frida and seeing them together made Alysse long for something that she suspected she'd never have with Jay.

She was honest enough to admit that she knew that inviting him into her house and her bed tonight would be a mistake. But it had been a long day, full of ups and downs, and she wasn't ready to deny herself Jay. She had the feeling that he'd be gone soon enough. She wished she could be more like a movie heroine and just not worry about tomorrow, but she'd never been that way.

"You're taking a really long time to get out of your car," Jay said, walking over to her.

"I'm trying to decide if I should invite you in," she said, speaking honestly. Tonight had made her realize that she still wanted all of those dreams that she'd shoved aside when Jay had left her.

The only problem now was she wasn't sure if Jay was the man she wanted to have them with.

"I'd love that but I followed you because it's late and I couldn't live with myself if I didn't make sure you got in okay. Also, I wanted to know where you live," he said.

"Is it what you thought?" she asked.

"No. I expected you to live closer to Sweet Dreams," he said.

He seemed subdued and maybe a bit tired himself. He ran his hand through his hair, which had been flattened by his motorcycle helmet.

"It's late," he said.

"Yes, it is. I didn't sleep at all last night and I had to get up early. You'd think I'd be tired, but I'm not."

He opened the door of her car. "Come on, let's go inside."

"I haven't decided if you're coming in yet," she said.

"What can I do to make you invite me?" he asked.

"I'm not sure," she admitted.

"What if I said I'll hold you until you go to sleep?"

"I'm not sleepy," she said. "And you holding me will only make me long for things that I can't have. We both know that."

She exited her car and Jay closed the door behind her and stepped in front of her, so that she was trapped between his body and the vehicle.

"I don't know that holding you is a bad thing, Aly. I think you aren't sure either, otherwise you would have been out of your car and in the house like lightning. You want me."

"I do. Too much, but tonight just proved that a real relationship—"

He kissed her, stopping the words that were on the

tip of her tongue and she shivered as the one embrace she'd been longing for all day was finally here. She'd missed this—intimacy, but to be honest they'd never had it before. Though she didn't want to admit it, she'd missed Jay. In Vegas, life had been a pretty dream.

Noticing his hand in hers, she laced their fingers together and for a moment simply enjoyed the fact that she was coming home with her man. Something shifted inside her and she knew that nothing would ever be the same again if she brought him into her bed.

He slid his hands up and down her arms before they settled on her waist. She tipped her head back and let the magic wash over her. She forgot about all that her mind knew about Jay and let her heart lead the way, for tonight at least. She tunneled her fingers through his silky close-cropped hair and held him to her as her tongue moved against his. He lightly sucked on her tongue and she felt an answering response in her breasts as her nipples tightened. And lower in her most feminine area.

She wanted him—there was no denying it. Or herself, she thought. She was single and she wanted this man. She could have him.

He shifted his hips against her and she felt the tip of his erection nudging at her as the heat and passion swelled inside her. This was Jay—wounded warrior, sexy lover and the only man she'd never been able to forget. She wrapped her arms around him to hold him close. She had tried to pretend the emotions she felt for him were only lust, but she knew better. She couldn't lie to herself anymore. Jay's hand on her made her feel cherished and special to him. He tore his mouth from hers.

"Alysse…" He said her name on a long sigh and her heart skipped a beat.

"Do you want me?" he asked, whispering the question close to her ear.

"Yes," she said, surprised at the breathless quality of her own voice. She also wanted something that she was afraid to believe he could give her. She wanted his heart. "I've thought of nothing else since I saw you shirtless on the beach. You have a very tempting body, Jay."

"Then take me," he said.

She did want to take him, and yet at the same time learning about his past had made her afraid to really use him. Jay was more vulnerable than she'd realized. It was silly, because he seemed so strong and indestructible that it had never occurred to her he could be hurt.

"I will," she said. But she promised herself she would do her best to protect his heart, too. Because hurting Jay would only result in wounding herself.

She took his hand and led him up the lighted path of her small bungalow to the front door. She fumbled for her key and almost dropped it.

"Nervous?"

"Silly, huh?"

"Not so silly. We aren't strangers anymore."

That struck her. They'd married and divorced but hadn't really known each other. The impact of what she was doing held her still.

"I'll go," he offered.

If he left she'd never see him again—she knew it.

And she had to ask herself if she was going to hide away from life on the off chance that she might get hurt or if she was going to live it.

"No. Stay."

Jay smiled then, a real smile, and she felt that flood of emotion rushing through her again. He stooped, picked up her keys and handed them to her. She turned to put the key in the door lock and he came up behind her.

His hands were on her waist, his mouth on her neck dropping gentle kisses that stoked the flames of desire burning through her and convinced her she'd made the right decision in inviting him in.

She finally got the door open and they stepped into her foyer. Jay closed the door and leaned back against it. He stood there for a moment surveying her and her lovely house. He crossed his arms over his chest, his expression unreadable, and she wondered what he was thinking.

"Nice place," he said at last.

"Thanks."

There was awkwardness between them that hadn't been there before and she wondered if it was because in her mind this had all changed. She had admitted to herself how much she cared for him. There was no going back.

"Come here, Aly. Make me believe I fit in your world."

She took a step toward him and he pulled her into his arms. She held him closely, burying her head in his shoulder and inhaling his unique scent—the saltiness of the sea that clung to his clothes and hair, the earthiness that she always associated with Jay. He kissed her passionately and slowly, as if they had all the time in the world.

Then she felt him caressing her back, his hands roaming up and down her body, loosening buttons and zippers until they could slip underneath and touch her naked skin.

She shuddered. Oh, she'd missed his touch. She gasped as he spanned her waist with his hands and lifted her off the ground so that she was more fully pressed against him.

She pushed her hands under his shirt, rubbing his chest to tease him. Then he drew her closer still.

"Oh, Jay," she said, knowing her heart was in her voice.

He swallowed hard and she saw a brief hint of emotion flash in his eyes before he kissed her.

In an instant, their tender moment became one of white-hot lust. His mouth was on her neck, one hand on her breast and the other between her legs. She was shaking and on the edge of her climax in seconds.

His hand left her breast and she heard the sound of his zipper being lowered and then felt his hot cock between her legs. He turned her around, though she wanted to see his eyes, hold his face.

Behind her, he guided her hands to the door and then touched her intimately to test her readiness. She felt the tip of his cock and shifted backward to urge him inside. He'd aroused her; she wanted him, there was no doubt. And he didn't waste another second before he thrust inside her.

He tweaked her nipples and then reached lower to fondle her clit as his hips pumped faster and harder.

Blind desire consumed her.

But still the questions sped through her brain, still she wanted to see him.

Suddenly, she felt the intense contractions of her body as her orgasm began and his hands quickly went to her hips and to pull her into each of his thrusts. He sent her over the edge into a climax that made stars dance in front of her eyes.

He thrust once more, then twice again before his hot release came. Falling forward, he rested his head between her shoulder blades. She stood there until her breathing slowed and he slipped his arms around her waist and held her.

Eventually, he pulled away from her, but took her in his arms. "Bedroom?"

She put her hand on his jaw as she saw the haunted look in his eyes. For the first time she understood that he had no idea how to deal with the emotions she'd elicited in him.

She pointed down the hallway. She wanted to pretend she was just using him for sex, but when he came into her bedroom and lay down beside her, she knew it wasn't just sex. He might have been unable to face her when they'd made love earlier, but now he cradled her in his arms, cuddled her close and made her feel as if he wasn't ever going to let her go. She focused on his lightly hairy chest rising and falling until exhaustion claimed her and she fell asleep. It felt like a fantasy. She knew that this time with him wasn't real. She had to remember that, she thought, as she drifted off.

JAY DIDN'T SLEEP as he held Alysse in his arms, but he
did enjoy having her naked body pressed to his side.
She snored softly in her sleep and he couldn't for the
life of him remember holding her this way in Vegas.
If he had it hadn't been as important as it was now.

He knew he'd played into her thought tonight that
she was using him for sex. She wasn't. No matter what
Alysse told herself she didn't have it in her to use anyone, least of all someone she cared for.

He knew that if he were a better man he'd walk
away. He wasn't exactly sure why he didn't, except that
when he was with her, despite his indecision about the
future, he felt okay.

He stroked her hair and glanced at his watch, knowing he should go. She had to get up early and she might
not want him to spend the night.

But he was reluctant to leave. He didn't want her
to wake up alone and think he'd abandoned her again.
Damn, he was trapped. But it was the sweetest situation he'd ever found himself in. He felt his pulse slow
and his eyes grew a bit heavier.

He rolled to his side, pulled her closer and drifted
off to sleep. His dreams were dark and disturbing. He
found himself back in Afghanistan, lying in cover,
waiting for his target. He saw the dust rising in the
east as a caravan of fast-moving SUVs headed toward
him. He glanced at his scout and it was Alysse calling out the coordinates of the wind and the trajectory.
And instead of lying down in cover she was standing
next to him in her chef's jacket and hat.

What the hell was she doing here? Alysse should

never be in the battle zone. Damn. This was a huge mistake.

"Get down," he yelled. Rolling at her legs, knocking her to the ground so that she didn't present as large a target. She popped her head up and he pushed it down before tucking her underneath him. "It's dangerous."

"You were supposed to protect me," she spat.

"I'm trying," he said. But he knew they'd been spotted and heard the convoy stop below their position. She wasn't listening to his orders. She was putting them both in harm's way and he had no way to save her.

"Stop smothering me." She struggled against him and he felt the whiz of a bullet flying past his head. He grabbed her more firmly, keeping her in place underneath him.

"Stop moving or we'll die," he ordered. God, he couldn't let anything happen to her. He didn't want Alysse to die. He wanted her safe and happy.

He had to get her out of here. He wrapped his arms around her and scanned the area. He'd roll them down the hill to the safety of a small copse of trees.

"Jay?" she asked, her hand on his shoulder. "Wake up."

"What?" he asked. The dream faded away. He was in Alysse's bed, on top of her. She had her hands on his chest and lightly pushed against him. Dammit, he weighed at least a hundred pounds more than she did and he was crushing her.

"Sorry," he said, quickly rolling off her. He sat up and put his feet on the ground. With his head in his hands, he took several deep breaths.

"Are you okay?" she asked, gently touching his back.

"Yeah. I didn't mean to fall asleep," he said.

"That's okay. Do you want to talk about it?" she asked, pulling on a nightshirt and moving around to sit next to him on the edge of the bed. She wrapped one arm around his shoulders and he didn't want to let her comfort him. He'd scared her and jerked her out of sleep. He didn't deserve this, but he sopped it up. He needed her. And that was scary because as Alysse had said in the dream, he was supposed to be her protector and he had no idea if he could do that.

"Um…no, I don't want to talk about it," he said. Hell, the last thing he wanted was to relive a single second of that nightmare.

She glanced over at the clock and he saw that it was nearly 3:00 a.m. "I guess I should head out and let you go back to sleep."

"That's not necessary. I have to get up in about an hour anyway," she said.

He was still shaking a little and the effect of the dream was hard to dismiss. He had thought that he'd simply be able to waltz back into her life, answer a few questions for himself and then move on. But that wasn't the case.

"How about I cook for you?" she suggested. "I know it's early but we didn't really eat last night."

That sounded so normal and so comforting; she couldn't even know how normal and comforting. But he wasn't about to let himself stay here and put her in more danger. He knew there was no enemy waiting outside her door. The true enemy here was himself. He was a risk she didn't need to take. He finally understood why she'd wanted to use him and move on and he regretted that he'd thought he could change her mind.

She deserved a man who could hold her through the night and not wake her with nightmares, she deserved a man who could sit in her kitchen and watch her cook without feeling a need to escape. She deserved a better man than he was and he knew he had to leave now before she started to fall for him again.

JAY GOT UP AND PULLED ON his jeans and began to walk out but she was sitting on the edge of her bed, watching him, and he couldn't do it. He realized that this might have been why he'd left her when she'd been sleeping in Vegas.

"What are you thinking?"

"That I am a mess right now. I've never had a dream that real before. Not like that," he said, unable to stop himself.

"You aren't a mess," she said. "You're human. You're allowed to have cracks and to make mistakes."

He wanted to smile at her but didn't. Not now. But he'd always treasure this moment and recall it whenever he felt alone. He wanted to do something equally nice for her and decided he didn't have to run away after all. He could stay here for her until she left for work.

"So what are you going to show me how to cook?" he asked.

"I don't know," she said, getting to her feet.

She wore a nightshirt that said Kiss the Cook on it

and fell to just above her knees. Her hair was tousled
and her eyes still a little sleepy but she looked good.
The last thing he wanted to do was go and get something to eat. He undid the fly of his jeans that he'd just
fastened and pushed them down his legs.

"What are you doing?"

"Taking you back to bed where we both belong," he
replied, closing the gap between them and pushing her
back onto the bed. He came down on top of her and her
legs slid apart. His hips fitted nicely in the space there.

"We do seem to communicate better here than anywhere else," she said. "But I think you need to do something to get your mind off the dream you had."

"This is going to help. Believe me, making love to
you doesn't leave room for other thoughts."

"Really? Why? Are you thinking about me?" she
asked. She cupped his butt and arched her hips to rock.

"Like what?" she asked. "I'm thinking how right
you feel between my legs. And how I like the feeling
of your breath against my neck."

"I enjoy that, too," he said, reaching down to free
his cock from his underwear and lift her nightshirt so
that they were pressed, naked, together. It was easier
for him this way.

"I also think about how pretty your breasts are under
this shirt," he said, leaning down to rub his cheek over
her breast until the nipple hardened. He leaned up and
then put his hot wet mouth on her nipple, sucking her
through the fabric of her shirt. Then he slipped the tip
of his cock inside of her body.

"I love the way you feel when I first enter you, Aly.

When I'm not inside your body all I think about is when am I going to be able to make love to you again," he said, entering her slowly, inch by inch.

She pushed up, trying to rush him but he kept himself still. He wanted to drive them both crazy and make this last as long as he could. She shifted underneath him and then reached between his legs to cup him.

He moaned. "Oh, baby, that feels so nice."

"Good," she said, continuing to tease him. Then she bit lightly at the side of his neck and pleasure spread through his body. He felt his resolve weakening. He slipped another inch inside her until he finally gave up on going slow and took her, his entire cock filling her.

She shuddered and tightened her legs around his waist, lifting her hips. She groaned his name and he thrust again and again until he felt his orgasm about to wash over him. He reached between their bodies and found her clit. He rubbed it as he pressed into her again and this time her body contracted around his cock. She gripped his shoulders, and screamed his name, holding nothing back. Her release was complete.

He pumped into her once more before coming inside her. Seated, he lay there with his head resting against her breast, letting his breathing slow. He tried to shift to his side but she still had her legs around his waist and her arms around his shoulders.

"Don't go. Not yet," she said.

He moved sideways so that their bodies remained connected. The room felt cool now that the sweat on his body had dried, and though he knew he shouldn't stay, he ignored that voice. Instead, he pulled the comforter up from the end of the bed and tucked them both in it.

A part of him was more than ready to acknowledge that truly he didn't know how they might make a future together, but for tonight he was content to just hold her.

9

Saturday dawned bright and clear. It had been four days since the night at the beach and Jay had fallen into the habit of spending most evenings at Alysse's place. They'd taken his bike and gone for a long ride up the highway from San Clemente last night and while she hadn't been able to truly forget their situation, she had to admit she'd enjoyed it.

This morning, though, she really hadn't been able to think too much about Jay. The kitchen was busy with two additional bakers who were helping since she and Staci had an event.

Alysse and the part-timers finished loading the last of the cupcakes for the Dana Point anniversary party into the back of her van. She and Staci had hired the two college students for weekends primarily. Marissa and Courtney were both eager and followed orders well, and someday they hoped to have their own kitchens where they were in charge. Marissa had said as much to Alysse ten minutes ago when Alysse had made her redo the icing on one batch of the cupcakes.

Alysse had been hoping that with the bakery being

extra busy, she wouldn't be alone with Staci given what she and Jay had started…which was what? "Seeing each other" didn't sound right.

However, they had managed not only to see each other every day, but to spend their nights together, too. Still, there was no point to hiding; Alysse would be spending the next forty-five minutes alone in the delivery van with Staci.

She got behind the wheel and pointed the van north toward Highway 5 and the anniversary party. "Did you get your dish sorted?"

"Yeah, I think so."

"Good. Was it for something special?" Alysse asked, knowing she hadn't been paying that much attention to her friend's life lately as she'd been consumed with Jay.

"Actually, it is. I've decided to try out for *Premiere Chef*," she said.

"Really? Isn't that a pretty intensive show?"

"Yes," Staci said. "It is. If I get on I'd be gone from Sweet Dreams for ten weeks. I wasn't sure how to bring this up because you've been busy with Jay and everything."

Was Staci thinking of leaving Sweet Dreams? Alysse didn't know if she could handle that right now. "It's fine."

"You look pale and about ready to wig out. It's just that I'm getting restless."

Alysse concentrated on her driving. "When will you know if you're a contestant or not?"

"I'm going to L.A. tomorrow to pre-audition. How lame is that? You have to try out to try out," Staci said. There was a note of nervousness in her friend's voice.

"Lame," Alysse agreed with a laugh, trying to act as if she was cool with it when inside she was slowly going into a meltdown. "Why are you doing the show? You don't have anything to prove."

Staci ran her hands through her spiky hair and then shook her head. "I do. I hate the thought of those cocky jerks on TV, whom I know I'm better than, being named Premiere Chef. I mean, come on," she said.

Alysse just had to laugh at her friend's ego. But she'd tasted Staci's dishes at more than one dinner party and knew that she had the cooking chops to back up what she said.

"You're definitely a good chef, but the competition on those shows is stiff and you've been a baker like me for the last four years," Alysse said. Baking was different than the type of cooking that Staci would be required to do on *Premiere Chef.* She'd have to cook a meal in less than ten minutes and come up with unique dishes under pressure. It was a challenging environment.

"I'm getting bored," Staci said. "I've wanted to talk to you about it for a while. The timing never seemed right."

"Talk about what?" Alysse asked. She hated this. Every time she started to feel comfortable and as if her life was on the right path, something like this happened. "Are you leaving Sweet Dreams?"

"I don't know yet. I want to do this competition to see if I still have it in me to run with the big dogs, you know?" she asked.

Honestly, no, Alysse didn't know. She liked the quietness of the bakery and the familiarity of the repeat customers. "I don't see it, although I can understand that you want more. You are Cordon Bleu–trained."

"Yes. And I think I'm finally ready."

"For this competition? Or is it about being on TV?" Alysse asked, trying to understand exactly what Staci wanted.

"The competition. I was working in a Michelin-starred restaurant in Paris before things went belly-up and I ran back here to the States. I want that again. Last night I dreamed I was on the line and we were doing forty covers. The kitchen was crazy and I felt the energy…I miss it."

"Then you have to go for it. You shouldn't deny yourself the chance to pursue your dream. After all, Sweet Dreams was my idea and you helped me get it off the ground," Alysse said. "So what do you need from me?"

"Just some time off to do the show if I get through the first audition. We should probably hire someone to help out with the baking," Staci said.

"Yes. We'll have to make some changes, I'd rather spend more time in the kitchen than up front so maybe hiring a full-time counter person would be better," Alysse suggested.

"That might work. Sorry to spring it on you like this, but you've been busy every night after work." Staci turned and looked out the window at the passing hills of Southern California.

"Yes, I have been," Alysse admitted. She'd been busy trying to avoid Staci and her asking about the bad-boy Marine she was dating, whereas Staci had wanted to tell her about this *Premiere Chef* thing.

"It's Jay that's making you rush out the door every night, right?" Staci asked.

"Yes, it is. We've been trying to get to know each other again," Alysse said. It seemed that she and Staci were both heading off in other directions. Maybe they'd both done as much as they could together and it was time for them to try things on their own again.

"And is that working?" Staci asked. "To be fair, you seem to be pretty happy most days."

Alysse shrugged. "I like him. He can be a challenge sometimes and I'm not at all sure that he's someone I can spend the rest of my life with, but going out every night reminds me of all I've missed. I guess, like you wanting to get back into a Michelin-starred kitchen, I had shut myself off from a lot of things."

"Yes, you had. As I have pointed out on more than one occasion. But I'm glad to hear you admit it. I've been worried about you for a while because the bakery can't be your life," Staci said.

Alysse hated to admit it but Staci was right. She'd let the bakery become her entire life, and, to be honest, she was still doing that. She gave Jay the few hours at night before she went to bed, and then she rushed out in the morning while he was still sleeping.

She was glad for Staci though. The more they talked the less panicked she felt about Staci leaving to pursue a different dream. She would get through this change the way she always did—by finding a new comfort zone. She could and would do it.

"I know. To be honest, I think I was hiding there. It took so much effort to get the place up and running but now we have it under control," Alysse said. And that was what bothered her. She liked the fact that she'd gotten the bakery to a point where things went smoothly. There was a lot to be said for having something in your life that did what it was supposed to.

"That's why it seems like I should audition," Staci said. Her friend was looking at her with a sort of question in her eyes.

"You are so right," Alysse said to reassure Staci, but she found that she'd kind of reassured herself, too. "We both need to stop hiding in Sweet Dreams and go after the things that pushed us to create it in the first place."

"True. It's funny that we both were able to make something so successful and safe out of our disappointments," Staci said.

It was, and it spoke to the women they both were, Alysse thought. She and Staci had run away from their problems by going into the kitchen and creating something new. Something that no one else had any control over and Alysse realized that sharing Sweet Dreams with Staci had helped her to survive that first year after Jay had left.

"I've never said it, but thank you for being my partner," Alysse said. Staci had given her something other than winning to focus on. Without her dad or Toby in her life Alysse knew she'd have been moorless, just drifting from competition to competition, even though her mom had warned her she'd burn out.

"We're da bomb. I'm not leaving the partnership, just the day-to-day stuff," Staci said. "We've got a good thing going."

"Yes, we do," she said.

Alysse pulled into the parking lot at the Dana Point

Marina and drove toward the center area near the yacht club so she could park the van for unloading. And, as they set up their cupcakes under the tent prepared for them, Alysse realized that she had wanted life to be predictable and safe but it never was. Even while she and Staci had been hiding at Sweet Dreams their pasts were waiting there to spring up again.

She was very glad that she was ready for the change. She had to stop hiding from the truth about Jay. The truth was hard to face but as she stood in the late-afternoon sun she admitted to herself that she still cared for Jay and the last thing she wanted was for him to walk out on her again.

They'd been playing house together, careful not to talk about anything of real importance. He didn't discuss Company B with her any more than the one time she'd asked about it and he'd answered with a simple yes or no. So she'd stopped asking. She knew that they both needed to face some hard truths about their life together.

Now Alysse was thinking that Staci's bold move meant that it was past time for her to step up and make some changes. She couldn't just keep bumping along, because sooner or later she and Jay would have to talk about what they both wanted.

She knew she wanted more than what they had but she was afraid to admit it in case that would drive Jay away. By not admitting it, she wasn't going to have what she really wanted anyway.

JAY WAS STILL UNEASY about working out of an office, but Lucien had paired him with Donovan O'Malley on a basic mission where they would be guarding a foreign dignitary. It was right up Jay's alley, which was good because he found himself thinking about Alysse at the most inopportune times.

"What branch you with?" Donovan asked. He was about Jay's age and from Seattle.

"Corps. You?" Jay asked as he studied the other man from behind his aviator shades. The man was shorter than Jay and had more muscles. He had a buzz cut and a tribal-armband tattoo down his left arm. He wore jeans and a T-shirt and had done a good job of blending in with the crowd, even though Lucien had told Jay that Donovan didn't have any special recon training.

"Army. I'm an infantryman, what about you?" he asked.

"Sniper," Jay said. They had snipers in all the branches but he'd been trained by the best in the world, in Jay's humble opinion.

"Have you been to Afghanistan?" Donovan asked. "I did two tours myself, but I got a bit tired of all that sand. I'm used to lots of lush greenery and rain."

"I've been twice. I hear you on the sand. It gets in everything."

"Yeah. That's why I thought this job would be nice," Donovan said, scratching the back of his head. "I was tired of dusting dirt off my cot before I went to bed."

"Me, too," Jay admitted, although he hadn't slept any better the last four nights in Alysse's comfortable sand-free bed. That had nothing to do with the mattress or the sheets and everything to do with Alysse. He'd been afraid to sleep in case he had another nightmare.

"So what do I need to do next?" Donovan asked. "I

don't want to screw this up. And I've never done anything like it before."

"You won't screw it up. You any good with a camera?" Jay asked, pulling a Nikon from his backpack and holding it out.

"I'm fair enough. What do you need shots of?" Donovan asked, taking the camera from Jay.

"The entire building and all the entrances. Do it close up from the sidewalk and then walk across the street and get some there. I'm going to check out the buildings nearby."

Donovan nodded and started to walk away. "No problem. I'll meet you back in thirty."

"Sounds good," Jay said, but the other man was already gone. Donovan was very good at taking orders—the kind of man who would be an asset to any team he was on.

Jay liked to get the lay of the land by walking it. He'd done it a thousand times before with a scout at his side.

He made notes and sketched a few things. They were in Santa Monica and close enough to the ocean that the breeze would make anyone targeting the guy Lucien was guarding difficult to shoot. It wasn't an impossible shot, but most guys wouldn't be able to hit their target with one bullet.

He sat where he'd sit if he were assigned to take out the target and made notes of the wind direction and the patterns as it changed. And, though he knew it was impossible, he could swear the ocean breeze carried the scent of Alysse on it.

Damn, he had no idea what he was going to do with

that woman. He was no closer to figuring out his future than he had been when he'd ordered that special cupcake from her.

This job wasn't the solution to the restlessness inside him and he was coming to realize that Alysse wasn't either. It was as if he'd lost a part of himself when he'd been alone in the hospital recovering. He reached down and rubbed the top of his thigh where he'd had the injury. It didn't hurt but he continued to remember the sensation.

Maybe he'd been meant to die and being here now… that was the mistake. He'd seen men with a hell of a lot more to lose than him die over there and that had bothered him. Why had he been spared when no one would have mourned for him? When men who had wives and kids back home hadn't made it out?

There were some questions that were too hard to answer and Jay pushed them aside as he always did. For whatever reason, he was glad he was here now and that he had a second chance with Alysse. Maybe that was why he'd been spared?

His phone vibrated and he saw that it was a text message from Alysse.

Do you have plans for dinner? How does a sunset cruise from Dana Point sound?

I'm still working and won't have an idea when I'll be finished for another thirty minutes.

Okay. Text me when you know.

He finished his recon and met back up with Donovan. They'd driven up to L.A. separately so meeting Alysse wasn't going to be an issue of transportation, but he was feeling as though they were doing Vegas all over again, not really being themselves. A part of him enjoyed being with her, but he knew that wasn't going to be enough for her. And every day they were together he felt further and further away from her.

"Are the photos okay?" Donovan asked.

Jay took the camera from the other man and, using the small view window, scrolled through them. They were actually pretty good. There were one or two that showed some areas Jay thought might pose a problem.

"How was the visibility of this alcove?" Jay asked, pointing to an entryway on the side of the building that was covered.

"Not the best, but there is only one shadowy area and it's not big enough to hide a man."

"Are you sure?" Jay asked. The mission to protect the dignitary had been assigned to him, but the intel was going to be his. He wanted to give Lucien the best information he could. Make sure his friend didn't get caught out by anything that Jay or Donovan overlooked.

"I'm sure. I watched it for about ten minutes and there was a lot of traffic in and out. No one just appeared. There's a guard there, as well," Donovan said.

"Good to know," Jay said.

They finished chatting and then headed back to Oceanside and the Company B offices. Jay texted Alysse he was busier than he'd thought he'd be and that he'd get in touch when he was done.

She didn't text back. That silence made him wonder if he'd done the wrong thing and finally put her off. He pushed it to the back of his mind as he entered the conference room and sat down at the table with the rest of the team. Lucien was at the head of the table with Donovan and Jay next to him on the left. Across from them were two men whom Jay didn't know but he quickly learned they were both assigned to guard the dignitary.

The client was a foreign minister from Egypt who'd managed to escape the country before being arrested and was applying for diplomatic immunity.

After they reported on what they'd found in Santa Monica, Jay and Donovan both were done for the day and left the conference room. But Jay felt restless. He wanted to stay and offer his services as eyes in the sky. He knew that those two guards would do their job, but he felt that he could benefit the mission.

The only problem with that was that he didn't work for them. Today had been challenging and the kind of work he liked to do, but yesterday he'd sat in a control room and monitored security cameras, which had been a total bore.

He pulled his phone out of his pocket and saw that Alysse had texted him back that she was staying for dinner and if he decided to show up he could join her.

ALYSSE HAD ALWAYS STRUGGLED with being alone in public. Partly it was because she'd always felt so self-conscious that being alone made her feel exposed. But after Jay had left and she'd spent all those nights alone having to rebuild her confidence, something had changed. Her mom often said that it was as if part of Alysse stopped caring what other people thought. And Alysse didn't know if that was true, but she had finally stopped building her life around the romantic fantasy that had always existed in her head.

She was having a drink at one of the many bars in the marina area and sitting outside where she had a nice view of the Pacific. Staci had unexpectedly met up with one of her former boyfriends and gone with him when they'd finished the cupcake giveaway, and, instead of heading back to the bakery and her home, Alysse had decided to stay here.

She had a lot to think about, what with Staci wanting to go off and do her own thing. And Jay.

He'd been so accommodating a part of her had just expected him to say yes when she'd asked him to meet her, but then she guessed it was important to remember that he was busy away from her.

She took another sip of her wine and leaned back in the chair. The marina was busy with foot traffic— couples and families taking a stroll. In the distance she heard the sound of a reggae band playing. The marina committee had a full schedule of events that were going until late tonight.

She stretched and turned to signal her waiter and was surprised to see Jay approaching. He wore his habitual jeans and a T-shirt with a thick leather bomber jacket over it.

He pulled out the chair next to her and sat down. "Sorry I couldn't get here sooner."

"I didn't think you were coming," she said at last,

realizing that she hadn't gotten over her expectation that he would leave her.

"I wasn't sure I would either," he said. "The traffic from L.A. was nuts. I don't know how people drive here all the time."

"This job is demanding?" she asked. "You haven't said much."

He hadn't shared a lot of his life with her. In fact, if it wasn't something she pulled out of him, he never volunteered information about himself. She suspected he was just used to playing his cards close to his chest.

"Today I went and did recon for a job they're doing tomorrow. Guarding a dignitary at a dinner. I was checking out possible places where a shooter could set up in case...well, the guy's a target so there is no in case."

She heard some excitement in his voice as he talked about it. He ordered a beer from the waiter and then stretched his long legs out and looked over at her.

"Do you think you will take the job?" she asked. "It definitely sounds like your kind of thing."

"Today was. But other jobs they have aren't as interesting," he said, taking a swallow of his beer. "I don't know yet."

He wasn't going to make a decision that quickly and even if he did it would have no impact on her. Had things between them changed at all in the week they'd spent together?

She knew they had an electric sexual chemistry and she had to admit he'd let her use him for all the sex she wanted. But the truth was the more that she was with him, the more she wanted him. He wasn't curing her so she could move on. She was falling for him and that loner persona of his, even though she was trying not to.

"Would you like it if I took that job?"

"I don't think that's up to me," she said. "I don't want you to hold it against me if I say yes and you hate it."

"That's fair enough. Have you thought about us in the long term?" he asked.

She shook her head. "No. Have you?"

He didn't say anything, just took a long draw on his beer and she honestly had no idea what that meant. It occurred to her that while she'd been busy trying to cure herself of Jay, he'd been doing his best to protect himself, too. Maybe they just weren't meant to be together.

"What are you thinking?" he asked her.

"Nothing," she said. No way was she spilling her guts to him. He couldn't even talk to her about the simplest of things. Wouldn't give her an answer about anything connected with the two of them.

He shook his head. "You look sad."

"I'm not. I'm concerned about the bakery," she said. "That's probably what you're seeing."

"Why concerned? I thought everything was going well there," he said.

"It is. But Staci told me today that she wants to take a more backseat role in the day-to-day running of the store. It's going to be a big change," Alysse said.

"You can do it. What will be the biggest obstacle?" he asked.

She had been toying with that. "I think finding another baker. Most of the really good ones already have permanent jobs and it's so personal in the kitchen I need to find someone who suits my style."

"If it was me, I'd make a list," he said. Reaching into his pocket he pulled out a pen and a small notebook.

"Jot down the qualities you are looking for and then you can draft an ad or ask around to see if someone who matches them is available," he said.

She smiled at him because for the first time today she didn't feel alone. She hadn't anticipated that Jay would be able to give her this. She needed to feel as though she had a partner when she had these kinds of decisions to make. And frankly, given the way their relationship had been going, she hadn't had a clue that he'd step up to the plate this time.

She couldn't help staring at him and seeing some changes that made her care just a little bit more for him. Jay was the kind of man she could count on in a crisis and that shouldn't have surprised her because of his experience in the Corps.

For the first time she thought about Jay as someone who lived life on the edge, as someone who protected those he cared for. Yet she wasn't entirely sure he was going to be able to watch over her for any longer than his leave.

10

JAY WAS nervous.

He'd agreed to go with Alysse to the volleyball tournament and watch Toby play, which was no big deal, except that he'd also be meeting her mother.

"Ready for today?" Alysse asked as she and Jay headed for her car. The Saab convertible was perfect for the sunny California weather.

"I guess so. Why wouldn't I be?" he asked.

"My mom is coming today," she said. "I didn't mention it before because I didn't think anything of it until Staci texted me this morning that she was looking forward to the fireworks."

Great. "I guess your mom will be like your brother then?"

"What does that mean?" she asked.

"That she'll be angry with me," he said.

"Well, yes. That's her in a nutshell. She's very protective of my brother and me. When we were in school we could never let her know if someone teased us on the playground or gave us a hard time after school…

she'd head right into the principal's office and defend us."

"Sounds perfect to me," Jay said.

"I can see how you would think so given how your mom was," Alysse said. "But it was embarrassing."

"I get that. I…how should I handle her?" he asked. He wasn't too happy with the way that Alysse mentioned his past with his mom as if it was normal and okay. But her acceptance of it and of him made things easier on him.

"Just be yourself. Once she sees that you weren't out to hurt me she'll ease up," Alysse said, holding the key ring up and dangling it from one finger. "Do you want to drive?"

"Yes," he said. "You are a speed demon in this car."

She chuckled. "It's not my fault that it has really good pickup."

"No, but it is your fault that you like going fast," he teased, giving her a quick buss on the lips before opening her door. She slid into the passenger seat and he went around to the driver's side.

He was trying to behave normally, as if this was going to be fun, while truthfully, he was dreading it. Over the last week they'd done more things with her friends than he would have thought himself capable of. He'd chipped away at his defenses and, frankly, he believed it was making a difference.

"What exactly is the Cal King Tournament?" he asked once they got on the road.

"It's a series of semi-pro beach volleyball games. Toby and Paulo are on a team. Each team has two people and they play all day. There is a final at night.

The matches can be really competitive and a lot of fun to watch."

He wasn't convinced that going to an event that had all of Alysse's family at it was going to be fun. But he'd agreed mainly because he was test-driving normal life. He'd been working every day for the last week at Company B and spending most of his nights at Alysse's house.

There was a certain comfort to the days but every night he woke in a cold sweat. Since that first night when he'd woken Alysse up, he'd managed to get out of bed and leave her sleeping.

Today was a Sunday and the bakery was closed and Jay was helping Alysse cater for her family at the volleyball tournament. He wasn't looking forward to meeting Alysse's mom given the way Toby had reacted toward him, but he wasn't a coward and would do his best for Alysse.

"Thanks for coming today," she said as they started unloading the trunk of her car.

"No problem," he said, watching as she stacked items on her cooler with wheels. He was impressed at how well they all fit on there until he realized that she normally had to carry everything herself and she'd devised this method to move stuff quickly.

He felt ashamed at that. But set it aside. He was here now and he wanted to make up for the past, but that wasn't enough. He'd realized that at Dana Point. She did need a man who was there. Not someone who was off fighting in a war halfway around the world. So, he factored into his decision that if he wanted a future with Alysse he couldn't go back into the Corps.

She started to tow the cooler with all the stuff and he stepped around her, brushing her hand away and taking over control of the contraption.

The sun was warm and the crowds were heavy when they got to the beach. Alysse took her cell phone out of her pocket.

"I'm going to text my mom. She's been here since six saving a spot for us," she said.

"That's early."

"Well, she's all about family events. She'd have gotten here at midnight if she'd had to," Alysse said with a laugh.

Her phone vibrated and a minute later Alysse led the way to a large easy-up with a bamboo mat and a table under it. The woman waiting for them was tall and resembled Alysse. The two women hugged and Jay stood to the side.

"Mom, this is Jay. Jay, this is Candi, my mom."

"Jay," she said, holding out her hand. She wasn't friendly and didn't really smile at him, but that didn't bother Jay. He expected that Alysse's family would treat him coldly until he could prove that he had changed and wasn't back in her life to hurt her all over again.

"Ma'am. Where do you want the food?" he asked Alysse.

She motioned to the table and he started unpacking stuff. He supposed if he were a different guy he would have made some kind of small talk, but that wasn't his style and he knew it would sound forced if he attempted it.

He stayed to the side and watched as more of

Alysse's family arrived. They were all chattering away and he felt like an outsider.

"Hey," Alysse said, slipping up beside him. She wrapped her arm around his waist and he almost hugged her back but felt as if too many people were watching them.

"You okay?" she asked.

"Yes. Just a little outside of my comfort zone. When does the volleyball tournament start?" he asked.

She dropped her arm and stepped away from him. He felt like a cad but he thought it would be better if there were no public displays of affection while her mom was standing nearby with a disapproving look on her face.

"It's already begun," she said. "What's up with the cold shoulder?"

"Your mom looks like she's just waiting for an excuse to lay into me. And I don't think you'd appreciate a scene with your family and friends here."

"I wouldn't, but then I don't think she'd cause a scene," Alysse said. "What's this really about?"

"I'm not comfortable in crowds," he said. "There are too many people here. I can't relax like this."

"You did okay the other night when we went surfing with everyone," she reminded him.

"The beach wasn't this crowded," Jay said.

It was a hard situation to handle when there were this many people around. It wasn't just the strangers on the beach; it was Alysse's people under this tent. They were her community, her lifeblood and if he needed any proof that he and Alysse didn't belong together, well, here it was.

Alysse enjoyed this crowd and eating and talking and holding the babies and playing with the younger kids. And all he wanted to do was find a place with a wall that he could have at his back. They were so different and yet he was coming to need that smile of hers and her calming presence in his life.

"I didn't realize the crowds would make you edgy," she said. "Maybe after you've been out of the Marines for a while that will change."

He stiffened. He wasn't sure he'd ever lose his edge. "Maybe. You know I haven't made a decision yet on the Corps."

She gave him one of those odd searching looks of hers and he wished he understood what she meant by it. He hoped that she found the answer she wanted in his face. But when she sighed and turned away, he knew she hadn't.

"I know."

"Sorry," he said.

"It's fine. I need to remember that you aren't really here to stay," she said, shaking her head. "I think we've both been deluding ourselves that we were exploring options but really we've been playing house. And that's not all that different from what we did in Vegas."

"You're right. Here's not the time or place," he said.

"Agreed. I think Staci's just arrived and I'd like to have one day where I can pretend I'm like every other woman my age," she said.

"What do you mean?"

"You know, that I have a boyfriend and my family and friends are with me," she said before striding away.

He wasn't sure how he'd done it but he knew he'd just hurt Alysse again.

ALYSSE WANTED TO IGNORE Jay but that was exactly what she suspected he wanted her to do. He needed the silence and liked his solitary life. Why was she trying so hard to make him into something he wasn't?

And she *was* trying. She could have just stuck to her original plan and had sex with him every night until he went back to the Marines, but no, she had to have dreams and want more from him.

She was coming to believe that there was no way to cure herself of Jay and find another man, because, in reality, she only wanted him. That fact made her want to cry or scream or maybe punch Jay really hard.

But it was hardly his fault that he couldn't be what she needed him to be. If she'd been a different kind of woman she could have taken him as he was and been content, but she wasn't.

She wanted him to blend with her family and to fit in with her friends. Instead, he sat in a lawn chair drinking a beer, watching the game. She was mad at herself because all the growth she'd thought she'd achieved during the last four years was really nothing at all. She'd been fooling herself.

"Why are you glaring at the potato salad?" Staci asked coming up behind her. "I've tasted it and it's good."

She gave her friend a half smile. "No reason. Just not sure if I should put an ice pack underneath it."

Liar, she thought. Why didn't she ever really talk to her friends about her problems? She was just like Jay in that—she had to sort it out herself. Maybe that was part of the reason she was so attracted to him.

"Well, considering you've already got two under

there I'd say no," Staci said. Her friend took her arm and turned her toward her. "What's up?"

Alysse shrugged and fiddled with her sunglasses. She'd been pretending that she and Jay could have a normal life together but this afternoon was just showing her how wrong she'd been. They were different. Not just in little ways but in huge ones. And… "I guess I'm just facing reality."

"Ha. You are the most grounded person I know," Staci said, tapping her on the forehead. "You overthink everything. Is that what you're doing now?"

"Not really. I'm still clinging to a few girlish fantasies that I should have gotten rid of a long time ago," Alysse said. She didn't want to admit that she'd been hoping that Jay would completely change and become the kind of man that would suit her life the way it was. That wasn't Jay. He did his own thing. He had his own strengths and those were what had drawn her to him. But those strengths were also his weaknesses.

"I'm guessing this has something to do with your Marine," Staci said in her wry tone.

"It has everything to do with him," Alysse said, wishing that for once her romantic life would be easy. But it never had been. Even in high school she had struggled with dating. Her mom had said that once Alysse was an adult she'd understand what she really wanted from a man but she still hadn't. "I can't figure him out."

Staci threw her head back and laughed. "You are kidding me, right? Men are from another planet. You will never be able to understand why he does whatever it is that is upsetting you."

Alysse smiled, then felt just a tad melancholy thinking about Staci being up in Los Angeles while she was in San Diego. It was only about a three-hour drive but it would seem a world apart.

"I guess you are right. You know, I'm going to miss you when you're in L.A."

Staci hugged her. "I know. But don't sweat it. I'll be coming back to visit. And if I get kicked off the show early, I'll be back for good."

"I thought you wanted to try something new?" Alysse asked her. She was afraid that she was projecting her vulnerability at the thought of losing her best friend and Jay within a few weeks of each other. And it was beginning to seem more and more that no matter what career path Jay took he'd more than likely not be with her. Different people, different paths.

"I do, but that's not fair to you. You have to find a new baker and new staff for the front of the shop," Staci said.

A lot was changing all at once and Alysse had been sort of ignoring it to deal with Jay. But she knew that she couldn't let the rest of life fall away because of him.

"I can handle it. It's not that big a deal. And I don't want you giving up just because you're worried about me. I'm way stronger than I look," she said.

That was when she realized that she was putting Jay through a test to see if he'd sacrifice what he wanted for her. Why was she doing that? It was as if she was afraid to trust him.

Hell, she *was* afraid of that very thing and had been since she'd stepped onto the beach at the Hotel Del Coronado and found Jay waiting, instead of some stranger. And she knew that no matter what she did or said, she was never going to be able to treat him like some guy she'd just met.

They would always have their past and she wasn't able to let that go. She was trying to make him be a part of a life that she wasn't too sure he'd ever be able to accept. Why?

Because it would be safer for her. If Jay wanted the same things she did, then he wouldn't leave her and she'd be able to let her guard down around him. Instead, since she was treating him with kid gloves, he was edgy and so was she.

"You should go for it, Staci. Don't feel like you have to come back to Sweet Dreams. If you want to though, your station in the kitchen will be waiting for you," she assured herself and her friend.

"Thanks," Staci said. "It'll help me out, knowing you've got my back. I think that we can invite friends to attend some of the cook-offs. Would you come?"

"Hell to the yeah," Alysse said, being silly because now that she'd figured out what she was doing to herself and Jay, everything seemed a little brighter.

"I'll be right back," Alysse said.

She left the table area and headed over to Jay. It was one thing to realize they'd been playing house but another thing entirely when she admitted that she'd set it up to test him. Did she honestly think that if they lived together and had these pretend lives together, he wouldn't leave?

She knew that she had been playing games with herself and trying to entice him to stay by showing him her family and friends. Today she had got it—if she wasn't enough for him then all the cool people she surrounded herself with wouldn't make her satisfy him either.

Jay was searching for something and she couldn't give it to him. If he could fulfill that part of himself that had been missing with her, then maybe they had a chance. And if he couldn't, it was time for her to cut her losses and move on.

Alysse couldn't find Jay at first and then noticed her mom was missing, too. She scanned the beach and found her lover standing in the shade with a brick retaining wall at his back. She smiled at that, but the smile soon left her face as she spotted her mom standing next to Jay and talking very animatedly to him.

Jay was nodding and had his arms crossed over his chest. He was being respectful or at least it seemed that way to her from where she was. And she felt a moment's panic. What if this scared him into leaving her again?

She took a deep breath and then let it out.

There it was, she thought. The fear that dominated every second of her thoughts and lurked in the back of her mind. She hated that she was filled with fear, but even acknowledging it wouldn't make it go away.

The only thing that would was some reassurance from Jay and she knew that was asking the impossible. She walked briskly over to her mom and Jay and they stopped talking when they saw her.

"Am I interrupting?" Alysse asked.

"No," her mom said. "I was just telling Jay that I haven't seen you this happy in a long time."

Really? Then she looked at Jay and he was grinning. He'd enjoyed chatting with her mom about her. She didn't know how he'd done it but they both seemed to be getting along. "Well, I am happy right now."

"Good. I warned Jay that if he made you cry again I'd come after him and I might not have his skills with a weapon but I do know how to protect my own," her mom said.

"Candi, I can respect that," Jay said.

"Good," her mom said. She patted Jay on the shoulder. "Thanks for listening to me."

"No problem," Jay said. Her mom gave Alysse a quick hug and then returned to the picnic area.

"What was that about?"

"She had some things to say to me and needed to clear the air," Jay replied.

"Was it okay? Did she upset you?" Alysse asked.

"I'm a man, Aly, I don't get upset," he said.

"Then what do you get?" she asked.

"Pissed off. But your mom really loves you and only wants what is best for you, and I can't get mad about that," he said.

"Good. I wanted…I'm not sure how to say this," she said. Now that she was standing in front of him the words she wanted to say wouldn't form in her mouth.

"Just spit it out," he said.

"Are you planning to leave me again?" she asked in one long breath.

He looked taken aback and stood up straighter. "I don't know."

Those quietly spoken words weren't the ones she was looking for and they shot dread straight through her.

"It's time for your brother's match," Jay said. "We can talk about this later."

She let him lead her to the volleyball game and, though she pretended to watch, her mind was on his words and the fear in her heart just grew larger.

JAY PULLED THE CAR to a stop in front of Alysse's place. His bike was stored in her garage and he knew he'd be leaving tonight. He had enjoyed hanging out with her, but they both knew she needed something more from him. Something he wasn't going to be able to deliver.

He'd felt the disappointment in her when she'd asked if he was going to leave. He knew he should have just said no, but he didn't want to lie to her.

"You got too much sun today," he said. "Your cheeks are red."

"I always do," she said, the same cold shoulder she'd been giving him all afternoon. "No matter how much sunscreen I use."

"I just get more tanned," he said.

"Have we really come down to banal conversation? You don't have anything more to say to me than that?" she asked, and he heard the anger in her tone. She wanted a fight and he got that, but he wasn't sure he could accommodate her.

"Sorry, just trying to lighten the mood," he said. "I'm not good at this kind of thing. You should know that by now."

"Yeah, you should try harder. You don't encourage anyone to talk to you."

"It's not my scene," he said. "I never know the right thing to say and I always end up feeling like I'm an idiot."

"You are the furthest thing from an idiot that I've ever met."

"That's not what you were thinking earlier," he said.

"True," she said with a laugh. "Do you want to come inside?"

"Yes, but I thought we agreed we'd played this suburban fantasy long enough," he said. He didn't want to have to walk away again but they both knew that... what?

"Let's talk inside. I really don't want to sit out here in the car and have a long conversation."

"Okay," he said. "You go open the windows and I'll get all the stuff from the trunk."

She looked as if she wanted to argue with him, but then she just nodded and got out of the car. He watched her walk up the path to her cute little house and thought how idyllic this place was. The house was comfortable and cozy with a neatly manicured lawn. The neighborhood was friendly but not intrusive. The lady was sexy, sweet and just not right for a man like him.

He cleaned out the car and then walked up to the house. She'd opened all the windows and a nice breeze welcomed him as he stepped inside. He heard the sound of Jimmy Buffett coming from the patio and dumped the cooler in the kitchen before pausing on the threshold between the house and the patio to watch her watering the hibiscus which grew around the edge of her water feature.

A part of him craved this life more than he knew was safe. She'd become an obsession for him and he wanted her. He wanted to say to hell with all the people in her life and just scoop her up and take her away to somewhere special, just the two of them.

But that wasn't ever going to happen.

"Jay?"

"Yes?"

"Do you want a beer?" she asked.

"Nah, I'm good. This place is nice," he said stepping onto the patio and going to sit on one of her Adirondack chairs. She took a seat next to him and then stood up and paced around the garden.

"This isn't really working out, is it?"

"No, it's not. You were right when you said we were playing house, and the last week has been fun though it's not any different from our marriage."

"I know. Do you realize if you spend the night with me tonight it will be the longest we've ever been together?" she asked.

He hadn't realized that. But it explained why he'd been so restless and jittery all day today. "You know you're the only woman I've ever been with for this long."

"That's sad, Jay," she said. "You don't even want to stay longer than a week with me."

"I do," he said. "I'm just not sure how to do this. I want this to be real but for some reason it just isn't."

"I think part of the problem is me," she said. "Earlier when I was talking to Staci I had an epiphany about myself."

"What was it?" he asked when she was quiet.

"I am trying to make you into someone you aren't. I don't think it was a conscious thing, but I was definitely trying to force you to be a part of my group of friends even though I know you prefer being a loner. Even with me you are quiet sometimes and I get that you like that."

He stretched his legs out in front of him. "Why are you doing that?"

"I'm not sure. I don't think it's to punish you but I do think it's some kind of test. Something that I want to prove either to you or me, I'm not sure."

"I guess you still haven't forgiven me," he said.

"I guess not. I thought it would be easy just to ignore the past and somehow use you and get back a little of my own. But that hasn't happened at all. Instead of feeling whole again I just find myself falling deeper and deeper into something that I don't think is ever going to work."

"Me?" he asked.

He knew exactly what she was getting at because he felt the same way. He wanted to be what she needed, but he wasn't about to actually let down his walls and take a chance on getting hurt. He knew she'd been right when she said that he'd purposely left before her in Vegas. That a part of him was always sure if he wasn't the first one out the door he'd be left behind.

And never had that seemed so hard to take than it did right now, looking at Alysse and knowing he wanted her with him for the rest of his life.

_11_

THE JIMMY BUFFETT CD had switched over to the smooth bluesy tracks of Adele singing about loss in a way that Alysse could relate to at the moment.

The closer she got to Jay the more she felt him slipping away from her. And she was definitely not helping things by trying to force an answer out of him on issues that he'd rather not confront.

At the small pond, she glanced down at the several koi swimming in endless circles. She liked her backyard and felt so comfortable here. She wondered if she would after Jay left. She should never have brought him to the sanctuary that was her home, because now she'd have a hard time not picturing him here.

"Where do we go from here?" she asked at last. She wasn't facing him because she couldn't bear the brutal honesty she saw in his eyes. It would be so much easier if he'd just lie to her a little bit.

"I don't know. I think we have to stop pretending…" he said. "I've been walking on eggshells around you trying not to do anything that will spook you and

apart from that one nightmare I had—I'd say I've succeeded."

She frowned as she remembered that nightmare and
how scared she'd been for him.

"You have been good about not scaring me," she
agreed. "I've been doing the same thing, sort of, trying to make sure you wouldn't leave me like you did
in Vegas, but to be completely honest, I don't know
what made you leave and hedging my bets isn't helping either one of us."

Hiding and hoping, she admitted it freely now, that
she could maybe be whatever she hadn't been before.
That was scary because she'd really thought she was
over him for good.

"I guess we both need to be just who we really are,"
he said quietly as he walked up next to her. He smelled
of suntan lotion and the sandy beach.

"Yes." Somehow that seemed so much easier to say
than do. She wanted to be free of her fear that he was
leaving her as soon as she let her guard down; however, that wasn't going to happen. "But I don't know
who I am."

Admitting it out loud seemed like the only thing to
do. She pivoted to face him and waited to see his response.

Now she knew why that whirlwind courtship had
worked out so well for her. She hadn't had time to think
or worry about the possibilities. But this time that was
all she'd done. And all that thinking had led her to a
place that made her feel as though she and Jay weren't
going to be able to cobble together the next few days,
much less a lifetime.

Yet she knew she'd grown to know him so much better now than she had before. He was complex. A loner who definitely needed her in his life. A man who would protect everyone around him but would accept no protection himself. A lover who was generous with his body but guarded his heart.

"You do know who you are," he said. "I'm muddling it up by staying here. Let's have breakfast in the morning, I want to spend the day just the two of us—maybe I'll take you on the balloon ride Paulo recommended. No thinking about our jobs or your family. What do you say?" he asked.

She didn't want to. She'd be alone with Jay and that was one thing she still wanted to avoid. "I'm scared."

"Why?" he asked. He glanced down into the koi pond and then put his hands in his back pockets and looked at her. His guarded dark chocolate gaze made her wary. Why couldn't he just trust her?

Why couldn't she just trust him? she asked herself, knowing that if she knew the answers to those questions things would be infinitely better between them.

"It feels as if I'm in one pond and you are in your pond and we just get together for sex. Is that what we're all about?" he asked.

"It's safer," she said. "There is absolutely no danger of me falling for you as long as you stay in your pond and do your own thing."

"I know," he said, taking his hand out of his back pocket and lacing their fingers together. "But neither of us wants a repeat of the last time we got together... do we?"

She looked up at him. The moment of truth. Was

she going to risk her heart on this man again? She'd already seen the proof of what happened when she did.

But if she didn't take this second chance with Jay, would she end up regretting it the rest of her life? Could she live with that?

"No, we don't," she said at last. "I'm willing to try again. Third time's a charm, right?"

"So they say," he said with a wry grin. "I know I wasn't the best when we met up with your friends so maybe we can do it again?"

"Sure. Why don't we invite them over next weekend? We can be the hosts so you'll feel more at ease and we'll have had another entire week to get to know each other. Oh my goodness, a week is hardly any time," she said.

"I'm sorry, I can't offer you more until I know if I'm going to reenlist," he said.

"It's fine. We do better on the fast track," she said. It was as if when she didn't have time to think, she trusted her instincts. She knew that she had something worth fighting for with Jay, but she was afraid to fight for him. Afraid to let him into her heart lest he hurt her again. And no matter how hard she tried to keep from falling for him, she knew she was.

"I don't know how we do better, but I do know that without you by my side…I'm missing something. And I've never had anyone mean that much to me before. I'm a little unsure of how to proceed. I don't want to take a chance on screwing this up," Jay said.

That was probably one of the most honest things he'd ever said to her. She wrapped her broken, fragile heart in those words he'd given her. She was touched by them more than she wanted to be. She understood this man far more now than she had in Vegas. She got that he had demons that she'd never expected and that he needed more from her than she'd been able to offer him.

"Lucien invited me to join him for drinks tomorrow night. Do you want to come along and meet him?" Jay asked.

It was the first time he'd invited her to be a part of his life. He'd gone to her things and talked to her about Sweet Dreams, but he'd never reciprocated much.

"Yes. That sounds nice," she said. "I've been dying to meet some of your friends. I thought maybe you were embarrassed by me."

"I never could be embarrassed by you. You are the best thing that's ever happened to me," he said.

"Really?" she asked. "Don't answer that. I meant to say thank you."

"You're welcome. So how about I pick you up in the morning very early for that balloon ride and then after lunch I will drop you back off…?"

"Okay," she said.

"We can have drinks with Lucien and then I'll take you out. What do you want to do?"

"Anything?"

"Sure," he said. "What's your dream date?"

"Dinner and dancing," she said without hesitating.

"Then that's what we'll do," he said. "I'll be back at six to pick you up."

He walked through her house to the front door and she followed him. She had a reluctant hope that this time maybe things were going to be better for them.

ALYSSE SLEPT RESTLESSLY without Jay by her side, but a part of her knew that she was better off this way. He wasn't ready to make a decision about his career or her. And she needed to be able to protect her heart.

She was awake at five so they could drive up to Temecula. It was very chilly, something she didn't realize until she was on the back of Jay's bike holding on to him. She started shivering and he pulled off on the highway.

"Why are we stopping?" she asked.

"Because you're freezing," he said. He took off his leather jacket and wrapped it around her. He wore a black sweatshirt bearing the Marine Corps emblem under his jacket.

"Will you be warm enough?" she asked.

"I'll be fine as long as you aren't shivering," he said.

"Thank you," she said. "I like your sweatshirt. I notice you don't often wear something with the Corps logo on it. Why is that?"

"People want to buy me coffee and stuff and it makes me uncomfortable," he said.

"They're just saying thanks for doing your job."

"I know that," he said. "But it's a job. The only one I'm trained to do and I'm nothing special."

"Yes, you are," she said.

"You think so?" he asked her.

She could tell he wasn't sure if she was joking around with him and that bothered her.

"Yes, of course I'm sure," she said.

They got back on the bike and finished the drive. There were three other couples waiting to go up in the hot air balloon. Jay had signed them up for a two-hour flight across the valley, and it had sounded fun to her until they climbed in the basket and she saw how fragile the basket was as they started to rise.

"I'm not sure about this," she said.

"What aren't you sure about?" he asked.

"That we won't fall," she said.

"It'd be bad for business if I let you fall," the pilot said with a laugh.

Jay moved to stand behind her, wrapping his arms around her body. He leaned down close to her ear and said, "I've got you and you know I won't let anything happen to you."

She relaxed against him. She might not be sure whether he would stay with her forever, but she knew that he'd protect her with his life. It was still and quiet as they rose up from the valley floor. The sun was just starting to peek over the mountains below. They floated higher and she was almost afraid to speak; the only sound was the occasional hiss of the fire used to inflate the balloon.

"Do you know which vineyard is Paulo's?" Jay asked.

"I don't," she admitted. "I haven't been to visit him and Frida because I'm always so busy at the bakery."

"You work too hard," he said.

"I'm a small-business owner," she said. "If I don't do it, no one else will."

"I don't like that you have to work so hard," he said. "You don't have enough time for yourself."

"That's just the way my life is. You work hard, too," she pointed out.

"But that's different."

"Why? Because you're a man?" she asked.

The pilot chuckled at her tone and Jay tightened his arms around her. "I know better than to answer that question. I just wish that I could pamper you a little bit."

She did like the sound of that. "That'd be nice, but I like my job. If I wasn't working at Sweet Dreams I'd be baking at home and then what would I do with all the baked goods?"

"If I were there I'd eat them," he said.

If he were there. She tried to live for the moment, but she couldn't. She had the feeling he'd already made up his mind to leave. She knew it.

"Time for your champagne brunch," the pilot said, handing them each a glass flute filled with sparkling wine.

Jay took his glass and she took hers. As she stepped out of his arms the gondola rocked a bit, making her reach for him to steady herself. He let her and then arched one eyebrow at her. "What are you doing?"

"I wanted to have a toast," she said.

"Okay," he said.

"To the best ten days we've ever had together," she said at last.

He clinked his glass against hers and took a sip and she did the same. They drank their champagne quickly and Jay pulled her back into his arms. When the pilot told them to look up and smile they did. He handed them a photo a few minutes later; they looked happy, she thought. They looked like a couple who were planning a life together.

Not like two people who could barely manage two

weeks together. She felt sad and didn't enjoy the rest of the ride, but she stayed where she was with Jay's arms around her. She wanted to be able to remember this day and have a nice memory of it.

When they landed, Jay helped her out of the basket and they bought a picture frame from the souvenir shop before getting on his bike and heading back to Oceanside. She was tired and rested her head against his shoulders. She wished there was some way to see into the future, but there wasn't. And when he dropped her off at her house and gave her a quick kiss goodbye, she made herself watch him leave.

She knew he was coming back later to pick her up for their date, but she still wanted to watch him go. Maybe she'd build up an immunity to him leaving so when he finally left for good she wouldn't let him take all of her soul with him.

JAY SENT LUCIEN a text that he was bringing Alysse and the other man had decided he'd bring his girlfriend, too. Drinks turned into dinner and a long, lovely evening. Lucien's girlfriend, India, was tall, almost six feet, and of African descent. She had beautiful skin, close-cut curly hair and the most exotic-looking eyes that Alysse had ever seen.

She felt like a pale plain Jane next to India. It would have been easy to fade into the background except that India wasn't the type of woman who left anyone out. She worked in the fashion industry as a hand model. Honestly, why this woman's face wasn't in front of the camera was beyond Alysse.

Lucien was more guarded, but still, he was relaxed

and he smiled easily whenever India said something that amused him. They were openly affectionate with each other and, in an instant, Alysse realized what she wanted her relationship with Jay to be like. This was how a couple should be, she thought.

Even Jay was a bit more at ease. She'd never say he was relaxed, but instead of being completely silent, he and Lucien had a steady conversation going the entire time they were eating dinner. Occasionally he'd glance over at her.

"How long have you two been together?" India asked after they were seated at a nightclub and the men went to get them drinks.

"It's complicated…we were married for a week and then divorced and now we've been together ten days."

India laughed, a big booming sound that made heads turn. "That *is* complicated. So what's your story? Why are you with Jay?"

No one had ever talked to Alysse that way. "I don't know. He's so different from everyone else in my life and I can't help being attracted to him."

"He is a hottie," India agreed. "But then so is my Lucien."

"You two seem like an interesting couple," Alysse said. Lucien was tall and bald and had a jagged scar running down his forearm. He wore expensive clothing but he still looked rough, as though he'd put a fresh coat of paint over his dents and scratches but she could still see them.

"That's an understatement," India said. "Like you, it was attraction that brought us together first. Then we got to know one another. Underneath all that hotness is a solid man."

"What do you mean by that?"

"Lucien is always there when I need him. I don't even have to say it sometimes and he just shows up," India said. "You know?"

"Yeah, I guess I know what you mean," Alysse said, but she wasn't sure. Jay was still figuring out where he wanted to be.

"You don't," India said, but not unkindly. "Why did you two divorce?"

"He left me," she said. "I know you probably think I'm crazy for trying this again."

"I don't judge another person's heart," India said. "When Lucien and I have our problems, they are monsters and we fight like it's the end of the world, but he's still the man I dream about and I don't think anyone else will do."

"I don't want it to be that way for me," Alysse admitted. "I'm afraid to fall for Jay until he knows what's going on with him. I just want something nice and normal like what you and Lucien have."

"Nothing is nice and normal in love. It's bold and passionate," India said. "Can I give you some advice?"

"Sure," Alysse said.

"Holding back is probably not going to bring you the results you want. Yes, it's safer to try to wait until he knows what he wants but if you aren't being honest with yourself and with him, he's never going to want you. You can't wait for him to be ready for you, you might not still be together if you don't go for it now," India said.

Her words echoed in Alysse's lonely heart. If Jay was her great romance…if they were truly meant to be together, then holding herself back and trying not to love him, well, that wasn't going to help her.

She watched Jay weaving his way through the crowd and she saw his face with its familiar lines of tension and stress. But then he smiled when their gazes met and she understood that she could give him something that he'd never had before. Jay had admitted to being abandoned by his mother. Would the only way he was going to feel safe enough to stay with Alysse be if he felt that she would never leave him?

Her hands literally started sweating and she felt a wave of fear wash over her as her stomach dropped. She didn't know if she could take a huge step like this. She was going to have to put Jay in front of her own dreams of family and happiness and what if this didn't work out? Could she ever trust a man again?

Jay handed her drink to her as Lucien put his and India's drinks on the table.

"Come on, baby. Let's dance," Lucien said, and India slid out of the booth to follow him.

Alysse took a sip of her drink, waiting for Jay to do the same but he was just staring at her.

"Aly, dance with me?" he asked.

"Yes," she said. It seemed as if he was reaching out to her in a way he hadn't before. Today had marked a turning point for both of them. They'd started to let their own guard down. For the first time since she'd woken up alone all those years ago, Alysse felt a tingling near her heart.

"Thank you for today," he said.

"What did I do?" she asked. Not sure where he was headed with this.

"You made me realize how good life can be when you share it with the right woman."

She blushed, knowing her happiness was broadcast on her face.

"You're welcome."

THE LAST OF HIS UNEASINESS from Afghanistan faded away as he pulled Alysse into his arms on the dance floor. The music was upbeat and many couples danced with distance between them, but Jay didn't pay any attention to them. He needed to hold Alysse and to feel that she was still his.

He put his hands on her waist as they swayed together to the music. Lucien had complimented him on being lucky enough to have a woman like Alysse in his life and Jay had been quiet. He had never believed in luck.

No unseen force had ever been looking out for him. He'd managed to get to where he was today by determination and sheer force of will. And as he held this sweet, sexy woman in his arms, he knew that he had to change. It was why he'd thanked her and he could see by her reaction that he'd said the right thing. He had to let her in. Had to enjoy these moments together because he didn't know how long they would last.

He had been searching for some kind of sign. He shook his head and leaned down to kiss her as she glanced up at him. He didn't care that they were in the middle of a crowded dance floor, he only knew that he needed her. He was tired of playing silly games that neither of them could win.

"What was that for?" she asked, leaning up on her tiptoes to speak into his ear.

"Because you make me happy," he said. "No one else ever has."

She hugged him close. "Good. I'm glad."

She pulled back as the rhythm of the music changed and they danced close together, bodies bumping and grinding until Jay thought he was going to explode. He enjoyed the teasing anticipation and could tell that Alysse did as well, because she kept brushing her hands intimately over him.

When it got close to midnight, they said goodbye to Lucien and India and walked hand in hand back to her car. He unlocked her door and then pulled her into his arms, kissing her slowly and seductively.

She held on to him as he tipped her head back and languidly moved his mouth over hers. It was intoxicating. He couldn't get enough of her.

The honking horn of someone driving by pulled them apart; for the first time that he could remember, Jay hadn't been aware of his surroundings.

"Take me home," she said.

He nodded and opened her door for her and helped her get seated. By the time he walked around to the driver's side she had her head tipped back against the seat rest and was staring at him with dreamy eyes.

"You okay?" he asked in his kindest voice.

"Yes. Everything felt right tonight, didn't it?"

He reached over and took her hand, kissing it then putting it on his thigh before he started the car. "Everything was very good tonight."

Her fingers stroked up and down his leg, teasingly dipping to brush against his cock, which was becoming more and more hard with each of her touches.

"India said that I can't hide…"

"What are you hiding from?" he asked, realizing that the fun evening with relaxed company had loosened her tongue.

"You," she admitted. "I don't want to love you again."

His heart stopped. He'd been hoping that she would love him again. That he'd be able to have that sweet attention from her and find somehow that he was worthy of it.

That was what he'd been searching for, he now understood. There was a reason why she didn't want to love him and that was that he'd ruined that emotion for her a long time ago.

No amount of pretending could change his life or rectify the past. He had to face the fact that he needed to leave. That the only solution was to walk away from her.

He glanced over to find her sleepily watching him and he knew that he didn't want to hurt her again. But a part of him was just selfish enough to want to stay. Why should he worry about Alysse and put her needs above his? He didn't know why. He only knew that he did.

She twined their fingers together and leaned her head against his shoulder. They exited the vehicle and she led him to the front door of her cute bungalow. Her perfect normal life and he wasn't strong enough to turn away.

12

Alysse didn't want to let go of Jay. The night had come alive for her. She'd let her emotions run instead of bottling them up, and she felt almost high from them. God, why hadn't she realized before how good this felt?

As soon as they were in her house she went to him. She'd missed him last night and she was finally able to really admit it. She'd been worried he was going to see her to the door and then leave again.

Having him inside with her made her bold. She knew he was nearing the deadline to decide what he was doing and where he was going and she wanted to make damned sure he knew she wanted him to stay.

"Dance with me here."

"Um, are you sure?" he asked.

She could tell he wanted to retreat and go back to his safe hotel room, but she wasn't going to let him. If Jay left her this time it wasn't going to be without knowing every detail of what he would be missing for the rest of his life.

"Yes. I really liked the way you felt next to me," she

said, leading him into her living room. She hit the light switch and the two side-table lamps came on.

The room was cast in a soft intimate glow and Jay stood in the center. He looked sexy and serious as he waited for her. She smiled at him, a soft sensual expression that he answered.

She went to the iPod dock that she kept in her living room hooked up to speakers. She had always liked music and hadn't scrimped on the sound system when she'd purchased it. Now she was glad because she wanted every detail of this night to be perfect. It was the only way she was going to be able to convince him to stay.

She flipped through her playlists and found what she was looking for. The song she wanted to dance with him to had been playing in the lounge the first night they'd gone for a drink in Vegas. She only listened to it when she was feeling nostalgic and a bit melancholy, but she wanted that to change. She wanted to reclaim the song as she felt she'd reclaimed the man.

As Michael Bublé crooned the tune "For Once In My Life," she moved slowly toward Jay.

"It's our song," he said.

"Yes," she agreed. "I didn't think you would remember."

"I remember every detail of that week with you. I can't have a steak without remembering eating a bite off the end of your fork. Or taste a strawberry without remembering the way you crushed them on your breast and invited me to lick them off."

She shivered remembering how free she'd felt with him back then because she'd trusted him completely.

"I haven't been that daring in a long time," she admitted.

"That's my fault," he said.

He held his hand out to her and met her halfway, pulling her into his arms and swaying gently with the song. His hands moved up and down her back.

"Do you remember our wedding?" she asked.

"I do," he admitted. "You wore the simplest white sheath dress that had a deep V in the front like this."

He drew his finger along her collarbone and then pulled the fabric of her neckline down until it was between her breasts.

"The slopes of your breasts were visible and as soon as you walked into the chapel it was all I could look at."

"Really?"

"Yes. I wanted to do this," he said, lowering his head and dropping very soft kisses against the globes of her breasts. "But then I looked up at your neck and saw the line of your jaw and that mouth of yours. You have the most luscious mouth. All I can think about when we are together is kissing you."

"Then do it," she said.

He leaned in and rubbed his lips over hers. She sighed and felt the magic of the evening deepening for her.

"What do you remember? First impressions of me in the chapel?" he asked.

"When I stepped inside and saw you waiting for me I couldn't breathe. You looked so handsome in your dress uniform. I didn't realize how good-looking you were until that moment. You stood so straight and at attention and then our eyes met and I felt a thrill all the way to my toes. I thought you were mine."

"I was."

But then he'd left. And she'd convinced herself that a feeling that strong could have been one-sided.

She wrapped her arms around his lean waist and rested her head on his chest. He put one hand on the back of her head and rubbed his palm over her back. Keeping her close. The song played on and they swayed together to the music.

It was a quick song, and when it ended she flushed as Marvin Gaye's "Let's Get It On" was the next song to start playing.

He chuckled. "We never danced to this one before."

"I know. It's not exactly the subtlety I was trying for."

"Hell, this is my kind of song," he said. Putting his hands on her hips and grinding against her. She did the same, moving her hands up and down his chest slowly loosing buttons until his shirt was open and she could touch his hard muscles.

"I love your chest," she said, pushing his shirt off his shoulders. His shoulders were broad and strong, his skin warm to her touch.

He let her have her way with him, caressing him however she wanted. She traced his spine and then let her fingers dip into his pants to caress the dusting of hair at the small of his back. He groaned. She slowly came around to his front trailing her fingers along that edge between bare flesh and cloth. Then she used her grip on his waistband to draw him closer to her. She tipped her head back and put her free hand around his neck and drew his head down to hers.

"I love the feel of your hands on my body. No one has ever touched me the way you do, Aly."

"Good," she said. She wanted to brand him all over so that he'd never forget her or these nights they'd spent together. He'd marked her deep in her soul a long time ago and she was just realizing that was why no other man could satisfy her the way he did.

His breath brushed over her lips first and then she took his mouth. His hands went to her back, drawing her as close as possible to his body until they were intimately pressed together. Their kisses were long and languid as they swayed to the music, not even noticing when it stopped playing.

The hand at her waist slowly gathered the fabric of her skirt and drew it up the back of her legs until she felt one of his big warm hands on her buttocks. She gyrated against him and felt him cupping her and pulling her closer to his rock-hard erection. She moaned as the tip of his cock hit her in just the right place.

She used the hand she had at his waistband to unbutton his pants, but didn't undo the zipper at first. Just teased him by resting a hand there. She felt his cock jump against her fingers as she stroked him before she lowered the zipper enough to slide her hand into the front of his pants.

He was so incredibly hard. She stroked the tip of his cock before letting her fingers drift lower to ride along the side of his shaft. She wished this moment with Jay would never end. She felt so alive, yet so in control.

With both hands she pushed his pants and boxers to the floor and he stepped out of them.

He was completely naked. She moved back to admire Jay. She understood that passion was the key to being truly free. Wasn't that what she'd discovered sitting in the club? And she felt passion as she looked at her man with his muscled chest and the light dusting of hair leading to his manhood, which stood proud and erect because of her.

She felt a surge of love and lust for him. She'd been completely crazy if she'd ever thought it could be just sex between her and Jay and then she'd move on. He was the only man she'd been unable to banish from her thoughts and dreams.

She walked over to him and he simply stood there. She took his hand and led him to the leather couch a few feet away. She pushed him back on the couch and he sank down with all the masculine grace she'd come to expect from him.

She went to kneel next to him on the couch but he stopped her. "Take your panties off."

Her pulse raced and she felt her pussy moisten at his words. Slowly, she lifted the hem of her dress to reveal first her thighs and then the edge of her panties. As she reached underneath, she slowly drew the tiny lace underwear down her legs.

She stood still, with her skirt held in one hand and turned so that she gave him a full view and bent low to pick up the scrap of cloth. She glanced over her shoulder at him and saw that he was staring at her butt. She tossed her panties on the ground at his feet and then moved back to his side.

He put his hands underneath her skirt, running his fingernails up and down the length of her thighs until she was panting in his grasp. He teased her by coming close to her intimate flesh but never touching it. She reached for his cock, caressing his entire shaft and then lowering her head to lick the tip of it before taking him into her mouth.

His hips jerked from the couch as she cupped him and continued to work his shaft with her mouth. He moved her body around until he could reach her clit with his fingers. She felt him separating her inner lips and then the light brush of his finger against her throbbing core. Moisture pooled between her legs and she felt his forefinger slip lower until he entered her. She moaned against his cock as he excited her, pushing her to the brink.

She sucked more strongly on his cock and tasted a salty drop of him and she swallowed it. But then he pulled her away.

"I don't want it to be like this when I come," he said, his voice rough and low. His skin was flushed and she was aroused to the point where she didn't know anything except desire.

"Come inside me, Jay. I feel so empty without you."

"Are you ready for me?" he asked, touching her between her legs again. All she could do was nod frantically, waiting for him to finish what they'd started.

"That's not ready enough," he said. "Unzip your dress."

She reached for the side zipper and undid it. The fabric gaped away from her body but still covered her.

She ignored it as she tried to climb on his lap, needing his cock inside her now.

He stopped her with his hands on her waist. "Take your dress off."

"Jay, we don't need to draw this out. I want you inside me now."

"No," he told her, his tone serious. "I want to take my time with you tonight, Aly. Do what I said."

His firm voice excited her that much more and she frantically ripped at her own clothing trying to get the dress off. Her arms got tangled in it and Jay helped her free herself. She was naked except for the lacy demi-bra she wore.

"Straddle me."

She did as he ordered, climbing on his lap. He lowered his head and kissed the full globes of her breasts, which were bared by the demi-bra. His hands slid down her back to her buttocks and he drew her forward so that she rode the edge of his cock.

Her grip on his shoulders tightened and she tried to shift around to bring the top of his erection to her opening and get him inside her, but he wasn't going to be rushed.

One of his hands slid up her back and unfastened her bra. The straps loosened and he used his teeth to pull the fabric away from her breasts. She felt the tip of his tongue on her areole, stroking it until her nipple tightened. Then she felt the warmth of his mouth on her nipple as he sucked on it.

She reached between them and took his cock in her hand and positioned him exactly where she needed him. She thrust herself onto his cock, driving him deep to the heart of her. She rocked her hips back and forth while he continued to suckle her.

He tore his mouth from her breast and looked up at her through half-closed eyes. His hands came to her hips and he began to thrust harder and quicker. She lost control of their embrace as he tilted her head toward his and slipped his tongue teasingly into her mouth as he came inside her.

She shuddered as her own orgasm overtook her. She kept on riding him to prolong her orgasm and then collapsed against him. She relaxed, tracing the lines of his pectorals and drawing a heart over it. She closed her eyes trying not to let her emotions get the better of her, but she knew the truth as soon as he looked her in the eye.

She loved him.

She wanted to say it but knew better than to say anything. She was still too afraid to trust herself or him.

India's words came back to haunt her. Where was the passion that she was using to embrace life? How was Jay ever going to know that she needed him to stay until she told him?

"Jay?"

"Shh…don't talk," he said. He lifted her, stood and walked down the short hall to her bedroom. He set her on her feet in the doorway of the bathroom, and she watched as he went to her garden tub and slowly turned on the taps.

"But I think there is something I need to say."

"I'm sure there is, but there is something magical going on between us right now and I don't want it to end. I want this one night, Aly. Is that okay?" he asked.

She nodded. She wanted it, too. She wanted to pretend that this was a world she'd never been in before. That all of her dreams were coming true with this man. She gathered candles from under the sink as he filled the tub with water and her rose-scented bubble bath. She lit the candles and set them on the edge of the tub.

Jay lifted her into water that was the perfect temperature and then climbed into the tub and sat down behind her. She lowered herself gently into the water and settled back against him. His arms were around her and she rested her head once again on his chest. She felt his big arms around her and knew that falling in love with Jay hadn't made any of her problems disappear. He was still a man at a crossroads, and who knew what path he was going to choose? But for tonight she didn't regret falling for him.

He had mended her broken heart and given her back some of the romantic dreams he'd stolen from her. He slowly bathed her and she felt tears sting the backs of her eyes as he treated her so tenderly. Jay was a rough man through the life he'd lived but tonight with her he was as gentle as any man could be and he'd found his way right back into her heart.

JAY DIDN'T ALLOW HIMSELF to think beyond this night. He'd had a few experiences in his life that he kept protected in his memory. Most of them involved this woman and he didn't want anything—not even himself—to mar this night.

She was special to him. More so than he'd realized when he'd come back to San Diego looking for answers. Now he had those answers and he knew without a shadow of a doubt that Alysse was the only woman in the world that he wanted to spend the rest of his life with.

And if life were as easy as television shows and Hollywood movies made it seem, that would be all it would take for them to commit themselves and spend the rest of their days together. But this wasn't a TV show or movie and he knew that despite his good intentions he'd never be the man that Alysse needed.

She knew it, he suspected, but because they'd spent so much time with each other she was probably thinking, as he was, that there was some way to make the magic last for them. But the truth was there was no elixir that would cure him of his past. No potion that would make his shattered soul whole and no real chance that he'd be able to live in this cute little suburban house with Alysse for the rest of his days.

The water was starting to cool, so he stood up and climbed from the tub, drying himself off quickly before helping Alysse. He dried her carefully from head to toe, lingering over her entire body because he'd never have enough of touching her. He dreamed of her skin and the softness of it when they were apart.

"Why are you treating me like I'm made of glass?" she asked.

He wasn't sure what to say. Didn't know what was the right or wrong thing and looking into her amazing blue eyes he settled for the truth. "To me you are the most precious thing."

She swallowed hard and then threw herself into his arms and he held her close, breathing in the floral scent of her skin. He closed his eyes and tried to figure out a way he could keep Alysse without shattering her dreams for the future.

But he'd seen the way she'd looked at Lucien and India tonight. He knew she wanted a relationship like that and he couldn't give that to her. He just wasn't that kind of man.

He found her nightshirt on the hook behind the bathroom door and put it on her before leading her to her bed. Once they were both settled beneath the covers and she was nestled close against his side, cuddled up on his chest, he felt her relax. She put her hand over his chest and kissed him right there over his heart.

"Thank you," she said.

"For?" he asked. He didn't think he'd done anything for her that she didn't deserve. Alysse had given him gifts that he'd just taken blindly before he recognized how much she meant to him.

"The best day," she said. "I have spent the entire day with you and it wasn't at all what I expected."

"It wasn't?"

"No. You were everything I ever dreamed you would be. I thought this morning that we were headed for a breakup tonight but the day turned around, didn't it?"

Her words were like a dagger to him. He couldn't give her days like this. Today had almost been the end of him because he'd felt too much. Men who had this much to lose never made it back.

"Today was nice," he said. "But it wasn't anything too special."

"It was to me. No one—not even my dad—has ever given me a day like this. You made me feel like a princess and not the little-girl kind."

"What kind then?" he asked her.

"Like a woman who can have it all. You were my white knight today. It was perfect."

She was killing him. She was unable to contain her excitement, and he knew that was because she'd started caring for him again.

And he didn't want to—hell, he wasn't going to let her down again. So if that meant that he had to stay here with her for the rest of his life then he'd do it. He didn't know how he'd do it but he'd figure it out.

For that smile he'd move the world.

"Why are you watching me like that?"

"Like what?" he asked.

"Kind of sad and sort of…scared almost," she said.

"Don't worry about it," he said. "And I don't know about being any knight. My armor is tarnished. Can't you see that? There is nothing hero-like about me at all."

She gently kissed him on the chest. "Everything about you is heroic."

He knew she was wrong. Still, he stayed where he was and held her as she drifted off to sleep. He was surrounded by Alysse and it was the closest thing to heaven that he knew he'd ever experience in this life or the next one.

Her breath stirred the hair on his chest and, as her sleep deepened, she snored softly and even that tiny imperfection just made him love her more. He held her as close as he dared so he wouldn't disturb her, and he felt the way he had back in that Vegas hotel room—afraid of her and for her. Afraid to be the man she clearly needed him to be because he wasn't sure he really had it in him.

He'd never in his life wanted anything more than he wanted to keep Alysse with him. But he knew just as surely as the desire formed inside him that he would hurt her, and he couldn't live with himself if he did that.

He tried different scenarios in his head, trying to figure out how he was going to be able to keep her safe and keep her in his arms at the same time, but there wasn't one that would keep her happy.

As the first fingers of dawn crept across the room he loosened himself from her hold and slid out of her bed. He found his clothing in the living room and dressed quickly, getting a hard-on from remembering the sexy dance they'd shared here last night.

And from the memories of their wedding night. He picked up his leather jacket, which she'd kept from the morning balloon ride, and the picture of the two of them that the pilot had taken fell out. He stooped to pick it up and then stood staring at them. He looked too hard for her.

She deserved that white knight she'd always wanted. A man who could love her and not worry about her leaving. A man she didn't have to worry would leave her. And if he didn't walk out this door today, Jay knew there was always a chance that he'd be taken from her life by war.

He had no other training and even if he worked with Lucien there was no guarantee that he'd be back home with Alysse every night. He'd promised her mother that if he couldn't ensure Alysse would be happy with him, he'd get out of her life and never come back.

At the time he'd hoped to find a way to stay with her but now it seemed there wasn't a way. And he knew exactly what he needed to do. But it was harder this time.

Last time it had only been lust between them and this time he had started caring for her, and that made each step he took heavy and hard.

He walked to the door that overlooked her backyard and remembered standing there with her at the pond and feeling maybe a little hope for the future. But he'd been kidding himself since the moment he'd returned here.

He was truly a loner and he only knew how to be comfortable in his own skin when he was on a mission in the field with his scout next to him. He liked the world through the view of his scope. It was safer that way. He could control everything when he was looking through the sight.

He knew that his life would always be gray after this, but it was better than attempting to be someone he wasn't and failing miserably. Better than trying to make things work with Alysse and breaking her heart again, only worse because he'd seen the real woman this time, not the girl on vacation. He slowly turned and looked around her living room before walking through it toward the door.

He had hoped to find answers here and he guessed that he had. He'd hoped that maybe this time he could make their ending different. He knew he was the one who was leaving, but he also knew it was just a matter of time before Alysse knew that he couldn't be the man she wanted him to be.

He'd got to the foyer when he heard the creak of the

bedsprings and knew he could either run out the front door as he had before or wait and confront her. And he wished he were a stronger man, but he reached for the front door, undoing the deadbolt and turning the handle as quietly as he could.

"Running again?"

13

ALYSSE HAD GOTTEN USED TO sleeping with Jay and sleeping lightly enough that when he got out of bed he'd waken her. She'd thought at first that maybe he was just getting a drink of water as he sometimes did, but then, as the time lengthened, she knew he was leaving.

She'd lain there in her bed debating confronting him and suddenly it seemed so cowardly for her to be lying there while he was sneaking out. So she'd gone to confront him and found him standing at the front door with his hand on the handle and her heart broke.

He wasn't leaving for work or an early meeting, he was leaving for good and they both knew it.

"I'm sorry," he said.

"Don't be. Just tell me why," she said.

"I think I'm going back into the Corps," he said.

As if that would explain everything and make this all okay somehow. "Really? Why did you stay last night then? What was that all about?"

She was beyond upset and well into angry now and she wasn't about to take this sitting down. He was leaving her twice. This was her worst nightmare and here it was coming true. Dammit, she had been planning to be the stronger one this time, why wasn't she?

"Can we not do this?" he asked. There was something in his expression that she couldn't read and that bothered her more than she wanted to admit.

"No, we're doing this," she said. "The last time I just let you walk out on me. Well, to be honest, I didn't hear you leave, but even if I had I would have lain there and let you go without a fight. But I'm not willing to do that this time."

He sighed. It was a heavy one as he finally came toward her. He stopped when there was six inches between them but it might as well have been a gap as big as the Grand Canyon. He was eons away from her and there was nothing she was going to say that would bring him back.

But last night she'd admitted she loved him. Last night he'd been the tender man she'd always dreamed of finding and she wasn't going to let him throw that all aside. She just didn't know what she could do to make him stay.

"Leaving isn't easy for me," he said. "But I can't stay. I saw your face last night when we were in the club with Lucien and India. I know that you hope that someday we will be that kind of a couple. But I can't be like that. I'm always going to be more inward and less social."

She shook her head. "I never asked you to change."

"I know that. You won't do it either. But I'd have to watch you wither and grow disappointed in me because I'm not the man you need me to be."

She wondered if that were true. But then she realized

that even if there were shards of honesty in that statement, the reason he was leaving was more complex. "I don't believe that's why you're sneaking out of here, Jay Michener. You're leaving because you're afraid you will like it here. That you'll start enjoying the life that we could have together. And you're afraid. Afraid to change and let yourself really feel something."

"And you're afraid to just let me go," he said. "As much as I enjoy being alone, you're afraid of that very thing. You surround yourself every hour of the day with family and friends, and you have to ask yourself why? What is it you are so afraid of?"

"I don't see that," she said. "You're grasping at straws because if you aren't looking at a target through the safety of your scope then you don't let yourself relax. You aren't living life. You are observing it."

He looked taken aback. And she felt a twinge of guilt at what she'd said, but there was no hiding from this. He was leaving and there was nothing she could say that would make him stay.

"You may be right," he said, a sudden quietness in him and in his voice. "But I don't think I can change. I'm sorry, Aly. I wanted a different ending for us. But I think I was fooling myself into believing I was a different sort of man."

She closed the gap between them and reached out to touch his beard-stubbled jaw. "You don't have to be a different man, you just have to be the man you are inside here."

She drew her hand down his chest and tapped lightly over his heart. She knew that as tough as he was on the outside, Jay was soft inside. And that was why he fought so hard not to let anyone in, even her.

She hugged him because she was going to miss him more than he could ever know. His arms stayed by his sides and she felt her heart break wide open. It wasn't his fault that he couldn't love her and there was nothing she could have done to make herself not love him. She'd thought she could bring her warrior in from battle and show him the beauty of being a part of her community, but he wasn't ready to give up fighting and she doubted he ever would be.

"Goodbye."

He stepped back and looked at her and she easily read the anguish in his eyes.

"I didn't mean to hurt you again," he said.

It bothered her more than she wanted to admit that he knew that he'd hurt her but somehow hadn't been able to see that she loved him.

"Is that really your only regret?" she asked.

"No, but we don't have time for me to list them all," he said, turning and walking toward the door.

"Coward," she said. "There's no pride in walking away now. You are just proving that you aren't all you can be."

"That's the army slogan," he said.

"I don't care whose it is. You pride yourself on being a soldier, a warrior, but you don't have the guts to stay and fight for something you said you wanted. Or have you changed your mind?"

JAY HADN'T EXPECTED Alysse to let him just walk out the door but he didn't expect this amount of anger. Why not? Was he that insensitive that he'd missed something important here? He knew that she'd been hoping—hell, he knew nothing. She was still a big mystery to him and it seemed as if she always would be.

"I'm not a coward. I'm doing this for you," he said.

"For me?" she asked, the incredulity in her voice enough to make him take a step back toward her.

"Yes, for you. Do you think I like knowing that even though you are with me I'm not the man you want? Do you think I like seeing disappointment in your eyes?"

"No. I never meant for you to feel that way," she said. "I can work on that."

She could try, but it wouldn't change the fact that he was always going to be who he was inside and she couldn't change that or accept it. He needed to make this break and never come back here again. He needed to walk away and keep Alysse tucked safely into his memories.

"You can't. We've been trying to build something out of nothing here. That's my fault. I'm sorry this didn't work out better."

"Sure," she said. "I guess it doesn't matter if I love you."

His heart stopped beating for a second. No one in his adult life had uttered those words to him and he wanted to hold them close and hold her close. Was there a way he could make this work? Could he be the man she needed him to be?

He'd thought about the job with Lucien but to be honest he was afraid to risk it and find that he couldn't stomach the job. He was a mess and had not been in the right place to start up his relationship with Alysse again. He'd made a mistake but he couldn't bring himself to say those words out loud.

She watched him carefully, he suspected she was looking for some kind of sign that he'd figure out how to work this through, but he was tired of keeping them both on this roller coaster. He just wasn't the right kind of man for the long haul. It didn't matter that he felt like he should want something more. He was too afraid to go after what it was he wanted. He deserved the moniker of coward that she'd given him.

"Your love is a gift I will treasure forever," he said.

She shook her head. "No, you won't. You'll shove it deep down inside you so you don't have to deal with it. I'm just sorry that I couldn't show you that life is more than your missions."

But she had. And that was the part that scared him. He stalked back over to her, putting his hands on her shoulders. "Of course I saw that. Do you think I don't crave this idyllic life with every fiber of my being?"

"Then why are you leaving?"

"Because I know how quickly this can be taken away. You know who makes the biggest sacrifices in Afghanistan?"

She shook her head.

"Those with the most to lose. Those with spouses and kids back home. It's never the loners. And I've been shown a lot of karma in this life. Who's to say if I try to make this work that we will have a lifetime together?"

"No one can guarantee that. No one," she said.

She lifted her hand toward him, brushing her fingers over his brow. Then down the side of his face.

"I'm willing to take the chance, Jay."

He knew he could make this easy on himself. Just open his arms and draw her into them. Pretend for her sake that everything would be okay. But he couldn't do it. He didn't want to cause her more pain by staying. And a part of him was sure he would. Or worse—he'd stay and she'd realize that the love she thought she had for him wasn't real. He didn't want to leave her. Hell, he wasn't an idiot. It was just that he knew that by going now he'd save them a much bigger heartbreak later.

"I'm not willing to."

Her arms dropped to her sides. She stared into his eyes with that electric-blue gaze of hers and he felt that she was peering deep into his soul. He hoped that she didn't really see into that bottomless well because he'd seen too much in this lifetime. Things he never wanted her to know about. She sighed and then nodded.

"Okay, then."

She walked around him to the front door and opened it. The sun was coming up over the horizon and the neighbors were out walking their dogs and getting ready for work. A perfect normal morning and yet he felt shell-shocked. As if he'd just withstood a barrage of enemy fire.

He wanted to pat down his body and look for holes but he knew exactly where the pain was coming from. He crossed the small hallway of her house and when he got to the threshold he knew that if he took one more step he'd never be welcomed back here again.

He was afraid of that step and hesitated. If he thought there was a way that he could have her and keep her for the rest of his life he wouldn't do this but he couldn't see it.

"Have a good life, Jay," she said. "I hope you find some peace."

He nodded, and as soon as he was outside on her front porch he heard the door close behind him with a finality that echoed down to his boots.

THREE DAYS LATER Jay went to the enlistment office on base to sign his papers, but the entire time his heart felt heavy and Alysse's words kept ringing in his ears. Was he afraid to change?

The weather didn't seem to notice his mood and stayed sunny and temperate as if to shame him with his own black thoughts. He missed Alysse more than he'd thought he would. He hadn't had a single night's sleep since he'd left her because he kept waking up to search for her.

Hell, he knew that was partly why he was right back here. This was the one place in the world that he trusted. Then he admitted that wasn't true anymore. He trusted himself when he was with Alysse and he should never have left her.

In fact, he loved her. He'd been in love with her for the last four years. He'd struggled to keep his distance from her only because he'd never felt good enough for her. He still wasn't sure that he was good enough for her, but the way she'd fought with him had told him that he was the man she wanted.

But leaving the way he had… Trying to sneak out on her again. He hoped he hadn't killed her love for him. It was going to be impossible to win her back.

He knew he could do it because she loved him, but he had to plan it. And do a better job than he had when he'd called her to the beach at the Hotel Del Coronado.

The first thing he did was to sign his separation papers for the Marines. Then he left Pendleton and headed toward the offices of Company B. Someone who worked as hard as Alysse deserved a man—a husband who worked just as hard, if not harder.

He pulled into the parking lot and felt a moment of sheer terror as he realized he'd left the only home he'd had since turning eighteen. To be honest, he hadn't had a home since his mother had left when he was eight. His dad had never been good with people, a trait Jay guessed had been passed on to him. But he was damned sure he was going to be good with Alysse. And he'd do everything in his power to make sure they were never apart again.

"You okay, Jay?" Lucien asked, coming out of the offices of Company B and standing next to Jay on his bike.

"No. I'm not. I just left the Corps." Oh, man. He was unsure of this decision as soon as he said the words out loud, but then he thought of going home to Alysse every night and some of the tension eased.

"Is that a good thing or a bad thing?" Lucien asked.

"It's going to be a very good thing if I can convince you to give me a job," Jay said.

"It's yours, buddy. I wanted you to work with me from the beginning," Lucien said. "Come inside and we can get the contract drawn up and have you sign it."

Jay got off his bike and followed Lucien inside.

"So what made you decide it was time to go private-sector?" Lucien asked him.

"Alysse," Jay said. He wasn't ever going to be comfortable talking about his personal life, but in this instance he didn't mind sharing it with Lucien. "I want to marry her again and do everything right this time."

"Good for you. Got an idea of how to propose?"

"No," Jay said. "And I screwed up so I have to win her back."

"Can I help?" Lucien asked.

"Be my best man?"

"I will."

It took forty-five minutes to get the contract drawn up and for Jay to sign all the paperwork that was needed. When he left the Company B offices he was an official employee.

Next on his list was a call to Toby. He needed Alysse's family on his side if he had any chance of pulling off his plan. He knew he'd never be able to trick her to the beach twice, and it was very important to him that he have all the details right this time. He wanted her to know how much she meant to him.

"Hello, this is Dresden."

"Toby? This is Jay Michener."

There was silence on the other end of the phone.

"Is Alysse all right?"

She hadn't told her family that he'd walked out on her again. He felt shocked and surprised. "Yes. I mean I think so. I messed up and I need your help to get her back."

"You need my help? What the hell did you do now?"

"Ran away again. But your sister held her own with me, which I'm sure isn't any surprise to you."

"No, it's not. Alysse knows how to give as good as she gets and she is brutally honest sometimes."

"She called me a coward," Jay admitted.

"Damn. You must have really upset her," Toby said.

"I did, but I want her back, Toby. Will you help me?" Jay asked.

There was a long silence on the other end of the phone. "If I help you it's because I love my sister and I know that she wants you in her life."

"Thank you, Toby. I want to be worthy of being in her life."

"What's your plan?" Toby asked.

He outlined what he had in mind and after a few minutes Toby agreed to assist him. "If she says no, that's it. I want you out of here for good."

"If she says no then I don't deserve her."

Jay drove back to the Hotel Del Coronado where Toby met him in the lobby. They spent the afternoon seeing to every detail and when the evening rolled around Jay got dressed in a tuxedo he'd purchased from Nordstrom's with Candi's help earlier in the day. He stared at himself hard in the mirror and he hoped that whatever Alysse had seen in him when he was in his dress blues, she'd see in him tonight.

He'd never needed another person as much as he needed her and it would be damned hard for him not to worry. He'd never depended on another person as much as he did on Alysse. And he had no idea how she'd react tonight.

14

"SWEET DREAMS BAKERY, home of the incredible red velvet dream cupcakes," Alysse spoke into the phone. It had been the longest three days of her life and now that it was almost closing time on Friday afternoon she wanted to get out of the bakery and go back to her home and hide away.

But she couldn't do that because her home was now filled with memories of Jay. She couldn't believe he'd left her once again. Worse, that she was still in love with him.

"Hello," the caller said. His voice was very familiar.

"Toby?"

"Yes. I have a dessert emergency," he said.

"An emergency?" she asked. "What kind of emergency?"

"It's Molly's parents' anniversary and I told her I'd order a replica wedding cake and deliver it to the Hotel Del Coronado tonight by six."

"Toby! I can't make a replica wedding cake in four hours," she said.

"It doesn't have to be huge or perfect or anything like that. I just need something. Maybe two layers."

"Two layers. I don't know. I have some cakes that I baked for a wedding tomorrow that I could use. If you want me to do this, you have to come down here with a photo so I can decorate it properly."

"Fine, but then I need you to deliver it because I have to get back to their party, which you are invited to, as well. Dress fancy."

Her brother was a lunatic. "I am supposed to bake a cake, haul it across town for Molly's parents and get dressed up, too?"

"Yeah. Is there a problem? Mom said she'd drop off your dress."

"Isn't that great. Anything else?"

"Nope, that's all. Will you bring Jay with you?" he asked.

She bit her lower lip. "I think he's busy tonight. So it'll just be me."

"I was wrong about him," Toby said. "I'm glad you gave him a second chance."

She wasn't. Hell, that was a lie, of course she was glad she'd given him a second chance. The last two weeks of her life more than made up for the previous four years of being alone. The only bad part was that they weren't together still.

"Don't forget the photo."

"I'm emailing it to you. Check your phone," Toby said. "Thanks, sis, you're a lifesaver."

"Yeah, right. Love ya."

"Ditto," Toby said, finishing the call.

She opened the attachment on the email from Toby

and was taken aback by the cake they'd selected. It matched the one from her wedding to Jay in Vegas. There was no way anyone in her family could know that because they hadn't attended the ceremony or even seen the cake, but it made her tear up as she looked at it.

She put two more cakes in the oven to replace the ones she was using for Molly's parents. And then got to work decorating a cake that made her heart break.

She finished the anniversary cake just as her mom came through the back door with a garment bag over one shoulder. Alysse was alone in the shop because Staci had gone to L.A. to do some more prep work for her audition on *Premiere Chef.*

"Hello, honey," her mom said, coming over and giving her a kiss.

She kissed her mom hello then shooed her hand out of the frosting bowl as Candi swiped her finger through it. "You look nice."

"Thanks. Toby is in the hot seat tonight," her mom said. "Molly just found out about this last-minute stuff with you. She was not pleased."

"He should have said that he asked me to do it a while ago," Alysse said.

"He couldn't lie to her. Would you lie to Jay?" her mom asked.

"No," she admitted. But apparently she had no problem lying to the rest of her family. She hated that she hadn't told her mom or brother that she and Jay weren't together anymore, but she was so afraid of looking stupid.

She put the cake in the van while her mom tidied up the kitchen. Then she got dressed in a pale yellow dress that she knew hadn't come from her closet. Her mom loved buying her things and, to be honest, Alysse didn't mind.

"Okay, I'm ready to go."

"You look beautiful, sweetie."

"Thanks, Mom."

When they arrived at the hotel Toby was waiting in the lobby. "I need Mom to come with me. Will you take the cake down to the beach?"

"Sure," she said. "I need a valet cart though. It's kind of big."

"No problem," Toby said. He took care of getting her a cart and helped her with the cake. Then he hugged her close.

"What was that for?"

"Just because I love you," he said.

"Love you, too, Tobe. But if you make me do this again I'm going to strangle you."

"I will never ask you to do this again," he promised.

As she followed the path to the beach she couldn't help but remember the last time she'd been here, supposedly trying to rekindle a romance and instead finding Jay waiting for her.

She wished that would happen again. But she knew that she would have better luck wishing for snow right now than Jay being here with her.

She got close and saw that the beach was set up for a dinner party with tables and chairs and in the middle a dance floor with a table nearby that she assumed was for the cake. A man stood there with his back toward her. He wore a formal jacket and there was something distinctive about the breadth of his shoulders.

She stopped abruptly and stared. "Jay?"

He turned around and a cascade of emotions ran through her. "What are you doing here?"

"Waiting for you," he said.

"Waiting for me?"

"Yes. I set this up. I wanted to do things right this time."

"I'm not entirely sure what you mean," she said.

He came to her and took her hand, leading her to the middle of the dance floor.

"I was a coward for leaving again. Even as I walked out of your door I knew I loved you, but I was so afraid to stay. Afraid I couldn't be the man you needed me to be," he said.

"What changed your mind?"

"You did," he said. "You have haunted me every single second since I left you. And I know now that I need you with me, Aly. I don't want to be alone anymore."

"But—"

"I know I haven't given you much to believe in, but I want you to know that I am changing. I quit the Corps and got a job with Company B. I confessed to your mom and Toby that I'd hurt you again."

"Oh, I hadn't mentioned that to them," she said.

"I think you did that because you knew I wasn't leaving for good this time," he said. "You took a big chance on letting me go and had to hope that I loved you enough to come back this time. And I do. I love you."

She blinked at the tears that were stinging her eyes and looked up at him. "Are you sure?"

"Yes. Very sure. Do you think I can redeem myself and be your hero again?"

"Yes," she said. "I love you, Jay Michener. If you ever try to leave me again I might have to hurt you."

"I never will," he promised. "In fact, I want to do something…will you wait here a minute?"

"Yes," she said.

While Jay strode up the path she moved the cake onto the table so it was out of harm's way. Eventually, hotel staff showed up to man the deejay booth and then her family and friends arrived. They all sat down at the tables and Jay came back to her in the center of the dance floor and got down on one knee.

"Alysse Dresden, in front of all of our family and friends, will you marry me and be the light in my life?"

"I will," she said.

Jay smiled up at her and pulled a small ring box from his pocket. Taking out the diamond ring, he slipped it on her finger and stood up to kiss her.

As he embraced her she knew she'd found something more than she'd ever expected. By taking that rush order for a redemption cupcake, she'd found the happiness she'd been missing. The man who was the other half of her soul.

* * * * *

SECOND-CHANCE SEDUCTION

BY
KATE CARLISLE

New York Times bestselling author **Kate Carlisle** was born and raised by the beach in Southern California. After more than twenty years in television production, Kate turned to writing the types of mysteries and romance novels she always loved to read. She still lives by the beach in Southern California with her husband, and when they're not taking long walks in the sand or cooking or reading or painting or taking bookbinding classes or trying to learn a new language, they're traveling the world, visiting family and friends in the strangest places. Kate loves to hear from readers. Visit her website, www.katecarlisle.com.

One

"You need a woman."

Connor MacLaren stopped reading the business agreement he was working on and glanced up. His older brother Ian stood blocking his office doorway.

"What'd you say?" Connor asked. He couldn't have heard him correctly.

"A woman," Ian repeated slowly. "You need one."

"Well, sure," Connor said agreeably. "Who doesn't? But—"

"And you're going to have to buy a new suit, maybe two," his brother Jake said as he strolled into his office.

Ian followed Jake across the wide space and they took the two visitors' chairs facing Connor.

Connor's gaze shifted from one brother to the other. "What are you two? The social police?"

Ian shook his head in disgust. "We just got off the phone with Jonas Wellstone's son, Paul. We set up a meeting with us and the old man during the festival."

Connor frowned at the two of them. "And for this you expect me to buy a new suit? You've got to be kidding."

"We're not kidding," Ian said, then stood as if that was the end of the discussion.

"Wait a minute," Connor insisted. "Let's get serious. The festival is all about beer. Drinking beer, making beer, beer-battered everything. This is not a ballet recital we're going to."

"That's not the point," Ian began.

"You're right," Connor persisted. "The point is that I've never worn a suit and tie to a beer festival and I'm not about to start now. Hell, nobody would even recognize me in a suit."

That much was true. Connor was far more identifiable in his signature look of faded jeans, ancient fisherman's sweater and rugged hiking boots than in one of those five-thousand-dollar power suits his two brothers were inclined to wear on a daily basis.

Frankly, this was why he preferred to work at MacLaren Brewery, located in the rugged back hills of Marin County, thirty miles north and a million virtual light years away from MacLaren Corporation in the heart of San Francisco's financial district. The brothers had grown up running wild through those hills. That's where they had built their first home brewery, in the barn behind their mom's house.

Over the past ten years, the company had grown into a multinational corporation with offices in ten countries. But the heart and soul of MacLaren Brewery still thrived in those hills, and Connor was in charge of it all: not just the brewery, but also the surrounding farmland, the dairy, the fishery, the vineyards and the brew pub in town.

And he wasn't about to wear a freaking business suit while he did it.

Meanwhile his older brothers, Jake, the CEO, and Ian, the marketing guru, took care of wheeling and dealing at their corporate headquarters in San Francisco. They both lived in the city and loved the fast pace. Connor, on the other hand, avoided the frantic pace of the city whenever possible. He only ventured into headquarters on days like this one because his brothers demanded his presence at the company's board meetings once a month. Even then, he wore his standard outfit of jeans, work shirt and boots. He'd be damned if he'd put on a monkey suit just to discuss stock options and expansion deals with his brothers.

Connor glanced at the two men, who were closer to him than any two people on the planet. "What made you think I would ever dress up for the Autumn Brew Festival? I'd be laughed off the convention floor."

True, the festival had become a very important venue for the fast-growing, multibillion-dollar beer production industry. In the past few years it had expanded to become the largest gathering of its type in the world. The powers that be had even changed the name of the event to reflect its importance. It was now called the International Brewery Convention, but Connor and his brothers still called it the festival because more than anything else, people showed up to have a good time.

It was a point of pride that the festival was held annually in their hometown at the Point Cairn Convention Center next to the picturesque marina and harbor. It was one of the biggest draws of the year, and the MacLaren men had done their best to ensure that it continued to be a not-to-be-missed event on the calendars of beer makers and breweries around the world.

But that still didn't mean Connor would dress up for it. What part of "good time" did his brothers not understand? The words did not equate with "suit and tie" in anybody's dictionary.

Jake gazed at him with a look of infinite patience. As the oldest of the three, he had perfected the look. "Wellstone's scheduled a dinner meeting with all of us and his entire family. And the old man likes his people to dress for dinner."

"Oh, come on," Connor said, nudging his chair back from the desk. "We're buying out their company. They're dying to get their hands on our money so the old man can retire to his walnut farm and enjoy his last days in peace and quiet, surrounded by nuts. Why would he care one way or another how we dress for dinner?"

"Because he just does," Jake explained helpfully. "His son, Paul, warned us that if Jonas doesn't get a warm and cozy, old-fashioned family feeling from the three of us at dinner, there's a good chance he could back out of the deal."

"That's a dumb way to do business."

"I agree," Jake said. "But if it means snagging this deal, I'll wear a freaking pink tuxedo."

Connor frowned. "Do you honestly think Jonas would back out of the deal over something so minor?"

Ian leaned forward and lowered his voice. "It happened to Terry Schmidt."

"Schmidt tried to buy Wellstone?" Connor peered at Jake. "Why didn't we know that?"

"Because Wellstone insists on complete confidentiality among his people," Jake said.

"I can appreciate that."

"And Paul wants it to stay that way," Jake continued, "so keep that news under your hat. He only brought up the Schmidt situation because he doesn't want another deal to fail. He wants our offer to go through, but it all depends on us putting on a good show for Jonas. Apparently the old man's a stickler."

Ian added, "Terry blew the deal by wearing khakis and a sweater to dinner with the old man."

"Khakis?" Shocked, Connor fell back in his chair. "Why, that sociopath. No wonder they kicked him to the curb."

Ian snickered, but just as quickly turned sober. "Jonas Wellstone is definitely old school. He's very conservative and very anxious that the people who take over his company have the same family values that he has always stood for."

"He should've gone into the milk shake business," Connor muttered.

"Yeah, maybe," Jake said. "But look, he's not about to

change, so let's play the game his way and get the old man firmly on our side. I want this deal to go through."

Connor's eyes narrowed in reflection. "Believe me, I want that, too." Wellstone Corporation was a perfect fit for MacLaren, he mused. Jonas Wellstone had started his brewery fifty years ago, decades before the MacLarens came along. He had been at the front of the line when lucrative markets in Asia and Micronesia first began to open up. Yes, the MacLarens had done incredibly well for themselves, but they had to admit they were still playing catchup to the older, more established companies. Last year, the brothers had set a goal of acquiring a strong foothold in those emerging territories. And here they were, less than a year later, being presented with the opportunity to purchase Wellstone.

So if all it took to attain their objective were some spiffy new clothes, the decision was an easy one. Connor would go shopping this afternoon.

"Okay, you guys win." He held up his hands in mock surrender. "I'll buy a damn suit."

"I'll go with you," Jake said, adjusting the cuffs on his tailor-made shirt. "I don't trust your taste."

The hand gesture Connor flipped his brother was crude but to the point. "This is the reason I hate coming into the big city. I get nothing but grief from you two wheeler-dealers."

Ian stood to leave. "Spare us the country bumpkin act. You're more of a cutthroat than we are."

Connor laughed and stretched his legs out. "My rustic charm conceals my rapier-sharp business skills."

Ian snorted. "Good one."

Jake ignored them both as he checked his wristwatch. "I'll have Lucinda clear my schedule for this afternoon."

"Fine," Connor said. "Let's get this over with."

Jake nodded. "I'll swing by here around three and we'll

head over to Union Square. We've only got a week to buy you a suit and get it tailored. You'll need shoes, too. And a couple of dress shirts."

"Cuff links, too," Ian added. "And a new belt. And a haircut. You look like one of Angus Campbell's goats."

"Get outta here," Connor said, fed up with the whole conversation. But as his brothers headed for the door, Connor suddenly remembered something. "Wait. What was that you said about needing a woman?"

Ian turned back around but didn't make eye contact. "You need to bring a date to dinner. Jonas likes to see his partners in happy relationships."

"And you didn't tell him that's a deal breaker?"

Ian scowled and walked out as Jake and Connor exchanged glances.

"Just find a date," Jake said finally. "And don't piss her off."

Definitely a deal breaker, Connor thought.

Abandon hope, all ye who enter here.

There should've been a sign announcing that sentiment, Maggie Jameson thought as she stared at the massive double doors that led to the offices of MacLaren International Corporation. But Maggie wasn't about to give up hope. She was on a mission, so rather than whimper and crawl away, she summoned every last bit of courage she could muster and pushed through the doors to announce herself to the pleasant, well-dressed receptionist named Susan at the front desk.

"He's expecting you, Ms. James," Susan said with a genuine smile. "Please follow me."

James? You had to give them a fake name to even get near him, the voice inside her head said, jeering. *Walk away before they toss you out on your ear.*

"Shush," Maggie whispered to herself.

But the sarcastic little voice in her head wouldn't stay silent as Maggie followed the charming receptionist down the wide, plushly carpeted halls. And as if to amplify the mental taunts, everywhere she looked there were signs that the MacLaren brothers had succeeded beyond anyone's wildest dreams. Huge posters of the latest MacLaren products hung on the corridor walls as she passed. Lush plants grew in profusion. Glassed-in office spaces boasted state-of-the-art furnishings and technology.

Maggie was even treated to the occasional stunning view, through wide windows, of the gleaming San Francisco Bay in the distance. Just in case she forgot that this was the penthouse suite of the office building owned by the MacLaren Brothers of Point Cairn, California. As if she could.

Despite her best efforts, Maggie felt a tingle of pleasure that Connor MacLaren had done so well for himself.

Yeah, maybe he'll give you a nice, shiny medal for doing him such a big favor.

Maggie sighed and glanced around. The receptionist was many yards ahead of her down the hall, and Maggie had to double her speed to keep up. How long was this darn hallway anyway? Where was Connor's office? In the next county? She should've left a trail of bread crumbs. If she had to leave in a hurry, she'd never find her way out. Heck, she could wander these corridors for years. It was starting to feel as if she was stuck on some kind of never-ending death march.

Stop whining. Just turn around and walk away before it's too late.

If she had a choice, she would take her own subliminal advice and hightail it out of there. She'd taken a big risk coming here and now she was regretting it with every step she took. Hadn't she spent half of her life avoiding risks? So why in the world was she here?

Because she didn't have a choice. She was desperate. Truly, completely desperate. Connor MacLaren was her last hope.

But he hates you, and for good reason. Walk away. Walk away.

"Oh, shut up!"

Susan stopped and turned. "Is something wrong, Ms. James?"

Yes, something's wrong! That's not my real name! Maggie wanted to shout, but instead she flashed a bright smile. "No, absolutely nothing."

As soon as the woman continued walking, Maggie rolled her eyes. Not only was she talking to herself, but now she was arguing with herself, too. Out loud. This couldn't be a good sign.

Her life truly had descended to the lowest rung of the pits of hell, not to be overly dramatic about it.

Even the cheery receptionist had caught on to the desperation vibe that hung on Maggie like a bad suit. She had taken one look at Maggie's faded blue jeans and ancient suede jacket, and smiled at her with so much sympathy in her eyes that Maggie wouldn't be surprised to have the woman slip her a ten-dollar bill on her way out.

Treat yourself to a hot meal, sweetie, Maggie imagined the woman whispering kindly.

Unquestionably, Maggie had been hiding out in the remote hills of Marin for way too long. Glancing down at her serviceable old jacket and jeans, she realized that she'd lost the ability to dress for success. Her boots were ancient. She hadn't been to a beauty spa in more than three years. True, she hadn't exactly turned into a cave dweller, but she certainly wasn't on top of her fashion game, either. And while that wasn't a bad thing as far as Maggie was concerned, it was probably a mistake not to have factored it in when she was about to go face-to-face with one of Northern California's top power brokers.

The man whose heart everyone believed she'd broken ten years ago.

Someday she would find out why Connor had allowed everyone in town to believe it was her fault they'd broken up all those years ago. It wasn't true, of course. They'd had what could charitably be called a mutual parting of the ways. She could remember their last conversation as if had happened yesterday because Maggie was the one who'd ended up with a broken heart. Her life had changed drastically after that, and not in a good way.

Why had her old friends turned their backs on her and blamed her for hurting Connor so badly? Had he lied about it after she left town? It didn't seem like something Connor would have done, but she had been away such a long time. Maybe he had changed.

Maggie shook her head. She would never understand men and she wasn't even sure she wanted to. But someday she would ask him why he did it. Not today, though, when she had so many bigger problems to deal with. She didn't dare take the risk.

Turn around. Walk away.

"Here we are," Susan the receptionist said cheerfully as she came to a stop in front of another set of intimidating double doors. "Please go right in, Ms. James. He's expecting you."

No, he isn't! He's not expecting a liar!

Maggie smiled stiffly. "Thank you, Susan."

The woman walked away and Maggie faced the closed doors. She could feel her heart pounding against her ribs. The urge to walk—no, *run*—away was visceral. But she'd come this far on sheer nerves, so there was no way she would walk away now. Besides, even if she did try to leave, she'd never find her way out of this office maze.

"Just get it over with," she muttered, and praying for strength, she pushed on the door. It opened silently, gliding across the thick carpeting.

At her first glimpse of Connor, Maggie's throat tightened. She tried to swallow, but it was no use. She would just have to live with this tender, emotional lump in her throat forever.

He sat with complete ease behind an enormous cherry wood desk, unaware that he was being watched as he read over some sort of document.

She was glad now that she'd made the appointment to see him here in his San Francisco office instead of facing him down back home. Not only would she avoid the gossip that would've invariably erupted when people found out she'd been spotted at the MacLaren Brewery, but she also would've missed seeing him backlit by the gorgeous skyline of San Francisco. Somehow he fit in here as well as he did back home.

For a long moment, she simply reveled at the sight of him. He had always been the most handsome boy she'd ever known, so how was it possible that he was even more gorgeous now than she remembered? He was a man now, tall, with wide shoulders and long legs. His dark, wavy hair was an inch or two longer than was currently fashionable, especially for a power broker like him. She had always loved his remarkable dark blue eyes, his strong jawline, his dazzling smile. His face was lightly tanned from working outside, and his well-shaped hands and long fingers were magical...

A wave of longing swept through her at the thought of Connor's hands and what he was capable of doing with them.

Maggie sighed inwardly. Lovemaking was one aspect of their relationship that had always been perfect. Yes, Connor had taken too many foolish risks with his extreme sports, and yes, Maggie's fears for his safety had driven her crazy sometimes and had ultimately led to their breakup. But when it came to romance, theirs had been a match made in heaven.

Maggie remembered her grandpa Angus saying that the MacLaren brothers had done well for themselves. Now, observing Connor in this luxury penthouse office, she could see that Grandpa's comment had been a gross understatement. She probably had no right to feel this much pride in the brothers' accomplishments, but she felt it anyway.

At the thought of her grandfather, Maggie dragged her wandering mind back to the task at hand. Grandpa Angus was the main reason she was daring to show her face here today.

Connor hadn't noticed her yet, and for one more fleeting moment, she thought about turning and running away. He would never have to know she had been here and she would never have to experience the look of anger and maybe pain in his eyes. And he would never know to what extent she'd been willing to risk humiliating herself. But it was too late for all that. She had been running from her mistakes ever since she first left Connor, and it was time to stop.

"Hello, Connor," she said at long last, hoping he couldn't hear the nerves jangling in her voice.

He looked up and stared at her for a long moment. Had she changed so much that he didn't even recognize her? But then one of his eyebrows quirked up, and not in a "happy to see you" kind of way.

He pushed his chair away from the desk and folded his arms across his muscular chest. After another lengthy, highly charged moment, during which he never broke eye contact with her, he finally drawled, "Hello, Mary Margaret."

The sound of his deep voice made the hairs on her arms stand at attention. Amazingly, he still retained a hint of a

Scottish accent, even though he'd lived in Northern California since he was in grade school.

Anxious, but determined not to show it, she took a few steps forward. "How are you?" Her voice cracked again and she wanted to sink into the carpet, but she powered forward with a determined smile.

"I'm busy." He made a show of checking his watch, then stood. "I'm about to go into a meeting, so I'm afraid I don't have time to talk right now. But thanks for stopping by, Maggie."

She deserved that, deserved to have him blow her off, but it hurt anyway. She took slow, even breaths in an effort to maintain her dignity, for she had no intention of leaving. "Your meeting is with me, Connor."

He smiled patiently, as though she were a recalcitrant five-year-old. "No, it's not. Believe me, I would never have agreed to meet with you."

She said nothing as she watched him study her for several long seconds until she saw the moment when realization struck.

"Ah, I get it," he said evenly. "So you're Taylor James. Inventive name."

"Thank you," Maggie murmured, even though she could tell by his tone that he wasn't the least bit impressed by her cleverness. She'd managed to use part of her real last name and had come up with a first name that could be male or female. She tugged her jacket closer. Had the temperature dropped in here? Probably not, but she felt a chill right down to her bones.

"Why the subterfuge, Maggie?"

She kept her tone as casual as she could manage. "I wanted to see if I could make it in the business without leaning on my family name." It was the same lie she'd been telling herself for the past three years she'd been back in Point Cairn. The truth was too embarrassing to admit.

"How intrepid of you," he said dryly.

She watched for a smile or even a scowl, but Connor revealed nothing but indifference. No real emotion at all. She had anticipated something more from him. Hurt. Anger. Rage, even. She could've accepted that. But Connor didn't appear to be fazed one way or the other by anything she said or did.

That's where the chill came from. She shivered again.

But honestly, what did she expect? Happy hugs? Not likely since she'd found out that he'd considered her departure such a betrayal. But if his current mood was any indication, he had obviously moved on long ago.

And so did you, she reminded herself.

He circled his desk and leaned his hip against the smooth wood edge. "I heard you've been back in town for a while now. Funny how we've never run into each other."

"I keep a low profile," she said, smiling briefly. The fact was, she'd spotted him a number of times on the streets of their small hometown of Point Cairn. Each time, she'd taken off running in the opposite direction. It was self-protection, plain and simple, as well as her usual risk aversion.

She'd returned to Point Cairn three years ago in a low state, her heart and her self-confidence battered and bruised. There was no way she would've been strong enough to confront Connor on his home turf. Not back then. She was barely able to do so right this minute. In fact, she could feel her thin facade beginning to crack and wondered how much longer she could be in his presence without melting down.

"How's your grandfather?" he asked, changing the subject. "I haven't seen him in a few weeks."

She smiled appreciatively. He and his brothers had always had a soft spot for Angus Campbell, and the feeling was mutual. "Grandpa is…well, he's part of the reason I've come to see you today."

He straightened. "What's wrong? Is he ill?"

Maggie hesitated. "Well, let's just say he's not getting any younger."

Connor chuckled. "He'll outlive us all."

"I hope so."

He folded his arms again, as if to erect an extra barrier between them. "What is it you want, Maggie?"

She reached into her bag and pulled out a thick folder. "I want to discuss your offer."

He reached for the folder, opened it and riffled through the stack of papers. They were all letters and copies of emails sent to someone named Taylor James. Many had been signed by Connor, himself, but there were offers from others in there, too. He looked at Maggie. "These were sent to Taylor James."

"And that's me."

"But I was unaware of that fact when I made those offers. If I'd known Taylor James was you, Maggie, I never would've tried to make contact." He closed the folder and handed it back to her. "My offer is rescinded."

"No." She took a hasty step backward, as though the folder were on fire. "You can't do that."

For the first time, his smile reached his eyes. In fact, they fairly twinkled with perverse glee as he took a step closer. "Yes, I can. I just did."

"No, Connor. No. I need you to—"

In a heartbeat, his gaze turned to frost. "I'm not interested in what you need, Maggie. It's too late for that."

"But—"

"Meeting's over. It's time for you to go."

For the briefest second, her shoulders slumped. But just as quickly, she reminded herself that she was stronger now and giving up was not an option. She used her old trick of mentally counting from one to five as she made one last effort to draw from that sturdy well of self-confidence she'd fought so hard to reconstruct.

Defiantly she lifted her chin and stared him in the eyes. "I'm not leaving this office until you hear what I have to say."

Two

He had to admire her persistence.

Still, there was no way Connor would play this game with her. At this point in his life, he wanted less than nothing to do with Mary Margaret Jameson. Yes, they'd been high school sweethearts and college lovers. At age twenty-two, he'd been crazy in love with her and had planned to live with her for the rest of his life. But then she'd left him with barely a word of warning, moved to the East Coast and married some rich guy, shattering Connor's foolish heart into a zillion pieces. That was ten years ago. At the time, he vowed never to be made a fool of again by any woman, especially Maggie Jameson.

Except it now looked as if she'd succeeded in fooling him again. All it took was a convenient lie. But then, he'd found out long ago just how good Maggie was at lying.

The last time they'd spoken to each other was on the phone. How screwed up was it that Connor could still remember their final conversation? He'd been about to go on some camping thing with his brothers and she'd mentioned that she wouldn't be there when he got home. How could he have known she meant that she *really* wouldn't be there? Like, gone. Out of his life. Forever.

Well, until today. Now here she was, claiming to be the very person he'd been trying to track down for months.

Odd how this mystery had played itself out, Connor thought. Eighteen months ago, a fledgling beer maker began to appear on the scene and was soon sweeping medals and gold ribbons at every beer competition in the western states. The extraordinary young brewmeister's name was Taylor James, but that was all anyone knew about "him." He never showed up in person to present his latest formulation or to claim his prize, sending a representative instead.

Taylor James's reputation gained ground as the quality of his formulas grew. He won more and more major prize categories while attracting more and more attention within the industry.

And yet no one had ever seen him.

Connor had been determined to find Taylor James and, with any luck, buy him out. Or hire him. But he hadn't been able to locate him. Who was this person making these great new beers and ales while continuing to hide himself away from his adoring public? For the past year, Taylor James had continued to beat out every other rival. Including, for the first time ever, MacLaren's Pride, the pale ale that had put the MacLaren brothers on the map and helped them make their first million. Losing that contest had been a slap in the face and had made the MacLarens even more determined to find the mysterious beer maker.

Through one of the competitions, Connor was able to obtain Taylor James's email address and immediately started writing the guy. He received no answer. From another competition, Connor unearthed a post office box number. He began sending letters, asking if the elusive brewer would be interested in meeting to discuss an investment opportunity. He never heard a word back—until this moment.

Now as he stared at the woman claiming to be the reclusive new genius of beer making, Connor was tempted to toss the fraudulent Ms. James out on her ear. It would be even more fun to call security and have her ignominiously escorted out to the sidewalk. The shameful exit might give her a minuscule taste of the pain and humiliation he'd endured when she walked out of his life all those years ago.

But that would send the wrong signal, Connor reasoned. Maggie would take it as a sign that he actually cared one way or the other about her. And he didn't. The purely physical reaction to her presence meant nothing. He was a guy, after all. And he had to admit he was curious as to why she'd hidden herself away and worked under an assumed name. She was a talented brewer, damn it. Her latest series of beers and ales were spectacular. And why wouldn't they be? She came from a long line of clever Scottish brewers, including her grandfather Angus, who had retired from the business years ago.

So he'd give her a few minutes to tell her story. And then he'd kick her excellent behind right out of his office.

With a generous sweep of his hand, he offered her one of the visitors' chairs. Once she was seated, he sat and faced her. "You've got five minutes to say whatever you came to tell me, Maggie."

"Fine." She sat and cleared her throat, then smoothed her jacket down a few times. She seemed nervous, but Connor knew better. She was playing the delicate angel, a role she had always performed to perfection.

He scowled, remembering that he used to call her his Red-Haired Angel. She still had gorgeous thick red hair that tumbled down her back, and her skin was still that perfect peaches and cream he'd always loved to touch. God, she was as beautiful as she was the day he met her. But she was no angel. Connor had learned that the hard way.

"My formulas have won every eligible competition for the past eighteen months," she began slowly, picking up speed and confidence as she spoke. "I've singlehandedly transformed the pale ale category overnight. That's a quote from the leading reviewer in the industry, by the way. And it's well deserved. I'm the best new beer maker to come along in years."

"I know all that." Connor sat back in his chair. "It's one of the reasons why I've been trying to hunt down Taylor James all these months. For some reason, *he* didn't feel compelled to respond."

"*He* wasn't ready," she murmured, staring at her hands.

Connor was certain that those were the first truthful words she'd uttered since walking into his office.

She pursed her lips as if weighing her next sentence, but all Connor could think was that those heaven-sent lips were still so desirable that one pout from her could twist his guts into knots.

His fists tightened. He was about to put an end to this nonsense when she finally continued to talk.

"Here's my offer," she said, leaning forward in her chair. "I'll sell you all of those prizewinning formulas and I'll also create something unique and new for MacLaren. It'll be perfect as a Christmas ale and you'll sell every last bottle, I guarantee it."

"At what price, Maggie?"

She hesitated, then named a figure that would keep a small country afloat for a year or two. The amount was so far out in left field, Connor began to laugh. "That's absurd. It's not worth it."

"Yes, it is," she insisted. "And you know it, Connor. You said it yourself. The Taylor James brand is golden. You'll be able to use the name on all your packaging and advertising and you'll make your money back a thousand times over."

She was right, but he wasn't going to admit that just yet. He stared at her for a minute, wondering what her real motivation was. Why had she come to him? There had to be other companies that wanted to do business with her. Or rather, with *Taylor James*.

"Why now, Maggie?" he asked quietly. "Why do you want to sell those formulas? And why sell to me?"

"Why?" She bit her luscious bottom lip and Connor had to fight back a groan. Irritated with himself as much as he was with her, he pushed himself out of his chair and scowled down at her. "Answer me, Maggie. Tell me the truth or get the hell out of here. I don't have time for this crap."

"You want the truth?" She jumped up from her chair and glared right back at him. "Fine. I need the money. Are you happy? Does it fill your heart with joy to hear me say it? I'm desperate. I've been turned down by every bank in town. I would go to other beer companies, but I don't have the time to sift through bids and counteroffers. I need money now. That's why I came to you. I've run out of choices. It's you or…"

She exhaled heavily and slid down onto the arm of the chair. It seemed that she'd run out of steam. "There. That's it. Are you happy now?"

"At least I'm hearing the truth for once."

She looked up and made a face at him. He almost laughed, but couldn't. She'd expended all her energy trying to finagle a deal with him and she just didn't have it in her. She might well be the worst negotiator he'd ever dealt with. And for some damn reason, he found it endearing.

For his own self-preservation, he'd have to get over that feeling fast.

"Where did all your money go?" he asked. "You must've gotten a hefty settlement from your rich husband." He gave her a slow up-and-down look, taking in her faded jeans and worn jacket. "It's obvious you didn't spend it all on shoes."

"Very funny," she muttered, and followed his gaze down to her ratty old boots. After a long moment, she looked up at him. "I know what you must think of me personally, but

I'm too close to the edge to care. I just need a loan. Can you help me or not?"

"What's the money for?" he asked.

She pressed her lips together in a stubborn line, then sighed. "I need to expand my business."

"If you're selling me all your formulas, you won't have a business left."

"I can always come up with new recipes. My Taylor James brand is going strong, growing more profitable every day. And my new Redhead line is popular, too."

"Then what's the money for?" he asked again, slowly, deliberately.

"I need to upgrade my equipment. I need to hire some help. I need to develop a sales force." She sighed and stared at her hands. "I need to make enough money to take care of my grandfather."

He frowned. "You mentioned Angus earlier. Is something wrong with him?"

It was as if all the air fled from her lungs. Her shoulders slumped and God help him, he thought he saw a glimmer of tears in her beautiful brown eyes.

"He's been to the hospital twice now. It's his heart. I'm so worried about him. He runs out of breath so easily these days, but he refuses to give up his goats. Or his scotch."

"Some things are sacred to a man."

"Goats and scotch." She rolled her eyes. "He insists that he's hale and hearty, but I know it's not true. I'm scared, Connor." She ran one hand through her hair, pushing it back from her face. "He needs medication. They have a new drug that would be perfect for someone in his condition, but we found out it's considered experimental. The insurance won't cover it and it's too expensive for me to pay for it."

Connor frowned. This wasn't good news. Angus Campbell was one of the sweetest old guys he'd ever known. Connor and his brothers were first inspired to make their own beer while watching Angus at work in the Campbell family pub. That brew pub had been on Main Street in Point Cairn for as long as Connor could remember. Growing up, he and his brothers had all worked there during the summer months.

Then five years ago, Angus lost his beloved wife, Doreen. That's when Maggie's mom sold the pub to the MacLaren brothers. Angus insisted that she move to Florida to live with her sister, something she'd been talking about for years. But that left Angus alone with his goat farm, though he got occasional help from the neighborhood boys. This had all happened during the time Maggie was living back east with her rich husband.

Now Maggie was back home and the only family she had left in Point Cairn was her grandpa Angus.

Connor made a decision. "I'll pay for that medication."

"We don't need charity, Connor."

Her words annoyed him at the same time as he admired her for saying them. "I'm not talking about charity, Maggie. Call it payback. Angus was always good to us."

"I know," she said softly. "But he's almost eighty years old. There'll be lots more medication in the future, along with a hundred other unexpected expenses. I need cash going forward to get my brewery up and running. That way, I'll be able to generate enough funds of my own to pay for Grandpa's health care needs." She started walking, pacing the confines of his office as if she couldn't bear to stand still any longer. "I'll also be able to hire some workers for both me and Grandpa and maybe make a few improvements to the farm. I'm looking to arrange a business deal, Connor. A fair trade, not a handout. And I need to do it right away."

"What happened at the bank?"

"I expected them to come through, but they turned me down. They explained that with the economy and all…" She gave a dispirited shrug.

Connor had been watching her carefully. He had a feeling there was something she wasn't telling him. Why wouldn't the bank loan her the money? Even though she was divorced, she must have received a hefty settlement. Her beers and ales were kicking ass all over the state, so she had to be considered a good risk. Was she hoarding the settlement money away for some reason?

And another thing. She and her grandfather owned at least a hundred acres of prime Marin farmland that would make excellent collateral for any bank loan.

She might not be lying to him at the moment, but she was holding back some information. Connor would pry it out of her eventually, but in the meantime, a plan had been forming in his mind as they talked. If he wasn't mistaken, and he rarely was, it would be the answer to all their problems. She would get her money and he would get something he wanted.

Call it restitution.

"I'll give you the money," he said.

She blinked. "You will?"

"Yeah." He hadn't realized until Maggie showed up today that he still harbored so many ambivalent feelings for her. Part of him wanted to kick her to the curb, while another more rowdy part of him wanted to shove everything off his desk and have his way with her right then and there.

He thought she had a lot of nerve showing up here asking for money. And yet he also thought she showed guts. It was driving him nuts just listening to her breathe, so why shouldn't he pull her chain a little? Just to settle the score.

"What's the catch?" she said warily.

He chuckled. Once again, she'd thrown him off base. She should've been doing cartwheels, knowing she'd get the money, but instead she continued to peer suspiciously at him.

"The catch," he explained, "is that it won't be a loan. I want something in return."

"Of course," she said, brightening. "I've already promised you the Taylor James formulas."

"Yeah, I'll take those formulas," he said, "but there's something else I want from you."

Her eyes wide, she took a small step backward. "I don't think so."

"Take it or leave it, Maggie," Connor snapped.

"Take or leave what?" she said in a huff. "I don't even know what you're talking about."

He shoved his hands in his pockets. "It seems I need a date."

"A date?" she scoffed. "You must know a hundred women who would—"

"Let me put it this way. I need a woman who knows a little something about beer. You more than meet that requirement, so I intend to use your services for a week."

"My…*services?* What are you talking about?"

"I'm talking about taking you up on your deal. I'll pay you the entire amount of money you asked for in exchange for your formulas, plus this one other condition."

"That I'm at your *service* for a week? This is ridiculous." Agitated, she began to pace the floor of his office even faster.

"It's only for a week," he said reasonably. "Seven days and nights."

"Nights?" she repeated, her eyes narrowing.

He shrugged lightly, knowing exactly what she was thinking. Sex. "That's entirely up to you."

"This is blackmail," she muttered.

"No, it's not. I'm about to give you a lot of money and I want something in return."

"My services," she said sarcastically.

KATE CARLISLE   31

"That's right. Look, the Autumn Brew Festival is next week."

"I know that," she grumbled.

"I need a date, and you're the perfect choice. So you will agree to be my date the entire week and go to all the competition events with me. I'll also want you to attend a number of meetings and social events with me, including the Friday night gala dinner dance."

That suspicious look was back. "Are you kidding?"

"What? You don't like to dance?"

She looked stricken by his words but quickly recovered. "No, I don't, as a matter of fact."

That was weird. Maggie had always loved dancing. "Doesn't matter," he said. "You're going to the gala."

"We'll see about that." Her eyes focused in on him. "And that's it? We pal around for a week at the festival and I get the money?"

"That's it. And I'll expect you to stay with me in my hotel suite."

She stopped and stared at him. "Oh, please."

"You want the money or not?"

"You know I do, but I can drive in and meet you each morning."

"That won't work. I expect us to keep late hours and I have a number of early morning breakfast meetings scheduled. I don't want to take any chances on you missing something important."

"But—"

"Look, Maggie. Let me make it clear so there's no misunderstanding. I don't expect you to sleep with me. I just expect you to stay at the hotel with me. It'll be more convenient."

She frowned. "But I can't leave Grandpa for that long a time."

"My mother will look in on him," he said, silently patting himself on the back for his split-second problem-solving abilities. Deidre MacLaren had known Angus for years, so Connor knew she wouldn't mind doing it.

"And at the end of the week," he continued calmly, "I'll give you the money you asked for in full."

"And all I have to do is stay with you for a week?"

"And be my date."

"In your hotel room."

"It's a suite."

"I'll sleep on the couch."

"You'll be more comfortable in a bed."

"And you'll sleep on the couch?"

"No."

Her eyes widened. "Stop kidding around."

His lips twitched. "Am I?"

"Wait," she said suddenly. "I'll get my own room."

"The hotel is sold out."

A line marred her forehead as she considered that for a moment, and then she brightened. "We can switch off between the couch and—"

"Take the deal or leave it, Maggie."

She flashed him a dark look. "Give me a minute to think."

"No problem."

She took to pacing the floor again, probably to work out the many creative ways she would say *no* to his outlandish offer. But she would definitely say no, wouldn't she?

Hell, what in the world was he thinking? God forbid she agreed to his conditions. What would he do in a hotel suite with Maggie for a week? Well, hell, he knew what he *wanted* to do with her. She was a beautiful woman and he still remembered every enticing inch of her body. He'd never forgotten all the ways he'd brought her pleasure. Those thoughts had plagued him for years, so living with her for a week would be a dangerous temptation. It would be for the best if she refused the offer.

And once she turned him down, Connor would go ahead and pay for Angus's medication, even if he had to sneak behind her back to do it. And as for Maggie getting a loan to grow her business, he figured that would happen eventually. She'd either find a bank that would agree to it or she'd tap one of the other brewery owners.

That thought didn't sit well with him, though. He didn't want anyone else getting their hands on her beer formulas. Or her, either, if he was being honest.

And in case he'd forgotten, he still needed a date for the Wellstone dinner meeting. As much as he hated to admit it, Maggie would be perfect as his date. Jonas Wellstone would fall in love with her.

So maybe he'd gone too far. If she turned him down— hell, *when* she turned him down, he would simply renegotiate to get those formulas and to convince her to be his date at the Wellstone dinner. That's all he really wanted.

Meanwhile, he had to chuckle as he watched her stomp and grumble to herself. A part of him wanted to take her in his arms and comfort her—in more ways than one. But once again, that wayward part of him was doomed to disappointment, because other than the obvious outward attraction to her, Maggie meant nothing to him now, thank goodness. He counted himself lucky that he'd gotten over her duplicity years ago. This offer of his was just sweet payback, pure and simple. It felt damn good to push some of her buttons the way she'd pushed his in the past, saying one thing but meaning something else. Keeping him in a constant state of confusion. Now it was his turn to shake her up a little.

"So what's your answer, Maggie?" he asked finally.

On the opposite side of the room, Maggie halted in her pacing and turned to face him. A big mistake. She could feel his magnetic pull from all the way over there. Why did he still have to be so gorgeous and tall and rugged after all these years? It wasn't fair. She could feel her hormones yipping and snapping and begging her to take him up on his offer to spend a week together in that hotel suite of his.

What was wrong with her? Unless she'd missed the clues, he was clearly out for revenge, pure and simple. Imagine him insisting that she provide him *services* for a week. Even though he'd assured her that she wasn't expected to sleep with him, she had a feeling he wasn't talking about a plain old dinner date here and there.

Services, indeed!

At that, her stomach nerves began to twitch and buzz with excitement. *Services!*

Oh, this wasn't good.

"Maggie?"

"Yes, damn it. Yes, I'll do it," she said, waving her hands in submission.

He hesitated, then took what looked like a fortifying breath. "Good."

"But I won't sleep with you." She pointed her finger at him for emphasis.

He tilted his head to study her. "I told you I don't expect you to."

"But…the hotel suite." She let go of the breath she didn't know she'd been holding. "Okay. But…never mind. Good. Fine. That's fine." She stopped talking as she felt heat rise up her neck and spread to her cheeks. She tended to turn bright pink when she was embarrassed, so Connor probably noticed it, too. Even though he'd made it clear he didn't want to sleep with her, she'd assumed…well. That's what she got for assuming anything. Apparently he just wanted to keep tabs on her.

If she'd thought about it for a second or two, she would've realized that he could have any woman he wanted. They probably waited in line outside his door and threw themselves at him wherever he went. Why would he want to sleep with Maggie, especially after he'd spent all these years thinking she had betrayed him? All he wanted was a date, someone who knew something about the brewery business. And that description fit her perfectly.

"I misunderstood," she admitted.

"Yeah, you did," he said, his tone lowering seductively as he approached her. "Because if you and I were to do what your mind is imagining, Maggie, there wouldn't be much sleeping going on."

Staggered, Maggie felt her mouth drop open. "Oh."

"So it's settled," he said, breezily changing tempo again as he tugged her arm through his and walked her to the door. "I'll pick you up Sunday morning and we'll drive together. Be sure to pack something special for the gala and a few cocktail dresses. We'll be dining with a number of important business associates, and I want them to walk away impressed."

She refused to mention that she only owned two simple cocktail dresses and nothing formal, having given away most of her extensive wardrobe to the local consignment shop three years ago. Instead she turned and jabbed her finger in his chest for emphasis. "Just so we're clear, Connor. I'm not going to have sex with you."

He looked down at her finger, then up to meet her gaze. "Still negotiating, huh?"

She whipped her hand away and immediately missed the sizzle of heat she'd gotten from touching his chest. She told herself it meant nothing. It had just been a while since she'd touched a man. Like, years. No wonder she was getting a contact high.

"I'm serious, Connor," she said, hating that her voice sounded so breathless. "I'll share your room with you, but that's it."

"It's a suite," he corrected, and slowly leaned over and kissed her neck.

Dear Lord, what was he doing? She knew she should slap him, push him away, but instead she shivered at the exquisite feel of his lips on her skin.

"Say it with me," he murmured. "Suite."

"Suite," she murmured, arching into him when he gently nipped her earlobe. This had to stop. Any minute now.

"Sweet," he whispered, then pulled her into his arms and kissed her.

Three

The heat was instantaneous. Maggie felt as if she were on fire and she reveled in the warmth of his touch. She couldn't remember feeling this immediate need, not even years ago when she and Connor first made love. And certainly not in all her years with Alan Cosgrove, her less than affectionate ex-husband.

Good grief, why was she thinking about a cold fish like Alan when Connor's hot, sexy mouth was currently devouring her own?

She gripped his shirt, knowing she ought to put an end to this and leave right now. Talk about taking a risk! This was madness. She had to stop. But oh, please, no, not yet. For just another moment, she wanted to savor his lips against hers, his touch, his strength, his need. It had been much too long since any man had needed her like this.

Connor had always been a clever, considerate lover, but now he was masterful as he maneuvered her lips apart and slid his tongue inside to tangle with her own, further melting her resistance. His arms encircled her, his hands swept up and down her back with a clear sensual awareness of her body as his mouth continued to plunder hers.

And just at the point where she was ready to give him anything he wanted, Connor ended the kiss. She wobbled, completely off balance for a moment. She wanted to protest and whine for him to kiss her again. But she managed to control herself, taking time to adjust the shoulder strap of her bag and straighten her jacket.

Then she glanced up and caught his self-satisfied smile. He looked as if he'd just won a bet with someone, maybe himself.

She remembered that smile, remembered loving it, loving him. Times changed, though, and just because they'd shared an amazing kiss didn't mean she had any intention of sleeping with him. Still, at least she knew what she was up against now. Was she crazy to have such strong feelings for him after so many years? No, it would only be crazy if she acted on those feelings. She needed to remind herself of the only thing that mattered: getting the loan, by almost any means necessary. Which meant that she would walk through fire to get it. And Connor MacLaren was fire personified.

She took a deep breath and struggled to maintain a carefree tone. "I guess I'll see you Sunday, then."

"Yes, you will." And with a friendly stroke of her hair, Connor opened the office door. "Drive home safely."

"I will. Goodbye, Connor."

She strolled from his office in a passion-soaked haze. But despite her earlier concerns, she somehow found her way out of the large office maze and down to the parking garage. And before she knew it, she was driving toward the Golden Gate Bridge and heading for home.

The kiss meant nothing, Connor assured himself as he closed his office door. He'd just been trying to teach her a lesson. Testing her. Keeping her on her toes. He'd wanted to prove she was lying when she claimed she wouldn't dream of having sex with him. And, he told himself, he'd done a hell of a job. She had practically ripped his shirt off right there and then. Hell, if he hadn't put an end to the kiss when he did, they would be going at it naked on his office couch by now.

And didn't that paint a provocative picture? Damn. The

image of her writhing in naked splendor on the soft leather couch was stunning in its clarity, causing him to grow rock hard instantly. In his mind's eye, he could almost touch the gentle slope of her curvaceous breasts, could almost taste her silky skin.

"Idiot," he muttered, straining to adjust himself before settling back to work. "Explain again why you stopped kissing her?"

At the time, it had made sense to stop, he argued silently. But now, as he hungered for more...he shook his head. Maggie had always had the ability to tie him into knots and now she was doing it again. Damn it, he was a different man than he was ten years ago. Stronger. Smarter. He wasn't about to let her call the shots again. He would be the one in control of the situation while they were together next week.

But the voice inside his head began to laugh. *Control. Good luck with that.*

He ruthlessly stifled that mocking voice. So maybe he hadn't always had a firm grip on things when he was with Maggie before. Things were different now. He still didn't trust her as far as he could throw her, which was pretty far, seeing as how she'd lost some weight since he'd last seen her. She was just as beautiful, though. Maybe more so. When he first looked up and saw her standing in his office doorway, she had taken his breath away. She'd always had that power over him, but he was older and wiser now and not about to fall for her charms again.

He wouldn't mind kissing her again, though, and was momentarily distracted by the searing memory of his mouth on hers. And it went without saying that he would do whatever it took to get her into bed with him. He was a redblooded man, after all. Didn't mean he cared about her or anything. It was just something he'd be willing to do if the occasion presented itself—and he had every intention of making sure that the occasion presented itself.

Absently, Connor checked the time. Damn, he only had twenty minutes before Jake would show up to drag his ass out to shop for a new suit. He figured he'd better get some real work done in the meantime so he'd be ready to go when Jake got here. His brother had already warned him that he'd be on the phone with the Scottish lawyers this afternoon, and that always put Jake in a foul mood.

The lawyers from Edinburgh had been trying to convince one of the MacLaren brothers to fly to Scotland to take care of the details of their uncle Hugh's estate. Whoever made the trip would be stuck there for weeks. But that wasn't the real reason none of them wanted to go there. No, it was because Uncle Hugh had been a hateful man. Jake, Ian and Connor couldn't care less about the terms of Hugh's last will and testament, despite the fact that they were his beneficiaries, in a manner of speaking.

Even though Connor and his brothers had grown up around Point Cairn in Northern California, they'd been born in the Highlands of Scotland. They were the sons of Liam MacLaren and heirs to Castle MacLaren. But when Connor was a baby, their uncle Hugh, an evil bastard if ever there was one, swindled their father out of his inheritance.

Their dad never recovered from the betrayal and died a few years later, leaving their mother, Deidre, a widow with three young boys to raise. Unwilling to live in the same area as her despised brother-in-law, she moved with her boys to Northern California to be near her sister. Connor had no memory of any other home except the rugged hills that overlooked the wild, rocky coast of Marin County.

Connor stared out the office window at the stunning view of the Golden Gate Bridge and the Marin shoreline beyond. Maybe in some small way, their uncle had done them all a favor because Connor couldn't imagine living anywhere else in the world. Hell, he never would have met Maggie Jameson otherwise, he thought, and then wondered if that was a good thing or a bad thing. He wasn't ready to decide on that one, but he couldn't help smiling in anticipation of spending the following week in a hotel suite with the gorgeous woman.

By the time she arrived home, Maggie felt relatively normal again. Her heart had finally stopped hammering in her chest, and her head had ceased its incessant buzzing. All that remained from Connor's onslaught was a mild tingling of her lips from his devastating kiss.

Mild? That was putting it, well, mildly. But never mind his kiss. What about his demands? For someone so risk-averse, Maggie still couldn't believe she'd entered the lion's den and put herself in such a perilous position. After all the lectures she'd given herself and all the positive affirmations she'd memorized, she had taken one look at Connor and practically rolled over, allowing him to take hold of the situation and make choices for her.

She pulled her car into the garage next to the barn and walked across the circular drive to the large ranch-style home she shared with her grandfather. The afternoon sun barely managed to hold its own against the autumn chill that had her tugging the collar of her old suede jacket closer to her neck. She still took a moment to appreciate the land that rolled and dipped its way down to the sheer bluffs that overlooked the rough waves of the Pacific Ocean. Despite some sorry choices in her past, she had to marvel at her own good luck. She was home now, living in a beautiful house in a magical location. Her darling grandfather, despite some tricky health issues, was still kicking, as he liked to put it. She was proud of herself, proud of how she'd finally arrived here, both emotionally and physically.

Connor MacLaren had no idea how much it had cost

her to show up at his office door with her hat in her hand, and Maggie had no intention of ever revealing that to him. She'd fought too hard to get to where she was today, and she wasn't about to gamble it all away on some *tingling* feeling she'd received from a simple kiss.

She jogged up the porch stairs and into the house, where she checked the time on the mantel clock. Her grandfather would be out in the barn milking his goats. Dropping her bag on the living room chair, she went to her bedroom to make a phone call. She was determined to avoid sharing a hotel room with Connor—even if it *was* a luxurious penthouse suite, as he had emphasized more than once.

But when she called the convention hotel to make a reservation, she was told that they were sold out, just as Connor had warned. And when she called the next closest hotel, she was quoted a price that was so far out of her range she almost laughed out loud at the reservationist.

She merely thanked her instead and hung up the phone. Then she spent a few minutes at her computer, searching for information. Finally, with nervous fingers, she dialed Connor's number.

"MacLaren," he answered.

"It's Maggie and I've been thinking, Connor," she began. "It's probably best if I commute to the festival from home after all. Grandpa isn't well and I'd rather be home each night to see him."

"I've already talked it over with my mother, Maggie," Connor replied dryly. "She plans to stop by your place twice a day and spend the night there, too. I know Angus won't put up with two women fussing at him day and night, so you'll be doing him a favor by staying away for the week."

"I'm not sure if—"

"And besides," he continued in steamroller fashion, "you've already agreed to be my date for the week, remember? In exchange for which I'm going to give you a lot of money. I think that's a pretty good deal for you."

"Pretty good deal," she echoed darkly.

"Maggie, I explained all this to you and I thought you had agreed. I'm going to need you to accompany me every day, starting with breakfast meetings and going into the late evenings with all the social events I've got to attend."

She frowned into the phone. "You never liked all that social stuff before."

"That was true ten years ago," he said smoothly. "Now I figure it's a small price to pay to get what I want."

"The price of doing business?"

"Exactly. And it won't hurt you to be seen with me, Maggie. It'll be good for your business to meet the people I know, too."

She knew he was right about that. But still. "Okay, but I'm not going to the dance."

"You're going with me, Maggie."

"You don't know what you're asking."

There was a moment of silence, and then Connor said, "Are you saying this is a deal breaker?"

Her shoulders slumped as she recognized that hard-nosed tone of his. She wasn't about to break their deal, but she still had no intention of attending the stupid dance. Especially because it wasn't just a dance. Maggie had looked it up on the festival website. The dinner dance was actually a formal affair, a gala event, meant to celebrate the culmination of the festival year and probably as snooty as any high-society ball she had ever attended in Boston. But since she didn't want to argue anymore, she left it alone for now. After a minute more of conversation, she disconnected the call.

She couldn't tell him that she didn't mind being his date for all the events during the week. That wouldn't be any problem at all. But the thought of having to share his hotel suite with him? It made her want to run through the house screaming. She didn't know how she would manage it, but unless another hotel room opened up in the next few days, she would soon find out.

But even another hotel room wouldn't fix the somewhat smaller dilemma of her not attending the dance. Maggie groaned and pushed that little problem away. If they managed to make it through the week together, Connor would just have to understand.

None of this would've been necessary if the banks hadn't turned down her loan. But the money was critical now. Even though Grandpa insisted that he was still hale and hearty and fit as a fiddle, Maggie was so afraid that one of these days he would need more care than she could afford to give him. She had gone through most of her meager settlement money fixing the roof of the house and then she'd bought a number of replacement items for the brewery.

She had been hoping to use the remaining funds as collateral, but now that Angus needed expensive medication and possibly even surgery someday, she'd reached the point of desperation. Her business was on the verge of expanding into a wider market, and that would bring in more money eventually, but before that happened, she needed to raise some capital to keep things going. And that was where Connor came into the picture. Negotiating and trading her beer formulas for cash was better than going to the bank. This way, she wouldn't have to pay back a loan.

She suddenly felt so tired and gazed at her comfortable bed longingly. How nice it would be to climb under the covers and take a long nap, but first she wanted to help Grandpa feed the goats.

As she stripped out of her "nice" jeans and pulled on her old faded pair, she had to laugh at herself. A few years ago, she wouldn't have dreamed of wearing jeans to a meeting in the city. Not even her "nice" jeans. But happily, jeans and work shirts had gradually replaced most of the clothing she'd worn during her marriage.

Alan, her ex-husband, had expected her to dress up every day, usually in smart skirts and twin sweater sets with pearls. It didn't matter what she was planning to do that day.

"You must always be seen wearing fashionable yet sensible clothing," her ex-mother-in-law, Sybil, was forever reminding her, usually in a scolding tone of voice.

Three years ago, when Maggie first arrived back in Point Cairn after her divorce, she'd had no idea what an emotional mess she was. She just knew that her marriage had gone disastrously wrong and she was determined to get past the whole experience and move forward. She wanted to catch up with old friends and explore the town she'd missed so dearly. So one day, shortly after she'd returned, she drove into Point Cairn to do the grocery shopping.

While at the store, she ran into some of her old high school friends she hadn't seen in years. She was thrilled to reconnect, but they quickly put her in her place, telling her they wanted nothing to do with her. They were still resentful that she had turned her back on the town. More important, they were livid that she'd hurt Connor so badly all those years before. Her friends had made it clear that while Connor was still universally loved and admired by one and all, Maggie was most assuredly *not*. One friend put it more succinctly: Maggie could go stuff it as far as they were concerned.

It was another blow to Maggie's already fragile self-esteem and she had limped home to cry in private. For a full month afterward, she lived in her pajamas, wandering in a daze from her bed to the couch to watch television and then back to bed again. The thought that she might've hurt Connor was devastating to her, but the notion that Connor had lied to her old friends about their mutual breakup was just as bad. Why would he do that?

She remembered tossing and turning at night, unable to sleep for all the pain she might have caused—without even meaning to do so!

Then one day, her grandfather told her he could really use her help with the goats.

Maggie's spirits had lifted. Grandpa needed her! She had a reason to get dressed and she did so carefully, choosing one of her many pastel skirts and a pale pink twinset with a tasteful gold necklace and her Etienne Aigner pumps.

When she walked into the barn, Grandpa took one look at her and asked if she thought they were going to have a tea party with the goats. He chuckled mightily at his little joke, but Maggie jolted as if she'd been rudely awakened from a bad dream. She stared down in dismay at her outfit, then ran from the barn and stumbled back to the house in tears. Poor Grandpa was bewildered by her behavior and blamed himself for upsetting her.

But Maggie knew where to place the blame. It was her own damn fault for being so weak, so blind and so stupid. She'd been well programmed by her manipulative ex-husband and could still hear his sneering voice in her head, telling her what to do, how to behave, what to wear and what she'd done wrong. As soon as their wedding vows were exchanged, Alan's disapproval began and never let up. It had come as such a rude shock and she realized later that she'd been in a terribly vulnerable state after leaving Connor. Otherwise, she might have recognized the signs of cruelty behind Alan's bland exterior.

During her marriage, she'd occasionally wondered why she ever thought Connor's love of extreme sports was too risky for her when compared to the verbal assaults she received constantly from her husband and his mother.

Maggie still couldn't get the sound of their menacing intonations out of her head.

She had thought that by moving three thousand miles

away from her ex-husband and his interfering mother, she would be rid of their ruthless control over her. But the miles didn't matter. Alan and Sybil were still free to invade Maggie's peace of mind with their disparaging comments.

That moment in the barn with Grandpa provided Maggie with a sharp blast of reality that quickly led to her complete meltdown. For days, she couldn't stop crying. Grandpa finally insisted on taking her to the local health clinic to talk to a psychologist. But how could she make sense of something so nonsensical? All she knew was that everything inside her was broken.

Gradually, though, Maggie came to realize that she was not to blame for succumbing to Alan's masterful manipulations. Through the outpatient clinic, she met other women who'd survived similar relationships. And she discovered, quite simply, that if she stayed busy with chores and projects, she didn't have time to worry and fret about the past. Oddly enough, it was Grandpa's quirky flock of goats that helped her get through the worst of it.

Lydia and Vincent Van Goat, the mom and dad goats, didn't care what Maggie was wearing or whether she was depressed or flipping out. They just wanted food, and Lydia and the other girls needed to be milked. The milk had to be weighed and recorded, then taken to the local cheesemongers to be turned into goat cheese and yogurt. The goats demanded fresh water to drink and clean straw to sleep on. Their hooves needed trimming. The newest goat babies needed special care and eventually, weaning.

They couldn't do any of it by themselves; they needed Maggie to help them survive. Maggie soon realized that she was dependent on them for her survival, too. The goats gave her a reason to get out of bed every morning. She had priorities now, in the form of a flock of friendly, curious goats.

For the next six months, much of Maggie's energy was spent tending the goats. She filled out her days by preparing meals for Grandpa and taking long walks along the cliffs and down on the rough, sandy beach. She grew a bit healthier and happier every day.

Eventually she was able to acknowledge that Grandpa was perfectly able to do most of the work with the goats himself. Thanks to Grandpa, Maggie was nearly back to being her old self, which meant that it was time for her to find a real job and make some money. Sadly, the idea of working in town where she could run into her former friends was just too daunting. That's when Grandpa suggested that while she was figuring things out, she might enjoy dabbling in her father's old family beer-making business.

The microbrewery equipment lay dormant in the long, narrow storage room next to the barn. Her father had called the room his brew house, and it was where he used to test some of the beers they served at their brewpub in town. The storage room had been locked up for years, ever since her dad died.

Maggie had fond memories of following her father around while he experimented with flavors and formulas to make different types of beers, so the idea of reviving his brew house appealed to her. Within a week, she was hosing down and sanitizing the vats, replacing a few rusted spigots and cleaning and testing the old manual bottling and kegging equipment her father had used. She spent another few weeks driving all over the county to shop for the proper ingredients and tools before she finally started her first batch of beer. And it wasn't half bad.

That was three years ago. Now Maggie could smile as she tapped one of the kegs to judge the results of her latest pale ale experiment. She had entered this one in the festival and fully expected, or *hoped,* anyway, to win a medal next week.

Once her glass was filled, she made a note of the liquid's

light golden brown appearance, then checked its aroma. Next, she tasted it, trying to be objective as she tested its flavor and balance.

"Perfect," she murmured. It just might be her best formula yet. Finished for the day, she closed off the valve and cleaned up the counter area, then took her small glass of ale out to the wide veranda that circled the house. There she relaxed and finished her drink as she watched the sun sink below the cliffs.

At this time of the afternoon, it wasn't unusual to spot a family of black-tailed deer or the occasional tule elk foraging its way past live oak trees, arroyo willows and elderberry shrubs. Maggie spied a brush rabbit scurrying across the trail, seeking cover from a red-tailed hawk that glided in the sky.

Maggie loved the wild beauty of these hills, loved the scent of sea salt in the air. She never got tired of staring at the windblown, impossibly gnarled cypress trees that lined the bluffs at the edge of the property. When she was young, she'd been certain that elves lived in those trees. Everything was magical back then.

The magic seemed to disappear after her father died. His death had marked the beginning of too many bad choices on Maggie's part. In the past few years, though, she had managed to turn things around and was now determined to bring some of that old magic back. That was one reason why the revival of her father's beer-making legacy was so important to her.

The upcoming Autumn Brew Festival would be the culmination of all her struggles to establish herself as a key player in the industry her father had loved. Maggie had come a long way and was proud to be the owner and operator of "possibly the best new small brewery in Northern California," as one critic had called her burgeoning enterprise.

But her smile faded as she was reminded again of the deal she'd struck with the devil, aka Connor MacLaren. If Maggie's old high school friends had anything to say about it, Connor should feel entirely justified in seeking his revenge next week. The slightest negative word from Connor would be enough to destroy Maggie's standing among her industry peers.

If Maggie was being honest, though, she would have to admit that it wasn't Connor's style to be vindictive or mean. On the other hand, he had blamed her for the breakup and might be willing to do something to get even with her over the next week.

But while the possibility of dirty tricks and sabotage alarmed her, Maggie's real concern was Connor himself and his dangerous proximity. How was she expected to survive a full week in the same hotel suite with him? For goodness' sake, the man had only improved with age to become the sexiest creature she'd ever seen. Maggie knew full well that he had every intention of luring her into bed with him. Could she possibly resist his sensual onslaught? Did she even want to?

She left that question unanswered, but she was adamant that whatever occurred, it would be by her own decision. She would never again allow herself to be coerced by a man. She was no longer a weak-kneed, passive girl but a confident, successful woman in control of her own destiny. And she would decide if that destiny included a sexy roll in the hay with Connor MacLaren.

The strong, confident woman giggled at that image as she went inside to start dinner.

Later, as they dined on meat loaf, mashed potatoes and freshly harvested green beans, she and her grandfather talked about the festival. "I'm afraid I'll be gone all week, Grandpa."

"I'm glad you're getting out and having some fun," he

said jovially. "And don't you worry about me. I'll be fine while you're gone."

"I won't worry," Maggie said, "because Mrs. MacLaren has already promised to stop by for a visit every day."

"That wasn't necessary," Grandpa muttered, but Maggie could tell his grumbling was just for show. He and Deidre MacLaren, Connor's mother, were lifelong friends and would have a great time visiting. More important, Mrs. MacLaren was a retired nurse so she would be able to tell in an instant if anything was wrong with Grandpa.

Maggie thought the rest of the week would drag on forever, but almost before she knew it, Sunday morning arrived and so did Connor MacLaren. She met him outside as he pulled up to the house in a shiny black pickup truck. Ignoring the sudden rush of heat she felt as she watched him approach, she carried her overstuffed suitcase awkwardly down the porch steps. He met her halfway, took the bag and easily lifted it into the back of his truck.

"I hope you have room for my kegs," Maggie said.

"That's why I brought the truck," he said, and followed her to the beer house. They made several trips back and forth, carrying the heavy kegs and securing them in the truck bed.

"Just one more thing," Maggie said, running back to the beer house. She emerged a minute later with a dolly loaded with three cases of bottled beer for the official judging.

"I guess I don't have to ask if you've entered the competition yourself," he said dryly.

"I honestly wasn't sure I would until the last minute," she admitted. "But the festival is so important I had to give it a try. But don't worry, I'm only entered in the small brewery category so I won't be competing with MacLaren."

"Good," he muttered. "You beat our asses off last time."

"I did, didn't I?" She smiled broadly.

As he loaded the cases, he noticed the markings on the box tops. "You've entered under your real name?"

"Yes." She sighed. "I decided it was time to come out of the shadows."

"Good. People should know who they're dealing with."

Was he talking about himself being deceived by her false name? Maggie kept silent, figuring the less said about that, the better.

He opened the passenger door and held her arm as she climbed up into the cab. Maggie almost groaned as her arm warmed to his touch.

"Should be an interesting contest," Connor said lightly, and slammed her door shut.

Something about his tone aroused Maggie's suspicions and they grew as she watched him circle the truck and jump into the driver's seat.

"Let me guess," she said, her heart beginning to sink. "You're one of the judges."

It was his turn to smile as he slipped the key into the ignition and started up the truck. "Yeah. Problem?"

"Oh no," she said glumly. "What could possibly go wrong?"

"No need to worry, Maggie. It's a blind tasting."

"Then why are you wearing such an evil grin?"

As Connor chuckled, she settled in for the ride.

Four

As soon as they arrived at the convention center hotel, they stowed their belongings with the bellhop, who would hold everything until their room was ready. One of the festival handlers took her kegs and assured her that they would be delivered to the beer garden, where many of the brewers served their latest beers to the festival goers all week long. Maggie took personal custody of the dolly that held the three cases she'd designated for the competition. Then Maggie and Connor went their separate ways.

Maggie could finally breathe again. The tension in the truck had been palpable and she wondered for the umpteenth time how she would survive a week in a hotel room with him. After only twenty minutes in the close quarters of his truck, she'd been *this* close to begging him to pull off to the side of the road so she could have her wicked way with him.

She could still feel the shivery vibes coiling in her spine as she recalled him coming to a stoplight, then turning to stare at her.

I want you.

He didn't have to say the words out loud. She simply knew it—and felt it. His eyes practically burned with intensity.

Goose bumps tickled her arms, heat filled her chest and—she still blushed to think about it—a tingling warmth grew between her thighs as she became aware of what he was thinking.

God help her, but she wanted him, too.

Slowly Connor had begun to grin, as if he could read her mind, damn him.

Then the signal changed to green. He'd turned away from her and stepped on the gas. And the moment was gone.

But he hadn't stopped grinning like a lunatic.

Maggie's first impulse had been to jump out of that truck and run as fast and as far as she could go. But she'd talked herself out of that plan, shook off her feelings and pulled herself together. She could handle this!

They had spent the rest of the ride making small talk, chatting about his mom, her grandfather, the goats, anything she could think of to keep herself from dwelling on Connor's sexy mouth, his dark unfathomable eyes, his impressive shoulders.

And she still thought she could avoid him for a whole week in the intimate confines of a hotel suite? Was she out of her mind? Maybe. But she'd already called the hotel twice to check on available rooms. There was nothing. In fact, there were no rooms anywhere in the area. She was stuck.

But on the other hand, maybe the hotel would have a few cancellations today.

During the ride, she had confessed to Connor, "Once we get to the hotel, I'm going to try one more time to see if there's another room available."

"Not ready to give up yet?"

"No," she said, and felt a twinge of pride. Why should she give up trying to stand on her own two feet?

He glanced at her sideways. "Fine. But you're doomed for disappointment. I have every intention of sharing the suite with you."

"But why?"

He shrugged. "I want to keep an eye on you. It's a big hotel. Anything could happen."

"What's that supposed to mean?" she demanded. "I'm perfectly capable of taking care of myself, Connor."

"I know," he said patiently, as if she might've mentioned it once or twice before. Well, maybe she had, but it bore repeating.

She continued. "I just think it's wrong for us to be…"

"Sharing a bed?" he said, finishing her sentence. "Living in such close proximity? Breathing the same air? What's the matter, Maggie? Don't think you can handle it?"

"I can handle it," she protested.

"Can you? Aren't you afraid I'll melt your resistance and have you begging for my body tonight?" He flashed her that cocky grin. "I don't blame you for being worried. Let's face it, I'm awesome. I'm smart, I'm wealthy, I'm hot, I'm, like, the perfect guy. It'll be a real challenge for you."

She burst out laughing. "Right. You wish."

Smiling agreeably, he took hold of her hand in what should've been a casual gesture, but it sent electric shock waves zipping up her arm and had her stomach muscles trembling with need.

"Look," he said. "We can check the room availability if you insist, but even if they do have something, I'd rather we stayed together. In case you forgot, you're my date for the week. You agreed to that, remember?"

"I remember." How could she forget when he kept reminding her? And she *had* agreed to abide by his terms of the deal. Not that she'd had a choice, but it was too late to whine about it now. She sighed inwardly. He was just doing this to get back at her for leaving him ten years ago. He wanted to teach her a lesson. Fine. She could handle his little power trip. If staying with him meant that she would obtain the loan money, she was willing to do whatever it took.

That money was vital to her future.

As she crossed the hotel lobby, it was clear to Maggie that as long as she kept looking for a way out of their deal, Connor would fight her at every step. And she wouldn't put it past him to fight dirty, either. So was it worth her time and energy to keep trying to pitch a flag on this hill? Probably not.

But that still didn't mean she would sleep with him, no matter what he might be planning.

After confirming with the reservationist at the front desk that there were definitely no rooms available, Maggie needed coffee. She was in luck; there was a coffee kiosk right in the lobby. After slugging down a medium café latte, she again felt capable of adult conversation.

She spent the rest of the morning on the lower level of the conference center, checking in with the judging officials. It took a long time to go through all the necessary paperwork and get her cases of beer unloaded and marked. She didn't mind the rules and procedures. The officials wanted to make sure that the so-called blind tastings were carried out in a forthright and aboveboard manner.

It was common knowledge that anyone who won a festival award was practically guaranteed thousands of additional orders along with a tremendous amount of free advertising and marketing. So to ensure that each entrant's beverages received a fair review, the festival operators went to great lengths to set up numerous firewalls and protective measures.

Maggie had no idea security would be so elaborate. Because of her need to remain anonymous, she'd managed to personally avoid the contest circuit for the past three years, so she almost laughed when she was instructed to step behind a thick red drape in order to shield herself from the curious eyes of other contestants in line.

Once behind the privacy curtain, she was greeted by a tall, beefy fellow in a tight black T-shirt who wore a name tag that read Johnny. He looked like a bouncer. "Got your copy of the entry form?"

Maggie handed him the multipage form and waited while he checked off boxes on a sheet of paper clipped to an official-looking clipboard.

"You're with Redhead Brewery?" he asked in a low voice to avoid being overheard.

"Yes," she whispered. The paranoia was contagious.

"I've never heard of Redhead Brewery and I've never seen you around here."

"It's a division of Taylor James," she said defensively, and was proud of herself for thinking fast to invoke the false name she'd used recently.

"Yeah?" Johnny looked impressed. "I love his stuff." He turned to the table next to him and sifted through one of many storage boxes filled with thick, sealed envelopes. He finally found the one he wanted and pulled it out. "Okay, I gotcha."

"Good," Maggie murmured, relieved.

Johnny glanced at her, took in her long red hair tied back in a ponytail and nodded. "Redhead Brewery. Now I get it. So what're you? Chief Executive Redhead?"

"That's right," Maggie said with a smile.

Johnny grinned as he leaned forward. "Okay, Red, here's the deal. You got three beers entered in the Small Brewery category. Tell me if these are the right names." He read off the quirky names of her pale ale, amber and lager.

"Yes, those are mine," Maggie said.

"Good." He opened the envelope and pulled out three index cards with printing on one side. "These are the official numbers the judges will use to review your entries. No names. Just numbers."

She watched him take a thick marker and write the corresponding numbers on each of her cases of beer.

Then he handed the index cards to her. "Don't let anybody see those cards, got it? We wouldn't want anything to compromise the outcome."

"Got it."

"I'm Johnny," the guy said, tapping his name tag as if she hadn't seen it before. "You got problems, you come see me."

She picked up her tote bag and purse. "Okay, thanks."

"Hold on, Red," he said, grabbing her arm. "I want to see you put those cards away where nobody else can see them." He wiggled his eyebrows at her, adding, "We don't want someone voting for you just because you're pretty."

"What? No." She whirled around to see if anyone had overheard him, then felt a chill skitter up her spine as she realized what she was doing. She was looking for her ex-husband! Alan used to freak out whenever anyone complimented her. He would accuse her of flirting and tell her she was turning into a whore. It wasn't fun. But good grief, she'd been away from him for three years. Enough already.

Would she ever be a normal person again? The thought depressed her, but she took in a few deep breaths and managed to work up a warm smile for Johnny as she slipped the cards into her purse. "Thanks, Johnny. I appreciate your help."

"You bet," he said, then jerked his head in the direction of the exit. "Now get outta here. And have a nice day."

Three hours later, Maggie sat on the sunny lobby level near the coffee kiosk. She had no idea where Connor was or when he would text their room number to her. But she figured she had enough time to enjoy her vanilla latte before she had to face the real challenge of the week: Connor MacLaren.

She'd had a busy day already. After signing in with Johnny at the judges' hall, she'd spent over an hour touring the huge convention floor, watching dozens of volunteers at work setting up booths, arranging kegs and glasses and signage. There was a band stage and a dance floor set up at one end of the room. The spacious beer garden overlooked the stage. The energy and excitement were infectious and she thought about volunteering next year.

After a while, she'd found an empty conference room, where she sat and studied the judges' guidelines again. Then she pored over the official program, highlighting the seminars she hoped to attend during the week. As she got up to leave, four brewpub owners walked in and she ended up having a spirited conversation with them about the industry and everything that was good and bad about it. Maggie had walked out in a cheery mood, feeling as though she was on her way to becoming part of a warm, friendly community.

As she had approached the escalator, another man joined her, grinning as they both stepped on the moving stairway at the same time.

"Enjoying yourself?" he asked.

"Yes, I am," Maggie said as she studied him briefly. He was nice looking in a passive, nonthreatening way. "I'm Maggie Jameson."

"Nice to meet you, Maggie." He gave her hand a hearty handshake. "I'm Ted Blake. I haven't seen you around the festival before. Are you in the business or just visiting?"

"This is my first time at the festival. I run my own microbrewery and I've entered some of my beers in the competition."

"How many workers do you have?"

She was a little taken aback by the direct question, but then figured he was just making friendly conversation. After all, they were all here to share information and grow the industry. "I'm it, for now."

"That's got to be hard."

"I enjoy it."

"What about your sales force?"

She frowned a little. "It's just me."

"Huh." He handed her a business card. "When you get tired of doing all the heavy lifting by yourself, give me a call."

She stared at his card, then looked up as they reached the main floor and stepped off the escalator. At that moment, Maggie noticed a pretty brunette staring fiercely at her from a booth a few yards away. The woman looked vaguely familiar—and she continued to glare directly at Maggie. Maggie was so surprised by the angry frown directed at her that she couldn't look away. After another long moment, the brunette tossed her hair back and turned away.

What in the world was that all about?

Nonplussed, Maggie glanced at her momentary companion. "It was nice meeting you, Ted."

"Hey, don't rush off," he cajoled.

But Maggie was desperate to spend a few minutes alone. "Sorry, but I'm meeting someone."

Now, as she sipped her vanilla latte by the wide plate-glass window, she tried to shake off the irritation she still felt from that woman's odd reaction to her.

Beyond the patio terrace and swimming pool area, the picturesque Point Cairn Marina bustled with activity. The small port had started life as a fishing village, and fishing was still a staple of the region. Fishing boats chugged their way back into the marina after a long day, pulling up to the docks to unload their catch of the day. Sailboats motored past on their way out to the ocean, where they would unfurl their sails and battle the strong winds and waves. In this part of Northern California, sailing was a sport for adrenaline junkies.

One sleek, teak-hulled yawl brought back memories of her father and his first sailboat. Maggie was ten years old when she and her mom and dad first started sailing together. It had been thrilling to skim across the water and feel the breeze ruffle her hair. That first summer on his new sailboat had been so much fun, with her father barking out orders and Maggie and her mom saluting and laughing as they trimmed the sails and adjusted the rigging according to his commands. They would sail to a small inlet where the waters were calm and the winds light. There they would drop anchor and have a picnic lunch. Once they even spent the night out on the water. It was magical.

But after that first season, her dad began to seek out rougher waters and more turbulent weather conditions. Maggie was ashamed to admit it, but she was too afraid to go with him after that. Her mother stopped going, too, and more than once, she tried to explain to Maggie why her father needed to seek bigger, more challenging adventures. White-water rapids, rock climbing, hiking the tallest mountains, parasailing. Her father tried it all and kept searching for wilder and more dangerous tests of will.

Maggie never did understand why being with her and her mother hadn't been enough for him.

Shaking off the melancholy, Maggie turned away from the marina view and glanced around the bustling lobby. The hotel was beginning to fill up with festival visitors and she wondered if she might recognize a friendly face or two. But she didn't see anyone she knew. Not yet, anyway. One of her goals for the week was to talk to and get to know as many people as she could manage.

Of course, she was also hoping to avoid any locals who might be less than happy to see her.

"Because I need something else to worry about," she muttered, shaking her head at the different directions her thoughts were taking her.

Since she wouldn't have much spare time later, Maggie pulled her schedule out of her purse and studied it one more time. Then she checked her judging number cards to make sure she hadn't lost them. They were still tucked inside her purse and she smiled as she pictured Johnny's stern look as he pretended to threaten her if she showed them to anyone. He might've been big and intimidating, but she knew he wouldn't hurt a flea. Johnny was the classic tough guy with a heart of gold.

She frowned as she recalled her own reaction to his offhanded remark about her being pretty. It annoyed her to know that she could still cringe at comments like that, a holdover from her years with Alan. Back then, if a man had complimented her, Alan would accuse her of having an affair with the guy. Once at a party, she and two other women had been joking about something. Later that night, Alan had wondered if the three of them might be forming a prostitution ring. She was so shocked she laughed at him. That had been a mistake. She learned quickly to avoid being friendly with other women and became an expert at discouraging attention from other men.

"Pitiful," she said, shaking her head. Even after three years back home, she was still living her life in the shadows, still trying so hard to be invisible that it came as a complete shock when a man noticed her, let alone complimented her.

But she refused to be depressed about it. She was so different from the woman she'd been even a year ago. She was happy to be at the festival and she was staying there with a gorgeous man, even though he had sort of blackmailed her into it. She had no intention of doing anything with him except sleep, preferably in a separate bed or on the couch. Still, it was exciting to be here.

Her phone beeped and she knew what that meant. Connor had sent her a text. Taking a deep breath, she read the message. Room 1292. Luggage is here and so am I. See you soon.

Suddenly she felt light-headed and wondered if it was caused by the caffeine or by Connor's message.

Did she really have to ask? It was Connor. Definitely.

Grabbing her tote bag and purse, she stood and tossed her empty coffee cup in the trash and headed for the elevator banks. Once in the elevator, she checked her purse again to make sure the number cards were still inside the zippered pocket.

Johnny would be happy to know how paranoid he'd made her.

Still, she was grateful for all the protective measures the festival had taken to ensure complete anonymity in the judging. Connor would never be able to figure out which entries were hers.

She frowned. She wasn't truly worried that he would try to sabotage her, was she? That wasn't his style, was it?

She brushed her concerns aside, but they creeped back in. How could she not worry just a little? Even though he'd been a perfect gentleman so far, they were still on shaky ground. Who knew what he really had in mind? Maybe he harbored a secret plan to humiliate her in front of the entire industry. Maybe he was going to all this trouble, only to destroy her fledgling reputation. Who could blame him? From his point of view, she'd apparently betrayed him all those years ago, left him behind with nothing but a broken heart.

It wasn't true, of course. He had been perfectly happy to break up with her. So why had he taken it so hard? At the time, Maggie had thought he was relieved to be rid of her. After all, he'd been the one to urge her to take that trip back east.

But she had obviously been wrong about his feelings. If her former high school friends were to be believed, Connor hadn't taken her departure well at all. So now she had to figure he might want to take her down a notch if the opportunity arose.

Would he stoop to searching out her secret judging numbers? Maybe he didn't even need to know them. Connor had worked for years in this business, tasting and testing and reformulating. And he'd been taking part in contests for all those years, too. He could probably decipher most of the different nuances of every brand and style of beer on the market.

Had he studied her particular formulas and techniques? He'd been following her progress for months—even though he'd thought he was following Taylor James, not Maggie. But didn't it stand to reason that after paying such intense attention to her techniques, Connor might be able to discern which beers were hers? And if he could, then why wouldn't he think about pushing her out of the running?

He certainly had strong motivation to sabotage her—and not just because she was his competition. No, Maggie figured that even after all this time, he might see this as a chance to get back at her for leaving him.

Revenge, after all, was a dish best served cold.

"Just stop," she muttered. She would drive herself crazy if she kept up that line of thinking. It would help if she could keep reminding herself that she had been with a good guy and a bad guy, and Connor was definitely one of the good guys. Besides, she had a bigger problem to deal with than the beer competition. Specifically, how to get through a whole week with Connor living in the same suite as her.

The elevator came to a quiet stop at the twelfth floor, otherwise known as the penthouse level. Maggie stepped out into the elegant hall and paused, taking in the parquet marble floor, the crystal chandeliers, the Louis XVI rococo furnishings. For a guy who preferred denim work shirts and blue jeans to an Armani suit, Connor MacLaren certainly liked to live in style. Maggie didn't know whether to be impressed or amused.

"Let the games begin," she muttered, and strolled toward the suite, once again wondering what in the world she'd gotten herself into.

* * *

Connor heard the water in the shower turn off and estimated that Maggie wouldn't be much longer. He reminded himself once again that he had shown excellent character earlier when he'd resisted the urge to follow her into the bathroom and join her in the shower like he'd wanted to.

While he waited, he glanced around the sitting room of the hotel suite. Earlier that day, in the hope that adding some romantic touches would somehow convince Maggie to fall into his bed, he'd arranged with the hotel florist and catering staff to bring bouquets of fragrant flowers and some champagne on ice to the room. Now soft jazz was playing in the background and a delectable dinner had been ordered. The kitchen staff was standing by to prepare and deliver it as soon as he placed the call.

This wasn't the first seduction scene Connor had arranged. If memory served, he'd done something similar the first time he'd made love with Maggie all those years ago. He could still remember the day as if it were yesterday. The lavish picnic on a deserted beach at sunset, aching desire, sweet hesitancy, shy touches, her giggles, his need, their bliss. For a while, anyway.

Connor ruthlessly shut off those flashes of memory and concentrated on his plans for right now. This time, he thought as he glanced around the room, at least he would know what he was doing.

As he double-checked that the champagne was properly chilled, he accepted that there would be no pretense of "making love" this time around. No, this time when he and Maggie got around to doing the deed, it would be good old-fashioned, sweaty, hard-driving sex—and plenty of it. That was the plan, anyway, despite Maggie's words of protest. The way she kissed him in his office told a different story. At least he hoped so.

And what about that searing hot gaze she'd cast his way

that morning in the truck? If that was any indication of her feelings, he figured it wouldn't be too hard to bring his plan to fruition. So to speak.

They both seemed to be on the same wavelength. And why not? After all, he mused, as he carried a large vase of stunning red roses over to the mantel, this wasn't their first rodeo together. They'd done this before. So why not do it again, for old times' sake? They were two consenting adults, right?

And in case she didn't see it that way, Connor figured the flowers and champagne would go a long way toward softening her attitude.

He didn't mind putting on a romantic show for a woman when the situation called for it, as long as it worked out in his favor. And yeah, by that he meant sex. He wasn't ashamed to admit that that was the bottom line.

Connor stared out the window at the sun setting over the ocean view and frowned. Was he starting to sound callous or deceptive? Because he wasn't that guy. He didn't expect Maggie to say yes simply because he was loaning her some money. He grimaced at the very thought. He would never make sex a condition for the loan, for Pete's sake. He didn't have to, he thought with a grin. His charm and persuasive abilities would take care of any qualms she might have.

Although why she would have qualms, he didn't know. She wanted him as badly as he wanted her, that much Connor knew. Maggie's expressions were still easy for him to read, so he figured he wouldn't have to work too hard to make it happen.

"This is a beautiful room."

He whirled around. Maggie stood near the doorway to the bedroom, using a towel to fluff her still-damp hair. She was dressed casually in a cropped T-shirt and a pair of those sexy yoga pants some women wore that fit like a second skin. Connor gave a brief prayer of thanks for that current fashion choice.

"I was in such a rush earlier," she murmured, and took her time meandering about, touching a knitted throw rug hanging off the sofa, studying the artwork, smelling the roses. "Oh, the flowers are gorgeous, aren't they?"

Connor couldn't help staring at her as she moved with supple ease around the room. Her feet were bare, her petite shoulders straight. Her hair, thick and healthy, became lighter and more lustrous as it dried. He could see the outline of her breasts as they rose and fell with each breath she took.

His groin tightened.

How had he forgotten how sexy her toes were? How perfect her skin was? To give himself some credit, he'd never forgotten her breasts.

As beautiful as she was, Maggie seemed more fragile now than when she was younger. She was quieter, too. Or maybe it just seemed that way because they were getting to know each other all over again. He would have to wait a few days to decide if that was true or not.

Only one thing marred the perfection of her face, and that was her eyes, where he caught the slightest hint of sadness that didn't seem to fade, even when she smiled.

He glanced down at her feet again, then rubbed his hand across his jaw when he realized what a complete fool he was. Damn it, he wanted her as he'd never wanted anyone before—except her, of course, all those years ago. At the same time, he wanted to lash out at her and demand to know why she'd left him, why she'd betrayed him, why she'd broken his heart ten years before.

But he would never say those words aloud. She didn't need to know how ridiculously vulnerable he was in her presence. Hell, she'd been driving him crazy ever since she walked into his office last week. He'd thought about her all week, at every hour, no matter where he was or what he was doing. She didn't have to be in the same room with him or, hell, the same city. He couldn't get her out of his mind. But he would. Once they'd slept together again, Connor would be able to rid himself of these lingering feelings and get on with his life.

Maggie had circled the room and was now standing in front of the ice bucket holding the bottle of expensive champagne. She turned to him. "What's this for?"

"Us," he said, crossing the room to open the bottle. "Champagne. I thought we'd celebrate."

She blinked in surprise. "Celebrate what?"

He thought quickly. "This is the first time you've attended the festival, right?"

"Right."

"So we're celebrating."

"Okay. Let me get rid of this first." She took the damp towel back to the bathroom and returned in seconds. "So, what's the plan tonight?"

"I thought we could dine here in the room." Connor pulled the chilled bottle out of the ice and wrapped it in a cloth. "Do you mind?"

"I don't mind at all. It sounds perfect."

"Good." He removed the metal cover and wire cage, then carefully twisted the cork until it popped. After filling two glasses with the sparkling liquid, he handed one to Maggie.

"Cheers, Mary Margaret."

"Cheers," she murmured, and took her first sip. "Mm, nice."

"I hope you still like steak," he said.

"I love steak."

"Good, because I've taken care of ordering dinner for us."

She swallowed too fast and began to cough. Setting

her glass down, she breathed in and out a few times and coughed to clear her throat.

"You okay?" he asked, ready to pound on her back if necessary.

"I'm fine." She folded her arms tightly across her chest and pinned him with an angry look. "You had no right to do that, Connor. I can order my own food and pay for it, too."

He shrugged. "I guess you could, but I already took care of it."

She stomped her foot. "How dare you?"

"Dial it back a notch, will you?" he said, his annoyance growing. "It's just dinner. Besides, how did you plan to pay for it? You came to me for money, remember?"

Her eyes widened as she clenched her teeth together. She looked about ready to scream, but seemed to swallow the urge and just stood there staring at him.

"What's the problem here, Maggie?"

Instead of answering him, she whirled around and paced, muttering under her breath. Connor could only hear every third word, but it didn't sound flattering to him. Abruptly she stopped in her tracks, inhaled and exhaled once, then again, and continued her pacing.

What in the world had just happened to her?

On her third pass, he grabbed her arm to stop her. "What the hell's wrong with you? I didn't order you gruel, for God's sake. Besides, you can order anything you want, you know that."

"Do I?" she asked.

Incredulous, he instantly replied, "Of course you do." Surprised by his own anger, he took a long, slow breath, then continued quietly. "But why should you? I ordered all your favorite foods. Steak, medium rare, baked potato with butter *and* sour cream, lightly grilled asparagus. Chocolate mousse for dessert. I thought you'd be happy. You used to love all that stuff."

She gaped at him for so long it was almost as if she was seeing him for the first time. Then she sucked in a big gulp of air as if she'd been underwater for too long. As she exhaled slowly, her anger seemed to deflate at the same time.

"You okay?" he asked, searching her face.

"Yes." She shook her head, clearly dismayed. "Yes. I'm fine. And I'm sorry, Connor. That was really stupid."

"No, just confusing," he said, flashing her a tentative smile.

Still breathing deeply as though she was centering herself, she ran her hands through her hair and then shook her head. Her eyes were clear now and she smiled. "Dinner, um, sounds great. You have a good memory. Those foods are still my favorites."

"Glad to hear it," he said cautiously, and handed her the glass of champagne she'd forgotten about. "But there's something I did that set you off. Tell me what it was so I don't do it again."

She took a healthy sip of champagne. "It's nothing you did. It's just something that I... Never mind." She walked to the window, then turned. "Just...thank you for ordering dinner. I know it'll be delicious."

"Oh, come on, Maggie," he said, losing patience. "After all this time, we can at least be honest with each other. Tell me what I did so I don't make the same damn mistake again."

She chewed her lower lip and Connor wondered if she might start crying. *Crap.* "Maggie, please don't cry. I'm sorry for...whatever I did."

"For goodness' sake, Connor, I'm not going to cry. And you didn't do anything. I just get a little carried away sometimes."

"If you say so."

"I do."

He watched her for another moment, then said lightly,

"Okay, I'm glad it's nothing I did. But I want you to know you've got the green light to yell or cry if you feel the need to."

"A green light? To cry?" She nodded, biting back a smile. "I appreciate that, but I have no intention of crying."

"You never know." He gave a worldly shrug. "Happens all the time."

She laughed. "Somehow I don't picture women bursting into tears around you."

"Not so much," he admitted, adding to himself, *Not ever.* The sophisticated women he'd dated over the past ten years would never dream of revealing their true emotions, let alone break down in tears. If for no other reason than it would ruin their expertly applied makeup.

And that was fine with him. Emotions could get messy and out of hand, and he wasn't interested in that. That's why, despite being a fairly casual guy with a laid-back style, he preferred to go out with worldly women who knew the score, who knew they could count on him for a great evening of dining and dancing, always followed by great sex, and that was it. What more could he ask for? No mess, no fuss.

"Tell you what." He took her arm and led her over to the sofa. "Come sit and relax. Enjoy your drink. There's no pressure here."

She did as he suggested and sipped her champagne. He sat down at the opposite end of the couch and she turned to him. "You must think I'm a fool."

He stared at her for a moment. It would be a mistake to get lost in those big brown eyes and that perfectly shaped mouth, but he wanted to. He really wanted to. Maybe later. For now, he wanted some answers. "I don't know what to think, Maggie, because you won't tell me."

She gazed at the bubbles in her glass, and Connor could tell her mind had gone a thousand miles away. Fine. She wouldn't reveal anything to him. And why should she? They weren't exactly friends anymore. She was only here because she needed the money. So what did that make them? Business partners? Hardly. Jailor and prisoner? Absolutely not, although she might look at things differently.

After another minute of silence, he figured he might as well send for dinner and reached for the telephone.

"My ex-husband," she began quietly, "also used to choose my meals for me. Among other things."

"Ah." Connor still wasn't clear about the problem, but he was glad she was finally talking. "Did he force you to eat liver or something?"

She laughed. A good sign. "No, he ordered what he thought I should eat. He didn't think I was capable of making my own decisions."

"Was he some kind of a health nut?"

"No. He was just convinced that he knew better than I did what I should be eating. And drinking. And wearing."

"Huh," he said, frowning. "Sounds like a control freak."

"Oh, *control freak* doesn't begin to describe him," she said, struggling to keep a light tone. "He made all my decisions for me. So when you said you ordered my dinner for me, I guess I flashed back to a different time and place and…well, sort of lost it."

"Sort of."

She reached over and touched his arm, gave it a light squeeze. "I'm sorry."

"Stop apologizing. I just wanted to know where that reaction came from. Now I know where I stand and we can move on. And I promise I won't make any more decisions for you."

She laughed for real this time and her eyes twinkled with humor. "Oh yes, you will."

He grinned. "You're probably right. But you can always punch me in the stomach if you don't agree."

"Thank you. You have no idea how much that means to me."

"Hmm." He rubbed his stomach. "I'm afraid to find out."

With a lighthearted chuckle, she held her glass out to his. "Cheers."

"Cheers," he said, clinking his glass against hers and then taking a drink. He was relieved to see her relaxed and smiling again and he wanted her to stay that way. So as much as his curiosity was gnawing at him, there was no way he would bring up the subject of her ex-husband again tonight. Besides being an obvious buzz kill, the guy sounded like a real jackass.

Okay, so the evening hadn't started out exactly as he'd planned, but that didn't mean it couldn't end up exactly where he wanted it to.

With Maggie in his bed.

Five

The dinner was fabulous, as Connor knew it would be. The steak was cooked to perfection, the chocolate mousse was drool-worthy and their conversation was relaxed with plenty of laughs and easy smiles. Connor had kept the champagne flowing and had consciously avoided any talk of ex-husbands and old betrayals.

Sated, he sat back in his chair and watched Maggie as she savored the last luscious spoonful of chocolate mousse. He'd enjoyed the dinner, too, but had found himself getting much more pleasure from observing her delight than from his own meal. Maybe too much pleasure, if the relentless surge of physical need that had grabbed hold of him was any measure to go by.

But what could he do about it? He was mesmerized by her luxuriant tumble of reddish-brown hair that floated over her shoulders and down her back. And her face, so delicately shaped and porcelain smooth, begged to be touched. Her lips were soft, full and voluptuous, and Connor's fervent desire to taste them again was driving him dangerously close to the edge.

He cursed inwardly. His famous self-control was slipping. He had to find a way to pull the reins in on his rampant libido. But how could he look away while Maggie still licked and nibbled at her spoon, lost in her own little world of chocolate mousse goodness, for God's sake?

She was killing him. He wouldn't survive another meal. Not until he'd had her in his bed.

Soon, he promised himself. Very soon. For now, he forced himself to stop watching her pink tongue darting and nipping at the spoon. Instead he glanced up and tried to appreciate the elegant and somber artwork on the wall while he shifted unobtrusively in his chair, carefully adjusting himself so she wouldn't notice the rather prominent bulge in his pants.

When he finally could speak in coherent syllables, he said, "So, I take it you enjoyed dinner?"

"Oh yes," Maggie murmured as she set down her spoon. "Delicious. Thank you, Connor."

"My pleasure." Connor was just glad she'd put down that damn spoon. One more lick and he would've been a dead man.

She lifted her teacup and took a sip, then set it down and smiled at him. "This has been so nice."

Nice? he thought. He was barely grasping hold of the edge of madness and she was having a tea party.

He needed to get a grip.

"Why don't we move over to the sofa?" he suggested, standing and reaching for her chair. "We can talk some more and you can finish your tea."

She hesitated a moment, then nodded. "Yes, all right."

They settled at their respective ends of the comfortable sofa. Maggie seemed a bit shy again, now that she didn't have the safe barrier of plates and food between them. But Connor kept the conversation light and she eased back into it.

Every time Connor thought about what Maggie had told him about her ex-husband, he felt more and more bemused. She hadn't been living the high life as he'd always assumed, and now he didn't know what to think. Really, though, how bad could it have been? The guy was worth millions. Should Connor feel badly for Maggie because the guy she ended up marrying turned out to be kind of a jerk?

After twenty minutes of safe conversation centered mostly on goats, beer, Angus and Deidre, Connor's mom, Maggie yawned. "It's been a long day and tomorrow will be a busy one. I think I'd better go to bed."

She stood and reached her arms up in a stretch that caused her shirt to tighten dangerously across her perfect breasts. Connor had to look away or beg for mercy.

After a minute, she relaxed, picked up her teacup and took it over to the dining table. Connor followed her, but before he could say anything or make a move, Maggie turned and stopped him with a firm hand against his chest.

"You got your way, Connor," she said. "I'm staying in the suite with you. Dinner was lovely, thank you, but I'm not going to sleep with you, so don't bother trying to make me."

"*Make* you?"

"That's right, don't try to talk me into anything." She folded her arms under her chest in a stubborn move that only accented her luscious breasts. "I'm not going to change my mind."

He held up both hands innocently. "I never expected you to."

"Yes, you did."

"No, Maggie. You're the one who keeps bringing it up."

"What? Me? No, I—"

"And frankly, I don't think it's a good idea."

Her eyes narrowed in suspicion. "You…don't think *what's* a good idea?"

"Sex," he said easily, though he was cringing on the inside. "Look, we had a nice evening, but as you said, tomorrow's going to be another long day, so I think we should call it a night."

She frowned. "You do."

"Yes, I do." He nodded calmly, mentally patting himself on the back for putting on this show of levelheadedness. "Look, you said it would be wrong and I'm agreeing with you."

"You're...agreeing with me. Okay. Good." It took her a moment, but finally she gave him a tentative smile. "Well, then, good night. Thank you again for a lovely evening."

He glanced down at her hand still pressed against his chest. "Good night, Mary Margaret."

"Oh." She whipped her hand away. "Okay, good night."

"Wait." With an innocent smile, he reached out and took hold of her arms. "I'll sleep better if I can have a good-night kiss. Just one. For old times' sake."

She gave him a look. "Oh, all right." Then she seemed to brace herself as she puckered up for a chaste kiss.

But instead of kissing her mouth, Connor bent his head and kissed her shoulder. Then he moved an inch and kissed the small patch of skin at the base of her neck.

She was gasping by the time he reached her jaw line. "What are you doing to me?"

He nibbled and kissed her ear, then whispered, "We're not sleeping together, no matter how much you beg me."

"Beg you?" She stretched her neck to give him more access to the pale smoothness of her skin. "This is crazy."

"I know," he murmured. "I wish you'd stop it."

"I'm not..."

But she couldn't seem to finish as he began licking each inviting corner of her mouth. When she moaned aloud, he pressed his lips to hers in an openmouthed kiss more erotic than anything he'd ever experienced. She was sweeter than chocolate and more intoxicating than the cognac they'd shared earlier.

He realized his mistake immediately, tried to keep the kiss light, but it was no use. He wanted her with the intensity of a red-hot sun, wanted to pull her down on the couch and touch her everywhere, from the tips of her sexy pink toenails to the top of her gorgeous red mane. And each place in between, too. He could do it, he knew. She was willing and wanted the same thing he did. And damn, he needed her now, needed to be inside her, to spread her shapely legs and press into her, sheathing himself in her dusky depths.

Damn it. He'd set up this whole evening to be a romantic interlude leading directly to sex. But despite her body pressed tightly against his, he knew she needed time to get used to being with him again. So why didn't he stop? He knew with every kiss that he was making things worse for himself. He'd go insane before much longer if he didn't put an end to this right now.

But then she moaned and he reconsidered, and somehow his hand moved to cup the soft swell of her breast. And a part of him felt as though he'd come home after being away a long time. He recognized the sweet roundness and wanted nothing more than to get lost in her, nothing more than to touch his tongue to her beaded nipples and hear the familiar sound of her little gasps and whispers of bliss.

And if he didn't stop now, he never would. With unearthly strength of will, he forced himself to end the kiss and pull away from her soft curves. And immediately missed the warmth.

He ran his hands up and down her toned arms, then squeezed them lightly, before taking another step back. The only reward for his good behavior was her look of dazed wonder. He wasn't sure it was worth his sacrifice, but it was too late to change his mind.

"Time for bed, Mary Margaret." He wrapped his arm lightly around her shoulder and led her into the bedroom, where he gathered up a blanket and pillow.

She dropped onto the bed and watched him.

He smiled tightly and held up his hand in a sign of farewell, as though he were a soldier heading for battle. "Good night. Sweet dreams."

"G-good night, Connor. Thank you."

He walked out of the room and closed the door behind him.

So much for tactical retreats, Connor thought the next morning, after he tried to roll over in bed and slid off the couch onto the floor instead.

"Damn it," he grumbled, rubbing his elbow where it smacked against the coffee table. "Where the hell…oh yeah."

After a minute, he managed to pull himself up off the floor and sat on the couch with his elbows on his knees, head resting in his hands. As his brain slowly emerged from the fog of sleep, he played back the events of last night that had ultimately led to him sleeping on the couch.

At the time, it had appeared to be a brilliantly strategic move. After several long, hot kisses, he had no doubt Maggie had been tempted to give in to her desires and join him in bed. But no, Connor had decided that rather than moving in for the kill, he would leave her wanting more. His theory, which clearly needed work, was that with any luck, tonight she would be seducing him instead of the other way around.

It had seemed like such a smart idea at the time.

"Idiot," he muttered, scratching his head. "How's that strategy working out for you?" Cursing under his breath, he gathered up the blanket and pillow off the couch.

He entered the bedroom and found Maggie sound asleep. So she was still enjoying a restful night's sleep while he was wide awake and whining in misery. Glaring at her, all peaceful and snug in their comfortable bed, Connor vowed that it wouldn't happen again. There was no way he was sleeping anywhere else tonight but in this bed—with Maggie tucked in right next to him.

He quietly rummaged around in one of the drawers until

he found his gym shorts and sneakers and slipped them on, then took off for a bracing run along the boardwalk.

Halfway through the run, despite his determination to take in the crisp ocean breezes and enjoy the clear blue sky, he caught himself grumbling again. Uttering a succinct oath, he forced himself to shove the surly thoughts away and look on the bright side. So maybe last night hadn't gone exactly according to plan. It didn't matter. He was a patient man and he knew he would have Maggie in his bed soon. He'd stoked not only his fire, but hers, as well. She might've slept soundly but he was willing to bet he'd been a major player in her dreams.

Tonight, it was going to be different. He had all day to convince her that she wanted him as much as he wanted her. Maybe more.

Grinning now, he thought about Maggie and how she'd nearly succumbed to her own needs last night. It wouldn't take much to bring her to that point again. Hell, he loved a good challenge and she was nothing if not challenging.

He would prevail, of that he had no doubt. And with that happy thought in mind, he jogged back to the hotel to take a shower and get ready for the long day ahead.

Maggie heard the suite door close and checked the bedside clock. Connor had mentioned the night before that he might go running this morning, so Maggie figured she had at least a half hour to get ready for the day. She jumped out of bed and took a quick shower, then dried her hair and dressed in black pants and a deep burgundy sweater. She slipped her feet into a comfortable but attractive pair of flats because she had no intention of walking around the convention floor all day in heels. If Connor insisted that she dress up for dinner, she would come upstairs and change into her killer pumps. Otherwise, she was going for comfort.

Last week he'd made it clear that their week would be

more business-oriented than fun-filled, so she shouldn't be bothered to pack any blue jeans or work boots to wear this week. She mused that it should've bugged the heck out of her that Connor had dared to tell her what to wear, but after he'd explained what they'd be doing, it made sense.

But she'd still slipped one old pair of jeans and sneakers into her suitcase, on the off chance that she'd have some time by herself during the week.

The good news was that Connor would be forced to suffer in his business attire as much as she would, since, based on everything she knew about him, he lived in denim work shirts and blue jeans every day, too.

Maggie wrote a note for Connor telling him she would be waiting somewhere near the coffee kiosk downstairs. Then she grabbed her lightweight blazer and left the suite.

Forty-five minutes later, her heart stuttered in her chest at the sight of the smiling, handsome man walking right toward her. She could get used to that sight, she thought wistfully, but just as quickly, she banished the thought away. Getting used to having Connor around would be a major league mistake and she'd be smart to remember that. They were only spending this week together because she was desperate for money and he seemed to want to teach her a lesson.

Still, it couldn't hurt to look her fill.

He was so…formidable, despite his clean-cut outfit of khakis worn with a navy V-neck sweater over a white T-shirt. He should've come across more like the boy next door. Instead he looked dangerous, powerful, intense as he prowled confidently across the room like a sexy panther stalking his mate. Maggie noticed other women giving him sly looks as he passed, and part of her wanted to stand up and shout, "He's mine!"

But he wasn't *hers,* Maggie reminded herself, and he never would be again. The thought depressed her, but she pushed it aside instantly. She could be sad and whiny about that later. For now, for this week, she vowed to enjoy every minute of her time with him.

After convincing Connor to have a quick breakfast of coffee and a muffin, Maggie and he walked across the hotel to the convention entrance. She was surprised to see the convention floor packed with people, even though the festival was not yet open to the general public.

These first few days were mainly devoted to programs and workshops designed to appeal to those industry professionals in attendance. Maggie was looking forward to attending several of them and had them highlighted in her program booklet.

But already, hundreds of booths were doing a brisk business serving tastes of every type of beer and ale imaginable and selling all sorts of souvenirs. It was a clear sign that the beer-making community enjoyed partaking of its own products.

As they strolled through the crowd, Connor would occasionally take her hand in his to prevent them from being split up. Maggie tried to remember it didn't mean anything, but his touch was potent and unsettling. Each time, he seemed to set off electrical currents inside her that zinged through her system and left her dizzy and distracted.

It didn't help that every few minutes, Connor would run into someone he knew. He would stop and talk and introduce Maggie, assuring his friends that she was destined to be the next superstar in their industry.

Maggie wasn't quite sure what to think of Connor's kind words and she had absolutely no idea what to do with all the positive energy being directed at her from his friends and business associates. She smiled and chatted and appreciated it all, of course. Who wouldn't? These people could open important doors for her that had been closed and locked until now.

But it was confusing. Was this Connor's way of teaching her a lesson? Of getting back at her for breaking his heart ten years ago? If so, it was diabolical. He was killing her with kindness, the beast!

To divert herself, she concentrated on the swarm of festival attendees and the cheerful babble of twenty different conversations going on around her. She warned herself that if she thought it was crowded now, just wait until the weekend. The place would be packed wall to wall with people, and the noise level would be overwhelming with rock bands playing and even more demonstrations and activities going on. Maggie couldn't believe she was actually looking forward to the crush of humanity.

Connor continued to run into friends and associates every few seconds. It was amazing to see how many people he knew. But of course, he'd always been outgoing and charming. His mom used to say that Connor had never met a stranger, and it was true. Everyone he met became a friend.

He persisted in pulling Maggie over to introduce her to each new person, and she began to relax and enjoy herself, grateful that he would think to include her in both his business and his personal conversations with people. She hadn't expected it. Frankly, she was still trying to convince herself that she knew him, knew he was not the type to resort to sabotage. But was that true? May not be, but it didn't seem to be on his agenda today. At least, not yet.

And the fact that he was being so generous and inclusive and kind to her made it all the more difficult to cling to her determination not to sleep with him.

Not that she would have sex with him simply because he'd given her a few good business contacts. No way. Her gratitude didn't extend *that* far. But it was getting more and more difficult to ignore the fact that Connor MacLaren was simply a thoughtful, honorable man, a good person, just as he'd been when she knew him ten years ago. He hadn't changed.

It was Maggie who had changed. Who would have guessed that when she and Connor broke up, she was simply trading one set of risks for another worse set? The result was that now, after ten years, she was more guarded, more tentative, more jumpy. All those years with Alan and his mother had not been good for her.

But those years were over. It was all in the past and she was moving forward, living in the present and planning for the future. She was doing okay.

The fact that she'd stepped out of her comfort zone, taken the risk and faced down Connor MacLaren in his own office a week ago was something to be proud of. And, she thought as she gazed around at the festival crowd, she was actually out having fun. It was such a dramatic change from the way she'd been three years ago that she wanted to jump up and give a little cheer. Go, Maggie, go!

She smiled to herself. Good thing nobody was monitoring her goofy thoughts.

"Maggie," Connor said, interrupting her meanderings. "Come meet Bill Storm, one of the top-selling beer makers in the country."

"Aw, hell, boy," the older man drawled. "I'd be the *very* top if it wasn't for y'all and your MacLaren's Pride."

Maggie smiled at the man, who had what was quite likely the world's largest mustache and a personality to go with it.

She shook his hand. "Hello, Mr. Storm."

"Call me Bill," he said jovially. "Mr. Storm is my old man."

"Thanks, Bill."

"Now, Connor here tells me that some of the pale ales

you've been producing might just be the hottest beers to hit the market in years." Bill scratched his head in thought. "Don't mind me being a little skeptical, but I can see with my own eyes what your actual appeal to him might be."

Suddenly wary, she glanced at Connor, who merely smiled at his friend's good-natured teasing. Maggie decided that the old guy meant no offense and turned back to Bill with her business card in her hand. "I'll be glad to give you a personal tasting of my latest beers and ales tomorrow."

"And I'll be glad to take you up on that, Maggie." He handed her his business card, too, and Maggie slipped it into the pocket of her tote bag. Then Bill drew Connor into a more personal conversation about a mutual competitor and after a minute, Maggie decided to wander around a bit.

She stopped at several booths to check out the competition and met so many friendly beer makers and brewpub operators that she was reminded of something her father had once told her. The beer-making community was famously close-knit and friendly and helpful toward one another. Yes, there was plenty of competition, but they generally cheered their rivals on and supported each other.

At the fourth booth she came to, she stopped and stared and then began to laugh.

"That's the reaction I get most of the time," the guy said cheerfully.

His three featured beers had been given the silliest names she'd seen in a long time.

Maggie had learned early on that one of the joys of running a small craft brewery was coming up with a colorful name for the final product. Some brewers went for shock value, others enjoyed grunge and still others tried for humor.

The names of Maggie's beers were rather tame compared to some. This year she'd chosen the names of famous redheads to call attention to her Redhead brand. Her three competition entries were Rita Hayworth, Maureen O'Hara and Lucy Ricardo.

The barrel-chested, sandy-haired man running the booth turned out to be the brewery owner, who introduced himself as Pete. "Would you like a glass of something?"

"It's a little early for me to be tasting," she said with a smile. "But I was wondering who came up with these names of yours."

Pete beamed with pride. "My three sons come up with most of our names."

"Must be nice to have sons," she said. "Do they help you out with the brewing?"

"No way," Pete said, laughing. "Not yet, anyway. They're all under the age of seven. They're the creative arm of the company."

"Ah, that makes sense," she said, nodding, and picked up one of the bottles. "I was wondering what inspired you to name this one Poodle's Butt."

"That came from the warped mind of my five-year-old, Austin. But don't be fooled. Poodle's Butt is a fantastic, full-bodied beer with a hint of citrus and spice that I think you'll find unique and flavorful—if you can get past the name."

She chuckled. "I love the name. I'll try and come back for a taste later today." She pointed to another bottle. "Now, what about Snotty Bobby Pale Ale?"

"Bobby's my oldest. He came up with that idea last year when he had a cold. Laughed himself silly over his idea," Pete said, then added sheepishly, "I did, too. Guess they got their sense of humor from me."

Maggie patted his arm. "You should be very proud."

"I really am."

"Hey, Maggie."

She turned and came face to face with the quirky man she'd met the first day. "Oh, hello, Ted."

He flashed her a crooked grin. "I hope you thought about what I told you the other day."

"I really don't think I—"

"There you are," a voice said from close behind her.

Maggie whirled around and found Connor standing inches away. Her stomach did a pleasant little flip. "Hi."

But Connor wasn't looking at her. He was staring over her shoulder at Ted.

"Have you met Ted?" Maggie asked. "He's…" She turned, but Ted was gone. She spied him halfway across the room, jogging through the crowd.

"That was weird," she murmured.

"How well do you know that guy?" Connor asked bluntly.

"Not well at all."

"You might want to keep it that way."

Someone cleared his throat behind her. "Oh, Pete! Connor, have you met Pete? He owns Stink Bug Brewery."

Connor and Pete shook hands and talked for a minute or two, and then Connor grabbed her hand. "We should go. I want to check the judging schedule downstairs."

Maggie promised Pete she'd return later; then she and Connor left to find the escalators. Once they were descending to the lower level, Connor let go of her hand and glanced around. "This place is going to be packed by Friday."

"Isn't it fabulous?"

"Fabulous?" He gave her a curious smile. "Most people would be annoyed with all the crowding. But not you."

"This is my first festival, after all."

"Right. No wonder you're so excited." They stepped off the escalator and walked the long corridor toward the judges' hall. "So all this time you were entering competitions under your Taylor James name, you never actually showed up for any of the awards?"

She shook her head. "Not once."

"Why not?"

She really didn't want to have this conversation, but she owed him an answer, even if it was lame. "I'm shy."

He snorted a laugh. "You've never been shy a day in your life. What's the real story?"

Back when he knew her, no, she hadn't been shy. But over the years with Alan, she had learned to become invisible. She couldn't say that, though, so she tried to keep it simple. "Things change. I'd been away for so many years, and by the time I got back home, I didn't really know anyone anymore. Some old friends had left town. New people had taken their place. You know how it is. So I wasn't as sure of myself as I used to be. Especially when it came to competing in this business."

"But your father ran a brewpub. I remember he was always winning medals. You must know you'd be welcomed wherever went."

"If only that were true." She smiled reflectively.

"Okay, even if nobody knew you, you've got this business in your blood. You had to know that your product was excellent. Seems like you'd want to show up in person and get the accolades."

"You're right, I should've," she admitted, "but I didn't. My confidence was pretty low, especially after a few run-ins with people in town. It made me realize I wasn't ready to take on the general public, so my cousin Jane and her boyfriend agreed to attend the competitions on my behalf."

"What run-ins?"

Maggie cringed inwardly. Leave it to Connor to hone in on that key detail. She hadn't meant to blurt it out like that and she was wondering how to explain herself when they were interrupted.

"Hey, Red, is that you?"

Maggie turned and saw Johnny, the muscleman she'd met at yesterday's check-in.

"Hi, Johnny," she said, smiling. "Do you know Connor MacLaren?"

"Aw, hell," Johnny said with a grin. "Of course I do. How you doing, man?"

"Hey, Johnny." The two men shook hands. Then Connor looked at Maggie. "I'm going to head inside the hall for a minute to check the schedule."

"I'll wait out here."

"I won't be long."

He took off and Maggie chatted with Johnny for another minute until he had to get back to his line of people. Then she began to browse the long tables that had been set up to display the hundreds of promotional gadgets and giveaways. There were flyers, as well, and booklets that described the latest seminars and vendor products that might be useful to the industry professionals attending the festival.

She picked up a few clever gadgets and grabbed some flyers that looked interesting. Five minutes later, she glanced up and saw Connor waving at her as he exited the door at the far end of the judges' room.

Just as Maggie started walking down the corridor to meet him, three attractive women approached Connor from the opposite direction. There was a loud, feminine shriek and all three began to flutter and buzz around him. "Connor MacLaren! I thought it was you!"

"Ooh, it is Connor!" the blonde said. "Hey, you! You're looking good."

Maggie recognized the blonde as Sarah Myers, one of her best friends from high school. Sarah was also the first person to turn on Maggie when she returned home.

"Hi, Connor," the second woman said, and wound her arm around his. "I was hoping we'd see you here this week."

"Hi, Connor," the brown-haired woman said. She seemed more shy than the other two and as she got closer, Maggie recognized her. She was the angry woman who had stared at her the first day of the festival. The one who had glowered and glared and frowned, then flipped her hair and walked away.

And now she was staring at Maggie again. Maggie had an urge to rub her arms to ward off the chill.

Connor nodded at the brunette. "Hey, Lucinda. Are you working today?"

"No." Ignoring Maggie now, she grinned up at Connor. "Jake gave me the day off and we decided to check out the festival before it gets too crowded."

Did she work for MacLaren? Maggie wondered. If so, it was no wonder she wasn't quite as forward with Connor as her two friends were.

Sarah looked up at the Judges Only sign over the doorway. "Oh, hey, are you one of the judges? That's so cool!"

Maggie's stomach did a sharp nosedive. She felt ridiculous just standing there thirty or forty feet away from them, but she had no intention of joining the group and watching Connor be devoured by drooling groupies. There was no reason to be so annoyed. She had no claim on him, but that didn't seem to matter to her topsy-turvy emotions. She whipped around and took off in the opposite direction, praying that Connor hadn't seen her rapid retreat.

Maggie walked quickly, skirting the crowd until she reached Johnny's check-in line. She had resigned herself to the fact that she would eventually run into some familiar faces from town, but she didn't think it would happen until the weekend when the festival was opened to the public. Just her luck that Sarah and her posse had decided to show up early.

She slipped between the short queue of people waiting for Johnny and made her way farther down the hall to the ladies' room.

It was blessedly empty. Maggie stepped inside one of the stalls and locked the door. She leaned her forehead against the cold steel door and wondered how long she would have to stay in here. She felt like a desperate escapee trapped in here, but at least she was safe.

Safe?

"For goodness' sake, lighten up," she scolded herself aloud. Those silly women out there couldn't hurt her.

But they *could* hurt her, that was the problem. And she knew they would be more than happy to attack her again, only this time they would have an audience. Namely, Connor.

"They can only hurt you if you *let* them," she whispered. That was what the clinic counselor had told her a few years ago. Maggie knew those words were true, but knowing the truth hadn't made it any easier to ignore the taunts.

Maggie pounded her fist against the stall door. Damn it, wasn't ten years enough time to suffer for the presumed sins she'd committed against her high school boyfriend? Couldn't they behave like adults?

Even as she thought it, she had to laugh, since hiding in the bathroom wasn't exactly a grown-up move. She had to face this. Port Cairn was her home again and she couldn't spend all of her time running from people she'd once been friends with. Maggie had to find a way to convince Sarah to call a truce.

She would get to work on that right away, she thought with a soft laugh, as soon as she stopped shivering like a scared pup in this cold tiled bathroom. She wasn't exactly dealing from a place of strength at the moment.

She hated this feeling of shame. After three years of hard work and trial and error, she had accomplished so much and built an excellent reputation for herself. She should've been able to face her detractors with poise and confidence. But none of her achievements meant anything, as long as she was hiding in a bathroom stall like a sniveling coward.

"Not a pretty picture," she muttered, and with a defiant shake of her head, she straightened her shoulders. All it took was a little guts and determination to walk out of here with her head held high. And she would. Any minute now. It wasn't as if she was procrastinating or anything. But with the restroom still empty, this would be the perfect time to call and check in with her grandfather.

Pulling her phone out, she pushed Speed Dial and seconds later, Grandpa answered.

"Hi, Grandpa, it's Maggie."

"There's my sweet lass," he said, his Scottish brogue sounding stronger than she remembered. "Are ye having a bang-up time of it?"

"Best time ever," she lied. "Connor knows so many people and I've already made a lot of new contacts. Everyone is so nice and there's so much to see and do."

"Ah, that's lovely to hear, now."

"I miss you, Grandpa."

"Now, there's no need," he said. "I'm right here as always, tending to me darlings."

"Have you seen Deidre?" Maggie asked, anxious to make sure that Connor's mom had been stopping by.

"She interrupts me on an hourly basis," he grumbled.

"Good," Maggie said firmly. "I'm glad she's taking care of you."

"She's a good cook," he muttered. "I'll give her that much."

"She's a great friend."

"Yes, yes," he said impatiently, clearly not pleased that he'd been assigned a *babysitter*. "Now, Deidre mentioned that Connor's taking you to a fancy dance party. When is that?"

"It's Friday night, but I'm not going, Grandpa. You know I hate to dance. I didn't even bring a formal dress to wear."

"Ah, lass. You used to love to dance."

"Not so much anymore."

"You go to the dance," Grandpa insisted. "Connor deserves to dance with his beautiful girl."

"He'll have to live with the disappointment," she muttered, and quickly changed the subject. "How are Lydia and Vincent doing?"

"Och, they're randy as two goats."

She chuckled. "Grandpa, they *are* goats."

But he was already laughing so hard at his little joke that he began to cough.

"Grandpa, drink some water. You're going to choke."

"I'm fine," he said, but his voice was scratchy and he coughed another time or two. "Och, I haven't laughed like that in years. You're a tonic for me, Maggie."

She smiled. "I really do miss you, Grandpa."

"You'll be home soon enough, lass, soon enough," he said. "I'm pleased that you're getting out and about. You take some time and have fun with your Connor. And drink plenty of beer. It's good for you."

"I know, Grandpa. I love you."

"You're a good lass," he said softly, and Maggie understood it was his version of *I love you*.

They ended the call and Maggie sat and stared at the phone for a few seconds before she realized her eyes were damp. She wiped them dry; then with more resolve than courage, she left the stall, exited the bathroom and stepped out into the corridor.

"Maggie!"

She glanced around and spotted Connor waving at her from halfway down the football-field-length hallway. She didn't see any of the women with him, thankfully, so she waved and walked toward him. He met her midway.

"Where the hell have you been?" he asked.

"You looked busy a few minutes ago, so I went to use the bathroom and then called my grandfather."

"How's he doing?"

"He sounded fine. Your mom's already been there a bunch of times, so I know he's well looked after."

"Good." He slipped his arm around her shoulder, out of habit or companionship or something more significant, Maggie couldn't tell. But it felt so good to be this close to him. She breathed in the hint of citrus-and-spice aftershave, reveled in the protective warmth, loved that they fit together so perfectly, even if it was just for this brief moment. For so many years, she'd been unwilling to admit to herself that she had missed him, missed these moments of closeness with him. Life with her ex-husband had never been warm or cozy. Just cold. She shivered at the memory.

"Hey, Connor, over here."

They both turned and spotted Connor's two brothers coming their way with Lucinda, the same woman Maggie had seen with Sarah and her friend a few minutes ago. The same woman who couldn't seem to keep from frowning at her. Now she was holding a notebook and pen and didn't look happy about it. Had the brothers corralled her into doing some work? Probably so. That would explain her sour expression. Or maybe it was Maggie's own presence, she mused, but briskly brushed that thought away.

Connor quickly slid his arm away and Maggie felt foolishly bereft without his touch.

"Hey, guys," Connor said.

"You go ahead and talk to them," Maggie urged Connor. "I'm going up to the convention floor to look around some more."

"Stick around. You know my brothers." Connor grabbed her hand to keep her close by.

Maggie had a bad feeling about this little reunion, but she stayed with him and tried to think good thoughts.

"Is that Maggie Jameson?" Ian said as they got closer.

"Sure is," Connor said cheerfully.

"Hello, Maggie," the woman said tonelessly.

Maggie tried to smile. "Hi. It's Lucinda, right? You're Sarah's cousin. I remember you from high school. It's nice to see you."

Lucinda's lips twisted wryly, as though she didn't quite believe Maggie's words. "It's been a long time."

"Yes, it has," Maggie said, recalling more about the woman as they spoke. Lucinda had been a few years younger than Sarah, but she used to hang around with the group once in a while.

"I work for MacLaren now," she said, her tone proudly confrontational.

Maggie blinked. Lucinda made it sound like a challenge. As if she really meant to say, *These are my men. You keep your hands off.* Frankly, Maggie couldn't blame her. If Lucinda believed her cousin Sarah, she probably accepted the story that Maggie had destroyed Connor. Now she wasn't about to allow this witch to get near his brothers.

Jake and Ian exchanged glances and Maggie suddenly had a whole new reason for running again. They looked even less happy to see her than Lucinda did.

Naturally, Connor's brothers were aware that she'd left town all those years ago and probably assumed, as Lucinda and Sarah and everyone else in town seemed to, that she'd left him with a crushed and broken heart. If the accusations of Sarah and her other high school pals were the common wisdom around Point Cairn, namely, that Maggie had betrayed Connor with another man, then Jake and Ian most likely hated her as much as her old friends did.

So this would be fun.

"Hi, Ian. Hi, Jake," she said, trying to be upbeat. "It's good to see you both."

"Yeah, good to see you, too, Maggie," Ian said carefully. "How are you enjoying the festival?"

"I'm having a great time."

"Oh yeah? Did you enter something in the competition?"

"Yes, I've got three entries."

As she spoke to Ian, Jake leaned in to say something to Connor. Connor laughed, but Jake did nothing but stare stone-faced at Maggie.

She tried to block Jake from her line of sight as she attempted to continue the casual conversation with Ian, but it was impossible. She realized she could no longer stomach this level of judgmental scrutiny. Even Ian, who was at least willing to talk to her, was emitting the same reproachful vibes as Jake.

She reached out and touched Connor's arm to get his attention. "I—I've just remembered something I have to do upstairs. You can text me when you're finished down here and tell me where you want to meet."

"Wait," he said. "I'll only be a—"

But she couldn't wait. She had to go. She turned and walked away as fast as she could move, leaving the Mac-Laren brothers and their silent but palpable condemnation behind.

Six

Baffled, Connor watched Maggie dash off the convention floor. The urge to follow her was strong, but first he turned on Jake. "What just happened here?"

Jake shrugged. "Guess she didn't want to hang around."

"Don't pull that crap with me. You were freaking her out with your, whatever you call it, *evil eye* thing. And I don't appreciate it."

"You're awfully defensive," Jake said, standing his ground. "I thought you were never going to speak to her again. What changed your mind?"

"I grew up." Fuming, Connor glanced down the hallway. "That was over ten years ago, for God's sake. Let it go. And besides, you're the one who told me to bring a date this week."

"I was hoping you might bring someone who everyone could get along with."

"You could've asked me, Connor," Lucinda said.

Connor ignored her and frowned in frustration at his brother. "I thought you always liked Maggie."

"Well, sure, I liked her, until she screwed you over so badly that you could barely drag your ass out of bed for, like, a year."

"That's not true."

"Truer than you'd like to believe. Maybe that time was fun for you, but it wasn't for me. Or Ian, or Mom. Maggie ripped your heart out, man. We didn't think you'd ever recover. And I don't want to see it happen again."

Even if Jake's recollection was skewed, Connor could at least try to be grateful for his concern.

He suddenly realized that Lucinda was listening avidly to things he'd rather not share with anyone outside his family. With a tight smile, he said, "Hey, Lucinda, I thought Jake gave you the day off. Why don't you go catch up with your friends and have some fun?"

"That's okay, Connor," she said cheerfully. "I don't mind staying if you guys need some help."

"No, Connor's right, Luce," Jake said. "Thanks for taking those notes for us, but that's all we needed. You should go have some fun while you have the chance."

Lucinda smiled. "Okay, I'm off, then. See you guys around."

Connor watched her walk away, then turned back to Jake. "Look, I appreciate what you're saying, I really do, but there's no way Maggie will get to me like she did before. And I'm definitely not back together with her, if that's why you're so bent out of shape. This is just business."

"Business?" Jake said skeptically. "Didn't look like you were conducting business just now."

"I have to agree," Ian chimed in. "You two looked pretty friendly to me."

"Look, she's here with me because we made a deal. She's my date for the week and in exchange, I get her beer formulas."

Connor had informed his brothers last week that Maggie was the brains behind the Taylor James beers, so they knew how important those beer formulas were.

Jake pondered Connor's words for a moment. "Sounds like a pretty lopsided deal. What's she getting out of it?"

"The pleasure of my company."

Ian snorted. "Right. What's she really getting?"

"She needs to borrow some cash," Connor admitted.

"You're giving her money." Jake's eyes narrowed in on

him. "So basically, you're paying her to spend time with you. Do you know how sleazy that sounds?"

Connor rolled his eyes. "You're such a jerk. She needs the money for Angus."

"What?" Ian's eyes widened. "Why? Is he sick?"

"He's got something wrong with his heart."

"Damn it." Jake leaned his hip against the long conference table. "I hate to hear that."

Connor nodded. "Yeah, me, too. There's some new experimental drug that's perfect for him, but it's incredibly expensive and the insurance won't cover it."

"Then we should just give him the money," Ian said.

"Maggie's too proud to take the money without giving something in return. So she's giving up her recipes."

Jake was reluctantly impressed. "I guess that sounds reasonable."

"It is. So back off, because I've got this covered."

"Now you're scaring me again."

Connor ignored that. "And next time you see Maggie, be nice. Pretend Mom's watching."

"Aw, hell," Jake muttered.

"Yeah, and no more Vulcan death stare," Ian added, scowling at Jake. "You were even scaring *me* with that look."

Connor turned to leave. "I'll see you guys later. I've got to go find Maggie."

"Hey, wait," Jake said before Connor could get away. "Are you really sure she needs the money? I heard she was rolling in dough from her rich ex-husband."

"Where'd you hear that?"

"I don't know," he said, frowning as he tried to think about it. "One of her friends, I guess."

"What friends?" Ian scoffed. "I heard from Sarah Myers that all of Maggie's friends had turned on her."

"That's her own fault," Jake grumbled.

The fact was, Connor didn't really know much about what had happened, either, but that didn't mean he would put up with Jake's attitude. Connor smacked his brother's arm. "Whatever happened between Maggie and me is ancient history and none of your business, so stop being such a jerk about this."

"All right, all right," Jake said, holding his hands up. "I'll be nice."

"You bet your ass you will," Connor said ominously.

"But here's an idea," Jake said, his tone turning derisive. "Maybe you can fill us in on the *ancient history* one of these days." He used sarcastic air quotes for *ancient history,* as if he wasn't buying Connor's claim at all.

The sarcasm pissed Connor off to a whole new level and he made a move toward Jake. Ian quickly stepped between his two brothers, ever the peacemaker.

"Easy, there," Ian said, holding up his hands. "Both of you take a step back."

"Jackass," Connor muttered.

"Lamebrain," Jake countered.

"Don't sweat it, Connor," Ian said, then turned and gave Jake a fulminating glare. "We'll all behave ourselves like gentlemen."

"You're damn straight you will." Connor jabbed his finger at Jake. "And here's fair warning. I'm bringing Maggie to the Wellstone dinner tomorrow night, so you'd better treat her like a freaking goddess or you'll be watching the whole deal fall apart like a house of cards."

Connor decided to give Maggie some time to herself and, after wandering around the lobby for ten minutes, he stepped outside for some air. Crossing the terrace, he walked down to the boardwalk and headed south.

The sun was still bright, but the wind had come up and

turned blustery. Connor didn't mind the chill after so many hours spent inside the convention center.

He still wasn't sure why he had defended Maggie so stridently to his brothers, especially since most of what Jake had complained about was exactly how Connor had felt at one time. Didn't trust her, didn't understand her, didn't want to see her again.

But that was before Maggie had walked into his office a week ago. Since then, some of his opinions had shifted a little. And wasn't that perfectly natural? Especially after he'd found out that she hadn't exactly lived a charmed life all those years she'd been away. Still, he wasn't quite willing to cut her too much slack. At least, not until he found out exactly why she left him in the first place

He wouldn't mention it to his brothers, but he could admit to himself that he liked hanging out with her. Now and then, he caught glimpses of the old Maggie he'd known and loved, and okay, the fact that she was sexier than ever was a major point in her favor. So what was wrong with enjoying himself for a few days?

That didn't mean he trusted her, of course. There was no way she could ever restore the trust he'd once had in her. Nevertheless, when he heard his brothers talking smack about her, he didn't like it. Truth be told, their sniping had riled him up so much that he'd been tempted to punch out both of them. Not that Ian deserved it as much as Jake, but hey, Ian could always use a punch in the stomach, too, just on general principle.

The thought made him chuckle as he brushed his windblown hair back from his forehead. He loved his brothers, but sometimes they could be pains in the butt. Jake in particular had always been a hard-ass, especially when it came to trusting people. He was famous for saying that he hated liars, and once his trust was broken, he never looked back.

Connor didn't blame Jake for feeling that way. He knew

exactly where the distrust had come from. It was all thanks to their deceitful uncle Hugh and his damnable will. Hugh's relentless rivalry with their own father had extended beyond the grave, as the three brothers found out last year when it came time to read Uncle Hugh's last will and testament. A miserable man even on a good day, Hugh had attempted to pit Connor and his brothers against one another in an all-out fight for their inheritance.

So far, the brothers had outmaneuvered their uncle's Scottish lawyers and the ludicrous terms of the will. But all of that was irrelevant at the moment. Right now Connor just wanted Jake to lighten up around Maggie.

He did appreciate that Jake was worried about Maggie worming her way back into Connor's heart and maybe twisting it into a pretzel and leaving him for dead all over again. But Connor was a lot smarter and stronger now and he wasn't about to let that happen. So Jake had nothing to worry about on that front.

And besides, Connor reasoned, it wasn't as if Maggie had ever lied to Jake. Hell, Connor couldn't even swear that she'd ever lied to himself, either. She'd just left him. That was all. There had been no lies. No tears. No pretending. Maggie had simply walked out of his life one day and had never looked back.

Connor rubbed at a twinge in his chest and then swore crudely. This had to be heartburn or something. It couldn't possibly be the lingering memory of Maggie's desertion that was causing this stab of pain.

He sloughed off the ache and concentrated instead on the sight of a tarnished old fishing boat as it puttered into the harbor with its catch of the day. The crusty captain had a pipe shoved in his mouth and a bottle of beer in a handy cup holder next to the wheel.

Damn it. As much as it bugged Connor to admit it, Jake might have been right to question Connor's feelings for

Maggie. Especially since, like it or not, he still seemed to have a bit of a soft spot when it came to her. Which was a little ironic since he invariably turned hard as stone whenever she was around.

But that didn't mean he suddenly trusted her. He didn't, and wasn't sure he ever would again. And because of that, it wouldn't hurt to take a page out of Jake's book and be even more watchful around Maggie than he'd been before. That redheaded beauty was more than capable of slipping under his guard if he didn't remain on full alert from now on.

Connor walked back inside and immediately spotted her exiting an elevator and heading for the lobby. As he approached, she caught sight of him and stopped in her tracks.

"I was just going to go for a walk."

He took hold of her arm. "I just came in from a walk, but I'll go back out with you."

"That's not necessary."

"Yes, it is. You're my date, remember?"

"Oh, come on. You don't need me with you every minute of the day, do you?"

"Yes, I do." When her eyes widened, he quickly added, "Because we have a deal, in case you forgot."

"Right," she said, and sighed. "We have a deal. But that shouldn't mean I don't get a break once in a while. Especially after being the target of your brother's evil stinkeye stare."

He almost laughed but managed to check himself. He didn't blame her for ragging on Jake, but he wasn't about to tell her so. "I didn't notice."

"Oh, please! He was scowling at me the whole time I was standing there. He's about as subtle as a rhinoceros."

He shrugged. "Jake scowls so often I never think much about it. But admit it, it's not just my brothers that you have a problem with."

"What do you mean?"

"You think I didn't notice you racing in the opposite direction as soon as Sarah and her friends showed up? You left me to defend myself against them. That was cruel. They're your friends, not mine."

"They are not my friends," she said flatly, then began to chuckle. "And honestly? You're complaining about having three women drool all over you? Hang on to your every word? You didn't appear to be suffering, Connor."

He chuckled, then changed the subject. "Let's go upstairs and get jackets. It's chilly outside."

The elevator arrived and she stepped inside. Connor joined her and the elevator quickly filled up, so they kept their conversation mundane. A few minutes later, they stepped out on the twelfth floor and walked to the door of their suite.

As Connor keyed open the door, Maggie said, "I don't care what you had planned for dinner tonight. I'm going to the Crab Shack and I'm having a glass of wine."

Connor grinned. The Crab Shack was one of his favorite dive restaurants and it was only a half block away. "I'm up for that."

"You are?"

He opened the door for Maggie, then followed her inside. But before she could go any farther, he grabbed her arm. "Look, Maggie. I know Jake can be a jerk, but that's not really why you ran off, is it?"

"Of course not," Maggie said, not quite meeting his gaze. "I had things to do."

"Right."

"Fine." She draped her blazer on the back of the dining room chair. "Of course I ran off. Anyone would've if they'd seen the look he was giving me. If they'd felt the chill."

"The chill?"

"Yes, the deadly chill emanating from your brother that was aimed in my direction. Forget it." She shook her head in dismissal and walked into the bathroom to brush her hair. Connor followed her and leaned against the doorjamb to watch in the mirror while she brushed her hair.

"Okay," he conceded. "I might've noticed him staring at you, but he hasn't seen you in a long time. Maybe he was mesmerized by your beauty."

"You're funny."

"Not trying to be." Connor sat on the marble ledge next to the luxurious spa bathtub and made himself comfortable while she applied a fresh coat of lipstick. Her movements were so simple while being quite possibly the most sensual thing he'd seen in forever. It took every ounce of willpower he possessed to keep from grabbing hold of her and licking the color off her mouth, then covering every inch of her body in hot kisses.

Sadly, Maggie didn't look as though she'd be open to that plan at the moment, but he had all afternoon to convince her otherwise.

The thought had him growing hard again and he subtly adjusted himself while forcing himself to concentrate on business. "Here's the thing, Maggie. Tomorrow night, you and I and my brothers will be having dinner with some very important business associates. MacLaren Corporation is involved in a very sensitive and confidential transaction with this other group, and the last thing we need them to see is friction between you and Jake."

"If your meeting is so sensitive and confidential, why do you want me to be there? I know you don't trust me."

He stared at her for a long moment. She was stating exactly what he'd been thinking earlier, that he didn't trust her and never would. And yet…he did trust her. Maybe not as far as his heart was concerned, but this was different. "In this case, I do trust you. I know you wouldn't do anything to jeopardize our business."

She blinked in surprise. "Thank you. I appreciate that.

And you're right, I would never deliberately put your business at risk."

"So you'll play nicely with Jake."

"I'm happy to get along with everyone, Connor, but your problem lies with Jake. You need to talk to him." She waved a little wand thing as she spoke, then wiped the tip of it along her lips, causing them to grow even glossier and lusciously edible than before.

"I've…um." He gulped. It was getting more difficult to follow the conversation. "I've already given Jake an earful."

"Good, because the last thing I need in my life is more friction." She met his gaze in the mirror as understanding dawned. "So you *did* notice he was scowling at me."

"Of course I noticed. But like I said, that's his normal expression. I've learned to ignore it."

"It's pretty hard to ignore when you're the target."

Connor was forced to agree with her since he had also been the target of Jake's wrath within the past half hour. "I apologize for his idiocy. I hope you can overlook it and get along with him tomorrow night."

She zipped up her cosmetic bag and turned to gaze directly at him. "We'll be fine, Connor. I'm sure your brother wouldn't do anything to jeopardize an important business transaction."

"No, he wouldn't."

"And neither would I. So it's settled. Let's go to lunch."

"Wait." He gripped her shoulders lightly. "I want to make this official in case you didn't hear me a minute ago. I sincerely apologize for my brothers hurting your feelings. You didn't deserve it and it won't happen again. And if it does, one of them will have to die."

She beamed. "Thank you, Connor. I appreciate that." She was gazing up at him as if he were some kind of heroic Knight of the Round Table, which was so far from the truth it was laughable.

"I'm not sure you should thank me," he said. "I didn't punch his lights out or anything. I should've, but I didn't."

"Thank you anyway." She continued to stare at him, the soft trace of a smile on her lips, and he no longer had a choice. He kissed her.

He fought to take it slow and easy with her, even though he was consumed with a stark need for more. But the knowledge that Maggie might still be reeling from Jake's censure forced Connor to keep the contact light. And that was one more reason why he planned to knock his brother on his ass the next time he had the chance.

Knowing she hadn't expected his kiss and wasn't ready to take it further, Connor was nonetheless tempted to break down her barriers and fulfill his deepest need to take her. Right now. In every way possible. He wanted her clothes stripped off, her breasts in his hands, his mouth on her skin, her body slick with his sweat, her core filled with his shaft.

The image made his heart pound so hard and loud his eyes almost crossed.

Connor had never been the kind of man who required instant gratification. Stretching out the anticipation made the fulfillment of his goal so much sweeter, so much more worth the wait. But now the scent of her filled his head, intoxicating him, making it difficult to remember why he'd thought it better to wait. He burned for her, wanted her more than he'd ever wanted anything before. Now. He didn't want to wait another second.

He shifted and changed the angle of their kiss and covered her lips completely. She had the most incredibly sensual mouth he'd ever seen on a woman, and he couldn't get enough of it.

Ever since the night before when he'd been stupid enough to postpone their lovemaking, he'd been craving the touch of her lips again. Waiting and wondering when the right moment would come and he could take her in his arms and fulfill his most ardent fantasies.

A soft sigh fluttered in her throat, and Connor took it as a sign of her desire for more. He eased her lips apart with his tongue and plunged inside her warmth, where her tongue tangled with his in a pleasurable whirl of desire.

As they kissed, a distant part of Connor's mind flashed to the past when he and Maggie had been joined at the lip. They'd shared hundreds, maybe thousands of kisses back then, so why did her kiss today feel so completely different and brand-new? As though they'd never kissed before this moment.

They weren't the same people, he thought. They were older, definitely. Smarter, too, he hoped. Back then, Connor had worshiped the ground Maggie walked upon. He'd treated her like spun silk, a rare treasure, something to be cherished above all else. Maybe that was why she'd left him. Maybe he'd been too wrapped up in her to notice she wasn't happy. He still didn't know.

But the Maggie in his arms today was a flesh-and-blood woman. Complicated. Beautiful. Normal. He no longer had any expectations that she was anything other than that. And that made everything different.

Better, he thought again.

When she moaned, he ended the kiss and gazed at her. "In case you couldn't guess, I want you, Maggie."

She studied him for a long moment; then she sighed. "Does this mean I'm going to miss my dinner?"

He laughed and ran his hands up and down her arms. "Only if you say so. It might kill me, but I'm following your lead—for right now."

Tonight, though, he would be the one in charge. And there was no doubt in his mind as to how they would be spending the evening.

"So, what do you want, Maggie?"

"I want… I…" She closed her eyes and leaned her forehead against his chest.

"You want…" he prompted, using his finger to lift her chin so he could meet her gaze.

"Damn it, Connor, just kiss me again."

His smile grew and he pulled her closer. "Be happy to oblige."

His mouth took hers in a white-hot kiss and Maggie met him with the same level of passion, mixed with a new level of confidence and enthusiasm. It seemed to Connor that now that she'd made the choice, Maggie could relax and go with her instincts. Maybe it came from being the one to make the decision, or maybe she just needed to hear him say how much he wanted her. Not that she couldn't have figured it out on her own by looking at a strategic part of his anatomy, but it probably also helped that he'd voiced how ridiculously desperate he was to taste her and touch her.

He refused to question her change of heart. He was just pitifully grateful that she wanted the same thing he did.

She parted her lips to allow him entrance and met each stroke of his tongue with her own. As his hands swept over her back and dipped down to lightly grasp her gorgeous butt, she let out another soft groan and arched into him.

Connor gave a mental shout-out to whatever gods were in charge of the really important things—like Maggie's body. Her well-sculpted arms. The smooth line of her stomach. The shapely curve of her thighs. Not to mention her delectable mouth. She was temptation personified and he couldn't resist any part of her. Never could.

That was probably why it had taken him so long to get her out of his system. But he *had* gotten over her.

This time, things would be different, he thought, as he slid his hand up and cupped her breast.

This time it was all about physical pleasure, pure and

simple. No hearts, no emotions, no pain. No more thinking about the past. From here on, there was only pleasure.

"Connor, I want…"

"So do I, baby," he whispered, and swooped her up into his arms.

"Oh, you never did that before," she blurted, then laughed playfully and wrapped her arms around his neck.

"I must've been crazy," he muttered, and carried her into the bedroom, were he laid her down gently on the comforter.

He followed her down and pulled her into his arms, where they gave and took in equal measure as they rolled together, exploring, begging, melting into each other as they each demanded more and more.

Connor moved up onto his knees and straddled her thighs. "You're wearing too many clothes," he said, sliding his hands under her top. "I do like this sweater."

She smiled dreamily. "Thank you."

In a blur, he whipped it up and over her head and tossed it aside.

She laughed in surprise, then sighed as he ran his hands along her bare shoulders, down her sides and across her stomach.

"I like this better," he said.

"Me, too."

He cupped her breasts and leaned over to kiss the soft roundness. Swiftly unhooking her bra, he tossed it, as well. "Better and better."

"Connor," she whispered, and moaned when he used his thumbs to tease her nipples to peak. He moved in with his mouth, taking first one breast, then the other, sucking and licking, nibbling and tasting until she was writhing under him.

He moved lower, kissing her stomach and nuzzling her belly button as he slid lower still. He slowly unzipped her pants, planting more kisses as he exposed more skin. Pulling them off, he rose to gaze at her body. "God, you're beautiful."

"Connor," she said on a sigh.

"I'm right here." He gazed at her, saw that her eyes were bright with desire. Her thick red hair was spread out in waves across the pillow like an aura. Her lips were plump and wet from the touch of his own. All she wore now was a pair of skimpy pink lace panties, the stuff of male dreams. He slid two fingers under the edge to tease her, but only succeeded in straining his already shaky control. His body was hard and aching and he couldn't wait another minute to do the one and only thing he wanted to do. Bury himself inside her.

He jumped off the bed and undressed in a heartbeat, then found one of the many condoms he'd been smart enough to pack. He quickly tore it open and sheathed himself, then returned to the bed, where she was watching him with a hunger that matched his own.

"All dressed up and ready to go?" she said saucily.

"That's right." He slid closer and planted a kiss on her smooth shoulder. "Now, where was I? Let's see."

He moved lower again, kissing and licking his way down her body. He stopped to taste her breasts once again, filling his senses, then moving along the soft contours of her stomach and hips. She was breathless by the time he reached the apex of her sleek thighs.

"Ah yes," he murmured as he reached beneath her panties with his fingers to find her hot, moist core. "I was right here."

She trembled and moaned her need as his fingers began

to stroke her inner heat, taking her to the edge and back again, driving her to the brink of release, then pulling her back once more. Her soft pleas became groans of need and Connor was certain he'd never known such all-consuming desire before. Not even ten years ago when all he'd wanted was Maggie. This was more. This was bigger. He craved her with every fiber of his being.

He hooked his thumbs around the band of her panties and tugged them off slowly, killing himself with pleasure as he watched them slide over her curvy hips and down her shapely legs. When he reached her ankles, she nudged him away with one foot while she used the other to fling the panties across the room.

He laughed and glanced up at her. Her full lips were curved in a sexy smile and her brandy-hued eyes gleamed with feminine power and pleasure. She'd never looked more beautiful to him and he decided, in that moment, that he needed honesty between them.

"I've wanted you in my bed since I saw you last week," he said, moving closer and positioning himself. In one swift motion, he entered her and crushed his mouth against hers. She gripped his shoulders as their bodies rocked together in a sensual, synchronous rhythm that seemed to arise from within them and overtake them effortlessly.

He felt her heart beating in time to his, kissed the smooth surface of her neck and shoulders. He'd never felt more alive as he strained to bring her the ultimate pleasure possible while holding out on the same for himself for as long as humanly possible. But as her body strained against his, as her sumptuous breasts pressed into his chest, as her stunning legs wrapped more tightly around his waist, he felt a stab of need stronger than any he'd experienced before. He pressed more deeply, filling her completely, building up the hunger within them both until they were clinging to the edge of sheer passion.

She fell first, crying out his name and shuddering in his arms, leaving Connor overwhelmed by a bone-deep sense of fulfillment. With one last driving thrust, he echoed her cry with his own and a dark, wild rapture hurtled him over the edge.

Seven

What did you do?

She'd had sex with Connor, she reminded herself, with a mental cuff to the head. Wasn't it obvious? The man himself was still warm, sexy, naked and snuggled beside her in their big comfy bed.

Sex with Connor. It had been even better than she remembered. More than wonderful, it was spectacular. Better than fireworks. Or rainbows. It was awesome. The best sex she'd experienced in…forever? Hard to believe, but Connor was a better lover than he used to be, and he'd been pretty darned good back in the day.

Connor had always been wonderful, thoughtful and giving. But now he was so much more than that. He was powerful and agile and…oh, mercy. Did she already mention *awesome?*

But that wasn't the point, was it? The point was, she had done something horribly wrong and stupid. How many times had she reminded herself in the past week that Connor MacLaren was out for revenge, pure and simple? How many ways had she practiced saying *No!* to him?

And with one kiss, her stratagem had crumbled. Granted, it had been a very, very *good* kiss, but now what? She'd let go of every last qualm she'd brandished as a first line of defense and now she was left with, well, nothing. If she were smart, she would get dressed and go back home to her grandfather and the goats.

More than anything else, this proved what a hypocrite

she was. After all, she'd spent years trying to avoid risks, ridding her life of any little thing that might bring her pain, and here she was again, risking it all for a chance to...to what? Find a love to last a lifetime? Yeah, right. With the guy everyone—including him—thought she'd unceremoniously dumped ten years ago? Get real.

Maggie squeezed her eyes shut even tighter.

She wished she could blame Connor for coercing her, but he'd made a point of insisting that it was her decision to continue. Awfully clever of him.

Well, Maggie would just have to chalk this up as one more bad decision in a lifetime full of them.

Alan would say—

Stop!

Maggie cringed. She had a long-standing rule never to start a sentence with her ex-husband's name.

Connor stretched, then turned and leaned up on his elbow to gaze down at her. "You're thinking too much. I can hear your brain ticking away."

"Sorry. Sometimes my inner thoughts can get pretty loud."

Smiling, he brushed a strand of hair off her forehead, then slowly sobered. That couldn't be a good sign. "Maggie, that was..."

A mistake?

A horrible error in judgment?

Was he waiting for her to finish the sentence? Was there a multiple-choice response?

"Phenomenal," he murmured, and bent his head to kiss the tender skin beneath her chin. "Incredible. Mind-bending."

"Awesome?" she suggested lightly.

"Beyond awesome." He nudged the blanket down so he could kiss and nibble her neck and her ear and her jaw and, oh, sweet mother, Maggie's synapses were starting to sizzle. She wanted him all over again.

Phenomenal, he'd said. Would this be a good time to jump up and do a little happy dance? Maybe not. And really, even though the sex was good—or rather, damn good, phenomenal, awesome—it didn't change the bigger picture, the one in which Maggie knew she'd screwed up royally. So right now she needed to stop fooling around and think about her next move. She should leave. But what if he changed his mind about their deal? What if he changed the terms? Was it awful of her to wonder about that at a time like this? Yes, but…oh dear, should she pack her bags? Should she eat something first? She ought to think about—

"You are so beautiful, Maggie," he said, trailing kisses along her breastbone. Then he reached for her. "Come here."

She stared at his tousled dark hair, ran her hands along the strong muscles of his shoulders and back and pondered whether she was making another mistake again. Oh, hell, was there any doubt?

He lifted his head and met her gaze. "Trust me, Maggie?"

Biting her lip, she stared into his dark eyes and wondered if she'd ever had a choice. He smiled then, and so did she. Because of course, she'd always had a choice.

"Yes," Maggie whispered, and didn't have to think anymore.

As the sun was setting over the ocean, Maggie and Connor slipped on jeans, sweatshirts and sneakers and walked down the boardwalk to the Crab Shack.

With peanut shells on the floor and a monstrous grinning crab crawling on the roof, it shouldn't have been romantic, but Maggie loved it. They grabbed an empty table next to the full-length plate-glass window and ordered wine. The last arc of the sun shot coral and pink cloud trails across the sky until the sun finally sank beneath the horizon. Once it was gone completely, streetlamps began to twinkle to life along the boardwalk. Their server brought their wine along with a votive candle to shed some light on the menus.

"I don't suppose you want lobster," Connor asked after a minute of perusing the specials.

"I love lobster. I haven't had it in years." She closed her menu and took a sip of wine. "Yes, that's what I'm having."

"I figured you might've gotten tired of it after all that time you spent in Boston."

"Oh no, no," she said, chuckling. "Lobster was not allowed."

"Allowed?" He frowned at her. "Is this about your ex? Because I've got to tell you, Maggie, the guy sounds like a real jackass."

She smiled. "What a lovely description. It suits him perfectly."

Their waiter was back with bread and butter and took their orders.

After the waiter walked away, Connor leaned forward. "I've got to ask you something. If the guy was such an ass, why did you ever…" He flopped back in his chair and held up his hand to her. "Wait. Never mind. Don't answer that."

"No, it's okay," she said, sighing as she buttered a slice of sourdough bread. "Go ahead and ask whatever it is you're wondering about. You deserve answers."

He pulled off a hunk of bread and popped a small chunk of it into his mouth. Did he really want to hear all the reasons why she'd stopped loving him? Hell, no. But she was right. After all this time, not to mention the past four hours they'd spent in bed together, it would be smart to get some answers. "Okay, I'll ask. Why'd you leave me for him?"

She stopped chewing abruptly and tilted her head in confusion. "Connor, I didn't leave you for him. You and I had already broken up a month earlier."

He was taken aback. "No, we didn't."

"Yes, we did," she said softly. "We broke up the day you announced that you and your brothers were going to spend a week at some skydiving camp."

He wanted to ask her what alternative universe she was living in, but he kept it civil. "Maggie, that's just not true."

"Yes, it is. I remember it as if it were yesterday because I was devastated." She tapped her fingers nervously against the base of her wineglass. "I was so proud of myself because I'd managed to keep breathing when you went on that white-water rafting trip to the most dangerous river in the country. But then you went off with your brothers to climb El Capitan in Yosemite and I was breathing into a paper bag the whole time. When you told me about the skydiving, it was the last straw for me. I told you that if you went away, I wouldn't be here for you when you got back." She waved her hand in disgust. "Such a stupid, girlish threat, but I meant it at the time."

He frowned, remembering her words in that last conversation, but not realizing their full implication at the time.

She continued. "So after I said that, you said, 'That's too bad, babe. I guess we both have things we've gotta do.' And that was it. We said goodbye and you hung up the phone. Believe me, Connor. I remember that conversation. I remember staring at the phone and then bursting into tears. My mother probably remembers, too. I drove her crazy that summer."

Apparently everyone had grasped her meaning but him. "I thought you were telling me that you were going away for a while, like, on vacation. I figured, I'd be gone a week, come home and then you'd be gone a few weeks. So we'd miss each other's company for maybe a month, but we'd get back together at the end of summer."

Her face had turned pale. "No. I meant that I wouldn't be with you anymore."

He felt his chest constrict as he considered her words. "So you were already over me."

"Oh no! No, I loved you so much, but you scared me to death. Connor, don't you remember how I used to tell you that you deserved a woman who enjoyed taking risks? Someone just like you?"

He swirled his wineglass absently. "Yeah, you said it a lot. I thought it was a little joke, because I always thought we were perfect together."

Her eyes glittered with tears as she shook her head. "No, it wasn't a joke. I wish it was, but I couldn't stand it when you took chances with your life."

"My life?"

"You and your brothers were always going off to hike up some sheer cliff, or ski over some avalanche, or ride horses down a treacherous canyon path."

He gave a lopsided grin. "The Grand Canyon trip. Hell, Maggie, we used to do that kind of stuff all the time. Not so much anymore. But I don't see why it was such a big deal to you."

"Believe me, it was a big deal. I would sit at home holding my breath, waiting for the phone call from the morgue."

And that's when Connor suddenly remembered that Maggie's father had died in a hiking accident in Alaska. He'd always known about it, but had never connected the dots. Damn, no wonder all of his wild sporting activities used to freak her out. He sat back in the chair feeling wretched, his appetite gone. "I'm so sorry, Maggie."

"So am I." She smiled sadly. "When you said you were going skydiving for a week? Oh, my God, I almost fainted. I couldn't take it anymore. Most of my life, I've been afraid to take those kinds of risks. I was ultracautious, don't you remember? I didn't even try out for cheerleading because I thought I might get hurt. It was all because of the way my dad died. He was just like you and your brothers, always looking for the next big adrenaline rush. His death was so devastating to me and my mom, there was no way I was going to put myself through that kind of pain again with you."

"Damn, Maggie." He realized now that he must've scared the hell out of her on a daily basis. As the youngest brother, he'd always been the one to take on any stupid challenge or death-defying dare. He really was lucky to be alive. "I guess that was the last straw you were talking about."

"It was." She reached across the table for his hand. "I'm sorry I didn't explain things more clearly, but I guess at the time, I just panicked."

"I'm sorry, too." He squeezed her hand in his. "If we'd taken the time to talk it out, we might've...well, who knows what could've happened?"

She gazed at him and her smile faded. "It seemed too selfish to ask you to change your lifestyle for me."

He shook his head and stared out at the darkening vista. The ocean was rougher now and the choppy whitecaps gleamed like shards of ice in the reflected light. "I would've done anything for you, Maggie."

"I know," she whispered, and blinked away tears. "But it wouldn't have been fair."

The waiter arrived with two huge platters, each with a full-size lobster, drawn butter and baked potatoes with everything on them. He poured more wine for each of them, wished them *bon appétit* and left them alone.

Connor chuckled somberly. "Are you even hungry after all this depressing talk?"

Maggie sniffled as she looked down at her lobster and then over at him. "You bet I am."

He laughed. "That's my girl." And they both started eating, their appetites and humor instantly restored.

They spent the next few minutes in silence as they wolfed down the perfectly prepared food. Finally Connor took a break and sat back in his chair. He reached for his wine and took a sip, then said, "Mind if I ask you something that might put me in a happier mood?"

"But not me?" She laughed shortly. "Sure, go ahead."

"Why'd you marry this joker?" Then, even though he knew the answer, he asked, "And what's his name again? Albert? Arthur?"

"It's Alan. Alan Cosgrove, and that's the last time I'll use his actual name out loud. I'm afraid of summoning the devil."

He chuckled. "Like *Beetlejuice?*"

"Exactly!"

It had been one of their all-time favorite movies back in the day.

Maggie drank down a hearty gulp of wine and seemed to brace herself before answering. It was one more way Connor could tell that the guy had been a real piece of work.

"After you and I broke up," she began, "I cried myself silly for weeks."

"Good to hear."

She laughed. "My mother finally sent me off to visit my cousin Jane in Boston. Jane had a summer day job, so I spent my mornings wallowing in grief and my afternoons walking for miles around Boston. There were so many charming neighborhoods and I think I saw them all. One day I walked into a fancy art gallery in the Back Bay and that's where I met him."

"Ashcroft," he said helpfully.

"Yes." She giggled. "*Ashcroft* was wealthy, nice looking, seemed stable enough. He enjoyed quiet walks, art galleries and foreign films."

"Much like myself."

She gave a ladylike snort. "Right." She went on to explain that the guy she met had seemed safe and sane and unlikely to do anything that would worry her excessively.

"Unlike myself."

"Sadly," she murmured. "At the time, I thought it was important that he wasn't a risk taker. I was so stupid."

"We were both young," he said, giving her a break.

"I suppose," Maggie continued, "but despite how good Ashcroft might've looked on paper, in reality, he was a jerk and probably a sociopath."

There was no *probably* about it, Connor thought, but didn't say it aloud.

"It turned out that he was being forced into marriage by his iron-fisted mother, who had decreed that it was time for him to find a wife. Sybil—that's his mother's name," Maggie explained. "Sybil had suggested that he find someone pretty enough, who was malleable, penniless and had very few ties to Boston. It would be easier to control her that way, she said."

"Let me get this straight. His *mother* was telling him this?"

Maggie nodded. "Yes. She definitely knew her boy."

"This is creeping me out," Connor said. "But don't stop. I want to hear it all."

She grinned. "I'm not sure I can stop now that I'm on a roll." She took a quick bite of her baked potato, then continued. "A month after we were married, Sybil called me into her sitting room to let me know how well I'd met the criteria to be her daughter-in-law. Then she proceeded to tell me everything that was wrong with me."

"She doesn't exactly sound like Mom-of-the-Year."

"She was peachy," Maggie said, and shivered. "But the good news was that I had also fulfilled Ashcroft's requirements for a suitable wife."

"Can't wait to hear his list." He held up his hand. "He obviously wanted someone beautiful, right?"

"Thank you," she said with a grateful smile. "But you really need to hear the prerequisites he gave his mother."

"Oh, I get it," Connor said. "She was the one who was going to find him a wife."

"That was the plan."

"But then he met you."

"Yes, but I had to pass muster with his mother first."

Connor shook his head. "What a guy."

"You have no idea," she murmured, her lips curving into a frown.

Connor didn't want her going too far down memory lane over this jerk, so he shot her a quick grin. "Come on, let's hear it. What did Weird Al want in a wife?"

She chuckled. "That's a perfect nickname for him. Okay, he specifically wanted someone who wasn't fat, didn't speak with a pronounced drawl, didn't snore and didn't chew with her mouth open."

Connor stared at her for a few long seconds. "Come on. You're kidding."

"If only," she said, smothering a laugh. "Sybil told me that Ashcroft was very sensitive about bodily sounds and emissions."

Connor snorted. "Yeah, most obsessive-compulsive anal-retentive types tend to be that way."

"If only I'd known this before the wedding," Maggie said. "But Ashcroft knew how to put on a good act. He swept me off my feet, promised me the moon and convinced me to marry him. What an idiot I was."

Connor didn't respond to that one, since he wholeheartedly agreed. "So, once you were married, what happened?"

"If you want to hear the gory details, I'm going to need more wine first," she said, grinning ruefully.

Connor chuckled and reached for the wine bottle. "Yeah, I think I might need a little more, too."

"Okay, the day we got married, we moved into his mother's mansion in Boston's Beacon Hill."

"You lived with his mom the whole time?"

"Yeah," she said. "They were close."

Connor almost spit his wine out. "They were demented."

"That, too." She speared a chunk of lobster and popped it into her mouth. "Oh, and none of my family were invited to the wedding, did I mention that? And within a few days of the ceremony, he was insisting that I cut off all ties with them."

"The better to isolate and control you."

"Yeah." She gazed at Connor. "I wasn't really smart about any of this. I think I was still traumatized about breaking up with you and I just kind of went along with things. It wasn't easy, because his mother was really cold and unbending. And he got worse as time went on. I just couldn't do anything to please either one of them."

"I wish you'd called me."

"I do, too, Connor." She reached across the table and touched his hand. "But I was adrift. After our last conversation, I didn't think you were all that interested in hearing from me. I wasn't sure of myself anymore. They did a good job of whittling away at my confidence."

"They sound like experts."

"Oh, they were." Her eyes hazed a bit as she remembered more. "After seven long years, I finally grew some gumption and decided it was time to divorce them both. And the very day I made an appointment to see a lawyer, Sybil died of a massive heart attack."

"Whoa."

"She left all her money to Ashcroft. And on the day of her funeral, he informed me that he was divorcing *me*."

Connor let out a string of expletives. "He did you a favor. You know that, right?"

"Oh, I know it," she said fiercely. "But even on the occasion of his mother's death, he couldn't leave it alone. No, he had to go on and on, explaining how unsuitable I was for him. How I had been nothing more than a convenience to him."

"He should be glad he's still breathing," he muttered.

"A *convenience,*" Maggie repeated slowly, her hands tightening into fists. "That son of a bitch."

"Literally," Connor muttered.

She waved her anger away. "The divorce was a gift, frankly, because it meant I was blessedly free of him. He tried so hard to break my spirit, but he never broke my heart, thank God. And I'm so glad he saved me the trouble of trying to divorce him."

"Because he would've fought you to the bitter end."

"That's right." She chuckled. "Irony was always lost on Ashcroft."

"No sense of humor, that guy."

She laughed. "So I took my miniscule divorce settlement, swallowed my pride and came back home to Point Cairn. And here we are."

But Connor knew that wasn't the end of the story. His eyes narrowed on her. "Did he hurt you?"

"Physically?" She hesitated. "Not really." Then she added, "To be honest, he didn't care much for anything physical. He preferred to demoralize me mentally and emotionally."

Connor leaned forward. "We can change the subject, Maggie."

"No," she insisted, waving her fork back and forth. "I want to talk about it, because I never got to. Except to a therapist and that wasn't very satisfying. I thought when I came home, I would have my old girlfriends around to help me hash things out and get rid of those old feelings. But the girls weren't exactly happy to see me show up again."

Understanding dawned. In the years after Maggie left town, all of their friends had rallied around him and turned Maggie into the bad guy. Connor had never tried to change their opinions of Maggie because that's what he had thought, too. "That's why you ran in the other direction when you saw Sarah and the others."

She smiled tightly. "Pretty much."

"Jeez, Maggie, you've had a rough time of it."

"Oh, please, it's nothing I can't handle." She airily brushed away his concern but then began to laugh at herself. "Okay, yeah. It was really bad there for a while. Grandpa's goats became my best friends."

Connor chuckled as he poured the last of the wine into their glasses. "So you didn't have your girlfriends to hash things out with, but you've got me. I'm here. I'll help you get through it all. Tell me everything you went through with this clown Ashcroft."

She beamed a hopeful smile at him. "Really?"

"Come on." He gestured with his hand. "Come on, tell me the rest of it."

"Where shall I start?" She inhaled deeply, then said in a rush, "Okay. Well, he bought all my clothes for me."

"Hmm." Connor frowned. "I guess that's…nice?"

Her lips twisted sardonically. "Believe me, he didn't do it to be nice."

"Oh, right. That jerk." He took a sip of wine before advancing on the topic. "So…what kind of stuff did he make you wear?"

She laughed. "Probably not what you're thinking. No spandex or anything. He wanted me to be seen in expensive classics, knits and wools, sweater sets, a lot of plaids, skirts, shirtdresses, sensible shoes, pearls. Nothing garish or low class, like blue jeans or boots."

"Idiot."

"Thank you! You make a really good girlfriend."

They both laughed, and then Connor said, "Did you work during your marriage?" He struggled to get that last word out.

"Work?" Her laugh was a soft trill. "No. I couldn't work."

He nodded. "No jobs available?"

"Oh, I suppose there were jobs, but I had no skills."

He frowned. "Yes, you do."

She stared out the window for a moment, then gazed over at Connor. "But even if I could get a job, how would I get from my house to my workplace?"

"By car?"

"Oh no. I couldn't have a car because I might get lost or crash it."

"He told you that?" He squinted at her, puzzled. "But you were always a good driver."

"I know," she said with a sigh, and dunked a small piece of lobster in warm butter.

Connor took one last bite of his baked potato and it tasted like sand. He couldn't even imagine how his Maggie had lived through all this degradation and come out so healthy and normal. And what kind of vicious creep was Ashcroft to have a great girl like Maggie and treat her so badly?

"On the other hand," Connor hedged, "he had money, so you probably didn't need to work."

"True, I didn't need any extra money," she said breezily. "I would've just squandered it on frivolous things."

He studied her as he sipped his wine. "You never seemed like a frivolous person to me."

"I'm not. But he didn't agree. He thought I needed more discipline. His mother agreed with him that I was helpless in so many ways. Once we were married, he began to criticize minor things. Just here and there, you know? But after a few years, he was taking daily jabs at my appearance, my weight, my personality, my lack of social skills. You name it."

"God, what an idiot," he muttered, shaking his head in bemusement.

"That's putting it nicely. And as bad as he was, his mother could be downright evil sometimes."

"I wish I'd known. I would've rescued you."

"My hero."

The waiter placed a basket of fresh bread and butter on the table. Connor held the basket out for her, then took a piece of bread for himself. He took a bite, then waved at her to continue. "Come on, girlfriend, tell me more. Get it all out."

Maggie chuckled. "You're enjoying this too much."

"Believe me, I'm not." In fact, he was imagining finding this guy just to plant a fist in his arrogant face. "But it seems like the more you talk about how awful they were, the more relaxed you get. And I like to see that. So, anything else you want to tell me?"

"I'm afraid if I get started, I won't be able to stop." She took a quick sip of her wine. "I think what I hated most was that my opinions never mattered. They considered me either too naive or just plain stupid, depending on the situation. He always liked to tell me how sad it was that I was so intellectually challenged."

"That's it." Connor shoved his chair back from the table. He was only half kidding when he muttered, "I'm really going to kill him."

She laughed and clapped her hands. "Thank you. You're officially my best friend."

"Yeah, I am," he said, easing back into his chair, though it cost him to give her a smile. "And don't forget it."

The following afternoon, Connor stared out the bay window of the Marin Club, taking in the view of clear blue skies and tumultuous waves crashing against the sandy shore. Though he was here to meet with his brothers, all he could think about was Maggie, and not just because of the incredible sex they'd had that morning. No, she was on his mind because he couldn't forget the horror story she'd related at dinner the night before. He just wished he'd had an inkling of what she'd been going through. Damn it, he'd been so clueless back then he hadn't even realized they'd broken up. If he'd known how Maggie really felt, he would have canceled that stupid skydiving trip in a heartbeat. And he might have prevented her from running off and falling into the trap of that creep husband and his twisted mother. One phone call from Maggie and Connor would've jumped on a plane and rescued her from that hell house she'd been living in.

His thoughts were interrupted when the waitress came over and took their drink orders. Jake had called this impromptu meeting with his brothers to talk over some important family business. They'd decided to meet here instead of the festival hotel in order to avoid any big ears that might be tempted to listen in on their conversation.

The Marin Club wasn't actually a club at all, but a bar and grill the brothers had been coming to for years. The service was good, the drinks were cold and the food was great.

The waitress set their drinks on the table. "Here you go, boys. Scotch for you, Ian. Pint of IPA for Connor and your martini, Jake. Extra dry, lemon twist."

"Perfect," Connor said, taking the pint glass from her.

"You boys are so dressed up in your suits and ties this afternoon. Is there some big party I should know about?"

Jake grinned. "We've got a business dinner to go to after this."

"Ah," she said. "Not quite as exciting as I imagined, but I hope you have fun."

"Thanks, Sherry," Jake said. "You're the best."

She winked at him, slid the black plastic bill case onto the table and strolled away humming. She was an old friend of their mother's and could always count on the MacLaren boys for a large tip.

"Cheers," Ian said, holding up his glass. They all clinked their drinks together, then sipped.

"Okay, what's up?" Connor said after taking a satisfying taste of his drink, a well-crafted English pale ale that he'd been ordering for years.

Jake gave each of them his patented scowl. "I heard from the Scottish lawyers again."

"What's their problem?" Connor asked. "We've still got a few months before the terms of the will have to be met."

"They're getting antsy."

"No, they're getting pushy," Connor said.

"What do you expect?" Ian said. "They're lawyers."

"Yeah," Connor agreed. "But they're just going to have to wait until one of us can take some time off."

"It's not that I care what they think," Jake said, "but I do believe we're reaching the point where one of us will have to fly over there and survey the property, just to see what's involved."

"It's basically some land and a big old house," Ian said, shrugging. "We've all done real estate deals. What's the big mystery?"

Jake stared into his cocktail and frowned. "The lawyer mentioned something about crofters."

"We've got crofters?" Connor said.

Ian looked puzzled. "You mean, like squatters?"

"No," Jake said. "These are tenants who live and work the land around the castle. We pay them."

"We do?"

"Yeah, so whoever buys the land has to buy the crofters, too. They're a package deal."

Disgruntled, Ian said, "What if we don't want crofters? And it's kind of weird to be selling people, don't you think?"

"I doubt we're actually selling the people," Connor said dryly.

Jake shook his head in frustration. "This is why somebody has to go over there."

"One of you should go," Connor said immediately.

"Why not you?" Ian said.

"Because I've got boots-on-the-ground responsibilities up here. I've got twenty-seven new products ready to hit the market, we have three new farmers who want to join the artisanal league and we're training a replacement manager at the brewpub."

Ian looked askance. "Oh, so you're saying our meager office jobs are expendable, is that it?"

Connor grinned back at him. It was a long-standing rivalry among the brothers, with each of them claiming to work harder than the others. But in Connor's case, it was true. Maybe he didn't handle the corporate stuff, like finances or marketing or hiring, thank God. But he did have sole responsibility for the day-to-day production of eight different facilities, including the brewery itself and the brewpub in town, both of which had put their company on the map in the first place.

"You're the natural choice to go," Connor said to Ian. "You could check things out with the castle, then take a detour south and visit Gordon. Make sure he's still willing to grow our hops."

Ian flashed Connor a dirty look. "Everything's fine with the damn hops. The next batch will arrive on time, right after the drying season. So back off."

"Touchy," Connor muttered, exchanging glances with Jake. It always irritated Ian when they brought up the subject of his recent breakup with his gorgeous wife, Samantha. Her eccentric father, Gordon McGregor, lived in an ashram west of Kilmarnock where he grew the hops and many of the bitter herbs used exclusively in MacLaren beers. The trade winds that warmed the west coast of Scotland provided the perfect climate for Gordon's hops and they were among the finest the MacLarens had ever used for their beers. While Connor cared very much for his sister-in-law Sam and was sorry she and Ian had split, he knew that if they lost their main source for those rare Scottish hops, it could be disastrous.

"I can't go right now, either," Jake realized.

Ian rolled his eyes. "Why not?"

"I'm in the middle of planning the senior staff retreat," he explained. "I won't be able to go for at least three months."

"Look, we don't have to make up excuses for the lawyers," Ian reasoned. "As soon as one of us gets a break, whoever it is will go to Scotland, meet with the lawyers, check out the castle and list it for sale."

"Sounds good to me," Connor said. "I can't wait to get rid of it."

"And Uncle Hugh's bad juju along with it," Jake muttered.

Ian nodded. "Mom will be glad, too."

"She's been wanting the whole problem to disappear from day one."

"Yeah," Jake said. "Uncle Hugh pretty much ruined her life."

"But she rallied just fine," Connor said with a hint of pride. "She made a good life for all of us once she got over here."

At that, the three men spontaneously clinked their glasses together and drank in silence.

Despite acquiring the castle and all the land for miles around it after their father died, Uncle Hugh continued to be a bitter man to the very end. Since he'd never had children and hated his own brother, he fashioned his last will and testament to deliberately create an irreparable rift among his nephews, forcing them to compete against each other for their inheritance.

His will provided that all the MacLaren money, land

and power would go to whichever brother had acquired the most wealth by the twenty-fifth anniversary of their father's death. As the date grew closer, Jake was contacted by the Scottish lawyers, who required the brothers to send financial reports in order to determine which of them would eventually inherit.

That final date was coming up fast.

Connor, Ian and Jake had no intention of complying with their uncle's wishes. They had vowed at a young age not to fight against each other for the sake of a plot of land and a big old house, especially if it fulfilled their horrible uncle's wishes. Frankly, none of them could even picture the castle in their minds since Uncle Hugh had taken possession of it when they were all too young to remember it. Their mother called it "a cold, crumbling pile of Scottish stone" and cursed it on a daily basis.

The plain fact was, their home was Northern California now. They didn't want the castle or the land. So no matter which brother "won" Uncle Hugh's blood money, the three of them planned to sell the Scottish land and the castle and split the proceeds three ways.

Jake savored his cocktail. "I'll call the lawyers back and let them know that one of us will get over there within the next three months."

"Sounds good," Ian said, and glanced at his wristwatch. "So, everyone ready for this dinner with the Wellstones?"

"Yeah," Jake said, reaching for his wallet. "I'll be meeting my date at the restaurant a few minutes ahead of time."

"Sounds good." Connor stood and tossed a ten-dollar bill on the table. "I've got to get back and pick up Maggie. I'll see you guys there."

Maggie paced back and forth in front of the living room window of the suite, occasionally glancing up to check the time. Connor would arrive any minute now to take her to the important dinner with Mr. Wellstone and his sons. They planned to close a major deal tonight, and Maggie had to be on her best behavior.

So it might not be appropriate to stumble and fall on her butt.

That's why she was walking around, trying to get used to high heels again. It had been three long years since she'd been forced to wear anything like these killer stilettos. Not since the days when Alan—er, Ashcroft—required her to dress up for the fancy society balls and dinner parties they were constantly attending.

Along with her ex-husband and his crabby mother, Maggie didn't miss high heels at all.

The dress she wore was one of the few she'd salvaged from her marriage, a little black dress, short and beautifully beaded around the edges, with flattering cap sleeves and a sweetheart neckline that showed the barest hint of cleavage. She didn't mind wearing it now because Ashcroft and his mother had hated it.

Maggie was surprised at how much relief she felt after talking to Connor about her crazy marriage. There had been a few moments at dinner last night when she'd almost burst into tears, but it hadn't been because of the bad memories. It had been because Connor was so sweet to listen, so quick to take her side, so heroic in his defense of her. And the amazing sex afterward had helped, too.

One thing Connor had never asked, though, was why she'd stayed with the man for so many years. Why didn't she leave Ashcroft in the very beginning when he first started picking on her?

Maggie was so glad Connor hadn't asked because she would've found it difficult to answer him. Not because she didn't know the answer, but because part of the reason for staying was so nonsensical.

How could she explain that she'd stayed because a part of her thought she *deserved* to be punished? After all, she had broken up with Connor because she was worried that he would die someday, and she would be left alone. It sounded so selfish now, but back then, the possibility of her being devastated by his death had been too great a risk for her to take. So basically, she had ended her relationship with Connor because she was a coward.

And how ironic was it that she'd ended up marrying Ashcroft, who had seemed like such a safe, risk-free alternative? Big mistake. Because he hadn't just tried to hurt her. He had tried to *destroy* her, psychologically, bit by bit. There had been moments during her marriage when she didn't know if she would survive another day. After living with that, skydiving and rock climbing didn't look so bad.

"So much for risk aversion," she murmured. From now on, she was going to take the riskiest choice available, every time.

Her cell phone rang and she rushed to grab it, noticed the call number and said, "Grandpa, is everything okay?"

"Just lovely, Maggie. Any day I see sunshine and blue skies is a delightful day. And yourself? How's your day, Maggie, me love?"

Maggie bit back a smile. "Grandpa, did you enjoy a wee dram before you called me?"

"Before I called ye? Ha! Before, during and after's more like it." He laughed so hard he dropped the phone.

"Oh boy," Maggie murmured. It didn't take many wee drams to get Grandpa tanked up and raring to go these days. She was just glad Deidre would be by to make sure he made it to bed and didn't sleep on the couch all night.

The phone was jostled, and then a woman came on the line. "It's Deidre here, Maggie. Angus is doing just fine, not to worry. He's had a wee spot of the angel's tears, but that never hurt a flea."

Maggie chuckled. It sounded as if Deidre might be a bit tipsy, too. They were a pair sometimes. They had probably already changed into their jammies before pouring the first of what sounded like several nightcaps.

"I'm not worried, Deidre," she said. "I know you're taking good care of him."

"Aye, we're coming along just fine." She covered the phone to say something to Grandpa, then came back on the line. "How's my boy treating you?"

"He's a perfect gentleman," Maggie assured her, but her mind instantly raced to a vision of Connor and her, making sweet love last night. She decided she wouldn't be sharing that anecdote with Connor's mother.

Maggie would always be grateful to Deidre for welcoming her back to Point Cairn instead of shutting her out. She had a wonderful open heart and Maggie loved her for it.

"Now you've got the big dance coming up," Deidre continued. "And I know Connor is so looking forward to dancing with you. I hope you two have a beautiful time together."

Maggie frowned. Maybe it was the wee dram speaking, but Deidre sounded almost weepy with happiness. Maggie hated to burst her bubble, but nothing would come of this week with Connor. Other than business, they had no future together. Even though their long talk the night before had answered some questions, Maggie could still catch glimpses of suspicion in Connor's eyes. He'd spent ten long years feeling betrayed and angry with her, so while these past few days together had been lovely, Maggie didn't see how they could possibly erase the painful past.

Maggie heard her grandfather talking in the background, and Deidre said to him, "Well, of course she's going to the dance. Every girl loves to dance."

Grandpa said something and Deidre laughed. "Oh, pish

tosh, Angus. Children can make such a mountain out of a molehill, can't they?"

Angus's laugh was hearty and Deidre joined him. After a few seconds, she must've realized she was still on the phone. "Maggie? Hello? Are you there?"

"Still here," Maggie said.

"All righty, then. Goodbye, dear."

And she disconnected the call, leaving Maggie staring at the phone in befuddlement.

"All righty, then," she muttered, shaking her head as she slipped the phone into her small bag.

The door opened and Connor walked in, then stopped. "Wow. You look…incredible."

She turned and smiled, ridiculously pleased by the compliment. She kept the mood light, twirling around to show off her pretty dress. "So this will do?"

"Absolutely. I'm a lucky man." With a grin, he walked over and kissed her softly on the cheek. "If I were Jonas Wellstone and saw you walk into the room, I would give you anything you wanted."

She gazed up at him solemnly. "And all I would ask for is that he sign over everything to you."

Connor laughed as he helped her with her jacket. "I believe you just might be our secret weapon."

Eight

She hadn't embarrassed herself yet, Maggie thought, smiling inwardly, but the night was still young.

Other than her self-deprecating attitude, everything was lovely tonight. For the private dinner meeting, Mr. Wellstone had chosen a small but beautiful room that had once been an old wine cellar, with arched brick walls and stained glass windows. Candles enhanced the wrought-iron light fixtures, creating a warm, romantic feel, the perfect setting for an intimate dinner for two.

Unfortunately, there were eleven of them at the table and this meal was strictly business.

And the same could be said for her relationship with Connor. It was strictly business, too, in case she'd forgotten. No matter how wonderful their late nights together had been, they shared too much history, too many past mistakes, to risk calling this short time together anything more than business.

To be fair, though, he'd been wonderfully attentive all evening, so she couldn't complain. She just wished things could be different between them somehow. If only she had made some better choices along the way.

But that was ancient history. It was time to stop whining and apologizing about the past. She wanted to enjoy the evening and the rest of the festival. She wanted to savor every minute spent with Connor. And then she would go home and get on with her life.

"How do you like the wine?" Connor whispered next to her.

"It's wonderful," she murmured, reaching for her glass. "Everything is so nice. What do you think? Is it going well?"

Maggie followed his gaze around the table. Other than his brothers and their dates, the rest of the guests were Wellstone family members. Jonas, his son, Paul, and Paul's wife, Dana, and his daughter, Christy, and her husband, Steve. There were several small conversations occurring at once along with plenty of munching and savoring of the delicious stuffed pastry appetizers. Jake and Paul were debating the results of a recent football game.

Connor grinned at Maggie. "I think Jonas looks pretty happy, don't you?"

Maggie glanced over at the man holding court at the head of the table. "He's a kick, isn't he?"

"He's a great guy," he said quietly. "I wasn't sure I would like him because of all these hoops he was making us jump through, but I'm glad we did this tonight. I think everyone's having a good time."

So far, business had only been discussed on a general level. The state of the industry, the latest gossip, who was making waves, who had burned out. There hadn't been a mention of anything specific about the buyout.

Of course, Maggie hadn't expected any real business to be conducted tonight. The purpose of this get-together was to see if everyone got along and to make sure Jonas Wellstone approved of the MacLaren men well enough to sell them his multimillion-dollar brewery business.

The whole scene should've made Maggie unbearably nervous, but it didn't. After spending so many years faking the social niceties with Ashcroft and his snooty high-society crowd, tonight Maggie was dining with real people who laughed and drank wine and enjoyed food and each other's company. It was such a refreshing change. No wonder she felt so happy.

It dawned on her that this was the first time she'd actually been out with a group of people, *any* people, in over three years. She didn't know whether to laugh or cry at that odd little fact.

"Are you okay?" Connor asked. "You looked a little dazed there for a minute."

"I'm perfect," she said, smiling up at him. "I'm happy to be here. Thank you for including me."

"I'm glad you're here with me," he said simply.

As Maggie took another look around the table, Jonas's daughter, Christy, caught her gaze. "I've met a few successful female brewers, Maggie, but it's still pretty rare, isn't it? How did you get started in this business?"

"My mom and dad owned a brewpub for many years in Point Cairn. The same one the MacLarens own now, by the way."

"Hey, we couldn't let it close down," Connor said in defense of his brothers.

"Absolutely not," she said, chuckling. "Anyway, to supplement the brewpub, my father built a home brewery in our barn and I used to follow him around like a puppy, begging to help him. He would give me odd jobs every day, like sorting bottle caps or sweeping the room. At some point, I wound up doing every job there was to do."

"That's the best way to learn," Jonas declared.

"I agree. So a few years ago, I decided to refurbish the brewery equipment in the barn and try my hand at some of my own formulas. And I think I'm starting to make some pretty good beers."

"She's being modest," Jake said, winking at her. "She's been kicking our asses lately at every contest she enters."

Maggie was stunned, no, *flabbergasted* by Jake's compliment. She didn't know if it meant that he'd changed his opinion of her, or if he was just playing nice for Jonas's sake. She decided to take it as a true compliment and bask in the sweetness of the moment.

Under the table, Connor's hand found hers and squeezed gently, sending shivers up her arm and down her back. She glanced up at him and he flashed her a wicked grin.

She wondered if her desire for him was written all over her face. Did she dare to hope he felt the same way about her? Could she risk losing her heart only to find out he wasn't willing to trust her again? She wanted to believe herself ready to take a big risk, but this one might leave her devastated.

Jonas chuckled, interrupting her fantasy. "Competition is good for all of us. I always say a rising tide lifts all boats."

"True enough," Ian said, nodding in agreement.

"What's your father's name, young lady?" Jonas asked.

"His name was Eli Jameson," she said. "He died when I was thirteen."

"Eli?" Jonas's eyes widened. "You're Eli Jameson's little girl?"

Maggie blinked. "Did you know him?"

"Know him?" He chuckled. "Hell, yes. We were great friends back in the day. We first met at a gathering similar to this one, only not nearly as large or as boisterous. Back then, we were a fairly sedate crowd."

"Dad's always talking about the good old days," Christy said, patting her father's arm fondly.

"I loved those days, too," Maggie said. "I always felt so close to my dad when we were working to accomplish something together."

"Your dad and I were competitors," Jonas said, "but it never seemed to matter which one of us won a medal or a ribbon. We hit it off the first time we met and we stayed friends like that until he died."

"That's so nice," Dana murmured.

Jonas grabbed a bread stick and bit off a small chunk. "Your father was a fine man, Maggie. Quite an athlete, too. I went sailing with him a few times, but I couldn't keep up with him. I don't mind saying he scared the hell out of me a few times. I paid him back by dragging him out to the golf course once or twice, but that wasn't his thing. Too slow moving for him. He was what you might call an adventurer. Always looking for the next big challenge. I was sorry to hear about his death."

"Thank you, Jonas," Maggie said, smiling softly at the older man. "Your words brought him back to life for a few minutes."

"It was my pleasure," he said with a firm nod. "They're good memories."

Maggie gazed up at the wrought-iron light fixture and blinked back tears. "You know, I've always thought of my father as a larger-than-life character. But then I would wonder if that was just my own skewed perspective of a little girl in love with her great big father."

"No, he was that kind of man," Jonas assured her. "You should be very proud of him and the legacy he left behind."

"I am," Maggie said. "Thank you so much."

No one spoke for a moment, until Christy patted her father's strong, weathered hand. "That was a very sweet tribute, Dad."

He squeezed her hand but said nothing.

Maggie broke the silence, anxious to move on from the somber topic of her deceased father. "Paul, Connor tells me that you've started growing grapevines and plan to make wine. How is that coming along?"

"Yes, I've turned traitor to my heritage," he said, and his wife and father both laughed. "I'm having a great time with it. It's similar to brewing in that it's a tricky blend of science and art. But the real bonus for me is that picking grapes is so much more fun than picking hops."

"Not quite as many thorns," his wife added.

Everyone at the table chuckled at that.

"Have you bottled anything yet?" Maggie asked.

"We've scheduled our first official bottling next month at the winery. You know, we're just over the hill in Glen Ellen. You should all come join us for the celebration."

She glanced around at Connor and his brothers, who were grinning, no doubt pleased with Paul's offer.

"We'd love to join you," Connor said, speaking for everyone. "Thanks for the invitation."

Paul's wife Dana spoke up. "We've hired a chef for the winery who serves these fabulous little snacks with the tastings. I'm telling you, it's the most fun we've had in years."

"Sounds like you've got quite a setup," Jake said. "I'm looking forward to our visit."

Maggie suddenly wasn't sure if she was included in that group invitation, even though Paul had been responding to her question. It shouldn't matter. She could drive out to their winery any time she wanted to, but it would be so much nicer to go with this group of people she was starting to consider friends.

"Wineries." Jonas sighed. "Another reason why I'm selling the brewery, boys. My own son is deserting the company."

"Aw, come on Dad," Paul said guiltily.

He grinned. "I'm just teasing you, boy. I'm glad you've found something you enjoy as much as I love my brewing." His gaze slid from Jake to Ian to Connor. "Gentlemen, that's why I insist that whoever buys my company should love this business as much as I do. I don't want some buttoned-down pencil pusher running my plant and pissing off the loyal employees who've worked there all these years. I want someone who walks in every morning and takes a deep breath of that hoppy smell and actually gets excited at the possibilities."

Maggie smiled, knowing exactly what the old man meant.

"Who knows what can happen when you blend all those bitter herbs and malts together?" Jonas's eyes sparkled as he spoke. "Why, throw in a slice of lemon peel or some odd bit of vegetation and you could come up with something completely new that might dominate the industry for the next five years. I'm telling you, if you can't appreciate the scent, the shades, the taste, the…" He paused, then chuckled. "Hell, I sound like I'm talking about a woman."

Everybody laughed, but Jonas laughed the hardest. "I'm talking about beer, gentlemen. And ladies, of course. I love this damn business."

"Right there with you, Jonas," Connor said, raising his glass in a sentimental toast.

"It really is the best thing in the world, isn't it?" Maggie said dreamily. "At the end of the day, when you've hosed down the brewing station and steam-cleaned the pipes and you've tapped off your latest keg and you're hot and sweaty and you can finally sit down on the porch and taste the day's batch while you relax and watch the sun go down? I don't think there's a better moment that captures the essence of beer making than that one."

"Dang, Maggie May." Jonas grinned and she could see a sparkle in his eyes. He held up his half-empty wineglass for another toast. "That's pure poetry."

She laughed at her new nickname and held up her glass to meet his. "Here's to special moments."

"I'll drink to that," he said jovially, and chugged down what was left of his wine.

"I was right," Connor said later that night after they'd made love.

"About what?"

"You turned out to be our secret weapon," he said, reminding her of his comment earlier that night.

She gave him a puzzled look. She was stretched out on her back, her head propped on a pillow. He lay on his side, facing her, his hand resting on her smooth stomach.

"I don't know about that," she said as she absently ran her fingers along his shoulder and down his arm. "But it was fun to hear Jonas talk about my dad."

"Everyone enjoyed hearing about him," he said, earning a smile from her. "It was a good evening."

"Did you get an inkling of Jonas's decision yet?"

"Jake talked to Paul briefly while we were walking back to the hotel. "He thinks we've got a lock on the deal."

"That's wonderful."

"Yeah. I won't count any chickens yet, but I think there's a strong possibility that he'll sell to us. There's plenty of work to do in the meantime, but it would be a real coup to take over Wellstone."

"I'll say."

It struck Connor that this was an odd sort of "pillow talk" conversation to be having with a woman, but it was one more indication of how comfortable he was around Maggie.

And that wasn't necessarily a good thing, he thought suddenly, unable to keep his old suspicions from cropping back up. Yes, Maggie had given him a simple explanation for why she'd left him all those years ago. Connor completely believed that she had feared for his safety back then.

But had she truly explained the fact that, before he could even grasp that she was truly gone, he'd received the news that she had married another man? Okay, maybe she was telling the truth when she said she'd been awash in grief and made a really bad decision. But he had to wonder how "in love" with Connor she'd really been to turn around and do something like that.

It didn't matter. What was he doing, thinking about this stuff when he had a warm, beautiful woman in his bed? He should be celebrating the fact that his plan to get her into bed had succeeded. Now he could relax and enjoy the moment.

It wasn't as if they had mentioned anything about getting back together. This was a one-time deal. When the week was over, he would hand her a check and go back to his life.

He ignored the wave of melancholy that that thought brought on.

Hell, there was a simple explanation for all this angst he was feeling. He hadn't been with another woman in…gads, had it been six months? No wonder he was reeling from all these unwanted emotions. But it was about time to snap out of it, he thought. A beautiful woman was pressing her lush body against him and he had the unrelenting urge to bury himself inside her. Again. And again.

And why not? Shouldn't he be making up for lost time? And while he was on the subject, why shouldn't he and Maggie keep on doing it, as long as the sex was good? And it was definitely good. Hell, it was world class. So why should they go their separate ways once the festival ended? Connor wondered. They lived in the same town, so why not continue to enjoy each other's company? It didn't have to be a big deal. Nothing special or permanent. Or complicated. Why couldn't it just be for fun? They could be friends with benefits. Nothing wrong with that.

For now, he tugged her onto her side facing him, then rolled back until she was on top of him, straddling his solid length.

"Oh, how did I get here?" she said, teasing him.

"Magic," he whispered, and lifted her up until he could slide into her.

She sank onto him, moaning in pleasure. And there was no more pillow talk for the rest of the night.

* * *

At breakfast Friday morning, Maggie watched Connor scan his email as he finished his coffee. He was dressed more formally than usual in a black suit, white shirt and rich burgundy power tie. He looked so good Maggie wanted to rip off his clothes and have her way with him.

He set his empty coffee cup on the dining table and stood. "I've got two meetings back to back this afternoon and the second one will probably run late, so I'll meet you at the gala by eight o'clock."

Maggie stood, too, and adjusted his tie. "Connor, I already told you I'm not going to the gala."

"Let's not go through this again, Maggie," he said. "You'll be there. It's required."

She made a face. "No, it's not. I told you I didn't want to go. The truth is, I don't like these sorts of events. I didn't even bring the right kind of dress to wear."

"So what?" he said, snapping his phone into its case and shoving it into his suit pocket. "You can wear any one of the dresses you've already worn this week."

"No, I can't. The gala is formal. Nothing I have is suitable."

"I'm not dressing formally," he said, glancing down at his suit.

"Oh, please." Maggie's laugh sounded slightly desperate. "That suit's got to be worth five thousand dollars. I think you can get away with wearing it. But I'll be expected to wear a gown and I don't have one."

"You should've thought of that before now," he said as he walked to the door. "I don't care what you wear, but I expect to see you there."

"But—" She ran after him to the door. "Connor, please. I can't—"

He grabbed the doorknob, then stopped and turned.

"This was always part of our deal. It's not optional. It's business."

"But I don't dance."

"I don't care," he said heatedly.

"Why are you making such a big deal about it?"

"Because I can." He yanked her close and crushed her lips with his. She moaned and he softened the kiss, sweeping his tongue over hers. When he finally let her go, her knees wobbled from the pleasure of his kiss. "Please, Maggie," he said, touching his forehead to hers. "Please, I want you there with me."

"Big bully," she muttered, and touched her fingers to her lips to make sure that kiss hadn't been a dream.

"Coward," he whispered, then kissed her again, briefly and softly this time, and walked out, letting the door close behind him.

She absorbed the silence for a moment, then flopped onto the couch. "Now what?"

She wandered the convention floor all morning, listening to other speakers and catching up with some of the new acquaintances she'd made this week. She had lunch alone overlooking the marina, but instead of enjoying the view, she agonized over the gala. Connor simply didn't understand. Why would he? It was no big deal. Except it was, to Maggie.

Staring out at the sparkling blue water, she sighed. The thought of attending the gala should've filled her with excitement, but Maggie was filled with dread instead. It sounded ridiculously melodramatic to say she might not survive the evening, but that was exactly what she was afraid of.

The last gala event she had attended was the Hospital Society's Black & White Ball, back in Boston. Her ex-husband had been the chairman of the event and it was a huge success. He should have been flushed with happiness, but that was so *not* Alan. Maggie still wasn't exactly sure what she had done to set him off. Had she been too effusive in congratulating him? Had she danced too close to one of his lackeys? Had she spilled something on her ball gown?

Whatever small offense she'd shown, Alan was apparently intent on making sure it didn't go unnoticed, even if it meant exposing their unhappy relationship to the world.

Leaving her in the middle of the dance floor, Alan had approached the bandleader and ordered him to stop the music. He had an important announcement to make.

"My wife is a whore," he had announced to the crème de la crème of Boston society. He didn't stop there, but Maggie refused to play back the entire tawdry speech in her mind. And later that night in the foyer of their home, he struck her physically for the first time, smacking her face so hard that she fell and hit her head against the hard surface of a marble statue, and passed out.

Two days later, after her headache had subsided and she'd regained some strength, Maggie snuck out to a pay phone and called a lawyer to begin divorce proceedings. She knew it would be a vicious battle and she prayed she would survive it. Her prayers were answered when her surly mother-in-law died a few days later and Alan divorced her instead.

Maggie had never told another soul about Alan's physical attack. How could she, when she could touch her cheek and still feel the physical blow he'd delivered? And if she closed her eyes, she could still experience the rush of utter mortification she'd felt on that dance floor as her husband destroyed her in front of everyone she knew.

She would never allow herself to be so humiliated again. Even if it meant she would never stand on another dance floor again.

"Would you like anything else?" the waiter asked.

Maggie flinched. She'd been so buried in the past she'd forgotten where she was. She quickly recovered and smiled. "No, just the check, thank you."

She returned to the convention floor, but after stirring up all those unhappy memories, she was unable to enjoy herself. She went back up to the suite to take a nap, but she couldn't sleep. She was awash in misery and clueless as to why she couldn't just flick away the past, shape up, straighten her shoulders and power through this dilemma.

After fixing herself a cup of tea, she sat by the window and stared out at the calming view of ocean water and windswept sky.

The fact was, she wanted to be with Connor, even though she dreaded attending the gala. So brushing aside the dread, she focused on her present predicament. She didn't have a dress!

She mentally sifted through the practical issues before her, as if they were written on a list she could check off. First, she didn't have a proper gown or even an ultrafancy cocktail dress to wear because she'd given away all of her dress-up clothes when she left Ashcroft. For good reason. They all reminded her of horrible, embarrassing times spent with her ex-husband.

Second, now that she'd given everything away, she couldn't afford to run out and buy something new, especially something so fancy. Not to mention the shoes and jewelry to wear with it.

Third, when she first made the deal with Connor, she honestly hadn't thought it would matter whether she showed up for the gala or not. But they had grown so close during the past week, she didn't want to disappoint him.

But that brought her to issue number four. The real problem. She hated going to formal events. Hated dancing. Feared what would happen if she did the wrong thing. Over time, the fear and hate had grown into a phobia. She'd spent way too many years attending monthly charity balls and society dances with Ashcroft, trying to impress his mother and all their rich, snooty friends, knowing that no matter what she did, it was always going to be the wrong thing.

Besides the big ugly result of the final event with Ashcroft, there had been plenty of other nasty repercussions that had occurred after she'd made some miniscule faux pas at a society dance. Maggie cringed and rubbed her arms to calm the shivers she felt. She refused to dwell on the various creative, nonphysical ways her ex-husband had made her pay for her innocent social foibles.

"This is ridiculous," she whispered. She was obviously still suffering from Post-Ashcroft Distress Syndrome, which probably wasn't a real disease, but it should've been.

She really needed to snap out of it.

But she couldn't. Because of issue number five. This gala tonight was actually important to her career. There would be people at tonight's event who were vital industry contacts, business professionals, the very people she wanted to impress so badly. But how could she? She had nothing to wear. Which brought her right back to issue number one.

It was a vicious circle and Maggie's head was spinning out of control.

She yawned, exhausted from worrying so much. Sitting down on the couch, she leaned back against one of the soft pillows and tried again to close her eyes for a few minutes.

The doorbell rang, waking her up. Disoriented, she had to stare at the clock for ten seconds before it registered that she'd slept for almost two hours. So much for worrying that she wouldn't be able to fall asleep.

She ran to the door and pulled it open.

"Delivery for Ms. Jameson," the bellman said, and handed her a large white box.

What was this? She was almost afraid to take it from him, but she did.

"Thank you," she murmured, and quickly searched for a few dollars to give as a tip. Then she closed the door and set the box on the coffee table. It carried the logo of a well-known, expensive women's store. She stared at it for several minutes, unsure what to do. Was it really for her? Maybe it was something Connor had ordered for one of his judging seminars.

"You're being silly." She double-checked the box and saw her name on a label on the side, just as the bellman had said.

Finally she settled down on the couch and slowly pulled off the top and saw…a blanket of tissue covering the contents. Okay, that wasn't too intimidating. She waded through the paper and finally found the real contents of the box.

"Oh my." It was pink. That was the first surprise. It was also soft. And beautiful. She lifted the dress out of the box and held it up to her, then ran over and stared at herself in the mirror. It was strapless, with beading all over the bodice, to the waist. From there, layers of soft pink chiffon flowed in a soft column to the floor. It was formal, but sexy. And sweet. And perfect. She'd never seen a more beautiful dress.

It complemented her skin tone and her hair. It was simply ideal. Almost as if it had been made for her.

There were shoes in the box, as well. She slipped her foot into one of them and was amazed that it fit her. At the bottom of the box, she found a small pouch that held diamond earrings and a necklace.

She didn't have to guess where all of this had come from.

"Connor," she whispered, and felt a spurt of happiness that he would do something so thoughtful.

"Wait a minute," she said, as reality sank in. Why would

he ever dare to buy her a dress after she'd spent most of their dinner the other night complaining about Ashcroft doing the same thing?

So who could've bought her this beautiful dress? Connor was the only person who knew that she—

Her cell phone rang and she ran to answer it.

"Maggie love."

"Grandpa. Is everything all right?"

"Fine and dandy," he said. "And are you having a good time?"

"I am, Grandpa. Are you feeling well today?"

"Fit as a fiddle," he said, and she could hear him patting his belly.

It was an old joke. He was tall and thin and barely had a belly to pat.

Someone giggled in the background.

"Grandpa, who's there with you?"

"It's our Deidre, making dinner."

"That's nice. And how are the goats?"

"They're a delight as always," he said "But how are you, Maggie love? We wanted to call and check. Is everything hunky-dory?"

"Everything's fine," Maggie said, touched that he was so concerned. It was unusual for her grandfather to use the telephone unless he was forced to, so maybe this was Deidre's influence.

"And how will you spend your evening, lass?" he asked. "Any special plans?"

"Grandpa, don't you remember I told you…" She paused. Something was wrong. Every time she'd talked to her grandfather during the past week, he had asked her about the dance. So why was he…? Her eyes narrowed in on the pink dress. "Grandpa, did you send me something today?"

"Och, aye, lass!" he shouted excitedly. "So it arrived?"

"She got it, then?" Deidre said, clear enough for Maggie to hear. "And does it fit?"

Maggie plopped down on the couch, speechless.

"Are you there, lass?"

"Did she hang up?"

"I'm here," she whispered. "Grandpa, why? You know I don't dance anymore."

"That's just something you tell yourself, lass," he said softly. "For protection."

She blinked at his words, but before she could respond, Deidre grabbed the phone. "Now, don't blame your grandpa for speaking out of school, but I've heard a thing or two about a thing or two."

Maggie smiled indulgently as Deidre made her point. "I'll tell you a secret, Maggie. I still have the picture of you and Connor at your high school prom. Such a pretty pair, you were. You danced all night and I know you loved it. You love to dance, Maggie. I don't know why or how you decided to stop loving it, but maybe you should decide to start again."

"Is it that simple?" Maggie wondered aloud.

"Most things are," Deidre said philosophically. "And as long as I'm giving out free advice, I think it's high time you closed the door on the past and started living in the *now*. Live for yourself. Choose for yourself, Maggie. Now here's your grandpa."

Choose for herself? Maggie stared at the telephone and began to pace back and forth across the room. Choose for herself? But every time she'd made choices, she'd made mistakes.

But so what? she argued. Was she never supposed to do anything fun or risky, ever again? She might as well live in a glass bubble!

But making choices was the same as taking risks, and taking risks meant that she might get hurt. Or worse.

But if she didn't take the risk, if she didn't go to the dance, she knew she would hurt much worse. And Connor would be hurt, as well.

So it seemed she had no choice.

Oh, good grief! Of course she had a choice. She could choose to go to the dance and have fun with Connor.

Exhausted from arguing with herself, Maggie slid down onto the couch.

Angus came back on the line. "No more guff now, lass. Tell me, do you like the dress?"

"It's beautiful, Grandpa, but you can't afford to—"

"Och, there'll be none o' that," he argued. "I've a little something tucked away for a rainy day, and Deidre chipped in a bit."

"I'll pay you both back."

"You'll not pay us back," Grandpa grumbled.

Deidre grabbed the phone. "You'll pay us back by dancing your little toes off with my son. Now, you have a fancy dance to prepare for. Go. Get off the phone and go."

"Yes, ma'am," Maggie said, and laughed as she disconnected the call.

The elevator moved slowly on the trip down to the lobby, giving Maggie more time to worry about every little thing that could go wrong. She caught a glimpse of her reflection in the elevator's mirrored wall, and it helped remind herself that there were plenty of things that were going to go just right.

She had made a pact with herself that from now on, the past would stay in the past. It was time to forgive herself for the mistakes she'd made back then. She was ready to move forward, not backward.

And tonight she was going to dance. With Connor, of course, and with anyone else who asked. Deidre was right. Maggie refused to sit in a corner anymore, worrying whether she might make a mistake or do the wrong thing. It was a risk, but she was ready to take it.

Two hours ago, she had refused to even try on the pink dress because the very thought of walking into the dance tonight made her queasy. Would she have flashbacks? Would someone criticize her for laughing too much? Would people sneer at the way she danced? Would they think her dress was too sexy? Too sparkly? Too pink?

There would be hors d'oeuvres and desserts served at the dance, too. What if she spilled something? What if she used the wrong fork? Because Ashcroft had once punished her for using the wrong fork.

"Good grief," she muttered. The wrong fork? Seriously? Who the hell cared?

She began to laugh at herself, so hard that tears came to her eyes. Then she tried to picture Connor sniveling about the wrong fork, and she laughed even harder.

It was ludicrous. And worse, it was tearing her apart inside and destroying her hard-won self-confidence. So really, wasn't it about time she drop-kicked her asinine ex-husband and his bony old mother out of her memory banks? Yes!

"And take your wrong fork with you!" she said in a loud voice, shaking her fist in the air.

Recalling her minitirade, Maggie giggled again. It was a good thing she was alone in the elevator. Otherwise, she might've received more than a few strange looks from her fellow passengers.

Nine

"Where's your date?"

Connor glanced at his brother while he casually sipped a beer, refusing to reveal how concerned he was over the subject of Jake's question. "She'll be here."

"You sure?"

"Yes," he said with a nonchalance he didn't feel.

"Good," Jake said, and grinned. "Think she'll dance with me?"

He scowled at his brother. "No."

Jake looked affronted. "Why the hell not?"

"Because you were a jerk to her."

"That's ancient history," he said, brushing away Connor's comment. "I thought we got along really swell at dinner the other night."

"Swell, huh?" Connor looked at him sideways. "That's because I warned you to be nice to her."

"That's not why," Jake insisted. "She was great. Talkative, interesting, fun. She loves the business, so she's got some smarts. Besides, if you can forgive her, who am I to judge? And Jonas loved her, so that counts for something."

"Yeah, it does." Connor refused to mention the twinge of affection he felt at hearing his brother's kind words. Instead he kept scanning the room for the exasperating woman he wanted to have standing by his side at that moment.

The place was filled with old friends and business acquaintances, wealthy competitors and a few enemies, all decked out in their fanciest attire. The men were in tuxedos or black suits and most of the women wore gowns. And they were all working the crowd. This was business, after all.

There were occasional flashes of light as the local paparazzi caught people on camera out in the wide-open foyer. The photos would eventually appear in the various industry magazines and websites, so everyone took it in good-natured fun.

But still there was no Maggie. Damn it, was she seriously planning to stand him up? But wait, could he blame her? She honestly didn't want to come tonight and he had done everything to bully her into it. And that was after she'd been so honest with him, telling him about her vicious ex-husband's behavior.

"You're a moron," he muttered miserably.

"Just so you know," Jake continued blithely, "I'm okay with you and her getting together."

Connor's eyebrow quirked. "And what's that supposed to mean?"

"It means, you know, if you wanted to actually date her, I'd be okay with it."

Connor placed his hand over his heart. "That means everything to me."

Jake laughed out loud. "Yeah, right. I know it matters, so I'm just saying, Maggie's A-okay in my book."

"You're wrong," Connor said, grinning. "It doesn't matter to me."

"Of course it matters," Jake persisted, only half kidding. "I'm the head of the family, so it's a very special occasion when I bestow my blessing upon you."

Ian overheard him as he walked up to join them. "Head *jackass* of the family, maybe."

Connor chuckled. "Good one."

"So, what were you two blathering about?" Ian asked as he sipped from a glass of red wine.

Jake pointed to Connor. "I was just telling him I'm okay with him and Maggie hooking up."

Ian smirked at Connor. "I'm sure you appreciated those heartfelt words."

"Oh, you bet," Connor said. "You know how much I look up to Jake and hang on his every word."

"Go ahead and give me grief," Jake said loftily. "But I'm not too big a person to admit when I'm wrong. I take back what I said about Maggie. She's a lovely woman and she's obviously still in love with you, so I wish you two many years of happiness together."

"Whoa," Connor said, carefully swallowing the gulp of beer he'd almost choked on. "Slow down, dude. Who said anything about, you know, whatever the hell you're talking about?"

Ian ignored Connor's protest. "As much as I hate to utter the words, I have to agree with Jake. You and Maggie have a really nice vibe together. So don't screw it up."

"Yeah," Jake chimed in. "Just make sure she sticks around this time."

"It wasn't my fault she left," he groused under his breath. But it was a halfhearted protest. He was no longer opposed to the idea of being with Maggie, even as he pretended to be so in front of his brothers. He'd been doing a lot of thinking over the past few days and he'd come to the realization that maybe he did have some culpability, after all. It was hard to admit it because he'd spent so many years blaming things all on Maggie. But after the other night when they'd talked it out, he could see that he'd done plenty to drive her crazy back then.

With the arrogance of youth, he'd carelessly ignored the warning signs she'd been giving him all along. Now he could kick himself for not paying closer attention. And while he was kicking himself, he would gladly give himself the boot for not going after her in the first place. But his pride had gotten in the way and he'd ended up wasting all those years without her.

So now that he couldn't wait to see her, where the hell was she? Not only did he miss her, but he also had some important news to give her. He wasn't sure she would appreciate him sticking his nose into her business, but that was too damn bad. She would want to hear this.

Earlier that day, Connor and his brothers had spent an hour with their longtime local banker, Dave, to discuss some hometown investments. After the meeting had wrapped up, Connor had pulled Dave aside to ask if he knew the reason why his bank had turned down Maggie's loan application.

At first Dave had been reluctant to say anything. There were privacy issues involved, naturally.

"Come on, Dave," Connor had cajoled. "We've known each other since grammar school. You can be sure that anything you tell me won't leave this room."

"Hell, Connor." He scraped his fingers across his thinning scalp.

"Look," Connor said, trying another tack, "the truth is, I'm floating her a loan, so I'd like to know if she's good for paying it back."

"Of course she is," Dave insisted. "But you know how things are these days. Her credit report came back with one black mark on it and with all our red tape, the loan wasn't allowed to go through."

"A black mark? From where?"

"Some company back East."

"Remember the name?" Connor knew that their local bank was small enough that even as executive vice president, Dave would still go over each of the loans himself.

Dave thought for a moment. "Cargrove? Casgrow?"

"Cosgrove?" Connor said.

"That's it," Dave exclaimed. "Apparently she ran up

quite a debt with them, although I've got to admit I've never even heard of them. Must be some regional store or something."

"Or something," Connor muttered.

"I felt really bad, turning her down," Dave continued. "And Maggie was devastated. She walked out of my office without even asking for her credit information."

Connor wasn't surprised, but it broke his heart to hear it. Maggie's self-esteem had taken such a beating, it figured she would simply blame herself for her inability to get a bank loan, not even suspecting that her lousy ex-husband, Alan Cosgrove, had gone and screwed up her credit rating, just to twist the knife in one more time for good measure.

Connor really wanted to meet this psychopathic dirtbag and smash his face in. He had every intention of doing it, but that happy moment would have to wait.

The Big Band orchestra had been playing softly for the past half hour as people streamed into the ballroom, but now the conductor tapped his baton and the music burst into high gear. Couples began to fill the dance floor. The lines at all four bars were growing and the crowd in front of the appetizers and dessert tables were now three deep.

So where the hell was Maggie?

"I'll be back," Connor told his brothers, but he hadn't taken ten steps before he ran into Lucinda.

"Hi, Connor," she said breathlessly, taking hold of his arm. "Don't you look dashing tonight. Oh, but you're not leaving, are you?"

"Hey, Lucinda. I've gotta run out for a minute, but I'll be back."

"Oh, good." She smiled shyly. "I expect to dance with you at least once tonight."

"Sure thing," he said in a rush, then stopped abruptly. "Sorry. Don't know where my manners went. You look really nice, too, Lucinda."

"Thank you, Connor," she said, beaming at him. "That's sweet of you."

"I'll be back."

"Okay," she said, but he was already halfway across the room.

But before he could escape, he was flagged down by Bob Milburn, the mayor of Point Cairn, who wanted to discuss the amount the MacLarens planned to contribute to the annual Christmas parade and party the town held every year. Connor had to endure five long minutes of mindless chatter before Jake and Ian finally rescued him.

"Sorry to interrupt you two, Ian said briskly. "But we need to pull Connor away to discuss some family business."

"Sure thing," Bob said amiably. "See you boys around."

As soon as the mayor was out of hearing range, Connor let out the breath he'd been holding. "Damn, I thought he would never stop talking."

"We saw you floundering," Ian said.

Jake grinned. "You looked pretty desperate."

"I was." He glanced around the room again, then checked his wristwatch. "Listen, I've really got to go find Maggie."

Jake grabbed Connor's arm to keep him from dashing off. "That won't be necessary."

"Whoa," Ian whispered.

"Guess you were right, bro," Jake murmured. "She did show up."

Connor turned and spotted Maggie standing on the threshold of the farthest doorway from where they stood.

"Wow," Jake said reverently.

"About time she showed up," Connor muttered, then couldn't say another word, just continued to stare as she walked into the room. She was a vision in pale pink, so sexy and gorgeous he wasn't sure if she was real or just a hallucination of his addled mind.

Her strapless gown clung to her stunning breasts in

a gravity-defying miracle of sparkling pink and crystal beads. At her waist, the beads disappeared and the dress flowed in a wispy column to the floor. Her gorgeous hair was held up by some pins with a few tendrils allowed to hang loose and curl around her shoulders

She looked like a sexy angel, and never more beautiful than at this moment. And that was saying a lot, Connor thought, because she always looked beautiful to him.

Connor continued to watch her as he sauntered across the ballroom to meet her. As he got closer, his insides constricted at the memory of her moaning in pleasure as he filled her completely last night. His jaw tightened as he tried to estimate exactly how long he would have to endure this party before he could take her back to their bed, where he would soon have her naked and whimpering with need.

"Glad you could make it," he said when he finally reached her.

"I'm sorry I'm late," she said, tiptoeing up to kiss his cheek. "Forgive me?"

The orchestra began to play a jazz standard, and without another word, Connor took her hand and led her out to the dance floor, where he pulled her into his arms and began to sway to the music. When Maggie rested her head on his shoulder, he was certain that nothing had ever felt more right.

After a full minute, he leaned his head back and gazed down at her. "It was worth the wait, Maggie."

An hour later, Connor felt trapped by his own success. Maggie hadn't stopped dancing, not once. It seemed that every man Connor had introduced her to during the week now wanted to dance with her. First it was Jonas, then his son, Paul, then big Johnny from the judges' room. Hell, even Pete from Stink Bug Brewery had claimed a dance.

Connor had danced, as well, with Lucinda and Paul

Wellstone's wife, Dana, and two women he barely knew who were friends of Jake's.

He was so ready to blow this party off, grab Maggie and go back upstairs. But it was not to be. No, instead he got caught up in some off-the-wall conversation with Jonas about fruit-flavored ales. The old man was waxing on about boysenberries and ten minutes had passed before Connor noticed that Maggie was standing on the sidelines talking to someone. He couldn't see the man's face, so he shifted his stance until he could get a look at the guy. And he didn't like what he saw.

"Damn it," he muttered. "What's that about?" Maggie was talking to Ted Blake. It couldn't be a good thing.

"Something's wrong," Jonas declared. "You suddenly look like you just ate a bad-tasting bug."

"I'm sorry, Jonas," he said, "but I think I'd better go rescue Maggie."

Jonas's eyes scanned the room and then narrowed in on Maggie and Ted. He nodded slowly. "Good idea, son. That boy's nothing but trouble."

Connor's stomach tightened all over again as he watched her laughing and joking with the guy who had tried to destroy MacLaren. When Ted leaned in and whispered something in her ear, Connor's vision blurred in anger.

He thought he'd warned her about Ted Blake after he saw her talking to him the other day on the convention floor. But now he realized that he'd simply glossed over it at the time. And after that one time, he hadn't seen the guy all week. It was another reason why he'd had such a good time at the festival this week. No Ted Blake to deal with.

"Maggie."

She whirled around. "Oh, Connor, there you are. You've probably met Ted before, but we were just—"

"Yeah, we've met," Connor said curtly, and grabbed her hand. "Come on, babe, time to go."

"But…okay. Nice to see you again, Ted."

"Sure thing, Maggie," Ted drawled. "Maybe we'll talk again when you're not in such a hurry."

"Don't count on it," Connor muttered as he pulled Maggie closer and walked faster.

"Connor, please, can we walk a little slower? My feet are starting to whimper from all the dancing."

"Sorry, baby," he said, slowing down. "I just wanted to get you away from him. The faster the better."

"But why?" She glanced over her shoulder to get a last look at Ted. "He seems like a nice enough guy. A little bit quirky, but—"

"He's the furthest thing from a nice guy you'll meet here." Frowning, he added, "I can't tell you who to talk to or who to do business with, Maggie. But I would highly recommend that you stay as far away from Ted Blake as possible."

She studied his face for a moment, then nodded. "All right. I've never seen you react so negatively to anyone before."

"He tried to ruin us when we were first starting out," Connor said flatly. "Lucky for us, his reputation preceded him and a few of the people he talked to in his crusade to smear us didn't believe him. But a few of them did, and we had some shaky moments there."

"What a rat!" Maggie said, and suddenly wondered if Ted had known she was attending the festival with Connor when he first approached her. Did he think he could damage her business, as well? She remembered some of the odd questions he'd asked her that first time they met. Her shoulders slumped. "You'd think I'd recognize the species after living with one for so many years."

"The thing about rats is, they're really good at pretending they're something other than a rat."

"Too true," she murmured, shaking her head in dismay.

He pulled her closer, wrapping his arm around her as they walked. "Don't worry about it. There's a lot more to the story of Ted, but I'll save it for another time. Not tonight."

"Okay." She paused, then added, "But I feel like such a fool for buying in to his act. I thought he was sort of an odd bird, but he seemed harmless enough. Is there any chance he might've changed over the years?"

"No," he said flatly. "He's always been a lying snake, and the fact that he struck up a conversation with you is a sure sign that he hasn't changed one bit. He knows you're here with me. That's the only reason why he approached you in the first place."

"And here I thought it was my sparkling wit that attracted him to me."

Connor stopped and stared at her. Then he rubbed his hand across his jawline. "Hell, Maggie. I'm sorry. I didn't mean it the way it came out. Any man in that room tonight would be damn lucky to breathe the same air as you."

"I was just teasing you." She beamed a smile at him and wound her arm through his. "Let's forget about Ted. I just want to go upstairs with you."

"Sounds good to me."

"Mm, and I can't wait to take off my shoes."

"This might help," Connor said, and swept her up in his arms.

"I could really get used to this," she murmured, wrapping her arms securely around his neck.

So could I, Connor thought, but didn't say the words aloud as he carried her snugly in his arms across the lobby to the elevators.

It was crazy, Maggie thought as they lay in bed together. They'd spent almost every night of the past week making love with each other, but still she wanted more. Would this need she felt for him ever diminish?

They'd raced from the elevator to the hotel suite, and after tearing off their clothes, they'd fallen into bed and immediately devoured each other.

Now, just as she was slipping into sleep, Connor reached for her again. And she couldn't resist him.

She stirred and saw him, saw the sweet desire reflected in his eyes and knew he could see it in hers, as well. Knew he wanted the same thing in that moment that she did. It awakened her, filling her with so much love she could barely wait to hold him inside her again.

Purely and simply, she had fallen irrevocably in love with him and there was no escaping the truth. Maybe she'd known all along that this was where she would end up from the first moment she walked into his office and saw him sitting at his desk.

She'd first gone to see him thinking she would be unfazed by his charm. She had known she was taking a risk but was certain she'd gotten over him years ago. But clearly, she was wrong. The passion was still there, as real and palpable as it ever had been, even after ten long years.

She adored Connor's hands, loved the way he touched her, the way he stroked her everywhere, the way he continuously awakened her body to such pleasure and desire. And she prayed he would never stop.

He slid lower to taste her and with the first sensation of his mouth on her, she gasped and arched into him. Then her mind emptied of all thought and she could only feel and enjoy. His fingers and lips brought her to the brink of ecstasy, only to reel her back and start all over again. When he swept in with his tongue and flicked at her very core, she shuddered as a sudden climax erupted, threatening to engulf her in a pool of need and yearning.

"Again," he murmured, his voice edgy with hunger.

"But…I don't…I can't…"

His gaze locked on hers and she shivered with need. "For me, Maggie."

"Yes," she whispered.

"I want to watch you," he said in a raw, throaty whisper. "I want to feel you tremble in my arms. I want to see your eyes turn dark with pleasure." And he moved his fingers in a staccato rhythm that drove her straight to the edge of rapture and then beyond as she shattered in his hands.

Seconds—or was it minutes—later, he eased her onto her stomach and covered her with his muscled body. His flesh pressed against hers as he kissed her shoulder. And in a heartbeat, she was enflamed with need. She wanted him, wanted everything he had to give her, almost as if she hadn't just fallen apart in his arms minutes earlier.

He trailed kisses along her spine, stroked her as he lowered himself down to plant kisses on her behind, then continued down her thighs, licking and nibbling and exploring every inch of skin until she was breathless again.

"Please, Connor." She wanted to see him, watch him, kiss him. She started to roll over, but he stroked her back, silently urging her to stay this way awhile longer. He kissed her again at the base of her neck and began the tender onslaught all over again.

Maggie sighed, then moaned as his fingers moved to stroke her more intimately again. Then he suddenly shifted, lifted her pelvis and shifted her hips to allow him entrance. When he thrust himself into her, she gasped for air. He was hard and solid as he delved deeper, filling her completely until she was sure he had touched her soul.

She met his urgent movements with her own, could hear him gasping for breath, could feel his heated body scorching her skin, and hoped this feeling would never go away, prayed that this moment would never end.

Suddenly he stopped and she almost collapsed, but he

held her steady. He pulled himself away from her and she almost cried until he gently rolled her over onto her back.

"I have to look at you," he said, simply, and instantly thrust himself inside her. She gasped, and then immediately felt complete again with him sheathed within her.

He moved faster now, plunging deeper, thrusting harder, taking her along on a frantic ride to an inexorable climax that had her screaming his name within mere seconds.

Connor tightened his hold on her, driving into her. She could feel the immense coil of tension rise within him and stretch to the breaking point. Only then did he shout out her name and follow her into blissful oblivion.

Ten

Connor woke up the next morning with a beautiful warm woman snuggled beside him. His first impulse was to wake her up slowly, kiss by kiss, touch by touch, until she welcomed him gladly into her heated core once again.

Despite his rampant erection, he couldn't do it. She looked so peaceful Connor didn't have the heart to wake her. And he figured, from now on, they had all the time in the world to spend pleasuring each other.

For now, he climbed out of bed, careful not to disturb her, and prepared for the day. The awards ceremony would be early this evening and he still had some final round judging to finish before noon.

He was reading the sports section and drinking his second cup of coffee from room service when he received a text from Jake. Emergency. Meet us in judges room immediately. Come alone.

Maggie awoke slowly, happy but exhausted from their lovemaking the night before. She glanced across the bed and found it empty, so Connor was already up and out of bed. She must have overslept, she thought, stretching languidly. Every muscle in her body was groaning, but it was so worth it. No pain, no gain, right? She chuckled lazily and glanced at the clock.

"Oh dear." She really had overslept. She didn't hear Connor in the bathroom, so she walked out into the living room to check whether he was still eating breakfast. The suite was deserted, so she knew he must have left for the festival floor.

It took her a few seconds to remember what day this was. Saturday. The day of the final judging. Tonight was the awards ceremony. She needed to kick herself into gear.

Today would also be the busiest day of the festival with members of the general public coming in droves. She would need extra energy to fight the crowds, but all that was left of Connor's breakfast was a piece of leftover toast and one last cup of coffee. She grabbed them both, then raced to shower and dry her hair. She decided to dress a little more casually in capris, a short linen jacket and a pair of colorful sneakers.

Still hungry, she stopped at the coffee kiosk in the lobby and bought herself a quick breakfast burrito and a latte.

Then she went directly down to the judges' room to find Connor. She knew she wouldn't be allowed inside during the final judging round, but she just hoped she could see his face.

The doors to the hall were closed and the outer foyer was deserted. Maggie glanced around, looking for Johnny, but he was nowhere to be found, either.

She finished her latte and tossed the cup in a trash can, then decided to make a run to the ladies' room while she had a few minutes.

She slipped into one of the stalls, hung her tote bag on the hook and had to smile. She'd been in here before, the other day when she'd been too afraid to confront Sarah. She had dashed to the safety of the bathroom stall like a helpless ninny, but never again, she vowed. She was fed up with being afraid. She would never hide from confrontation again.

Before she could exit the stall, the outer bathroom door opened with a bang. Two women entered and stopped at the bathroom mirror to talk. Some protective instinct convinced Maggie to wait inside the stall as the women chatted in front of the mirror.

So maybe she was still working out some of those *helpless ninny* issues, Maggie thought, shaking her head. Baby steps, after all.

"So, what happened?" the first one said, her voice low.

"Oh, my God, you won't believe it," the other one said, her inflection classic *Valley Girl*. She sounded about twelve years old. "One of their contest entries was tainted."

"That's terrible," the first woman said. "How?"

"Johnny said that someone broke into the storage room last night and tampered with the MacLaren entries. It wasn't discovered until this morning during the semifinal round of judging, about an hour ago. A couple of the judges tasted the MacLaren ale and a few minutes later, they lost their breakfasts. The head judge sampled it and declared it was ruined."

"But how'd anybody get into the storage room?"

Huddled behind the stall door, Maggie wanted to know the same thing. Who would do it? Why? And how?

And despite her lofty thoughts from a moment ago about facing confrontation, there was no way she was leaving her hiding place until she heard the whole story.

"I'm not sure," Valley Girl said. "They either found a key or just broke in. Johnny's mortified."

"Poor guy, it's not his fault," the first woman said. "Wow, so someone deliberately sabotaged the MacLarens. I wouldn't want to piss them off. Do they know who it is?"

"You have to ask?" Valley Girl said, her voice dripping sarcasm. "Who else could it be?"

There was a pause, and then the first woman whispered, "Oh, come on. You can't be serious."

"Connor is absolutely certain that she did it," Valley Girl said, her voice hushed but confident. "And look at the evidence. It happened during the dance last night. She arrived really late. And then later on, I saw her talking to Ted Blake. And it wasn't the first time, either. I've seen them together before. Connor saw them, too. They were very tight and cozy, if you know what I mean."

"Ted Blake?" the first woman whispered. "He hates the MacLarens. Do you think the two of them planned it together?"

Maggie's heart sank. She knew they were referring to her. And it was true that she'd talked to Ted Blake a few times, but she hadn't known what a rat he was until Connor told her. Her eyes narrowed in suspicion, almost certain she knew who "Valley Girl" was.

"Oh, absolutely," Valley Girl insisted, then fudged a bit. "Or she planned it alone. Either way, she's guilty as sin."

"But why would she do that to Connor?"

"She's jealous," Valley Girl hissed. "She'll do anything to win the competition, and that includes cheating."

"It doesn't make sense. Why would she sabotage Connor? She likes him."

"Because she can't have him back."

"News flash," the first woman said dryly. "She's sleeping in the same hotel room with him."

"That's only because he's paying her."

Maggie wondered if she had fallen down a rabbit hole. Their conversation sounded like a bad soap opera, and her head was starting to spin. And worst of all, she was sick to death of standing by idly while her reputation was being torn to shreds.

"He's paying her to sleep with him?"

"Yes, and I would've done it for free," Valley Girl whined.

"Lucinda, you're delusional," the first woman said. "You've had a crush on him since high school and he's never even looked at you. Face it, he's just not that into you."

"He would be if she would just go away."

Maggie's head was going to explode. She had to get out of here. It was time to take a risk, stop hiding, stop running from her mistakes. She had to fight for herself, for her reputation, for her life. And for Connor. Taking a deep breath, she gathered her strength and shoved the stall door open. "Hello, ladies."

Sarah saw her in the mirror and blinked in surprise.

Lucinda whirled around, then froze. Her face blanched and she stuttered in shock, "Wh-what are you…what… you…"

"Oh, shut up, Lucinda," Maggie said, dismissing her as she stepped up to the sink to wash her hands.

Sarah slowly shook her head. "Wow. I did not see that coming."

"Hello, Sarah," Maggie said pleasantly as she grabbed a towel from the dispenser.

Her old friend began to laugh. "Maggie, I was wondering how long it would take you to find your spine again."

Sarah was smiling in real pleasure and Maggie realized that maybe she hadn't lost all of her friends after all.

"Well, I've found it now, so look out." Maggie tossed the towel, then straightened her shoulders and shook her hair back defiantly as if she were about to go into battle. She looked at Sarah in the mirror. "You ain't seen nothin' yet."

"Go get 'em, Maggie," Sarah said, still laughing as Maggie stalked out of the bathroom.

Maggie stormed down the wide hallway to the judges' room entrance. She didn't much care what someone like Lucinda thought. What bothered her was that anyone else might think that she would resort to cheating. With a firm tug, she pulled the heavy door open. She no longer cared about contest rules and regulations. She had to find Connor and find out the truth. She wasn't about to take the word of a silly twit like Lucinda again.

The room was bustling. Dozens of judges sat at twenty

round tables scattered around the room. Each judge had at least five small glasses in front of them, each one marked with numbers only and filled with a different beer or ale. They were in various stages of tasting and studying and Maggie couldn't help being drawn into the process.

Each judge had a clipboard listing all of the categories used to judge the entries. Maggie knew them by heart. Appearance, aroma, flavor, balance, body and mouth feel, overall impression and flaws.

These judges took their job seriously, and the brewers who submitted their products to the competition were even more serious. Taking home these prizes could mean millions of dollars to the winner. The judges were trusted with making those critical decisions. And someone had destroyed that trust.

And they were blaming it on Maggie.

If Lucinda was to be believed, they'd already put her on trial and found her guilty.

But Lucinda was an idiot. Always had been. Would Connor actually take her word over Maggie's? It wasn't possible. She had to find Connor and hear the truth from him. After all this time they'd spent together, after all they'd shared, he had to realize that she would never do anything to hurt him. He had to know that she could be trusted with his heart.

She thought he already did. But now…was he still unsure of her feelings for him? Was he still holding on to the hurt he'd felt for so many years? They had talked about it over and over this week. How could he still believe she'd betrayed him back then?

She had to find him. But would he believe her? Would he trust her? Would he listen and believe it when she told him she'd never stopped loving him? That she loved him more than life itself?

She was confident that if she could just look into his

eyes, she would see the answers and know that he truly believed her, trusted her, loved her.

So where was he? The room was filled with people, but she could've picked him out of any crowd. And he was nowhere to be found.

"Where are you, Connor?" she murmured anxiously.

At that very moment, as if he'd been summoned by telepathic command, Connor walked out of a smaller anteroom and into the larger judges' room. He was followed by his brothers, the three of them looking like warriors marching into battle. All that was missing was the blue war paint and their clan tartans wrapped around them.

Johnny and two older men she didn't recognize followed in the brothers' wake. Their expressions were all severe and Maggie wouldn't want to tangle with any of them. But it appeared that they were headed in her general direction.

Connor's face was stern and ashen. Jake stared ahead with fierce intent, and Ian was fuming, as well.

Her heart went out to them. They looked angry and ready to fight. Maggie could completely understand their feelings, especially after overhearing Lucinda's unfounded accusations in the bathroom.

Then Connor spotted her. He led the men straight to her, watching her the entire time as he walked closer. Maggie stared back at him, searching for that same spark of love she'd seen in his eyes the night before. But all she saw was…guilt?

Blame?

Censure?

She couldn't tell, but she backed away instinctively as they got closer.

"Maggie, wait," Connor said.

She stopped and straightened her shoulders. "For what?" Sarah was right, she thought. Maggie had found her spine and she wouldn't be treated like a criminal. "For you and your brothers to pronounce me guilty? No, thank you." She turned to leave and slammed right into Lucinda, who was standing inches behind her.

"Don't believe her, Connor," Lucinda shouted.

"Lucinda," Jake said. "We were just looking for you."

Lucinda shot Maggie a look of triumph. "I was just looking for you guys, too."

"Connor," Maggie said. "I just heard about the tainted beer. I'm so sorry." But Connor wouldn't meet Maggie's gaze.

Why? Wait. He didn't believe her? Couldn't even look at her? Without even listening to her side of the story? So this was it?

Instead of meeting Maggie's gaze, he was staring at Lucinda.

"Your entries weren't damaged, Red," Johnny chimed in reassuringly.

"Thanks, Johnny," Maggie said, not reassured at all.

"So you only care about your own entries," Lucinda taunted. "Kind of selfish if you ask me."

"Nobody asked you," Maggie said.

"That's enough, Lucinda," Jake muttered.

"Me?" Lucinda slapped her hands on her hips in outrage. "She's the one pretending to be innocent. I'm just trying to point out who's guilty here."

Maggie looked carefully at each of the men in front of her and saw nothing encouraging in their eyes. "So you believe her? You think I'm…guilty?" She almost choked on the words. "You really believe I could do this?"

But Lucinda wasn't about to let them talk. Instead she confronted Maggie face-to-face. "What time did you finally show up at the dance?"

"What does that matter?" she asked.

Lucinda whipped around to the men. "She was late because she was busy sneaking into the storage room. You saw her talking to Ted Blake, Connor, I know you did. And that wasn't the only time I've seen them together. They probably planned it from the start."

Maggie frowned. The men were all watching Lucinda. Were they actually taking her word for this? Connor still wouldn't look at her and Maggie felt as if she were facing another inquisition, as she used to call her confrontations with her ex-husband and his mother.

Well, screw that. That was the past, she reminded herself. She would never, ever put up with an unfair accusation from anyone, ever again.

She gazed up at Connor. "Do you think I would do this to you?"

He stared hard at her, then said, "No."

"Wow," she whispered. "It took you more than a few seconds to decide on your answer. So your first instinct was to believe I would hurt you that way?"

His jaw tightened. "No, Maggie, it wasn't."

But again there was that momentary pause and Maggie began to question everything. Did he believe her? Did he trust her? Did he honestly think she would do this to him? If he believed she was innocent, then why wasn't he grabbing her and kissing her and assuring her that he knew she would never hurt him again?

Because he didn't believe that.

Her heart was breaking and she wanted to cry, to scream and demand that he believe her, love her, trust her.

But that would give Lucinda too much satisfaction. So instead Maggie cast one more beseeching glance at Connor, and when she received nothing back from him, not even a glance her way, she couldn't remain there another second. She turned and walked away.

"Maggie, wait," Connor said.

She wanted more than anything to keep moving away

from him, but she'd just remembered something important. She whipped around and walked up to Johnny.

"I'm signing my three Redhead entries over to the Mac-Laren Brewery," she said tersely. "I owe them the formulas anyway, so now they officially belong to Connor and his brothers. If you need me to sign anything swearing to that, text me. You have my phone number on my entry form."

She cast one more glance at Connor. "Oh, and you should fire your secretary."

And then she walked away.

He fired their secretary.

It was a unanimous decision made by all three brothers, especially after they viewed the videotape that had caught the culprit red-handed, so to speak.

Luckily for everyone, the convention center had videotapes running twenty-four hours a day, in every single room of the massive structure, including the storage room. Who knew? Connor thought, giving thanks that the center was so security-minded.

Connor, Jake and Ian had viewed the tape with Johnny and the festival president, along with the local sheriff, who had shown up for the festival on his day off. They had all seen the moment when their secretary Lucinda had snuck into the storage room and tainted one of the MacLaren entries.

But even before Connor saw the evidence, he had known Maggie was innocent, although Lucinda had done everything she could to sway their judgment in Maggie's direction.

But when Maggie stomped back over to Johnny and told him she was signing over her entries to MacLaren, Connor felt his heart jump in his chest. He could swear he'd never seen anything so courageous in his life. He'd been ready to tear off after her, but Lucinda was still raving and the sheriff needed their united presence.

"Don't tell me you believe her!" Lucinda had cried after Maggie stormed off. "Just because she put on a show for all of you, it doesn't mean anything. She's still your most viable suspect."

"What's your problem, Lucinda?" Connor asked, fed up with the woman sniping at Maggie. "What do you have against Maggie?"

"She's trying to hurt you. I'm trying to help you, but you can just forget it. I'm through doing all your dirty work." She spun around and began to walk away quickly.

"Not so fast, young lady," the sheriff said, jogging after her and grabbing hold of her arm. She squirmed and twisted to escape, but it was no use.

"Something you want to tell us, Lucinda?" Ian had said.

She stomped her foot. "I don't know why you think I did something. Maggie was the one who was talking to Ted Blake. Didn't you see her? The two of them were probably plotting the whole thing together. And look how late she was for the dance. She had plenty of time to break in and destroy the entry."

"It's not Maggie," Connor had said decisively, putting an end to Lucinda's blathering.

But he knew the damage had been done. Maggie had arrived right after he and his brothers had viewed the tapes. They all knew who the guilty party was. The videotape was a powerful indictment. But the sheriff had suggested it would be easier to deal with Lucinda if she would just confess. Connor had been willing to go along with his request, but regretted it the second he saw Maggie's reaction to his silence.

"Damn it." Connor should've grabbed her in his arms the instant Lucinda began to spew her venomous accusations. He'd been glaring at Lucinda, but she'd been standing directly behind Maggie. So now he wondered if Maggie might've thought his glares had been aimed at her.

"No doubt," Connor muttered, and rubbed his jaw in frustration. Maggie would naturally default to the worst-case scenario, and he couldn't really blame her in this situation.

She'd been through enough trauma in her life. Connor was sick at the thought that he might've given her a reason to doubt that he was completely, utterly, irrevocably in love with her.

Now he needed to find her and convince her otherwise.

Maggie barely made it to the suite and got the door closed before the tears threatened to fall.

But she was sick to death of tears. Yes, her heart was breaking, but she refused to cry about it.

And to think that she'd gone downstairs to find Connor and tell him she'd fallen in love with him. She had foolishly thought he'd be happy to hear it and would respond by telling her how much he loved her, too.

How ironic. It seemed that circumstances had played a cruel joke on her. It wouldn't be the first time.

So much for taking risks.

"Now you're just feeling sorry for yourself," she muttered. "But don't you dare cry." She grabbed her suitcase and opened it on the bed. Then she began to toss her clothes into the open bag.

She couldn't wait to leave this damn hotel and go home to Grandpa and the goats.

"Goats? Really?" She sniffled a little at the thought of the goats, then rolled her eyes. How pathetic could she get? She was reduced to depending on goats to comfort and sympathize with her in her moment of misery. It just added to the misery.

She heard the suite door open and knew that Connor

had come back. Could things get any worse? She wanted to hide under the bed, but she'd been hiding for way too long. No more hiding, Maggie. She'd grown so much in the past few years, and these past few days had made her feel more powerful than she ever had.

Besides, it was a platform bed, so there was no place to hide anyway.

She really didn't want another confrontation with Connor, but she couldn't avoid it now and she figured it was long past due. But at least she knew that his last impression of her would not be of red-rimmed, swollen eyes and tear-drenched cheeks. Nope. She was not going to cry and look like some pathetic water rat.

But then, why would he care what she looked like? He thought she was a saboteur—or worse.

He stood in the doorway, watching her.

"Hello, Connor," she said, and dropped her shoes into the suitcase. "Did something else happen that you can accuse me of doing? Maybe I tainted the water supply? Released a dirty bomb? Stole your underwear? Take your best shot."

"I'm not here to accuse you of anything, Maggie."

"Good," she said, folding her arms across her chest defensively. "Because I'm not putting up with one more accusation from you or anyone else. If you honestly believe that I would ever do anything like that to hurt you, you're horribly mistaken." She grabbed another shirt from the closet and flung it into the suitcase. "My God, what you must think of me. One of those judges could've been killed. Do you really think I'm capable of that?"

"No."

"Right." She tossed a pair of pants into the suitcase. "Look, this has been fun. Well, most of it, anyway. The past hour or so, not so much. But other than that whole belittling, accusing thing that just happened downstairs, I had a really wonderful time and I'll always keep the memory of you in my heart."

And with those words said, she burst into tears. Damn it. She really didn't want to cry. She was stronger now. But the truth was bringing her to her knees. Connor had always been in her heart and he would remain there forever, even if they were apart.

Still, tears were not acceptable. She hastily brushed them away as she grabbed more clothes and threw them into the suitcase.

"I'm glad to hear it," he said, "because you'll always be in my heart, too."

"Thank you." She sniffled.

"And I owe you this," he said, handing her a piece of paper.

Her eyes were still a little blurry, but she could see it was a check with a lot of numbers written on it. He was paying her for her week of service. Another sob escaped and she had to struggle to speak. "Do you really think I'm going to take this?"

"That was the deal," he said.

She took a deep breath and wiped her eyes. Then she gazed at him for a long moment. "Forget the deal," she said finally, and tore the check in two.

"Maggie," he said softly.

"Connor, I saw that look of accusation in your eyes."

"That look you saw," he said with aggravating calmness, "was aimed at Lucinda, who was standing about two feet behind you the whole time."

"If you say so," she muttered.

"You know she was there, right?" Connor took one step into the room. "She was the one we were all looking at. We already knew she was guilty. We reviewed the videotapes a few minutes before you arrived. We saw her do it, Maggie."

"Videotapes?"

"Yeah. The center runs security videos in all the rooms," he explained. "So we knew Lucinda was guilty. But even before I saw the tape, it never crossed my mind to suspect you, Maggie. Why would I? You're in love with me. You would never hurt me."

She glared at him. "How do you know?"

He laughed, damn him. He wasn't playing fair. She'd wanted to be the one to tell him she loved him, had rushed downstairs to find him and let him know her feelings. But he'd guessed anyway before she could say the words. But wait, she thought. He hadn't said he loved her, too. Why? She knew he loved her. Or he *did,* before this day happened.

"You got caught in the cross fire," he continued. "The sheriff wanted her to confess, so he advised us not to say anything. But he finally got tired of her caterwauling and dragged her off to book her."

That got her attention. "Really? You had her arrested?"

"Hell, yes," he said, scowling. "You were right, Maggie. She could've killed one of those judges."

Her anger left her in a heartbeat and she had to lean against the dresser to steady her suddenly weak knees.

"So let me turn the question around on you," Connor said softly, taking another step farther into the room and disturbing what little equilibrium she had left.

"What question?" she asked warily.

He took a step closer. "Do you really think I'm capable of believing you could do such a horrible thing?"

"Oh." She stared at him in shock, then had to think about what he'd said. "No. Of course not, but we've had to overcome some history to—"

"I'd say we've overcome all that." Another step. "So now, do you really think I believe you could hurt me that way?"

She bit her lip. "When you put it like that, no. But I still think—"

"Don't think." He was inches away now, close enough to

reach out and tenderly sweep a strand of hair off her face. His fingers remained, lightly stroking her cheek. "Don't think, Maggie. Feel. Take a chance. Believe. In me. In us. I do."

"I do, too," she whispered. "I believe in us. I believe in taking a chance. Risking it all. For you."

He kissed the edge of her chin. "I'm so in love with you, Maggie."

"Oh." She had to catch her breath. "I—I love you so much, Connor. I don't think I've ever stopped loving you."

"I've never stopped loving you, either."

"I'm so sorry I wasted so much time being away from you."

"Let's make up for it now," he said. "Say you'll marry me, Maggie?"

"Oh, Connor," she said, staring up at him. Her heart filled with so much joy she wasn't sure she could hold it all. "Yes, of course I'll marry you."

"And love me always?" He kissed her cheek.

"You know I will," she whispered.

He nibbled her neck. "And have my children?"

"Oh, Connor." She blinked away more tears. "Yes. I would love to have children with you."

He licked her earlobe. "And pick out my clothes for me?"

She laughed and smacked his chest, then threw her arms around his neck. "Yes. Absolutely yes to all of the above."

"I'm glad you're packing your bags," he said, glancing around the room. "Let's go home right now and start our lives together."

"Please, Connor," she said as he swept her off her feet and into his arms. "Take me home."

Epilogue

"I heard from the Scottish lawyers again," Jake said, leaning back in his chair as he downed his beer. "They're getting more nervous about the property, so I told them that one of us would fly over to check things out."

Connor's brothers had come by his house to talk business and to try a taste of Maggie's latest award-winning ale. Connor had named it Maggie's Pride, a takeoff of their own MacLaren's Pride. "Ian's the logical choice to go."

Ian scowled. "Just because my ex-father-in-law lives there doesn't mean I'm the one who has to go. Forget it."

"Why not?" Jake asked.

Ian glared at him but said nothing. He'd been doing that a lot lately, Connor realized. Something had crawled up his butt, but he wasn't willing to talk about it. It wasn't too hard to figure out, though, since he and his wife, Samantha, were no longer living together.

"Well, don't look at me," Connor said. "I'm not leaving Maggie."

At that moment, Connor's beautiful wife walked into the room carrying two bowls of chips and salsa and set them on the table in front of the men. Her gaze went directly to Connor. "You're leaving me?"

Jake laughed. "No, he's not leaving you. He just married you. I haven't seen him wander more than five feet away from you since the wedding."

"Come here," Connor said, smiling up at Maggie. He grabbed her hand and pulled her gently onto his lap. Then he wrapped his arms around her waist and felt utterly content with life.

He hadn't announced the news to his brothers yet, but Maggie had been to the doctor yesterday, where they found out that she was pregnant. Connor wasn't sure he could contain all the love he had inside for his wife and the tiny baby growing within her belly.

It had barely been a month after the festival ended when he and Maggie were married on the beach with their family and a few trusted friends gathered around to celebrate. They had been apart for so many years that neither of them had wanted to wait any longer to begin their married life together. The small ceremony had suited Maggie perfectly. She'd already endured an extravagant society wedding with her ex-husband and didn't want to repeat the experience.

And speaking of her bizarre ex-husband, Connor had not been surprised to hear the news that Ashford had recently been arrested on suspicion of murdering his dear mother. According to the news reports Connor had seen, it appeared that the old woman hadn't died of natural causes after all. Her cantankerous butler had hounded the police until they agreed to investigate and finally discovered the truth.

Maggie snuggled closer and Connor kissed her neck, thankful again that she had come back home to him. The day she told him she was ready to take the biggest risk of her life and marry him, he knew he was the luckiest man alive.

"Jeez, you two," Ian groused. "Get a room."

Connor laughed, unfazed by his brother's bad mood. "Ignore him, he's jealous."

"He's especially cranky today," Jake said.

"Stop talking about me like I'm not in the room," Ian protested. "Besides, you would be cranky, too, if…never mind."

"If what?" Connor asked, growing concerned. He'd

never seen his brother more miserable. Ian had always been the most even-tempered of the three brothers, but ever since he'd separated from his wife, Samantha, he'd been unhappy.

Ian shoved his hand through his dark hair in frustration. "Never mind."

"Now you've got our curiosity piqued," Jake said mildly.

"You'll get over it," Ian muttered.

"I still don't see why you can't go to Scotland," Connor said, looking at Ian pointedly. "You loved it there last time. And Gordon is a great host."

"Yeah, well, last time I went, I was with Gordon's daughter," Ian reminded them. "Things have changed."

"No kidding," Jake said, took a last gulp of beer and set his glass on the table.

Maggie turned and gave Connor a look of concern, then glanced at his brother. "I'm sorry, Ian. Connor would go, but the timing—"

"No, love," Connor interrupted, not yet willing to share their baby news. He gave her a quick hug. "They understand that I won't be going this time."

Jake stood and stretched. "Fine, I'll go. I should've just agreed to go in the first place. Better than listening to Ian whine."

"I don't whine," Ian whined.

Maggie giggled.

"It's better if you go, anyway, Jake," Connor said. "You'll do the job quickly and get home."

"Yeah, I'll make it a fast trip, but I still want to stop in Kilmarnock for a day and visit Gordon. If Ian's really going to divorce Samantha, it's more important than ever to maintain a strong contact with her father."

"No," Ian said, more forcefully than usual.

"What do you mean, no?" Connor said. "Are you getting a divorce or not?"

Restless, Ian pushed his chair back from the table and stood. "I mean, no. You can't stop to see Gordon."

Jake whipped around. "Why the hell not?"

"Because he's disappeared," Ian said. "Nobody's seen him for days and they don't have a clue where he's gone." And with that bombshell dropped, he left the room abruptly.

Jake and Connor exchanged looks of apprehension. Then Jake shrugged. "You know Gordon. Chances are he slipped away to be with a woman. Let's not jump to conclusions."

"That's the most likely answer," Connor said, nodding in agreement. Right now he had to admit he was more concerned about his brother than Gordon McGregor's whereabouts. He wasn't sure what was going on with Ian and his in-laws, but it was something Connor would have to deal with later on. Much later, he thought, after he'd had more time to spend with his beautiful new wife and the unborn child they had created.

Maggie reach for his hand and whispered, "I love you."

"I know," Connor said, making her smile as he leaned over and kissed her with all his heart.

* * * * *